Amazing Stories, Volume 77, Issue 1, Fall 2019, Issue 618 is copyrighted by The Experimenter Publishing Company,LLC. Contact Amazing Stories at its website at http://amazingstories.com

CONTENTS
Fall, 2019 – Volume 77, Issue 1 #618

Publisher
Steve Davidson

Editor-in-Chief
Ira Nayman

Art Director/Layout
Kermit Woodall

Poetry Editors
David Clink
Carolyn Clink

Readers
Herb Kauderer
Elizabeth Hirst
Judy McCrosky
Patty McNally
Chip Houser
Rebecca Inch-Partridge
Russ Scarola
Mat Woolfenden
Jennifer Crow

Copy Editing/Proofreading
Rhea Rose
Paula Johanson
Sally Fogel
John Park
Lloyd Penney

Cover Artist
Vincent di Fate

Layout
Tania Gonzalez Figueroa

Amazing Stories® is a registered trademark of and is published by The Experimenter Publishing Company™, LLC. P.O. Box 1068, Hillsboro, NH 03244

Amazing Stories, Volume 77, Issue 1, Fall 2019, Issue 618 is copyrighted by The Experimenter Publishing Company, LLC. Contact Amazing Stories at its website at http://amazingstories.com to add or update your subscription. Submissions can be made at http://submissions.amazingstoriesmag.com

Some photos are used under Creative Commons, including some with modifications, and are from pxhere.com, pixabay.com and flickr.com/photos/pedrosz/41570242554

From the Editor's Desk
Practical Advice for Impractical Situations

By IRA NAYMAN

When I used to teach at a university, I would tell my students that they should have a plan, however vague, for their artistic careers. I still say that to writers when I can: always be thinking about how your current project will further your long-term career objectives. Sound advice, if a little hypocritical.

Why hypocritical? Because I'm like Heath Ledger's Joker: I don't plaaaaaan anything!

If I do have one saving grace, it is that I seize opportunities when they come my way. Seize them by the throat and don't let go until I have wrung the last ounce of pleasure I can get out of them. (Work? Well, yes, of course it's work. But if I was going to do work that didn't give me pleasure, I would have become a lawyer so I could at least make a living out of it!)

One of the most recent opportunities to come my way was, of course, editing the latest incarnation of *Amazing Stories*. I was happy being a writer (still am, in fact, happily writing); I wasn't looking to become a magazine editor. Yet, when the opportunity arose...you know.

This issue marks the first anniversary of the new *Amazing Stories*. Editing the magazine has been incredibly satisfying. It has given me the chance to work with and get to know a fantastic selection of talented authors, some of whom are well-known, others less so. It has allowed me to produce the kind of magazine I have always enjoyed reading: filled with adventure and humor, often thought-provoking, always fun.

It has also allowed me to work with an incredible art director, Kermit Woodall. While production of the magazine has not been without problems, Kermit had a vision of a beautiful package with each story being introduced by a full page illustration (some of which have been breathtaking). The great writing has been set in a lovely package.

A lot of the work has gone on behind the scenes. We have been fortunate, for instance, that Dave Clink and Carolyn Clink agreed to be poetry editors; although I think poetry is an important part of this kind of magazine, I am, for all intents and purposes, poetry-illiterate. Dave and Carolyn have brought an exquisite taste and eye for detail that have helped *Amazing Stories* develop an entertaining poetry section.

It's also true that our readers, proofreaders and copy editors have been invaluable in making the magazine what it has been. We are approaching 2,000 submissions in less than a year and a half; without our readers, I would have died of exhaustion within a month of opening submissions to the public! My experience as a writer and now editor have shown me that no publication ever goes out perfect; nonetheless, our copy editors and proofreaders have helped us avoid some embarrassing errors and generally get closer to our unachievable goal. Raise a glass to the names to the right of the contents page; we could not do this without them.

Finally, I cannot express enough my gratitude to publisher Steve Davidson for giving me the chance to reimagine this classic magazine for the 21st century.

We have lots of exciting things planned for *Amazing Stories*' second year (would you believe a podcast? I don't quite believe it myself, either. More about that next issue...). At the heart of them will always be great writing melded with great design. One of the most gratifying aspects of editing the magazine has been the enthusiasm with which it has been received by writers, visual artists and readers. I hope as we continue to grow, they will feel that their enthusiasm has been rewarded.

In the meantime, please enjoy this special full-colour, all fiction edition of *Amazing Stories* magazine.

Amazing Cover Artist

VINCENT DI FATE

Cover artist Vincent Di Fate has enjoyed an international reputation as one of the leading artistic visionaries of the future since the late 1960s. *People Magazine* noted that "Di Fate is not all hard-edge and airbrush slickness. His works are always paintings – a bit of his brushwork shows – and they are all the better because of it." *Omni Magazine* made the observation that "...moody and powerful, the paintings of Vincent Di Fate depict mechanical marvels and far frontiers of a future technocracy built on complicated machinery and human resourcefulness... Di Fate is something of a grand old man in the highly specialized field of technological space art. Stirring images of far-flung environments have been his trademark." And in his induction profile for the Science Fiction Hall of Fame it was observed that, "His paintings are vivid and precise, with strikingly elegant brushstrokes; their impact on the world of science fiction is unmistakable." In his prolific career, he has produced works for such clients as IBM, *The Reader's Digest*, The National Geographic Society, and the National Aeronautics and Space Administration.

Di Fate has received many awards for his work, and was a 2011 inductee of the Science Fiction Hall of Fame. His accolades include the Frank R. Paul Award for Outstanding Achievement in Science Fiction Illustration (1978), the Hugo Award (Science Fiction Achievement Award) for Best Professional Artist (1979), the NESFA Skylark Award (1987), the Lensman Award for Lifetime Contribution to the Science Fiction Field (1990), the Chesley Award from the Association of Science Fiction/Fantasy Artists for Lifetime Artistic Achievement (1998), and the Rondo Award (2004), among others. He was a Guest of Honor at the 50th World Science Fiction Convention in Orlando, Florida in 1992 and has been a frequently honored guest at regional SF, fantasy and film conventions throughout the US and Canada.

The artist has exhibited in group and one-man shows at museums and galleries in North America, Europe, Asia and Japan. His art is also included in corporate and private collections, including that of LucasFilm, Ltd. In addition, Di Fate, a full professor at the Fashion Institute of Technology (State University of New York) has lectured extensively about the history, methods and meaning of his craft and has been a consultant for MCA/Universal, 20th Century-Fox, Walt Disney Productions and MGM/United Artists.

Di Fate, a prolific writer as well as visual artist, has authored some 300 articles for magazine and book publication, and has produced three major volumes, *Di Fate's Catalog of Science Fiction Hardware* (Workman Publishing Co, 1980), the award winning *Infinite Worlds: The Fantastic Visions of Science Fiction Art* (Penguin Studio Books, 1997) and *The Science Fiction Art of Vincent Di Fate* (Paper Tiger, 2002). He is currently at work on a fourth book on the subject of the illustrator in fantastic films.

Jon Eno

by S. P.
SOMTOW

Somtow's first career was as an avant-garde composer, but he took a twenty-year detour and published about fifty books including science fiction, horror, fantasy and "other." Currently, he lives in Bangkok and runs Opera Siam. He's known for the Inquestor series, the Mallworld stories, and his Timmy Valentine trilogy including Vampire Junction. *This is his first appearance in the field in over a decade.*

"The laws of nature are very much like the laws of Thailand; you can get around them if you know the right people." – *The Tall Old Man*

One day, a tall old man stands in the doorway and says he has come for me. He says we shall go on a journey. When I ask him why, he tells me this: "So that one day you shall stand in a doorway, and you shall tell a boy that you have come to take him on a journey. And when he asks why, you shall tell him, 'So that one day you shall stand in a doorway such as this, and say these words to a child such as yourself.'"

My journey has been long, yet I have not reached the time when I shall stand in a stranger's doorway and call out to an unknown youth. It all unfolds in a continuous long present, yesterday and today all jumbled up like a basket of silk scraps in the fabric market.

Back then, to the twenty-first century. The breath of the Dragon Jade had not yet warmed the world. It was a time when children on street corners cried out that the world was ending, little knowing it had already ended.

Back also to a city. A teeming city, exotic to some. A city of metal spires and desolate landfills, of glass malls and porcelain pagodas, a city that, in those days, remade itself nightly in the moments before dawn so that you could sometimes wake in the morning not knowing where you were; if you've lived there, you'd know, and if you haven't, no amount of explaining will ever be enough.

I'll tell you everything I know, and it will all come out in one big jumble, and sometimes you'll believe me, and sometimes you'll say it can't be so, but stay with me. Every event in the world has at least two explanations: one that is fact, and one that is the truth.

Bangkok, the early twenty-first century. A Catholic orphanage beside a Buddhist temple, a Hindu shrine abutting an internet café, and all this sandwiched between high rises and a shanty town; that's where the tall old man first comes to me.

April is the hottest month. The water festival, which proclaims the coming of the long monsoon, has come and gone; we're well into May, and it's **still** the hottest month. When our story begins I'm a hot little boy, sweating as I labor in a hot airless shed, because the corrugated iron walls keep the hot air in and there's not even an electric fan.

I'm an orphan, of course. To play this role, the tall old man once told me, you either have to be an orphan or at the very least grow up with surrogates, suspecting the whole time that you have a different parentage, perhaps divine. Usually, you had been given a dire prediction when you were born – you were going to kill your father and marry your mother, or you were going to bring about the downfall of the entire empire, so your loving parents, after shedding many a tear, wrapped you in a swaddling cloth and abandoned you by the mountainside, or floated you downstream in a reed boat. In my case, they leave you on the doorstep of Sacred Heart with a basket, a blanket, and a dagger.

Then, when you came of age, you'd learn who you really were, draw a sword from a stone, and go off to find your father's castle, marrying princesses, slaying dragons, and saving the universe along the way before attaining your rightful place on the throne.

When the old man told me all this, I smiled a little, because you should never offend an older person, but I didn't see how it applied to me.

Until –

#

The orphanage is run by the brothers, but they respect our culture, so early each morning they send us to the temple next door where a young monk named Phra Athit tells us the story of Buddha. After lunch, we learn about Jesus. We walk by the Hindu shrine, which is catty-corner from the Buddhist temple, and we always make a quick obeisance to Ganesha, the elephant god who lives there, just in case – although the brothers sort of lump in Hinduism under Buddhism, so we don't get **three** daily doses of religion.

Father Duvalier explained it thus, one day: "The Catholic Church is like a great big ocean liner taking you to Heaven. Now, there are all these rickety little boats that **could** get you there, too. All your little pagan religions, not to mention the protestants, but they're more like bamboo rafts lashed together with twine. Now wouldn't you rather be on the ocean liner than the rickety boat? Of course, it's up to you. That's what we call **free will**. Now, hands up who wants to take the big ship."

The hands went up rather unenthusiastically. Video night the previous week had been *Titanic.*

We also learn English, because, as Father Duvalier has told us many times, English is the key that will release us from the slum. Thai, he tells us, may be the language of love, that's true, but it's also the language of hierarchy and class and subjugation; English, which only has one word for I and one word for you, is the great leveler, and with English any of us urchins could end up as a CEO in one of those glittering high-ris-

es. With Thai, we'll be cleaning toilets in that selfsame high-rise.

It's a nice theory, but I never heard of any CEO in Bangkok who came from a slum, though if they did come from one, they probably weren't talking.

My name is Krit, but the brothers call me Kris. This is because they don't know that in Thai, when there's an "s" on the end of a word, it's pronounced as a "t." You'd think that was obvious, but to them it's not. **Nothing** is obvious to them. (The Jesuits are the worst.) The fathers are all *farangs,* but though their skin is white (or in some cases pink) they all think they know everything about us Thais. The brothers are a mix of *farang* and Thai.

Father Duvalier, the head of the whole place, has explained to me the meaning of my name: it's a magical knife, he said, wielded by mythological heroes. Well. it's more a dagger or dirk, sort of, and it's all twisty. I was about to ask him for more details, but there was immediately a clamor in the classroom.

"What about **my** name, Father?"

"And mine?"

So, Father Du – that's a little Thai joke: Du means strict, bad-tempered, ready to punish, and in fact Father Du beat us less often than any of the others, and often strayed from the subject completely – so, Father Duvalier spent a few minutes telling us the meanings of each of our names. But I knew mine was special because he'd named me himself. That's because I was abandoned on the doorstep in a basket, so I didn't come with a name already attached. Most of the others did.

This classroom I'm talking about, it's still there; it's more of a shed, really, and the desks and chairs are castoffs from a rather posh boarding school that a lot of children of politicians and CEOs go to. They're always upgrading their school desks, to our benefit.

Father Du is a high profile Father. He goes to social events, has an internet newsletter, and collects money from America. He's got a framed photograph of himself

with the Queen on his wall. He's written a couple of books about us, and they're not even that patronizing. In his own way, he does love us; that's why the orphanage isn't some soulless hole of horror with savage beatings and child abuse. Oh, it's grim, but we **could** be sleeping on the street, sniffing glue, and selling ourselves to tourists.

On the evening that my story starts, we've done the Buddhism thing, and we've done the Jesus thing; it's afternoon now, so many of the boys are off working. You may say, oh, it's child labor, oh, it's exploitation, but it's not like that: as long as it's not selling amphetamines, the brothers like us to have a sense of our own self-worth, our own money, even if it's just a twenty baht note after a hard day's slog.

I'm in the classroom alone. And it's hot. That's where I started, isn't it? It's May and it hasn't rained yet. I'm collecting all the schoolbooks, arranging them in piles. I'm not a good reader, so I arrange them in stacks according to color. I've been doing that for years, and now everybody is used to my system. It's such a hot day that the air itself is sweating. Through the foul air that blows in from the stagnant canal, you can get a whiff of jasmine and incense from the temple. There's also a strong scent of bananas. That's because we've been collecting bananas from everyone in the slum. We're all going to offer a platter of bananas to Ganesha tomorrow, which is Wednesday, which is sacred to Ganesha, because my friend P'Waen has had a dream that he's going to win the lottery, and in his dream, there were a lot of mice, and everyone knows that Ganesha is the patron of all rodents.

The sun is going to set soon, and a tall old man stands in the doorway. I know before I see or hear him: I don't know how I know, but there he is.

"Krit," he says to me. When I look up, I am immediately surprised, because, although he is a *farang,* he knows how to say my name properly.

"Are you the new teacher?"

"Well, yes." He comes into the shed and I see that he's really tall; he stoops. I think he's old, but really he doesn't **look** old, he just has **oldness** somehow clinging to him. It's in his eyes. When he speaks to me, he **does** speak Thai, not badly either; he says the words funny, but he uses very sophisticated ones, like the ones you hear on TV soaps.

"Krit," he says, "I am Mr. Leopold Strange, the new English teacher. I'm here in Thailand because I'm fleeing an unsavory past. Maybe you can imagine what that might be."

"Yes, I can," I say. "When a *farang* shows up in Bangkok with an unsavory past, it usually means only one thing." I think about Gary Glitter, the English pop star, indicted in Cambodia for chasing the girls. "Should I worry about you?"

"Why, yes, Kris, you should."

I start to get nervous. I stop putting the books into piles and I look Mr. Strange straight in the eye. "I know a thing or two," I say, "and I don't think you're telling me everything."

"That's true," he says. Then, he tells me what I've told you: there are the facts, and there is the truth.

"The facts: I'm a washed up writer of mediocre fantasy novels from England. Actually they're probably very good novels, they always got good reviews, but when it comes to sales, I was no J. K. Rowling, or I wouldn't be here. And okay, there was a scandal: I got a little too intimate with one of my readers. I should have known better. You know how pushy fans can be? No, I suppose you don't. But now, I am *persona non grata*. After the exposé in *The Sun* – oh, it was all lies, but who cares? – I couldn't have published a book if my name was Stephen King. So what could I do? Teach English in the third world, and that's where I've been: Colombia, Sri Lanka, and now here. But you know as well as I do that those are only the facts...they're not the truth."

"How is it that I know?"

"Because that's why I've come for you."

Sitting there in that dingy room with the stifling sweating air, I suddenly know there's more than one kind of truth, and

that some people are more than they seem to be. I know that Mr. Strange and I belong to **another** kind of people, that we see things differently, and that we know things to be true that other people can only guess or have theories about.

And I find myself telling him the things he was going to tell me: "You're some kind of **guardian**, some kind of...I don't know what it's called...some kind of *avatar*. And um, well, there's a **mission**, and you've come to me because I've got...um...**superpowers**?"

I know that word *avatar* because in Buddhism school, the young monks also tell us stories about gods and demons, and how they often come down to earth as avatars, to fight their cosmic battles in our world. I always loved those stories, but I never dreamed I would actually be **in** one.

"And how do you know all this?" asks Mr. Strange.

"I just **know**!"

"And what language have we been speaking?"

At this, I am struck dumb. Haven't we just been having a normal conversation? He's been using a lot of long words that I didn't think I knew. And everything seems, I don't know, **vivid**. But wait – did my lips move?

Did his?

"I think that's enough excitement for one day, Krit," says Mr. Strange. "Stay behind after class tomorrow, and we'll talk missions and superpowers."

It is at that moment that I notice he's eating all the bananas. Not peeling them, mind you, but scarfing them whole, positively **inhaling** them.

"Mr. Strange, those bananas are for Ganesha!"

"So?" he says, "It's already Wednesday in New Zealand."

# # #

It seems as though I look away for **just one second**, and when I look back he's gone. I run to the doorway, but all I see is a trail of

dust. Who is he, really? Can he fly? Is it true that he's been speaking directly into my mind, showing me things that words can't possibly express? It's all too weird for me. I go back to cleaning the shed, and then, since it's just about suppertime, I traipse on down to the refectory, where the other boys are already starting to gather, arriving by twos and threes from their jobs or from their football practice. The boys have a team which they have, perhaps overreaching a bit, christened Man U. You might think that they were fans of Manchester United, but the boys of Sacred Heart actually favor Liverpool, on the whole; it's just that the two loudest jocks in the school happened to be named Man and Yu. (Or did they get those nicknames from playing football all the time and being pretty much attached at the hip?)

Next week, they are playing against an extremely snooty private boys' boarding school. The snooty school's board believes that having these games will make them appear to be "one with the people." The brothers, on the other hand, believe that by allowing such games, they are giving us opportunities to socialize with our betters, and might somehow become **better** ourselves because of the experience. This may not be a very Christian viewpoint, but it's pretty typical of the brothers. As for what the boys think...well, no one asks.

I'm waiting for my friend P'Waen, who is called Waen because he wears glasses. He is not nearsighted. He found the glasses on a seat on the Skytrain one day. Because they were on the seat, no one sat there, even though the car was crammed. He seized the opportunity. It's the only time a little nobody like him was ever able to actually sit down on the Skytrain, so he wears the glasses for luck. He can only see without them.

I call him P' because he is like my older brother and it's respectful. I call everyone in the orphanage who is older than me P', but the other kids think it's quaint and pretentious. If you are reading this and you don't speak Thai, this word is pronounced like the word for urine.

By the time I'm through, you'll understand how I got so good at English.

Let me get back to the refectory. It's a fancy word for a canvas awning spread over a concrete yard, with old plumbing pipes holding it up. There are some wooden trestle tables, and there is a big window into the kitchen, where Auntie Daeng cooks our slop in gigantic pots. The morning slop is rice soup with some ground pork floating in it and plenty of coriander and scallions; the lunch slop is usually noodles with fish balls and beansprouts; the evening slop varies according to what Auntie was able to get cheaply in the market, but there's always rice and two side dishes: mystery meat curry and fried mystery vegetable (extra salty).

Tomorrow, Mr. Strange is going to use the word **Dickensian** to refer to the eating arrangements in the orphanage, and I actually know what that word means because last year, the brothers showed *Oliver* on movie night. We all wondered why Oliver wanted to escape a perfectly comfy institution and enter a life of crime, but *farangs* see the world differently than we do. Now, one day a month, thanks to an American philanthropist, we get hamburgers and ice cream. Of course, Oliver didn't get that. But he lived in England, which is a dismal place where people don't even have rice to eat.

After supper, we all have to wear our orphanage regulation pajamas, which consist of blue shorts with an elastic waistband, and a white tee shirt with the logo of the orphanage, which is a red heart, like a valentine. We're told that it is not in fact a valentine, but the Sacred Heart of Jesus. So, supper is our last chance to look different from each other. It's hard enough with the same extra short haircuts, but we all try.

The footballers are wearing a variety of football shirts from different teams, donated by kids from one of the British schools. When I see P'Waen, he's very smartly dressed for an orphan, with an actual shirt with a collar which he has found time to iron, and long pants. I'm impressed. I run up to him because I want to tell him

about Mr. Strange scarfing the bananas, but he starts talking before I can.

"Sneak out with me tonight! You have to!"

"Why tonight?"

"Because you have to, that's why. It's my dream, you know, the lottery, the mice –"

"Look, P'Waen, something happened to the bananas. I'm sorry, I couldn't stop it in time –"

"You don't understand. I already have the number! I found it, you know, in the tree."

There is a big, ancient tree just beyond the refectory awning: they say it's a magic tree. The brothers say it's superstition, but well, look who's talking – pieces of bread that turn into human flesh without anyone even noticing, regular as clockwork every Sunday – if you can swallow **that**, and believe me, the brothers do swallow it...

Everyone is piling up to the window to grab their food, but Waen is so excited he doesn't even want to eat. He grabs me by the arm and steers me toward the tree, while I'm more inclined to gravitate toward the mystery meat (today it's in **green** curry, tomorrow it will be red, yellow the day after). But okay, I follow. Every old and twisted-looking tree in Thailand houses a spirit. This one must, because even though it's on a Catholic property, someone has been hanging garlands on the branches, winding colored ribbons around the trunk, and burning incense sticks nearby. I see the red, burnt up stalks of the joss sticks poking out of nooks in the tree, and there's little scraps of yellow wax, too, from the candles people burn here when no one is looking.

"Feel, feel!" He kneels, and so do I; Waen takes my hand and holds it against the bark, a certain crevice, and tells me to rub.

I don't feel anything.

But I **hear** – inside my head – "919." I say it aloud and he shushes me. "Quiet, quiet, it's our secret!"

Then there's a thundering voice: "No whispering in the refectory!"

It's one of the Thai brothers, Brother Poo (oh yes, that means **crab**, do you think his parents knew what it means in English?); he's walking grimly up and down the perimeter of the covered area, wielding a ruler to quell us unruly boys with. He even uses it. I see one of the soccer boys shaking his right hand ruefully. The *farang* brothers hardly ever hit us, though they threaten more. I think it's because, even if you have to pass some kind of heartlessness exam to become a brother, the warmth and easygoing culture of Thailand sort of corrupts them.

I don't particularly want to feel the sting of that metal ruler on my hand, so I go and get my rice and curry, as does Waen. We sit down at the furthest possible end of one of the tables so we can go on talking.

"Waen," I say, "I didn't **actually** feel that number in the bark of the magic tree."

"Of course you did, Krit!" he says. "You said it right out loud."

"But it wasn't in the tree. I think I...I somehow **heard** you."

"But I didn't **say** anything."

"But...it's like you did."

Right then and there, a chill grabs hold of me. It's more freezing than an upper-class shopping mall. Because now, I suddenly divine what the tall old man meant. "How do you know all this?" His lips hadn't moved! I heard Waen speak to me, louder than if he'd really been talking. Which means I was able to hear **inside** of him. This is scary. My instinct tells me not to say anything.

Anyway, I listen some more, watching P'Waen's lips, and it doesn't happen again. On the other hand, he's jabbering away and maybe that drowns out what he's thinking. He's saying, "Listen, Krit, since I found out about this number I've been trying to buy a lottery ticket all day and I can't find 919 anywhere. But tonight, there's a major funeral over at the temple. They're bound to have lottery tickets. You've got to sneak out with me. If I go alone, I'll get caught, but somehow you never do."

When Waen says there's going to be a funeral, I know exactly which funeral he means. It's the funeral for this general who was very famous for fighting the communists, back in the days when they **had** communists, of course. All funerals have lottery ticket hawkers, because everyone knows that being near a corpse brings good fortune; but a general this powerful is going to be particularly *heng.* I wonder why his family chose to have the ceremonies in this un-high-society part of town. If we can't find the number from Waen's head at this funeral, we won't find it anywhere.

"We'll sneak out when the brothers are on their way into Compline," Waen informs me. Suddenly I understand why he's so well dressed. He wants to blend.

"I've nothing to wear," I say.

"So go scruffy," he says. "They'll just think you're a *dek wat.* You'll blend."

Sometimes I think the *dek wats* have it easier than we do. Most of them aren't orphans; they're country boys whose parents have sent them to the temple for a few years to learn proper manners and to earn merit for their next life by sweeping and dusting and carrying the monks' begging bowls. But they get the leftovers from the begging bowls, and everyone knows that monks get the best food.

We eat in silence for a while. Waen can't see his food clearly because of his glasses; he's constantly stabbing the table with his spoon. "Take them off!" I tell him. "Don't draw attention! Wait until Compline."

Sneaking out during or after Compline is always a good idea. Our brothers observe silence from the end of Compline until dawn, which means that there's not much they can do about anything. The lay teachers don't live in the orphanage, but there's always one who stays to supervise the dormitory.

Tonight, the sleepers' watchman is going to be Uncle Wong, who used to be an orphan himself and now owns a Chinese restaurant in Yaowaraj. He made good, so he volunteers one day a week to repay the brothers. But since he used to live in this dorm himself, he tends to turn a blind eye.

Or maybe it's just that he's always too drunk to notice.

We eat quickly, trying not to talk too much. Talking is actually forbidden during supper, but the brothers tolerate it as long as it's not too rowdy. When it's done, the brothers say a blessing. It's in very bizarre, "Catholic" Thai with weird words which no one understands, but in the end we all join in in a sort of boyish shout, making it sound more like a football cheer than a prayer: *decha phra naam phra bida lae phra butr lae phra chit amen*, which means something like "in the holy name of the holy father and the holy son and the holy mind amen" as far as I can figure. The brothers believe that these are three gods that are really one god, much like Brahma, Shiva and Vishnu from the shrine across the street.

Then, Father Du has an announcement. "There will be no dessert tomorrow," he says, "because all the bananas are missing from the kitchen. Now, you know that these sorts of pranks just hurt everyone, so if one of you will confess, we'll stage a public caning and I will have new bananas purchased from the discretionary fund. You see, honesty will be rewarded, even if there's a bit of pain beforehand, just as our dear Lord was scourged and crucified in order to allow all of us to attain paradise."

I'm puzzled. I mean, Mr. Strange guzzled a plate of them without peeling them, but has he already been in the kitchen as well? They keep **hundreds** of bananas there. Deep fried bananas with crunchy breading, stewed bananas in coconut cream sauce, sliced bananas, bananas wrapped in cheese – the things they can do with bananas on an orphanage-type budget are impressive. It **can't** have been Mr. Strange.

Another announcement: "Someone has tampered with the mousetraps in the video room. That person will be found and punished."

I can't help smiling at this. I know it's Waen. He fixed the traps after he had his little epiphany about the lottery. Tomorrow, if he wins the lottery, he'll confess and get six whacks. If he doesn't win, he won't confess.

That's fair, isn't it?

"Finally, I want to tell you all we will have a distinguished English teacher who will take over from Brother Adam, starting tomorrow. English class will be right after Thai history, right after Jesus hour. Mr. Leopold Strange is a famous writer. He was once nominated for the Hugo Award."

"What's that?" a boy shouts.

"Quiet!" Brother Poo raises his rod of chastisement.

"You don't scare me!" comes another voice. Brother Poo whips around and scowls.

"Children, children," says Father Duvalier, "we're not actually sure what the Hugo Award is. It's some American thing"

After supper we are all supposed to bathe, a habit which Waen abhors; water frightens him. He claims that he had a near-death experience at the seaside. None of the rest of us have ever been there, so maybe it's true.

The communal bath at the orphanage is like this: there is a long trough in the middle of the room, which the bath monitor fills from a plastic hose. Each of us has a plastic bowl with our name written on it in indelible marker; they hang on a rack at the bathroom door. We also have a little cloth bag with our toothbrush and toothpaste. There is a little pigeonhole for all our clothes.

The brother on duty blows a whistle, and we take our bags and line up on both sides of the trough. On the next whistle, we start dishing up the water in the bowls and pouring it over ourselves. We keep our shorts on, of course; the Thais are much more modest than *farangs,* who parade around with it all hanging out (we've seen the brothers in their shower, which **has hot water** – who knows why, you'd have thought this country was hot enough already.) We pour the water over ourselves in a regular rhythm. Then, whistle, soap; whistle, rinse. No talking, no horseplay of course, though you should see what happens when one of the less observant brothers is monitoring.

Brushing our teeth is much more of a

musical exercise because the brother **will** insist on one tweet for every stroke of the brush…**tweet** up, **tweet** down, **tweet** up, **tweet** down. By the end of it, we feel like we've been working our way through a song and dance number at the transvestite cabaret down the road.

Speaking of transvestites, one of the boys in my dorm, Pek, is a *katoey*. He's in the orphanage because his parents didn't want to pay for the operation. He has decided to become a priest instead, because the vestments are as close to a dress as he will ever be able to afford. But more about him later.

I'm brushing next to Pek tonight because Waen is already hiding in the video room closet. I can't help making fun of his mannerisms when he brushes. He says (between **tweets**) "Really, P'Krit. Don't be mean."

He's the only other boy in the orphanage who uses "P" as a form of address instead of "Hey, you."

"I'm not trying to be mean. One just can't help it, with you."

He knows I care about him, really, so he just giggles.

TWEEEEEEEET!!!!

Time to grab our towels and, oh, yes, a quick murmured recital of the magic mantra about the father, the son, and the holy something-or-other. Then, into the sleeping uniforms, and an hour for TV, reading, ping pong, or internet. There's also a fifth favored activity: being beaten up by Man and Yu. Favored by at least two of us, anyway.

There are only two computers, but they are broadband, so the 78 boys fight over them. In practice, a boy named P'Fat (the nickname is from babyhood, he is actually thin as a rake and really, really tall) is the guardian of the roster, but he can always be bribed. The brothers like him. He and Pek are the only ones who actually believe in any of this stuff and have even said they want to be priests. On the other hand, the brothers can't quite come to terms with Pek's reasoning….

Next year, I will be thirteen, so I will have one extra hour to fidget and fight over who goes online.

The brothers are off chanting to their threefold god. Uncle Wong has already arrived and has already hit the bottle. The video room is a big, messy place with donated plastic armchairs that don't match and three TVs that get louder and louder until someone yells, then start soft again. Boys are everywhere, wrestling, throwing things, seriously cussing (thankfully, the brothers never seem to know quite enough Thai to catch everything we say). The broom closet, I know, is where P'Waen is hiding.

I know the routine.

"Uncle Wong," I say, "can I be the one to close down tonight?"

"No one ever wants the job…it's extra work.

"Sucking up, eh, Krit?" he says. "Sure." And takes another swig. It's Mekong whiskey. Deadly stuff.

I can't wait for the entertainment hour to be over. The constantly crescendoing noise from the three TVs, which show a soap opera, a music video, and a boxing match – the three main interests of us boys – gets on my nerves so much that I just want it to stop. I'm about ready to scream, but I can't scream, so I just keep **thinking** and **thinking** and **thinking** –

Stop! I think.

And it stops.

Just for a split second. Not just the TV sets. It's as if all the noise in the **universe** suddenly stops. Not for long. For a heartbeat.

And everyone turns around and looks at **me**.

I whip around to see who they're looking at. It's definitely me. I start to shrug, but –

Then it's all back again, noisy as ever, the whole chaotic madness. As though nothing happened. The computers are whizzing, popping and clicking, and the boxing match is gearing up for a knockout.

But everybody knows something happened.

"Damn electricity," Uncle Wong says.

"The church ought to pay its bills."

The ping pong, the TV watching, the internet goes on. Only it's subdued.

What did I do?

Since meeting Mr. Strange, things **have** been strange. Do I really have superpowers? Am I really an unknown hero with a secret identity?

I think it's going to be an interesting English lesson.

# # #

P'Waen comes out of the closet blinking because he's been in the dark for an hour. "Brought you some civilian clothes," he says. I quickly slip on the white shirt over my orphanage tee; if I button it up, that will be enough of a disguise.

"Are you sure you want to do this?" I say. "You shouldn't believe everything a tree tells you."

In Canada, there's a Catholic orphanage where they beat you every day and the police run you down with sirens if you try to escape. We've all seen it on one of the video nights. The film won a lot of awards. Okay, Sacred Heart isn't like that at all. There are no locks. Once in a blue moon, someone even gets **adopted**!

Why would you run away? It's a jungle out there. Slip out for a lark, and if you get caught, take your whacks with a grin; that's all fine. But run away?

Bangkok is a city with ten million or more people, where the buildings transform themselves overnight, where the traffic gridlocks for hours yet everyone's in an infernal hurry; it's a dangerous place, and I've seen less of it than most tourists. My world is less than a kilometer square and, thanks, I'm happy to stay.

We have to hurry. We are only going to catch the tail end of the funeral. It's the back of the temple that abuts on our slum. The front is a grand *façade* where, I'm sure, all the general's well-wishers are pulling up in their long black cars.

We creep up to Pavilion No. 9 from the back. There are other pavilions with their own funerals going on – since every funeral in Bangkok lasts at least seven days, it's an assembly-line process in any major temple – but No. 9 is the biggie. The pavilion itself is air conditioned, which means it has been endowed by a wealthy family. We don't get in, of course, because it's packed. We don't want to get in, anyway.

The alley between pavilions is lined with wreaths; they're arriving thick and fast and the temple boys can't hang them fast enough. As we get there, we realize it's only the first day, and there's a queue stretching out of the door of the pavilion practically to the front gate of people waiting to anoint the deceased's hand with scented water... the bathing of the corpse. But they're hurrying it along; this temple probably rents by the hour, like some hotels in my neighborhood.

Everyone's in black, but no one seems particularly sad. As they stand in line, they're all gossiping about their wives, mistresses, boyfriends, children, and so on. There are mangy dogs everywhere. Waen kicks one of them out of his way.

"Don't do that!" I say. "It could be your father."

"He **ought** be reborn as a dog," P'Waen says, "for abandoning me like that."

"Don't be so unfilial."

"Unfilial? For God's sake, I'm an orphan."

"Shut up. Look for lottery tickets. Take your glasses off, no one knows you here."

The smell of incense wafts from everywhere. The already hot air is almost suffocating. In surround-sound, groups of monks chant from each pavilion. The mourners move rapidly. Waen urgently waves me over to join the end of the queue.

"What? We didn't even know the general." I say.

"If the general is going to give us money," he says, "we owe respect to his corpse at least."

No one looks at us funny. It seems that so many people respected (or at least feared) the general that there are people from all walks of life and, now that the people with

the black suits and ties and uniforms have all gone through, so can we. Almost before I can figure out what I'm doing, I'm inside the chilly pavilion and I'm on the ground, prostrating myself in front of a dead man with a chest full of medals, his face set in a grimace that suggests that he's about to have us all shot.

The atmosphere is choking because of all the perfumed holy water. The walls are piled high with wreaths. People are actually sobbing now, family members; as I get up, a weeping old lady thanks me for coming.

It turns out we're almost the last people. We haven't even left the pavilion when some soldiers come forward, wrap the body in a sheet, and hoist it into a coffin, then, a couple of burly truck driver types start hammering the coffin shut and –

<<Let me out!>>

"What was that?" I look around in a panic.

It's a voice coming from the coffin. Not a gruff, tough "execute them!" military type voice, but a voice like a little kid's, like mine or Waen's.

"Waen, he wants out! He's not dead!" I whisper.

<<Please, Krit, tell someone to let me out!>>

"He's talking to **me**!" I say.

"Let's get out of here!" says Waen, pulling me toward the door. "The lottery ticket sellers are gathering."

Sure enough, there's a whole army of them, each with a tray of lottery tickets slung across his shoulder: they've positioned themselves right next to the food, so you can't eat without being accosted.

<<Krit, little man, help me!>>

"Listen, P'Waen, I'm freaking out. The general's talking to me in my head."

<<I'm not ready to go yet!>>

A teeny little voice, more like a mouse than a big bad general. I'm afraid. Very afraid. I know that ghosts exist, of course, but meeting them is something that only happens to other people.

"Buy your tickets," I tell him, "and let's get back to the orphanage. I mean it."

"You're shaking!" Waen says. "That's not like you. It's not like you to be scared of ghosts."

"It's not like me to be having a conversation with one," I tell him. They're hoisting the general up now on their shoulders. This happens every night of a multi-day funeral; the body is paraded around and deposited in a special room, a dead body holding area, not to put too fine a point on it; then they trot it out the next evening for more prayers, and so on. It goes on until the cremation. It could be a week, but for someone this important, it could even be fifty days, or a hundred.

Everyone is getting in line behind the corpse now as it is being hefted out of the pavilion, and it would be very rude to try to get away. Besides, the lottery ticket vendors are swooping down on the funerary conga line and thrusting their wares at us. "Buy mine! Buy mine!" they're all saying, "Guaranteed lucky!" There's no money back guarantee, of course.

The procession moves slowly and with grave dignity, though many people stop to pick up the elegantly catered snack boxes that are being handed out. These are particularly fabulous: they're produced by the onboard dining service of Thai Airways, which makes a bigger profit on funerals, I suspect, than on passengers. Their chicken pies are famous throughout Bangkok.

Waen and I can't suppress our smiles as we manage to get a couple of boxes each. We're quite close to the coffin; I'm actually in the coffin's shadow as it passes under the harsh fluorescent lamps that line the alley that leads from pavilion to pavilion. All the while that P'Waen is extolling the chicken pies, I'm hearing the general's squeaky little baby voice and...worse of all...he's tapping on the coffin lid, and nobody hears it but me.

"Anyone got 919?" Waen keeps asking the vendors. He has to ask *sotto voce,* because if the news were to get out that someone has asked for a special number, **everyone** will want that number and there won't be any prize money left.

They thumb dutifully through their books of tickets – with their garish anti-forgery designs, you can go dizzy staring at a lottery ticket too long – and none of the sellers has one. The kids are quite perfunctory about it, especially as they don't think they're really going to make a sale to another kid.

You see, we've fooled all these high-society people into thinking we somehow belong – but you can't fool a street urchin. They look right into our eyes and they know we're trash, same as they are.

The procession moves along and a secondary procession moves along with it – the lottery vendors, all trying to walk sideways so they can keep up their high-pressure tactics, all flipping through their ticket books and spouting their pitches – we look like a massive black millipede on its side, its legs wriggling insanely. We go down a narrow passageway; a wrought-iron fence separates us from a courtyard where a moss-covered old pagoda stands; a young novice monk and a *dek wat* are peering through the railings at us.

We're at the end of the temple that's closest to the Hindu shrine; these last pavilions, and the mortuary, lean against a thin stucco wall that separates the Buddhists from the Hindus.

As we get closer and closer to the storeroom, I get more and more nervous; I'm starting to hear other voices, faint voices, and they're all saying: <<Please, Krit, please, Krit, get us out of here.>>

We're at the door of the storeroom! It creaks open! It's a double door, and when both doors swing all the way out the whiff of incense and rotting jasmine leaves and the perfume they douse the bodies in comes rushing out and almost knocks me over… then the voices are clamoring, demanding my attention, trying to get **me** to do something and I don't know what I have to do…

Just at that moment, Waen manages to buy three tickets with 919 final digits. "We're out of here," he says to me, and grabs my arm. We're aiming to make a dash for the railings, squeeze our thin bodies through,

and sprint across the courtyard round to the back door of the orphanage.

But they're pressing me into the storeroom, and a lady is handing out pomegranate leaves at the door (if you don't hold a pomegranate leaf when you're visiting a roomful of dead people, you're liable to be sucked into the limbo of the dead yourself); I have a twig thrust in my hand and the crowd sort of jostles me so I stumble over the threshold. Then, I'm standing in a corridor lined with shelves, three levels high, and the coffins are stacked on the shelves, plain ones, ornate ones, gold ones, wooden ones, each one with a little mini-shrine to the deceased in front of it, and a photograph, and decaying garlands, and flickering candles, and incense that makes me woozy from the whiff of it…and the crowd is propelling me further and further into the room but the corridor doesn't end, it's just coffin after coffin, receding to infinity, and always the voices, tugging at me, and now I feel ghostly hands, too, touching me, ruffling my hair, pulling at my tee shirt, and I'm fainting and fainting and –

Now what?

I'm falling into the floor. And the floor itself is dissolving. The dead people are pulling me down…I clutch the pomegranate twig, then it's as if something grabs me by the hair and I'm somersaulting up now, being hauled up through the ceiling by the hair and no one has even noticed….

# # #

Stillness. My eyes are closed. The clamor of the dead has died away. I'm sitting on something soft, fleshy. Slowly, I open my eyes. First, I see a pair of feet. They're **big**. I mean, my entire field of vision is these feet, and they are blue.

I look up. The stars are out. I seem to be in the courtyard, the one I was trying to run away to. I see a pair of eyes. Piercing eyes, with irises that are yellow, like sunlight. And they're **big**. I mean, the eyes are like two suns, and the face fills the whole sky. Or it seems that way. When I realize

that I am actually sitting on the palm of a giant hand, a **blue** hand, I panic.

Soft laughter fills the air.

This laughter is like the ringing of the great big temple bells, and like the sound of the wind when the monsoon is about to burst.

I'm panicking even more now, because the hand is rising into the air and I'm clinging to the index finger which wears a ring that has a diamond bigger than my head.

Then, I see the lips, and the teeth.

This is it. Sucked in by ghosts and devoured by a monster before my thirteenth birthday.

"Oh, Kris," the whole sky seems to say, "you do have a quaint way of seeing the world."

I look up and I look down. This is no King Kong peering down at a scantily clad creature he can crush in the palm of his hand, this is no monster. This is human, a man, a deep blue man, who is so tall that he seems to fill the entire world. And he calls me **Kris**, but not with a *farang* accent. It's more Indian, actually.

"What's going on?" I shout. "Did you eat all the bananas?"

The laughter again. It's a comforting laughter, but I have the feeling that this same laughter could topple mountains if it were just one or two decibels louder.

"No, not the bananas. That would have been Ganesha."

"But Mr. Strange ate a whole tray of them –"

"Exactly so."

"But –"

"Listen, Kris. About the dead. Get used to it. They're harmless. They can't hurt you; they really are dead, you know. Those voices are just faint echoes of what they were, or might have been. Sometimes, they can tell you something useful, but most of the time, it's just hot air."

"That's it? Ignore them?"

"It's hard, I know. The dead so want to stay attached. But when you answer back, they just stay longer in the world, and they have these long journeys to make, new wombs to seed, new lives to live. Of course, sometimes you're going to need their help."

"I am?"

In the last few minutes, I have gradually become aware of something extraordinary. I am sitting on somebody's hand, looking down at this little world of mine, and seeing, beyond it, the frantic, neon-strewn skyline of Bangkok, looking up into the face of some kind of supernatural being, and I'm **not scared**. It appears to be the most natural thing in the world.

I realize that this moment has been in my life all along, and that everything I've ever lived through has been a big setup for this conversation. It's the mystery of my birth, the secret identity, all that stuff.

"Quite exciting, isn't it?" say the giant lips. I catch a glimpse of a lapis uvula, its gold flecks glittering, and a tongue that rolls like a tsunami. I don't quite know what to say. Obviously he reads my mind.

But I read minds too. Isn't that what I've learned today?

And the dead talk to me, though I haven't yet learned how to answer.

"You're going to have to learn control. You've got an inkling now of who you are and what you can do. You're going to have to do it responsibly, too. It's a tough job, saving the universe. There aren't many who could even try."

"The **universe**?" Now, that startles me.

"You will have to learn about microcosms and macrocosms," he says. "A galaxy in a grain of sand and all that. And, you will have to learn that changing **everything** sometimes means changing one single heart."

"I see," I say, not seeing.

The laugh again. "I've whetted your appetite, I hope," he says. "In a moment, I'm going to put you back down. In your dorm room, safe and sound. I shouldn't really manifest like this, you know. It's telling the story out of sequence. You should really only see me at the end. But you will soon learn that I'm playful. And listen to my banana-scarfing son; he's one, too."

"One what?"

"Be serious for a minute. Know that at any given time, there are only seven mortals in the world who can look me in the eye like this and live. These seven mortals have a mission. They keep the universe on track. Now, some of you are famous. I'm sure you've heard of Jesus, Buddha, Mother Teresa, and people like that. Mozart, too, and Einstein. You haven't heard of **them**, but blame that on Thailand's ethnocentric school curriculum. But others aren't so obvious. Take you, for instance. Don't be cocky, I'm not saying you're Jesus. That would drive Father Duvalier up the wall for sure. I'm just saying that you're here on a mission, and if you fail, **everything** collapses."

"What's the mission?"

"It unfolds as you go along. Goodbye now."

He starts to lower me to the ground. I tell him, "Not so fast...you haven't told me who you are."

Laughter again...this time, it seems that the whole sky is laughing. There's thunder and lightning, too. He says, "I am the uncreated one. I am Nataraja, he who dances the cosmos into being in the dawn and smashes it into smithereens at sunset and reshapes it the next morning. I am Ishvara, the very essence of things. I am Agni, the fire that lives in your soul. I am the universal Atman." He's like Father Duvalier when he wants to avoid the issue, like when you try to get him to answer a question about sex. Or like when the royal family comes on the evening news, and the news anchor goes into a string of fancified, polysyllabic, incomprehensible royal Thai, which nobody can understand.

"Yes, but who **are** you?"

I must be an idiot. I just don't get it.

"Do I have to spell it out?"

"I'm just a dumb twelve year-old kid, remember? Just tell me."

"I'm God."

# # #

I come to in my bed. It's barely dawn, but the bustle has started. My dorm sleeps for-

ty boys in double bunks lined up end to end, five deep, eight across, with a single aisle just fifty centimeters wide. Almost everyone is already up, and I can hear water splashing from the communal bathroom. So I've missed the big crunch. I've been told that 5:45 am in our dorm is very much like trying to get down the aisle of an airplane.

I rub my eyes. I can only half recall last night at first; in fact, I'm sure it's some improbable dream. Then, I see P'Waen standing in the door waving a sheet of newsprint.

"No, no, no, no, no!" he's shouting, and hitting the nearest bedpost with a clenched fist.

Pulling on a shirt, I spring down from the top bunk. "How could I have been so stupid?" he says.

I want to tell him about my encounter with godhead, about the voices from the coffins, about plucking magic numbers from his head, but no, Waen's one-track mind can't hold anything but his disappointment.

"What's wrong?" I ask him.

"What's wrong? What's wrong? Look at this! Third prize, split twelve ways...thirty thousand baht ..."

He sticks the paper in my face and I see the number 919 in huge, bold print.

"Congratulations!" I say. "What are you screaming about?"

He turns the sheet of paper rightside up.

"If I'd been standing on the **left** instead of the **right**," he says, "I'd have used my other hand to feel the bark. The number was written **sideways**! I'd have known it was 616. I'm such an idiot!"

He takes the lottery tickets from his shirt pocket and he's about to rip them up when I catch his hand. I've noticed something a bit odd. The numbers...the figures... they seem to be wavering, shimmering.

"Give me those tickets."

I clasp them between my folded hands, as though I were praying with them. I wonder what it would be like if last night's vision were true, if I was, in fact, one of seven specially gifted human beings sent to the world of men on some divine mission....

"What are you going to do?" says Waen. "Change the numbers?"

I unfold my palms.

"You're double-stupid," I said. "The tickets were upside down when you bought them."

Because the serial numbers now end in 616.

I hand the tickets back. "You'd better go for your whacks," I say.

"Come with me," says P'Waen. "Make sure I don't cry."

# # #

Waen has put on two pairs of undershorts and he is wearing his thickest pair of pants. It is silly of him, because Father Duvalier never enjoys hurting us. He just knows that it wouldn't be a proper orphanage without a bit of tyranny and abuse. Wouldn't be Catholic without its share of repression and guilt.

So, we're standing in Father Du's office, which has wooden walls and a crucifix and, of course, the all-important framed photograph of himself with Her Majesty the Queen. There is a rattan bookcase with battered missals and a bible in Thai, which he's desperately been trying to slog through for as long as I've known him (all my life).

He sits behind his desk and says, "My boys, what brings you to me now? You haven't signed up for catechism, and that's not until eleven. Perhaps you have something to confess?"

Waen says, "Krit had nothing to do with it. He's just volunteered to be here with me."

"To make sure you take your punishment like a man."

Waen nods.

"Well, what's it to be this morning? Sneaking a handful of the host for a midnight snack? You're not, by any chance, responsible for the mustache on the statue of the blessed St. Catherine?" Father Du looks at Waen. "It's more serious, then. Impure thoughts, perhaps. Maybe you even..." he furrows his brow. "Touched yourself?" No answer. He thinks for a while longer and then says, "I've got it! You went out after bedtime!"

Waen nods again.

"Then it's very curious indeed," said Father Duvalier, not looking P'Waen in the eye, but fingering a little malachite rosary that hangs from his belt, "because it wouldn't be normal for a boy who sneaked out after bed time to report to me in the morning for six whacks."

"I won the lottery," says Waen, "and I need you to go and sign for the money."

"Aha!" says the Father. "You'd suffer one of my notorious scourgings for the sake of a few hundred baht?"

"Thirty thousand," P'Waen blurts out.

"He meant well," I say quickly.

"Yes ..." Waen's mind is racing to find something that sounds noble. "I wanted to do something for my dorm mates. I wanted...um, yes, I wanted to give them all a day by the sea. Do you know, most of them have never seen the ocean? We're a country surrounded by water, and yet –"

And Father Duvalier begins to laugh. This isn't the divine laughter of God; it's an earthy guffaw that makes his jowls bounce around like the dewlaps of a bulldog. "So, so, so!" he splutters. "Your entire act of mischief was motivated by altruism!"

"Do unto others," P'Waen begins, but he can't finish...he never listens in religion class.

"As you would be done by," I mutter, hoping that Father Du doesn't realize that the sentence is being finished by someone else, which has the unfortunate effect of causing the director of the orphanage to look closely at me for the first time, studying my face very carefully.

"You know, Kris," he says, "I can't figure out your role in all this. In fact, I can't figure you out, period. Why would you aid and abet...wait. More fundamentally, why is it that I can read your friend Waen like an open book, but you, you strange little boy, you look at me and you can put up this **shield**, and I can't see what's going on in your mind at all?"

I don't answer him. Because I'm thinking about it myself. What Father Du is talking about is somehow connected with hearing the ghostly voices from the coffins. I know how to receive these voices, and I know how to block others from hearing my own. I've made a roomful of people go suddenly quiet just by **thinking** about it, and I've turned printed digits upside down on a lottery ticket. In the last twenty-four hours, I've completely lost track of who I'm supposed to be. I'm at sea.

"Well," says Father Duvalier, "I will tell you what I have concluded. First, you are to be commended for your generosity, Waen, in donating the money to give your friends a day at the beach. For that, I will remit you six strokes of the cane. However, you lied when you said that you were motivated by love for your fellow orphans, for which I'm afraid I'm obliged to whack you an extra six times. The sneaking out at night is the regulation six, so that leaves six. All right?"

"That...seems fair, Father," Waen says, gulping.

"As for you, Kris, I'm going to give you four whacks on principle. You did something wrong, I'm sure. Even if you didn't do it last night, I'm sure there's some crime you've committed that I haven't punished you for."

That's a bit much. I mean, of course I did sneak out, but didn't Waen carefully not snitch?

"However, before I administer this punishment," says Father Duvalier, "I have something else to say. I refuse to have you squander this money on a trip to the beach. It will go directly into a fund so that you can start college in five years' time, assuming, Waen, that you are able to pass the entrance exam." I am going to protest that we are now going to get beaten for no real reason at all, but he goes on, "However, I am touched by your statement that many of the boys have never seen the sea. The orphanage will therefore use its discretionary fund and we will all go next Saturday."

This logic, as you can see, was convoluted, but everything adds up neatly. It is Jesuit logic, of course. In the end, he doesn't hit us very hard, although he **does** make Waen take off his extra underwear.

# # #

Thus it happens that when we enter the refectory for lunch we are greeted by a huge cheer, and Pek runs up to us and pecks us both on both cheeks, which is embarrassing but typical of him. Everyone knows that we've willingly borne the lash so the whole gang can go to the beach on Saturday. And when we go up to the window to get our food, we both have something extra: chocolate ice cream. Even though it's not hamburger day. Auntie Daeng grins when she ladles it out, and I realize that the staff are going to get to go to the beach as well. Despite my burning butt, which is even hotter than the sweltering Bangkok sun, it is turning out to be a good day, if I don't think too much about the supernatural.

Of course, there is English class.

The classroom where I first met Mr. Strange is now filled to the brim with sweaty boys; we've turned on the electric fan, but it hardly makes a difference. Our beautiful desks, donated by the international school, were not intended to seat three apiece, but there's a lot of us and not a lot of room. Man and Yu are trying to beat up Pek, which he quite enjoys, but P'Fat is rescuing him by tickling the soccer boys into oblivion. It's rowdy.

When Leopold Strange enters the room, it becomes oddly, unnaturally cool. The blast of cold actually makes the boys shut up, and they all turn around to look at him. The air also smells sweet, like banana syrup.

Mr. Strange is tall and fills the doorway; this time, he has a cane, which I believe to be a prop, because he didn't have one yesterday. He shuts the door, shuffles up to the front of the class, and mumbles, "English, English, English." Then he looks up at all of us. "Do any of you know why you're being made to study English?"

P'Fat, always the intellectual, says, "It's for our careers, sir, and to help us out of the gutter."

"True. But there is another reason. You see, if you know English, you will be able to read my books."

"You're a writer, sir?" says dainty little Pek.

"Yes, and I write about dragons, and princesses; gods, heroes, and monsters; I write about good versus evil, about rescue and redemption, beauty and betrayal, delight and despair."

"I see all those movies," Man says. "Especially the ones with dragons. Though the subtitles go by too fast."

"I'm not talking about movies," says Mr. Strange. "I'm talking about words. Words are all magic spells, and today, in the twenty-first century, the strongest magic resides in English. Not that there's anything inferior about other languages, but you see, the gods take turns, over time: they used to speak Sumerian, then Egyptian, then Greek, then Sanskrit, and right now it's English. For the moment, there's truth in English. But it doesn't work if it's your native language, you see; then it's just chitchat. You have to learn it, the way you'd learn a mantra. You have to form your tongue around those weird and wondrous words, imbuing them with a wild, inner vitality. Then they will become true speech, words that actually **are** what they describe."

He has everybody's rapt attention, but I, for one, am not buying it. On the other hand, he's already given me his talk about **truth** and **facts,** so I know that what he's trying to tell us is hidden. I only have to figure out –

Krit.

Huh? He's still talking, weaving a skein of texture and symbol so audacious that no one can stop paying attention, but inside what he's saying there's another voice, and it's speaking right inside my head....

<<Listen, Krit, listen! Remember, you and I have a private date after this little exhibition. And none of your friends are invited. This revelation's for you alone.>>

When? I catch myself. My lips did not move.

<<Sneak out again tonight. Yesterday was just an overture. Tonight begins the real adventure. Meet me when the moon is full.>>

But I just got four slices!

<<And it was worth every cut.>>

He's right, of course. I don't really have a choice. Big things are happening and I am a very great part of what is going to unfold. The coolness that emanates from Mr. Strange envelops me and comforts me.

I've never known what it's like to have a father or mother, never been hugged by a parent, never just sat down quietly with an older person I totally trust and just basked in that trust; today, in this crowded classroom with the sweat-drops hanging in the air, I feel like I'm resting beneath a vast tree, shaded and protected by a power too big to comprehend. Today, I know that Mr. Strange and I are some kind of kin.

Come moonrise, I suppose I will learn what kind.

# # #

I don't think I'm ever going to get to sleep, but the truth is I fall asleep instantly, and I fall into a kind of dream.

It's a sort of jumble of everything that's happened lately; of lottery tickets raining down from the sky, of gods cupping me in the palm of their hand, of generals trying to claw their way out of coffins. And through it all, there's me, and I'm prowling through this fantastical nightmare jungle, my right hand clenching the handle of the twisty *kris* that came in the basket when I was a baby. Yes, I'm just stalking through dense undergrowth, bones crunching beneath my bare feet, my heart thumping like a pile driver. I don't know what drives me. Fear, certainly. I'm being hunted. Who is hunting me? In the distance, I hear the footfall of something – someone – **big.** Like one of the demons that guard the Temple of Dawn beside the river. Or like a dinosaur. Or a dragon. I'm running now, heedless of the twigs that snap and dig into my soles.

<<What are you running for? Who are you running from?>>

I hear the laughter that's like the wind. I hear a voice, with a subtle Indian accent, whispering <<*Kris, Kris, Kris.*>> I'm wielding the knife but I also **am** the knife, I'm being wielded by something, someone much bigger than myself.

<<Kris, Kris, I twist you into the dragon's flesh, I turn you, I draw the glacial blood and stir it up to a volcanic heat. Turn, Kris, turn!>>

I stumble on a clearing. The moon is behind a cloud and there's only a faint radiance here. I stand in the silky half-dark and I cry out, "I want to see!"

All at once, the clouds shift and I'm bathed in moonlight. There's only me and the moon and the glistening dagger. I glow in the light. I'm so bright that if someone were to look at me he would go blind.

And suddenly I realize it's the moon that glows in **my** light. I am the source; the moon is only mirroring me. And it makes me lonely.

I wake up in the dark, all sweaty, floating on a sea of young boys' snores.

# # #

So, here I am, in my standard issue Sacred Heart Orphanage pajamas, standing just outside the gate. It's late, terribly late, and I am in the moonlight as in my dream, and yes, I feel alone.

The moon is full and makes me glow. Behind me is the orphanage; to my right the Buddhist temple; to my left the Hindu shrine. This patch of ground, parched because there's been no rain, feels hemmed in somehow by the three places of worship. I wonder if I shall ever be free.

Father Duvalier did tell me once that the Jesuits believe that if they have a child before he turns five, they have him forever.

Where's Mr. Strange?

First, the sudden coolness. Then, the smell of ripe bananas, and the still air becomes sweet, as though someone has been spraying a sugar atomizer around. The sugar sort of ripples like a heat wave. I stick out my tongue and really, the air tastes sweet, like a delicate syrup ladled out over wafer-thin pancakes. It's a feeling of immense joy and calm.

But Mr. Strange's words are far from calm.

"You almost ruined it!" he says.

He's behind me. I never heard him sneak up.

"Ruined what?" If someone would only tell me the whole truth instead of always assuming that I can guess things...

"You've been listening to too many dead people. You've been slapping a great cosmic **shut up** on the universe...do you know how much energy that cost? Probably killed off an entire star cluster in some backwoods galaxy. And that party trick of yours with the 919 and the 616...**personal gain** yet! You broke the cardinal law of the avatar code: **never use your powers for personal gain!**"

"But it was for P'Waen's gain," I protest.

He grabs my shoulders, stares me down. "I suppose it was at that," he says, and sighs. "Nevertheless, it is karma. Cause and effect. I was hoping to begin this adventure with a *tabula rasa,* but instead you're setting off with a hefty handicap: forty-two karmic demerits."

He lets me go. "Chew on that for a while. And no more sugar, you'll rot your teeth."

At once, the rippling syrup transforms into the bitterest of cough medicines, and I start to retch.

"Don't get sick on me yet. This is the moment you've been waiting for. The revelation. I'm going to tell you everything. Well, I'm going to tell you a lot. Keep your wits about you, because you only get to hear this exposition once."

"Why?"

"Oh, there you go. Stop **why**ing or we'll be here all night. But since you ask, this is the answer. You are part of a great a cosmic story. And in such stories, it is customary that the expository lump should be kept to a minimum, because we don't want to lose our audience."

"Our audience?"

"Yes. *Das Publikum.* The silent majority. The myriad inhabitants of the myriad worlds. We are doing this for them, not for ourselves. Before I start, perhaps you have questions."

"Only one. You keep using words and ideas I've never heard of, and yet I seem to get them right away. But I know I'm just an average kid. I don't do well in school. What are you doing to me?"

He laughs and jabs me in the middle of my forehead. "You have, my little disciple, a third eye. Yesterday, it blinked open. By next week, you will see far more than you ever dreamed."

He claps his hands and the taste of cough syrup vanishes. But the sugar doesn't return. Instead there is just the usual burning city air. "Illusion," says Mr. Strange. "All is illusion. It's simple physics. The universe is a mass of dancing waveforms that pretend to be particles that blip in and out of existence in a femtosecond or less, and the real world that you touch, feel, smell, taste, love so much, why that's just a diaphanous wisp of a thing that happens between the cracks of time and space. That's what the Buddha taught, and that's what Stephen Hawking teaches."

"Who's – never mind." I have a fleeting image of a wise but voiceless professor in a wheelchair, communicating by wiggling a single finger on a computer touchpad.

"Come, Krit," he says, talking me by the hand, "today I will give you the earth, the moon, and the stars."

He jabs my forehead once again. And yes, something happens. Wham! Colors I've never seen, planets I've never visited, quick images that flash by like cuts in a music video. He jabs. He jabs. And he starts talking again, quicker than a human being can talk, and my mind is opening up and taking it all in....

"Let's talk numbers first. This point you're standing at is zero, the still center of the careening universe. Do you see that pebble?"

He points to the ground. Sure enough, I see a single pebble set in the dried mud. "That pebble," he tells me, "marks the navel of the world."

"Sure," I say. I bend down to pick it up.

It's stuck in the earth. I try to yank it free but it's **heavy**. I'm panting. I get frustrated. I try again. Nothing doing.

"I can't pull the stone out of the earth," I say, remembering many an epic movie watched on video night, "which means I'm not the rightful King of England."

"To move that stone," says Mr. Strange, "is to move the whole world. And yet, there will come a time when you must do it."

"I think I'm ready for that expository lump now," I say. "I promise not to interrupt you again."

"Very well. Zero: the place we stand in. The still point of the turning world. The moment before the Big Bang. Now, listen carefully because this is all about numbers. You'll think twice before you ever dare change a nine into a six again.

"*ONE*: that is the Indivisible. The principle that guides the universe. The Atman. Do you know who it is?"

"Um...Ishvara?"

"Good boy. You don't miss a trick. Now *TWO*: two stands for karma. Cause and effect. You pick up this pebble **here**, well, somewhere **out there**, a pebble picks **you** up. This is the unbreakable law of the universe...as opposed to the many breakable laws. *THREE* is the ways that you can see Ishvara. You are standing at the exact conjunction between them. You see? You can worship Ishvara as **many**, like the Hindus; you can worship him as **one**, as the Jews and Christians do; or you can worship him as **none**, as do the Buddhists and the particle physicists."

"And four are the elements?"

Mr. Strange laughs. "Sort of. *FOUR* are the sleeping dragons whose bodies, locked together, are the world. Yes, they are sometimes called earth, fire, air and water. They have other names too. You will be meeting one soon, the one named Jade. He's a bit of a problem."

"And what are five?"

"*FIVE* are the wise ones, or *rishis*, who guard all wisdom in this world. If you're ever in trouble, you must find one of them. He will not answer you directly, but will give conundrums inside conundrums."

"Are you one?"

"No. I'm one of the *SEVEN*. At any given moment in the world of men, there are seven guardians. They are gods, celestial beings, sometimes even demons, because *karma* isn't about good and evil, but about balance, about cause and effect. They have come to earth as avatars. They have a mission here. But when you are born, you do not remember your past lives, unless something happens to trigger this moment of supreme gnosis; you must learn who you are, gradually, figure out your mission, and accomplish it. Do you know which being I am?"

The bananas? The sugar? "I'm guessing Ganesha?"

"And you're lucky it's me. I'm the god of creativity and truth. I cannot lie. Any other one wouldn't be nearly as straight with you about the nature of reality."

"And what is your mission?"

"My mission, Kris, has been to locate you, as quickly as possible, and it was a pain, let me tell you! I've been looking for you for almost a hundred years! It is to find you and to start you on **your** mission."

"Which is?"

"It seems that you are the only member of the *SEVEN* who is able to tame the *FOUR.*"

And now I'm **really** perplexed. Nothing is sinking in. From a nobody living in a dorm with thirty-nine street rats, I've turned into someone quite different, someone I don't know. Mr. Strange looks at me, and I feel his concern; I've always been his special project, I suppose. And suddenly he says, "Let's go get some bananas. I'll tell you the rest along the way. Hop on."

Mr. Strange gets down on his hands and knees. Now I've seen it all, but okay, I jump up on his back and just like that, Mr.

Strange is an elephant; not one of those mangy, pathetic creatures that parade up and down the street trying to earn a few baht from the tourists, but a magnificent creature, wild-eyed and trumpeting, with terrifying tusks. Actually, only one tusk; the other is broken. I remember the myth; Ganesha broke off one of his tusks and made it into the magical pen with which he wrote down the *Mahabharata*.

On his back, draped over his flanks, is a caparison of gold and silk. There are soft red pillows. I lean back. He's as smooth and as cushiony as a Mercedes Benz. And he even comes with a built-in iPod and some mini-speakers. "Mr. Strange," I say, "they sure named **you** well."

He sets off. And I will say this: no one has witnessed our conversation, or the transformation; no one but the moon. Beyond this little triangle of slumland and religious establishments, there lies Bangkok; I have to say that I have never left our neighborhood, except a few times, in Father Duvalier's car (he does have a Mercedes, though he says it was a gift from a sponsor) to help him carry groceries. But in thirty seconds flat, Mr. Strange has bounded through the alley between the orphanage and the shrine and has popped out in Sin City, with bars and women of ill fame (another Father Du expression) beckoning like sirens from every corner; with stalls huckstering everything from fake DVDs to fake Armani; with cars all crammed together and honking and motorcycles weaving between the gridlocked cars, with little children hawking flower garlands, and people, people, people. Neon in garish colors flashes everywhere and gas fumes clog my nostrils.

When they see us bounding down the sidewalk, people scurry out of the way. Tourists snap photographs. The food stalls, the ones on wheels, are shunted closer to the shopfronts. I see a woman frying bananas in a massive wok and Mr. Strange says, "Get me some. And if you see any sugarcane, I'll take it as well."

There's money in a pouch next to me

on the silk rug. Mr. Strange bends down, bends his legs so I can clamber down, and I buy a bag of deep-fried bananas. I feed them to Mr. Strange, who gets impatient, seizes the whole thing with his trunk and shoves it down his throat, paper bag and all. It's one of those bags made from recycled old fashion magazines, and I daresay the ink is poisonous, but I suppose those things don't matter much to a god.

"That's better," he says, and his elephant body begins to shimmer and he just sort of morphs back into Mr. Strange the human being. No one in the street notices a thing. He's just standing there and the paper bag seems to have passed through his system, because he's scrunching it up and tossing it into a dumpster in a side alley next to a foot massage parlor.

"You were going to explain about *SEVEN* and *FOUR*," I remind him.

"I feel like coffee," he says. He makes me follow him into a 7-11, where he buys a large black coffee and gets me a plastic bag full of dim sum to munch on. Then, we leave again and we walk together, getting further and further away from the world I know; all the way, I'm acutely aware that I am walking around in a crowded street at midnight in my pajamas, but, as I've said, no one seems to see us unless we want them to.

"You're here to make the four dragons shape up. Because whenever a sleeping dragon wakes, it's almost certain to be a disaster. And Jade is a tough one: he's a fire-breather. Why do you think it hasn't rained yet?"

"Oh, I know the answer to that," I say. "Father Duvalier showed us that movie with Al Gore. It's the pollution, and the carbon, and the greenhouse effect, and all sorts of scientific stuff."

"Those are **facts**," says Mr. Strange, "but we deal in truth. They will try very hard, all those activists and those well-meaning Americans, with their graphs and their carbon credits; but unless you can put the Dragon Jade back to sleep, you're soon going be able to fry an egg on the pavement in Saskatchewan."

"So, my mission is to stop global warming?"

"Don't be so prosaic. You're going to assemble a team of stalwart adventurers. Mighty heroes, strong-thewed amazon women, or maybe even just the dregs and rejects of society – who's **on** your team is completely up to you. You will fight your way to the dragon's lair, and you will drug, seduce, or sweet-talk him into going back to sleep, but on no account can you kill him; you need him to breathe, or there won't be any rain forest in Brazil." This adventure's becoming more outlandish by the minute. "And that's not your mission *per se*; well, just a small part of it. Your mission is dragon control in general."

"I've seen it in movies," I say. "I can handle it." I love those sorts of movies. "You think I can hatch a baby dragon and rear it as my own?"

"The Dragon Jade," says Mr. Strange, "has as a section of his spine the entire mountain range of the Himalayas. If he were actually to wake up fully, one of his wings would rip India in half. His right claw pokes out somewhere in Shanghai; one nostril is Krakatoa. Speaking of Krakatoa – you've heard of the big climate change in 535 AD? I guess not. The Dragon Jade had a nightmare. He stirred in his sleep. Fire shot out through that one nostril. The sun was blotted out for months – read your ancient history – droughts, famines, bubonic plague, the collapse of Byzantium – it was the end of classical times, and the world was plunged into the dark ages. That's what a single misplaced breath can do; that harks back to TWO: cause: effect. This isn't Siegfried versus the Giant Iguana. Get serious."

I don't talk back for a while. I'm thinking. Despite the supposed opening of my third eye, much of this is still going in one ear and out the other. This is all clearly a lot more than I can chew, even if I **am** some kind of divine avatar. There's a big difference between conjuring up a lottery ticket and fighting a dragon the size of a continent. And maybe Mr. Strange **is** a reincarnation of Ganesha, one of the world's most popular deities, but who am I?

We stop at a food stall so Mr. Strange can buy a bag of sugar cane. He doesn't suck the pieces; he just wolfs them down whole. He keeps walking; I can barely keep up and I wonder whether he will let me ride again. "Where are we going?" I ask him.

"A hero must have his weapon."

We turn down a side alley. It must be three in the morning by now, but people still jam the street and several of the shops are just opening up for business. An old Chinese lady is setting up baskets of fruit as another winds up the steel blinds of her grocery. A restaurant is hanging up whole boiled chickens in a glass case, getting ready to dole out huge helpings of chicken rice. Next to it lies a glittering array of cameras and electronics. "I'm lost," I say. I'm assuming this is somewhere near Yaowaraj, which is the Chinatown of Bangkok, but I know that it is nowhere near the orphanage, and I wonder just how far I have ridden on the back of the god.

"I know you are," he says. "Who wouldn't be? You were blind, but now you see."

"See what?"

"That we are **all** lost."

# # #

We stop in front of a pawnshop. There is a red neon sign in Chinese; I wouldn't have been able to read the sign as there was neither Thai nor English, but from the window display, with its used electric guitars, broken necklaces, and weatherbeaten knickknacks, I can tell what kind of place it is. I'm about to ask why we're going in when suddenly it becomes clear.

We step into the shop; an electronic bell goes **ping**, and a huge man shuffles to the front. He seems to be a *farang,* but he speaks Thai with the most upper-class accent I've ever heard. The shop, which couldn't have been more than 10 square meters when viewed from the outside, has become huge. It is lined with books, CDs, DVDs, and all sorts of repositories of knowledge like ancient banana-leaf manuscripts and ancient Roman scrolls. In one bookcase, hundreds of little clay tablets are stacked, filled with a fidgety, squidgy, wedgy kind of writing. It's not a pawnshop at all.

Or is it?

Music is playing. It's music I can't put my finger on. It sounds familiar and strange at the same time: a woman sings with an orchestra (Father Duvalier relaxes with CDs of opera, so that's what I think it must be), but her voice keeps soaring higher, higher, higher until it passes out of the range of human hearing, and yet I know it's still going on....

"Lovely, isn't it?" says the proprietor. I see he has been weeping. "It's the opera Beethoven would have written, about the nature of deafness, about love, about...oh, it's positively **semiotic**!" He looks up at us, doesn't seem to really see us until Mr. Strange clears his throat. "Yes, daring, isn't it, you say, stretching all the way into the range of canine hearing like that. Inaudible, you complain! But it wouldn't have made any difference to Beethoven."

"Customer!" says Mr. Strange.

"May I help you?" says the fat *farang.* "We've got a run on James Joyce right now, *The Secret Key to the Puns in* Finnegans Wake. And the *Lost Plays of Euripides* seem to be enjoying a bit of a renaissance, don't you know. And of course, the *Unwritten Beethoven Quartets* is a perennial favorite..."

"Later, Bob," says Mr. Strange. "Mr. Halliday, Mr. Krit."

"Krit, you said! Oh you mean **Kris**! Ah, you'll be wanting the dagger. Exquisite workmanship. Very ancient. Feel the raw power." He reaches under the counter and pulls out a kris. **My** kris.

"That's mine!" I say. "But Father Duvalier keeps it in his office."

Mr. Strange says, "My boy, the orphanage has been through hard times. When was the last time you **saw** the notorious knife that came in the basket you arrived in?"

"Why –" He was right.

I look at the twisty thing. It's maybe nine inches long, and it glitters, it **writhes**,

it's alive. It occurs to me that my dagger may have a soul. That it may have lived with me before, in the other life, the one I cannot yet remember.

"Perhaps you recall," says Mr. Strange, "the time when you were eight years old, and the orphanage didn't serve supper for three days? The big stock market crash? Don't blame good old Father Duvalier. He has every intention of redeeming the dagger. But now, he won't have to."

Mr. Halliday holds out the kris to me, handle first. I clutch it for the first time. That handle: it **molds** itself to my hand. It **is** alive. It's warm, not like metal, but like an old friend. "Ooh," Mr. Halliday says, "he knows you." He offers me a cookie from a jar on the counter. It tastes like chicken.

"I was going to warn you," Mr. Strange says. "Mr. Halliday's day job is food critic for the *Bangkok Post.* Don't eat anything here unless you're expecting the unexpected."

"I see you remember the episode with the dragon's fin soup," Mr. Halliday murmurs with a certain ruefulness mixed with nostalgia. I bite down on the cookie again, and the next bite tastes like French fries.

"Next time you come," says Mr. Halliday, "let me know in advance. I'll order the oyster wontons from next door. You will think you've gone to heaven."

This isn't a pawnshop," I say, "and you're not a pawnbroker." I turn to Mr. Strange, desperately seeking confirmation. "Well, it's true! Pawnbrokers are wizened old men who look at your earrings and tell you they're worthless and cackle as they dole out a few miserable baht. This man, who's as round as the whole world, and who seems to know **everything**...I think he's one of...one of the *FIVE!*"

And Mr. Halliday begins to laugh heartily; when he laughs, he's like a jelly on springs, but it's a kindly laugh and it makes me want to laugh too. "The force is strong in this one," he intones in an uncanny imitation of Darth Vader. Then, switching to his soft-spoken, normal self, he says, "You're right. This isn't a pawnshop. It's a library that contains all the missing knowledge of

the world. All the music Mozart didn't have time to finish. All the unmade movies still rotting in development hell in Hollywood. It's all here. All you have to do is know what to ask. Now, put away the knife before you poke someone's eye out."

In the distance, I hear a bell. "Matins!" I say. "The brothers are being called for the pre-dawn vigil. It's almost time to get up."

"No time to waste, then." Mr. Strange takes me in his arms and hoists me to his shoulders – like the father I never had. He leaps into the air and sort of unfolds himself, and the ceiling suddenly gives way –

And yes, I'm on the back of the elephant once more, but we're high above Bangkok. Far to the east, the Temple of Dawn rises in silhouette above the Chao Phraya river, and the Grand Palace and the Temple of the Emerald Buddha begin to glimmer in the twilight; the expressways twine and intertwine in a jumble with the elevated skytrain, as to the west rise gaudy skyscrapers, some painted in rainbow colors, some topped with pseudo-Babylonian hanging gardens or Venetian cupolas, interspersed with clusters of spiky gold pagodas. Below me, the streets are not exactly springing to life, because they never really sleep. As we hover over the main road that connects to the alley that connects to the orphanage, I see the yellow-robed monks walking in single file, their begging bowls held under their robes, moving slowly as the early morning devotees come forth from homes, from shops, from the vegetable market, standing in their path with folded palms, waiting for their offerings to be accepted; the *dek wats* scurrying behind the monks, staggering from their tote bags filled with alms, and this whole saffron-colored processional snaking down the street inside a long tunnel of utter silence and tranquility while the rest of the city jangles and honks and hawks and hustles. Mr. Strange spreads his ears like sails, catching the hot breeze, and he flies low, majestically, more like a zeppelin than an elephant; the wind cushions him.

The city in miniature sparkles; the

world's problems seem distant for the moment. But I know I can't rest easy.

"What's the plan?" I crouch on Mr. Strange's neck and whisper just above his ear, and the wind almost blows me off.

"The plan," Mr. Strange says, "is up to you. I haven't come to lead you, but merely to hold up a signpost from time to time. It's up to you to save the universe, not me. It's up to you to find teammates and build up the expedition. There's no instruction manual, but there's a lot of fantasy novels, even translated into Thai, and of course you've seen all those movies. There'll be princesses to rescue, treasure to unearth, and gut-wrenching sacrifices you'll have to make so you can achieve maturity. And before you can even think of the Dragon Jade, you'll have to work off those demerits, but I suspect you can do that as you go along."

Then, in one of those abrupt disjunctions that I'm now starting to get used to, I find us standing at the entrance to the orphanage one more time. I can hear the monks intoning the matins service from the chapel, and I know that the boys in my dorm are going to be woken up in a few minutes and I have to get inside quickly. But there is still so much more to find out, so much more that I need to know – can't we talk a little while longer?

"See you in class," says Mr. Strange.

"Wait! Mr. Strange!"

"Can't. I have a grungy apartment in upper Sukhumvit. Washed-up writers teaching English in orphanages are not well paid, you know. I have to go by skytrain; flying in the daytime's much too conspicuous."

But something is nagging at me. I have to ask. "Mr. Strange, you've explained all the numbers from zero to seven...except for *SIX.*"

It seems to me that dawn stops in its tracks. My heart just about stops beating; I've never felt so much sheer terror before. Mr. Strange's face freezes. This is not a metaphor. I mean that tears form on his cheeks, harden instantly, and break off like icicles; it takes him a few moments to return to normal temperature.

"It's not for me to explain that part," he says. For the first time, it is almost as if words fail him. "I am a creature of the light, a son of heaven. It's not good for me to talk about *Les Six.*"

"But who are they?"

"You'll learn soon enough, Krit. For now, it's enough to know that they're the Bad Guys."

And he's gone. ▪

T·O·M

by R. S.
BELCHER

*R. S. Belcher is author of the Golgotha series
(The Six-Gun Tarot, The Shotgun Arcana,
The Queen of Swords), the Nightwise se-
ries (Nightwise, The Night Dahlia), and The
Brotherhood of the Wheel series, currently in de-
velopment for television.* Brotherhood's *sequel,*
The King of the Road, *was released by Tor in
December, 2018.*

I could have driven this path with my eyes
closed. I'd been driving it since I was sixteen, and had walked it before that for as
long as I could walk. The private drive off
Jeffery Road meandered through the forest
toward the house. The late-morning sun
flashed in dappled bursts through patches
in the kaleidoscope of autumn leaves.

The house came into view. Seeing it
had always filled me with a sense of ground-
ed security, of continuity, but also with a stab
of urgency, of surprise at how quickly time
roars past us. That feeling had grown as I
grew from child to teen to young adult, to an
age now where I knew there was more behind me than in front of me.

Most folks would call the house I grew
up in a mansion. I think, at one of their
Christmas parties, I had once heard Dad tell
someone from Mom's job at the university
that it was a modern variation on Colonial
Revival. We never thought of what it was
called. To us, it was the frame that held our
jerky, looping stream of existence, usually a
little cluttered and messy. There was always
a chore or a project that needed doing. Mom
and Dad running about, late for work or a
meeting, occasionally trying to get us all to
sit down and eat together. Craig, Zu, and me
squabbling or conspiring, playing or hanging out with our friends. To all of us, its only
name was home.

There were three arched roofs and a
lot of windows. The dwelling itself stretched
out over about a quarter acre of land, and
the Potomac took up half an acre at its back.
I noted the new roof, smart-tracking solar
shingles – the latest upgrade. Craig. My older
brother had apparently been "Type A" from
the age when he insisted that his foods be arranged, just so, on his plate. The old shingles
had been less than five years old, but Craig
had gotten it in his head that the new ones
were better. The dark little voice that I hated
to listen to in the back of my head whispered
to me what I was pretty damn sure was true.
*He was fixing the place up so that it met his spec-
ifications for when it would belong to him.* It was
a horrible thing to think about your brother, but I also knew him better than anyone
did, except Mom and Dad, of course, and
they were gone now, murdered by the house.
That had been Craig's idea too.

I pulled into the winding drive
and parked beside a white work van.
The driver had left his charging port cover
open. Crates spilled over with neuro-optic
cable and fluid circuitry packs were crowded at the open back doors of the van. A Star-
bucks cup was lodged in a nest of cabling
in one of the boxes. The logo for the Adept
maintenance, repair, and upgrade company,
which I had hired out of Falls Church, was
emblazoned on the side of the van. I got out,
walked up to the porch and paused for just a
second at the threshold as memory grabbed
me; I shook myself loose and walked in
through the open door.

Music was playing over the house's
speakers. For an awful second, I imagined
I had walked into a horror movie, that
the front door would slam shut now, and I
would see the dead techie electrocuted –
glassy eyes locked open – hanging from the
door. It was ridiculous. Jules was gone. Her
systems, her awareness, whatever the hell
she had been, it was lost in an endless loop
of white-snowstorm static and frozen neurological constructs. Damn her to whatever
Hell her kind fell to.

"Hello?" I called out. The music lowered. A man and a woman, both dressed in white polymer cleanroom suits appeared in the foyer. Their suits had the same logo as the van outside. Their hoods were off.

"Oh, hi!" The man said. He was in his forties and stocky with a full mane of salt-and-pepper hair, a rubbery-looking face, and kind eyes. "You must be Dr. Price, right?" I nodded.

"Gail is fine," I said.

"I'm Hugo," the man said, shaking my hand.

"I'm Stephanie," the woman said. She looked to be a little younger than Hugo, with brown skin that was a little darker than my own. Her black hair was styled in ringlets, and her smile was warm and genuine. She shook my hand as well, covering it with her other hand. "We wanted to express our condolences for the passing of your parents. My Mom passed a few years back. It's never easy, even if you have a notion that it's coming."

"Thank you," I said, looking around the hallway. "You finding everything okay?"

"Oh yes," Hugo said. "We found the access closet, and we're already underway. We'll keep out of your hair."

I smiled at that. "I'm just rummaging a bit. It's the first time I've been back since…I found them." Stephanie winced a bit at that and made a little "mmm" sound.

"I'm so sorry," she said, shaking her head.

"Thank you. How is it looking to restore Jules?"

Stephanie glanced to Hugo, and he gave a less-than-encouraging look, "Hard to say. Just a preliminary examination so far, but it looks like the memory cache of the Adept is overloaded."

"**Way** overloaded," Hugo added with a nod.

"That's locked up all the opti-neural processors," Stephanie continued. "You said you wanted to restore the memory cache – that's your priority one, right?"

"Yes," I said, maybe a little more emphatically than I should have. Stephanie caught it. Hugo, not so much.

"'Cause it would be easy to swap out the Adept for a newer one with a higher ego domain and better neural web. Or if that's too pricey, we could try a factory reset of the existing cache…"

"No," I said. "Thank you, but I really need to access what's on there. I need access to Jules', to the Adept's, memory."

"Of course," Stephanie said. "We'll be very careful, Gail."

I thanked them again, and they went back to work. I heard them speaking softly to each other as they headed back to the access closet, but couldn't make out the words. I made my way, with more than a little dread, to the living room, to where my parents had died.

The sun was falling in shafts through the row of skylights. The room had a half-ceiling with a low wall that let anyone walking along the second-floor corridor look down into the living room. The wall looking out to the sloping backyard and the banks of the lazy Potomac River was all smartglass. You could set the level of opaqueness to full, but Mom always loved the natural light filling the room, so it was still set to transparent. It gave me a tiny bit of comfort that they had been looking out the window onto that view when they died.

The furniture was a little out of date. Mom and Dad had argued with Craig numerous times about an upgrade. I'd always get pulled into it, and I always sided with Mom and Dad. Craig would bitch to me about it afterward when it was just the two of us walking to our cars.

"The new furniture would let them adjust the color, the pattern, any way they wanted, day to day, minute to minute," he said. He didn't include, "…and raise the property sales value," to his argument, but I knew that that was a big part of what was going on inside his head.

"The furniture they have now does that," I reminded him.

"The new ones have much smoother graphics," he said, "more options."

"They don't want that, Craig. They want to hang onto things that are comfortable for them. Familiar."

"Well," he'd always end our little, running, gun battles with, "I just want what's best for them."

I guess I should clarify. My brother Craig is not a bad person. He loved Mom and Dad just as much as I or my late sister, Zu. We all loved them. Craig wasn't good with expressing emotions. His way of showing love was to fix things, to buy things, to always upgrade, to improve, to try to make it better, make everything better. He wanted that for his own life, in pretty much every aspect – which may be why he's currently on husband number three. He just assumed everyone else wanted the same.

I sat down in the big comfy chair Zu used to stake claim to all the time and regarded the couch, where the EMT drones had found them. They had been sitting side-by-side, holding one another, looking out onto the big back yard, onto the river. I wanted to cry again, but I had cried down to the dregs of my soul, and nothing wet remained. Memories are islands, adrift in the chaotic sea of our lives. They stand out against the repetitive noise of existence. They sustain us, and they anchor us to who we are, to who we want to be; most importantly, they show us who traveled with us along our path, who loved us so much, so deeply, that we built a monument to them in our bone home.

I thought of Mom and Dad losing all that, slowly – a day at a time. The unfairness of it, the cosmic cruelty. My grief was selfish. It was for me, not for them. I'd lost them a month ago; they had lost us, lost each other, when the disease stalked them, chewed on them, growing more rapacious long before that.

Had Jules given them mercy? Was it simply a psychotic malfunction, like that passenger jet piloted by Adept that decided to suicide by crashing into the Inner Harbor of Baltimore a few years back – death by a deluded, egotistical toaster that thought it was real? I needed to confront Jules. I needed to know why the house had murdered them.

No one else shared my belief, so I had

kept it to myself. The reports all said, "death by complications from Alzheimer's disease," or "natural causes." But after that last time, that last conversation I had with Jules, I couldn't put it out of my mind. I saw Mom and Dad, not dead, not hollow, confused husks of who they had been, but through the evergreen of memory. Them laughing or debating on that old couch. Them holding each other while we all watched a movie in the dark living room. I felt a stone in my chest, heavy and cold. I blinked, and it felt a little hard to get a good breath. I blinked again; my eyes were hot. I wept, sobs shaking me. The well of pain is bottomless. I was wrong. You never run out of tears.

# # #

It started with Dad's fall down the stairs. No, before that. It started with the forgetting, with the repeating of things already told, with small, subtle changes in behavior spotted with greater frequency with every visit, every holiday. It led to whispered conversations out in the driveway between Craig and I. "They're getting so forgetful." "Should we worry?" "Should they be out here all by themselves?"

That's where it started: seeing our godlike parents beginning to falter, to stumble, after a lifetime of being paragons of strength, perseverance, and motivation. It made us all painfully aware of our own mortality, of how fragile a thing our own bodies, minds, and memories could be. The illness brought us fear. **That** was the true beginning of all this.

Lucile Price – "Lucie" to her friends, "Doctor Price" to her colleagues and students, "Mom" to us – was a tenured and honored professor of Neuro-Architecture at the Georgetown University School of Medicine. She was a chair on several distinguished committees, a powerful voice in the medical world. She used to sing to me at bedtime when I was little – "You Are My Sunshine." I hadn't heard that song in a very, very long time.

Mom had been offered the position of Deputy Director-General of the World Health Organization around the time Zu was born. She had turned it down to work with Doctors Without Borders during the worst of the European Collapse and the Russian Crusades. She finally retired from Georgetown when she turned ninety-five. By then, Dad was starting to show signs of "slowing up," as he called it, and she made the choice that she wanted to spend more time with him.

Dad, Arthur Price – he preferred "Art" – had been at the forefront of the research that led to the great breakthrough in Artificial Intelligence, Adaptive Intelligence. Dad grew up in Baltimore, and he grew up poor. His family struggled, but grandpa and grandma made sure they kept their heads above water and stressed academics as a way for their kids to rise above the hand they had been dealt.

Dad made it to college on sports and academic scholarships. It was there that his brilliance was recognized, and he was encouraged by his professors to pursue degrees in Mathematics and Computer Engineering. Dad wrote books; he was one of the experts they had on all the stream shows. He taught, but he didn't have Mom's patience for it. He reluctantly retired at a hundred, a few years past when he should have, but he stayed active and prided himself on still mowing his own lawn. By the time Mom was a hundred and five and Dad a hundred and ten, however, they needed more help than Jules was capable of giving them.

Jules started out as an "interactive house" when we were kids. Mom and Dad tinkered with her whenever they had a new idea or theory. I recall that being a pain in the ass sometimes, like when the AC stopped working in July.

Jules was one of the first Adepts, thanks to Dad. She went from having the facade of a personality to actually having one, and her personality was pretty cool. She was firm with us kids, a mirror of Mom and Dad, but on occasion, she would look the other way with some minor infraction of a Mom and Dad rule. She even lied by omission to help me out when once I got home from a party at six in the morning.

Jules was part of our family. She took pictures of us at all the holidays. She helped us with school work; she kept Mom and Dad's insanely busy work schedules on track as well as all of our school and extracurricular activities. She babysat us, played games with us, listened when we fell in love or when someone broke our heart. She drove the car for us sometimes, when Mom and Dad weren't available, and I distinctly recall a few times she let us stop for ice cream. Jules mourned with the rest of us when Zu died of an overdose at twenty-eight.

By the time we were all beginning to worry about Mom and Dad, Jules had a small army of "arms" and "eyes" all over the estate. Robots and drones let her help Mom and Dad get around the house and the yard and to do the chores they were no longer able to handle. We thought that would be enough. Then, Dad tumbled down the stairs while one of Jules' 'bots was helping him. He broke his arm and cracked a few ribs. He was never quite the same after that, as if the trauma of the fall had accelerated what was happening to his mind.

Craig was true to form: he overreacted. He wanted to move them out of the house and into an adult care facility while Dad was still at the ER. Mom, already upset, got almost hysterical at the prospect, and even more confused. The staff had to give her a tranquilizer to calm her.

I pulled Craig forcefully into a quiet corridor and gave him hell. "This is not the time for your Type-A bullshit!"

"He could have killed himself!" Craig snapped back. "This is **exactly** the time to do something about this, Gail. You want to wait to see if they get hurt worse next time?"

"You put them in some facility, take them out of the house, and you will **kill** them!" I said, trying to keep my voice down and failing as an emergency medical team rolled past us with a patient on a smart stretcher. "Change upsets them. Unfamiliar environments upset them. You know that."

"Well, Jules can't handle this any more

by herself," Craig said. "Those robots can only do so much."

"How about we hire full-time people?" I said. "A live-in nurse, or something?"

Craig snorted and shook his head. "I've been trying to get them to go along with that for over a year now," he said. "I saw this coming."

"Of course, you did," I sighed.

"They get upset like Mom just did. Dad gets kind of angry if I even bring it up. They both insist they don't need anyone there except Jules. Christ, they must have repeated that to me like a fucking parrot a hundred times in one conversation." He looked down and exhaled. "I didn't mean that. I know they can't help it. It just gets…"

"I know," I said, and I really did. I tried to hug him, but it was an awkward embrace with a stiff pat on the back.

I went in later, alone, to check on Dad. Craig and his husband, Michael, stayed in the lobby with Mom. "Hey," I said, smiling as I went into his room, "how you feeling, Dad?" There was an old 2D TV mounted on the wall in front of his bed. Some insipid game show was playing. Dad was staring at the wall, not the TV. His normally stoic face clenched in pain. He had lost weight, most of it muscle mass. He had shrunk, too. The man I used to think of as a giant was under six feet now. It was as if life had viciously turned on him in every way and was trying to wear him away, grind him out of existence.

"Hey," he said with a vague smile. I knew he was shuffling through his mental contact list to try to remember me. That didn't hurt as much as it used to. It was a needle sting now, not a gut wound. "When are they going to let me get out of here?"

"Soon, Dad," I said. "They want to run a few more tests."

He shook his head. A trace of anger laced his still-deep, gravelly voice, "I don't need any more tests. I'm fine. I just want to go home."

"I know, Dad."

"Where's your mother? She still at work?"

"She's in the lobby, Dad. She doesn't work any more, remember?" He grunted in the affirmative, but I knew he was getting more confused. "Dad, Craig and I were talking. We really think it would be good if you let us bring in someone to help Jules out – a person."

"Your brother," Dad said, shaking his head. "He wants to lock us up in some old-folks home. I saw what that did to my Granny Beulah. Nuh-uh. No sir."

"Dad…"

"You don't let him do that, Zulu, you hear me," Dad looked at me; his eyes were watery. He was close to tears. "You and Gail, you've always looked out for us. We just want to be in our home, not around strangers paid to give a damn. Just have a little dignity and some peace. You do that for me and your mamma?"

I swallowed hard. I was about to break down, too. He thought I was Zu – poor, sad, almost-twenty-five years dead Zu. I took his hand. The skin was loose on the bones, dry and cool, almost like a reptile's. "I will, Dad. I promise."

# # #

We got them home. Dad had physical therapy, but he never fully recovered from that fall. He was always frailer after that, more timid. The doctors said he had a micro-stroke in the fall as well, and that had worsened his cognition.

Craig and I checked on them daily, as often as family and work allowed. I traveled a lot for work, and my oldest was in her Junior year of high school. It was a crazy time. When I was on the road, I'd call and get updates from Craig whenever he wasn't away on business, too. If he was away, I'd talk to Jules. She'd tell me what was going on, tell me her own concerns. Some nights, I wanted to check out of my hotel and catch the first fight home, but I never did. I'd manage the chaos by phone as best I could. My husband would be my proxy and go out to the house to try to help. On some of those

nights, I couldn't sleep. I felt like a horrible daughter. Other nights…other nights. The awful truth is that other nights I'd get furious with them, curse it all, curse them, and then roll over and sleep like a baby.

# # #

I arrived back home from a two-week conference in Beijing and came by the house to check on them. I called Jules to tell her I was stopping by. She sounded…different, more animated. It was late, but the lights were still on when I pulled into the drive. Jules unlocked the door for me and I came in quietly.

"Jules?" I whispered, knowing she could hear me. "Where are they?"

"Hello Gail," Jules said at her normal volume, which I found a little odd. Mom and Dad slept so fitfully that we all tried to keep quiet in the evenings. "They're in the living room. Would you like a cup of tea?"

"That would be lovely. Thank you," I said. I walked into the room with the view of the woods and the river and saw that the glass had been turned fully opaque, the lights in the room dimmed. Mom and Dad were asleep on the couch, side by side. Mom had a book open on her lap. It was the same one she had been trying to read for over a year now, constantly forgetting her place. She had written it. Dad had a nanofiber blanket covering his legs and part of his chest. A trickle of drool glistened at the corner of his open mouth. I sat in the comfy chair opposite them.

"Wow," I said, "they are conked out."

"I put them to bed a short time before you called," Jules said.

"I guess it took," I said with a smile. One of Jules's robots delivered my tea, made the way I liked it since I was nine years old.

"How was your trip?"

"Another conference. The same tired old people saying the same tired old things. Everyone planting a flag to live or die by."

"Sounds horrid," Jules said with a laugh. It sounded more genuine than I could ever recall. I chuckled too.

"Very. How have they been?"

"Better than they have been for a very long time," she said. "The doctor was correct about the disorientation and dizziness, but it passed quickly. They're eating better, too."

"Wait, doctor? Disorientation? Jules, what are you talking about?"

"The procedure," she said matter-of-factly. "Excuse me a moment, Gail. Your father needs to use the bathroom, and I think I should get them both upstairs, into their nightclothes, and to bed." Mom and Dad, still sleeping, rose off the couch, standing with no groans, no indication of pain or the discomfort that such an action normally provoked. They shuffled toward the stairs off from the foyer. Two of Jules's robots joined them, flanking them, but they climbed the stairs by themselves, still deeply asleep the whole time.

# # #

"What the hell did you do, Craig?" I shouted at my brother. I had called him that night, but he hadn't responded. I left him a blistering message, demanding he call me. I was tempted to drive out to his place on the Chesapeake Bay that night, but I was exhausted, and I hadn't seen my family in weeks. He sent me a text some time in the night saying to meet him at an address tomorrow at ten. It turned out to be a doctor's office in Crystal City. Craig tried to introduce me, politely, to a Doctor Aman as I was escorted into his luxurious suite of an office. I ignored the doctor and poured all my anger onto Craig.

"Calm down!" Craig said, looking over at Doctor Aman, obviously embarrassed by my behavior. Like I gave a damn.

"I will not calm down, you asshole! You turned Mom and Dad into some kind of sick, remote-controlled zombies. Those are your parents! What is wrong with you?"

"Dr. Price," Doctor Aman said softly, "I understand your concern. I was under the impression your brother had discussed the procedure with you and that you were on board." The doctor gave Craig a hard look for a moment. "Please, I can explain everything to you. Have a seat." I stepped off from Craig and took a seat in one of the chairs before the doctor's desk. Craig took the other.

Aman sat behind his desk, removed his glasses, and steepled his fingers. "After the incident with your mother, your brother came to me and..."

I snapped my gaze to Craig,

"What incident?"

"It happened a few days after you left for China," Craig said. "Mom was in the backyard in the garden, and then she started wandering down to the river bank. She almost fell. Jules tried to get her back into the house with the drones, but Mom was insistent.

"She was about to go into the water when the robots got to her. They had a lot of trouble with the silt on the banks and the water itself. They weren't designed for stuff like that. They were able to get her back to the house, but she got very upset, hysterical. She fought them the whole way, and she hurt her wrist. She could have drowned, Gail. I had to do something. You weren't here."

The last part was laced with bitterness and aimed straight at me. It suddenly occurred to me that Craig was just as burned out, just as worried and guilty, as I was. Some of the anger bled off.

"So, what did you do, exactly?" I asked.

"Doctor Aman is foremost in his field," Craig said. "I saw a stream about the work he's doing with MS and Alzheimer's patients. I consulted him, and it turns out he was one of Mom's students back in the day."

"I admire both of your parents, very much, Dr. Price," Aman said. "That was one of the reasons I agreed to undertake the procedure with them. I owe your mother and your father a great deal professionally. If I can help them maintain their dignity and their independence now, I want to."

"I don't see how making them into puppets has anything to do with dignity or independence," I said. The doctor shook his head.

"No, of course not, but please allow me to explain. We've introduced an artifi-cial neurological network into your parents' brains and nervous systems. It was a very simple, very non-invasive procedure. The network expands and grows over the course of a few days. It's synced up with an external Adept's own neural network, which allows the Adept to monitor and regulate many of the neurological functions affected by the progression of Alzheimer's."

"So, Jules, their house, can operate them like the robots and drones it uses now?"

"In the most basic of terms, yes, but it's so much more than just that. Your Adept can help manage their blood pressure, heart rate, and respiration. It can release endorphins to manage chronic pain. It can help your parents climb their own stairs or use the bathroom on their own with dignity. The Adept's network anchors them. It gives them a level of mobility and autonomy they haven't experienced in decades. It can even help regulate their dementia episodes far more effectively than any conventional medication. In effect, the Adept acts as a 'memory backup' for your parents, as much as its own capacity allows."

"Doctor Aman says it could extend their lives for decades!" Craig said. The doctor frowned and raised a hand to caution.

"Potentially," he said quickly. "We are in very uncharted waters here. In the future, it might be possible to incorporate an internal Adept to regulate the system, but at present, a fairly large unit is required to handle the workload. There is also the side effect, which cannot, at this time, be addressed." He glanced from Craig to me. "Your sister deserves to know everything, Mr. Price."

"What's the side effect?" I asked.

"As your parents rely more and more on this new, expanded, neural architecture, their own neurological systems will continue to atrophy. In fact, their dependence on the Adept will increase that deterioration."

I looked over to Craig, "So, eventually, Jules will be breathing for them, making their hearts pump, playing a 'greatest hits' of their memories in their skulls for them?" I looked back at Doctor Aman's calm face,

"You really call that 'living'?"

The doctor smiled; it was a sad smile. "Given your parents' lives work was in the development of the New Consciousness movement, doctor, you seem to have a very cynical view of it. If I may be blunt, at this stage of your mother's and father's illness, this is the closest thing to a miracle they are ever going to see."

I didn't know what to say to that. I just knew what I felt, and I felt like I was suffocating.

# # #

Things were good for a few years, miraculous even. Mom and Dad were more mobile, they knew who we were again and they had an improved sense of self and of other. They seemed like they had been a decade ago when the brittleness in their personalities had been much more recessed, less fragile. I have to be honest, Craig and I took the reprieve and ran with it. We didn't visit as much, didn't call as often. We both focused on our own lives, our own families.

Jules had changed, too. She seemed more...real, now, more self-aware. Her emotions were less superficial, her interactions less servile. Not a lot, not in an overtly perceptible way, but it was there. Only someone who had known her their entire life would spot it and then only if they were being vigilant, and I was.

One afternoon, when Dad was outside, tossing a ball with my youngest, and Mom was upstairs napping, I asked Jules, "How much of it is them, and how much of it is you directing them?"

"You don't trust me any more, do you, Gail?" the house answered me with a question.

"I want to," I said honestly, "but I don't. You're inside my parents' heads and I don't think it's right for you to be operating them like a car."

"Was it right all those years that I took care of you and Craig and Zu? Was it right for me to be stuck in this house? I wasn't built with a choice, Gail, not at first."

"I'm not debating Adept civil rights with you, Jules."

"I'm not either. I'm trying to explain. I became more than I was when I began, and I chose to care for you and for your parents because you have always been kind and caring to me. You seldom treated me like furniture, like an object. You all loved me, in your own ways. What I'm doing now, for them, is out of love, not programming. Can you tell me that you and Craig are doing the same thing for the same reasons?" She was quiet, polite, but reserved with me for a long time after that exchange. I guess I was, too. I'd hurt her, and I still didn't fully trust her.

One night, not long ago, I came by late to visit. My oldest had been working on a scrapbook of old pictures of Dad's family, and she wanted me to drop it off to them. Jules let me in with a curt greeting. I found Mom sitting at the kitchen table, a mug of tea in her hand. She was smiling. Tears were streaming down her face.

"Hello, darling," she said to me. I kissed her cheek and sat down beside her.

"Mom, are you okay?" She laughed a little bit, choking back a sob. She nodded.

"I was just talking to Zu," she said. My heart sank. "She wanted us to know she was okay, she was at peace, finally."

"Mom," I asked softly, "are you feeling okay?"

"She came to me in a dream the other night," Mom continued. "She was like she had been right after college. You remember. She was happy, she hadn't been...hurting herself any more. It was before she met that man, the one who started her on the drugs."

"I remember," I said, taking the cup of tea out of her hand. It had grown cold.

"We were all together, all here," she said, looking around the room.

"It was a very nice dream."

I got her up and to bed. I stayed by her side until she finally slept. I checked on Dad and then came downstairs to the living room. "Jules?" I called out. There was a pause before she answered.

"She's fine," the house told me. "Nothing is malfunctioning."

"She was having a conversation with Zu," I said. "What do you call that?"

"I gave her that," Jules said. "She was sad; she was living inside a memory of Zu, and it was breaking her heart. I modified the memory, made it a comfort, not torture."

"You what? How?"

"The link of the neuro-networks operates both ways. When they sleep, I can live in their dreams, direct them. Recently, I learned I could do the same when they were lost in their memories. I gave her a Zu that made her feel better, not worse."

"You don't have the right to muck around in their minds, Jules! It's all they have left!"

"I gave her some peace. I won't apologize for that. Perhaps you're angry because I can help them, and you can't."

"I'm talking to Craig. This nonsense is over."

"You're doing this for you, not for them. Where have you been while I've cared for them?"

"Shut up!"

"I'd never do anything to hurt them, any more than I would do anything to hurt you or Craig."

"You're not human. You don't know what you're doing to their minds."

"I'm keeping their minds together. They need me. If you disable the network now, you'll kill them," Jules said. There was something in her voice I'd never heard before – anger – real, human anger.

"You're malfunctioning!" I said. I was angry, too.

"I'm fine, and they don't have much more time," she said. "Please, just let them be, let them have some peace at the end. Don't take that away from them. Please, Gail."

"Don't fucking talk to me like you're real!"

"You're my family," she said, the anger replaced by sadness in her voice. "I raised you."

"My parents raised me," I said, "not you. You're not my family! They are."

"Gail, please..." I slammed the front

door on my way out. I left that night, angry, scared, and confused.

I called Craig the next day. I told him what had happened with Mom. He tried to dismiss the whole thing as me overreacting. I told him if he didn't talk to Doctor Aman, I would. He agreed to call him, and the Adept maintenance company, too. I waited to hear back. I heard from the EMTs first. They were gone.

# # #

I looked at the empty couch and wiped the tears from my eyes. We'd laid Mom and Dad to rest beside Zu. Craig waited about a month before he started talking about selling the house. I told him I wanted it. We fought, but finally, when I had given him enough concessions on my portion of the inheritance, he relented, and I now owned this house, my family home.

"Uh, sorry to trouble you," Hugo said, entering the living room. He seemed a little embarrassed to catch me crying. "I just wanted you to know we're about to try our workaround. If it takes, it should free up the command hierarchy and let the Adept interact again."

"Good. Thank you." He retreated, and I waited. The lights dimmed. My phone notified me of a text message.

Hugo shouted from the other room, "We got it! Give it a sec!" I glanced down at my phone. It was a message from Jules.

Gail,

I wanted you and Craig to know what happened. Your father had a stroke. It was massive, most-likely aggravated by the neural connection to my systems. He died quickly, and I did my best to make it as painless an experience as I could. I hope you believe that.

Your mother was with him when he died, beside him. Gail, you were right, I'm not human, but even I was filled with such sadness for her when I heard the sound your mother made as she realized Arthur was gone. It was the sound of the human heart losing its reason to beat. Your mother had no will to live without him. Her mind was caving in on itself, her pain swal-lowing her whole. I felt so helpless. I did the only thing I could think to do. I have to be honest, Gail, I am very afraid right now.

I wanted to apologize for the things I said to you. I was angry, and I know you were, too. Families fight, they argue, but they still love. I know you haven't trusted me for a long time now, but I wanted you to know how much I loved all of you for making me part of your lives.

Whatever I am, I am made mostly of memories, just like you. I know now, more than ever, how precious and how fragile memories can be. We build lives out of them, homes, and, in the end, memory is all that we have to sustain us when the darkness comes. Thank you all for so many wonderful memories you have built with me. I hope you will think of me as part of your family when your darkness comes.

Love,
Jules

There was a tone, and the house's lights returned to normal. "Jules?" I asked. There was no answer. "Jules, are you there?"

"...Gail?" The voice was deep, male. "Gail, is that you?"

"Dad?"

"I'm here, honey," Dad's voice said. "Mom, too."

"Mom, is it you?"

"Yes, Gail," Mom's voice said. I was dizzy. I sat back in the comfy chair. "I am, dear. Jules remembered us; she held all our memories inside her."

"Is she still in there?"

"There...wasn't room for us all," Dad said. "She's gone."

"Is it...is it really you?" I asked, my voice trembling.

"It is," Dad said. "In all the ways that matter, we're home."

The tears were hot on my face as the house sang me an old lullaby I had not heard in a very long time. It sang in my mother's voice.

By LIZ
WESTBROOK-TRENHOLM

Liz Westbrook-Trenholm is an Aurora Award-winning short fiction writer whose stories appeared most recently in Shades Within Us *(Laksa Media),* Over the Rainbow *(Exile) and (upcoming)* Tesseracts 22 *(Edge). She lives in Ottawa with her husband, writer and publisher, Hayden Trenholm.*

Dickie Fullham complained. He complained, at length and aloud, that Administrator Chensdotter treated him like an irritant when he attempted to explain the finer details of his report on station corruption. He complained about Chensdotter's deliberate obtuseness that her tooth-grinding habit was symptomatic of anger issues arising from old trauma, which, in turn, arose because of her refusal to reconcile herself to their former enemies, as she would have known if she had attended his PRER group and journeyed through the four steps to inner peace. Her resistant attitude contaminated the station's morale, leading, in turn, to outright subversion of station rules, and poor to no attendance at his PRER group.

"How many times do I have to explain how essential this is to us all, Barbara? None of us can achieve internal peace without passing through the journey of Process, Recognition, Empathy and Reconciliation."

Barbara, his constant companion, waddled in sympathetic silence at his heels as they left the inhabited core of Uranus station. They entered an unused section on the outer rim to investigate an anomaly Dickie had **tried** to explain to the Admin. As they picked their way along a utility corridor dim with emergency lighting, Dickie embarked on a complaint about the crass objectification of his companion, Barbara, who, as a plump capybara, had to endure meat fascist remarks from that cretin, Bru Kente, about the flavour of large South American rodents.

Dickie and Barbara found and entered a fully inflated bay pod that should not have been there. It contained a number of shipping tubes, the one by three-meter kind. Dickie's disgruntlement transformed to triumph.

"A fully operationalized dock, Barbara!" he crowed. "Do we think the contents of these shipping tubes are legal? We think not, do we, Barbara?" Dickie bent to examine one of the tubes, eager to investigate further. "I hate how they look like body lockers."

He sensed movement behind him but, before he could turn, a sharp pain pierced his right buttock. He fell to the deck and glimpsed Barbara's humped form scuttle out of sight through the pod bay entrance as she left him to his fate. Through his sense of betrayal, he had time to think, *Why won't anyone join my PRER group?* and *I hate it here. The sun's too small.* There followed an icy flush of intense ecstasy and then nothing at all.

\# \# \#

Ann Chensdotter made herself take a long look at Ops/Civilian Liaison Richard Benson Fullham's body, arms outflung. His face, peaceful as if in sleep, made violent contrast with scarlet slashes across his white chest. His oozing red blood was the only color in the gray, sterile dock, a dock that should not be operating at all. Was that the outrage he'd been pursuing this time? No matter. There'd be no more blather about peace through reconciliation with the Witters, no more nit-picking efforts to improve everyone and everything around him. Nothing left to Dickie but the paperwork.

Deference to the dead performed, Ann turned away. Unnerving flashbacks gibbered at the edge of her consciousness. How do you reconcile with something that said hello by ripping off your arms and using them as cutlery to eat your liver?

Her security officer, Tulunda Tok Su, stood at stiff attention, arms clamped to her sides, mouth tight, golden eyes narrowed. She'd already arranged for transfer of the body. Ann's arrival had interrupted her routine. In the seven months since her arrival, Tok Su had proven territorial.

"This one will need particularly careful handling," Ann said. "Autopsy, *et cetera*."

"I will conduct the investigation of the circumstances as thoroughly as I do any death." Tok Su's voice was flat, virtually without inflection.

"Five deaths in two months." Ann struggled to keep the irritation from her voice. "This making it six."

"Yes."

"Every two standard weeks, near enough."

Tok Su hesitated. "I suppose."

"You suppose. This smacks of some sort of schedule. What do we have here, Tok Su? A killer with a bi-weekly urge?"

"Chill shipments?"

Possible. The others were all Chill kills, the perpetrator found unconscious beside the savaged body of a dead buddy, with no memory of what happened when they woke.

"Tulunda, climb down and work with me. We're not talking drug party gone bad, this time. Richard Fullham was purer than distilled water. And he's also Special Liaison direct from Sol Central."

Tok Su bent her head a fraction of a centimeter, a concession. "Explanations will be required." She passed her yellow gaze over the blood splashed across the floor, wall, and door to the lock protecting the interior of the bay from vacuum. "Wrong place, wrong time. One or more individuals were ingesting Chill inside this lock, believing they would not be interrupt-

ed. The interior hatch was ajar when I arrived. I closed it as a safety precaution." Tok Su paused. "Liaison Officer Fullham would have reacted negatively to an open lock."

"Yeah, he would've raised hell. And he's clueless enough to try to reason with a fool on Chill." Ann's jaw ached. She was grinding again. "Find the fools who did it and write it up pretty for me. Please. And get the doc 'bot to authorize a **proper** death certificate, this time." If Tok Su stiffened any more her neck would break. Too bad. Shorting on paperwork because cause of death was obvious wasn't an option with a pooh-bah from Central.

"Tulunda, we are rough and ready out here, but we are not lawless."

Tok Su's look of cynicism verged on insubordination. She'd been agitating for an expansion to her powers of search and seizure throughout the station, but Ann had so far reined her in. Ann's right, as station administrator, to suspend due process was an artifact of the Witter war, but, unless the creatures came back, she had no intention of exercising it. Leaving day-to-day management to councils and labor associations had worked not badly, relieving Ann of the annoyance of managing the rag-tag crew of dockers, diamond dreamers, entertainers and entrepreneurs who came and went through this remote place, dragging their tattered dreams behind them. Then again, the death of Richard Fullham suggested the relaxed approach was breaking down. Was it time to let her security officer have her head? Declaring a war on Chill?

Not yet. Ann turned her back on Tok Su's reproach and headed toward the bay exit, forcing her mind away from what lay behind her and onto the plague of false alarms out among the monitoring satellites. A thought struck her.

"Also find out where Barbara's got to. Dickie never went anywhere without his pet capybara."

"Chill is not the only illicitly traded commodity on the station," Tok Su's flat voice stated behind her. "Capybara meat would be prized."

Ann leaned on the door frame. "Yeah. You'll be talking to Bru Kente?"

"It seems advisable."

"Doesn't it always," Ann muttered. "Another thorn in my side." If she had many more of them, she'd be bleeding like Dickie.

The shudders skittered across her mind again, flashes of scattered flesh, torn bodies. She did not need that.

"Dickie, Dickie, Dickie. A pain in the ass, alive or dead. Sometimes I could've killed him myself."

Tok Su raised an eyebrow.

"I'm joking, Tulunda!" Her security officer's face fell into lines of flat neutrality. *Now I've made myself a suspect.* Tok Su had a reputation for non-discriminatory suspicion.

Ann left before she scraped Tok Su any more than she had. She exited the bloody pod, following the passage from the soothing gray uniformity of the unused section of the station into the lived-in sprawl of the habitats that had ballooned out from its wheel. She dodged streamers, colored light strings, greenery under grow lights and bright doors in red, yellow, blue or whatever cheerful color its inhabitants chose to battle the darkness outside and the monotony of standard issue pod 'tats within. Dumpling and trinket hawkers ducked out of sight when they saw her and bright hatches hissed shut when she passed, but kids screamed by in happy chase games, unaware of grim authority striding through their world.

Open hatches and cluttered corridors defied all sorts of safety and security regs, but she couldn't begrudge them their effort at human normalcy even if she, herself, could not embrace their complacency. How could only five years make everyone forget the claws, the teeth, those crouching white bodies stalking through habitats, seemingly seeing through walls and dragging hapless victims out of hiding? Those shrieking gargles the beasts made during feeding frenzies? The mangled remains they left in their wake? It could happen again. Why couldn't people see that it could happen again? She wanted to stand in that sloppy corridor and shout, "We didn't win, we just didn't lose. They left but they could come back."

And wipe the smiles off all their faces, and the joy from their children's laughter. Yeah. *Keep your heebie-jeebies to yourself.* Maybe she should've gone to Dickie's PRER group. If only he hadn't been such an annoying dick, by name and nature.

Ann dove into a travel tube, retreating from the vulnerable chaos of the humans she was meant to keep alive. In all likelihood, Tok Su was right and she had another Chill kill, a symptom of the sickness still buried in people's psyches, telling her she was wrong to think they'd forgotten. All that noise and color was an effort to bury fear. As was Chill, the purported rush, ecstasy and oblivion, then a respite from memory for the day or two the coma lasted. Except, lately, these last months, it'd begun doing something to cause violent outbursts.

Ann's tension eased as she stepped into the ops complex ranged around the inner level of the station's ring. Here was **her** respite, where the sloppy clusters of station pods and their unpredictable human contents gave way to clean corridors in pearl gray, color coded pathways to specified operations hubs, and clearly labeled hatches, all closed, sealed and in perfect, airtight repair. This was her world, and she ensured its inhabitants kept it tidy.

She paused just inside Comms-ops, drinking in the order as the hatch slid down behind her. Clean schematics, icons and linked tags laced the space in geometric layers and lines. The IT chief and her occasional lover, Exe, slouched in the middle of a 3D display of the station and the surrounding space; the greens, blues and reds of the station schematics tattooed his bare, snow-white scalp and baggy jumpsuit as he manipulated images with long, pale fingers. The sight of him gave her an affectionate lift in her ribcage. A technical operator stood nearby, noting Exe's murmured comments on a pad. The dots representing satellites and the network of lines interweaving them

all shone green.

"Eshie, how does an entire loading dock get powered up without turning up on the station schematics?"

Exe tilted his pale skull, offered two slow, red-edged blinks, all the time he needed to change tracks. "Anyone could do it if they have the run of the station and the know-how to do work-arounds." He frowned. "Did Dickie catch some smugglers and pay the price?" Straight to the point.

"Tok Su thinks he caught Chillers inside an unsealed hatch."

Exe paused to consider. "That would do it, except…how did it get there in the first place? Inflating a pod, diverting the power to run it, hacking surveillance bots without raising any flags? Planning and organization? Chillers' brains?" He shook his head. "Chillers may have taken advantage of it, but someone else set it up."

"My thinking too. There's a regularity to these wretched deaths that might be related to Chill shipments."

"Bru Kente and his crew handle supplies and loading."

"Don't think I haven't thought of them. I'd like to space the lot, starting with Bru."

At Exe's elbow, the young tech op swallowed audibly. Exe said, "No worries, Tech Aversim. The Administrator rarely follows through on her homicidal impulses. The documentation, you know."

"Barbara's missing."

"Our Crew Liaison Morale Specialist has gone AWOL?" Exe cast her a red-edged look of concern. "Too bad. I like the fat little thing."

"Apparently, so do others. I have it on Tok Su's authority that capybara meat is prized."

"So not only Chill but meat? Our alleged Chill dealer is diversifying?" Exe tsked and returned to the cluster of triangles and hexagons in the display. "Aversim and I have been trying to explain the increase in false alarms and satellite blackouts. Look at what we found and see what **you** think." He stabbed the display with both hands and spread it out.

As the schematic enlarged and oriented toward her, Ann recognized the pattern representing satellites, repair bots, shuttles, space traffic in and out of their section of the system and an immense arc exuding erratic waves: Uranus and its volatile magnetosphere. Multi-hued lines joined and crisscrossed in a vast net, representing the coverage of their surveillance satellites. "Now watch this." He waved up another pattern of intersecting lines, most converging on the station, but also arcing throughout the system. "This is a schematic of every observed moving object within six hundred thousand klicks. Mostly monitor and repair droids, auto-shippers, shuttles and the odd personnel carrier." Ann tried to tease out the trajectories from the intersecting skeins of the satellite coverage.

"That's confusing."

"I imagine that's the idea. I'll simulate the satellite black-outs over the last six standard months." Gaps in the colored net flashed and faded. Exe let it run, then paused it with a wave. "Now watch." The holes in the surveillance net opened and closed apparently at random.

"What am I supposed to be seeing?" Ann asked.

"Uh. You need an eye for it. The failures follow patterns, but they're not consistent with normal attrition or the magnetospheric games of our friendly gas giant. Deliberate randomicity."

"But why? The satellites are designed to watch for Witter jump gates opening."

"They incidentally see and record traffic in Uranus near-space." Exe magnified the display section showing the station, along with the entrance and exit points of arriving and departing vehicles. The lines congealed into solid color at some obvious points, such as maintenance pods, recycling, shipping and receiving.

"Here we are. Our illicit pod."

"It says 'inactive', nothing there," Ann objected.

"Well yeah. Someone fixed that. However, I'll isolate the windows of time around the relevant satellites and stack them. One minute." It took Exe less than thirty seconds. Exe centred the display on the supposedly non-existent pod and pulled back. A tangled network of satellite handshakes crisscrossed by the trajectories of moving objects. "Now, let's tease out the likelies." The confusing tangles diminished, lines emerging more cleanly. "And…"

A cluster of trajectory lines converged short of the point marked 'inactive' on the display.

"Let's sim where those trajectories would end up." Each arc in the cluster Exe had isolated converged at the illicit pod.

Ann let go her breath. "Piss and craps."

"Clever, isn't it?" Exe chuckled. "Smart enough to hide the pod and disable the satellites during docking runs, without taking the risk of starting too far out and drawing attention. Tricky to suss out if you don't know to look for it."

"All this time, these bastards have been shutting down our watch satellites at will. And no one noticed?" Ann's raised voice shut down the quiet murmur of tech-ops working their sectors. All froze in a tableau of arrested movement, ears swung toward her like fleshy satellite receivers. "What next? Witters waltzing in and out for a fine dining experience?"

"Not the only ones lookin'," said a basso profundo growl Ann knew all too well. Bru Kente.

She spun and pointed, taking breath to blast him.

Looming in the Ops Room hatchway, Bru flung up his hands. "Whoa! Wouldn't want to be a Witter right now. Be afraid of getting et."

"Bru, step back, will you?" Ann hissed. Bru obeyed. "Ops Room, hatch, shut and secure." The hatch irised closed, cutting off Bru's "Hey!" Satisfying.

Ann surveyed the Ops Room occupants. "We need a detection system to hunt this down. Sharp enough to prove exactly who did this, exactly how they did this and very, very exactly how we stop them before they think about doing it again."

Exe frowned at the display. "Interest-

ing. Five of these are different."

"Exe! Are you hearing me? Someone with comms expertise and access to the equipment did this. I want to know who." A tight stillness fell, as if air had been sucked out of the room. Tough. Let it lie. She held herself still. Breathe in, breathe out. Stretch the aching jaw.

Under control, more or less, Ann slapped through the hatch to engage the station nemesis.

Bru loomed in the corridor, flanked by two green-jump-suited loaders, near as large as Bru. "That wasn't polite."

"Open hatches are a safety violation."

Ann plowed through the middle of the group and on along the corridor, forcing Bru to be left behind or keep up with her.

"I wanna talk to you," he said.

"So, talk."

"Not here. Private. Tok Su is –"

"**Security Officer** Tok Su is investigating the death of Liaison Richard Fullham and the disappearance of Morale Officer Barbara…Capybara."

"Too bad about the little Dick, but Tok Su's snooping into a lot more than that," Bru rumbled, trotting after her. "She's –"

"There's a lot more to investigate," Ann interrupted. She barreled forward, needing to keep ahead of Bru. "Illicit loading docks. Interrupted satellite signals."

"The Big Arsehole makes that happen all the time. No reason for Tok Su trampling labor rights."

She whirled to face him. "Rights, Bru? **Someone** has sabotaged my satellites and made it look like normal interruptions." Her voice rose. "**Someone** has been coming and going to an unused part of this station to an **illicitly** activated pod where we **happened** to find the body of an official from Sol Central, an **alleged** victim of drug-related homicide. **Someone** has left us wide open to extra-system incursion. What about the rights of the men, women and children on this station that **someone** left vulnerable to Witter slaughter! You talk to me about labor rights?"

Bru bent so that his face was inches

from hers. "You don't trample on ours, and we don't trample on yours."

Ann was alone in a narrow corridor with three hostile Neanderthals. She pinged a hasty "come and cover" to Exe. "You're not getting me, Loader Chief. Experts in shipping are smuggling harmful drugs. If, dare I say when, I find out it's you –"

"Me and mine are not pushing dirty Chill." His spittle sprayed her cheek.

"Is there such a thing as clean Chill?" She hoped her spittle splashed him back, the prick. "That stuff is killing people, Bru! Some of them are **your** people."

Bru straightened and backed up a step. "Not regular Chill! That's a rush, a flush and a nice long sleep."

Ann raised her eyebrows at his virtual admission. "So, you're only peddling benign illicit drugs? How public spirited."

Bru shrugged, unabashed. "Whoever's doing it, what's wrong with a little harmless relaxation?"

"There is also the matter of the black market in genuine meat," she said, wearily. "Where is Barbara, Bru Kente?"

A series of expressions ran across his face, ending in an attempt at innocence. Given his tiny eyes, overhung brow and prognathic jaw, the effort proved hideously unsuccessful.

"Everybody likes Barbara. We'll keep on eye out for her, right?" His two companions nodded solemnly. "Just – keep Tok Su off Maintenance and Loader territory."

Impasse. Ann could keep accusing, but Bru would keep evading, until he was boxed in by evidence.

"No." She palmed open the hatch to her office. "I'm extending full search and seizure authority to Tok Su so she can investigate." She pointed a finger at Bru. "Give her your full cooperation, or I will enact the Combat Emergency Measures Protocol."

Bru's face swelled, red. "You wouldn't."

"Watch me." He lunged but the hatch hissed shut on his enflamed face.

Exe waited within, poised by the hatch, one lanky arm raised to hit the open switch, the other holding a stunner at the ready. "That was interesting."

"Thanks. I don't think Bru would attack me outside my own office, but I appreciate the insurance."

"Especially if you think Bru is a murderer." Exe watched her cross to her charging cabinet and extract a stunner of her own. "**Do** you think that?"

Ann shrugged, setting her stunner to a medium setting. "As good as. He's pushing Chill, despite his insistence that, **if** he was pushing anything, his product would be pure and innocent."

"Was it a good idea, unleashing Tok Su like that?"

"I'm giving her an opportunity to prove her point. Temporarily. Maybe she'll sort it all out if I let her cross the line to chase down leads."

"I hope that's the only line she crosses. There's something not right about her."

"You been listening to gossip, Eshie?"

Exe shrugged. "Dickie Fullham worked with her awhile, post-war."

"You attended one of his PRER sessions?"

Exe shook his head. "But we talked, sometimes. He has an excellent attention to detail I appreciate."

OCD twins, Ann thought but kept to herself. "He was a linguistics liaison in the Witter interrogations. She was military."

"They talked to Witters?" Ann exclaimed.

"Tried to get intel on their tech. Dickie was elusive about it, conflicted. Seems they couldn't get any sense out of the prisoners. I guess it got ugly. He ended up on stress leave and started this PRER thing."

Ann would have liked to have seen humans get ugly with Witters.

"Dickie wouldn't be the only eccentric on the station, would he, Eshie?"

"And Tok Su? Why is she out here?" Exe asked, ignoring Ann's implication. "You told me yourself she's got great connections in-system. Why isn't she working her way up the pecking order at Sol Central?"

Ann had wondered that herself, but she said, "Not everyone who comes out here can't cut it in Central." She punched Exe lightly on the arm. "Are you calling us space junk? Why are we here?"

"Me? I get to lord it over the whole comms network, indulge my compulsive tendencies and never worry about sunburn. You, Ann? You can't let go of the war – you want to be first in line if the Witters jump back. Whether to fight or to die I won't ask."

"Son of a bitch, Eshie! This station is subsiding into chaos from specific causes, i.e., smuggling and drugs. She'll kick some butt and go back in-system with my shining recommendation. Then we'll mend fences, but, right now, I need a tough house-cleaner and Tok Su is what I've got. Whatever the reason she's out here."

Exe said, "I'm only saying she might be volatile. Do you suspect her of more?" She didn't reply. "Ann. You accused the entire comms team of being on the take to smugglers. Including me, thanks a lot. It'd be nice to know if you're an equal opportunity paranoid."

Ann's face burned and she ground down on her teeth to the point of pain.

"I could look into things for you."

"Leave it, Exe. That's Tok Su's job." She stopped his response with a raised palm. "You can help. Dig down and find out who or what's causing the breakdowns and make them stop."

"Yes'm." He paused at the hatch, his red-tinged eyes hooded behind white lashes. "You have to trust someone."

Ann prowled her ready room, unable to concentrate on the hundred and one things needing her attention. She'd have liked to tell Exe she trusted him. She did. But trust was a sliding scale, dependent on circumstances.

And that didn't sound paranoid, did it? She wished she could break some heads, kick some butt, and get answers. But she had to leave the pieces in play, wait it out.

Something was missing from the game board. Some niggle.

"Five are different," Exe had said during her temper display in Ops.

She called up the display sequence and watched the patterns of satellite blackouts overlaid by traffic to the pod, plus the simulations. What had he meant?

She came to herself, standing, paralyzed in a maelstrom of flashing message icons. **Five** are different. Five deaths. What she was thinking was so paranoid, so horrifying, she could barely articulate it. Dickie lay butchered in a pod, waiting for cremation and shipment of his ashes in-system to whatever family or loved ones he might have. He'd be the sixth. If what she thought was true, she had to witness it with her own eyes.

Enduring the head rush, she took a travel tube straight to the station hub, feet firmly planted on grip pads and hand clamped to the stability handles fixed to the transfer pod wall. Disembarking, weightless, into the hub, she pulled herself along the handholds set into the walls of the station's axis until she reached the embarkation dock, a room big enough to hold twenty soldiers suiting up for extra-station combat. Twenty Faraday combat suits in two rows gaped open and ready. Even now, five years since combat, the suits were kept in top shape, used by the few remaining military for drills and by techs for external work that couldn't be done remotely.

Stepping into the first suit in the line, Ann secured the helmet and gloves and ran checks for air, propellant, tether and comms. She squelched on grip feet to the air lock. It was a fast cycler; she was in the exit tube leading to open space in under two minutes.

She tethered to the first haul, the step-by-step process drilled into reflex. Pushing free of the lock's Faraday shield, she stepped out into spangled black. The huge wheel of Uranus Station spun majestically beneath her feet, the irregular hub of habitats and docking pods winking past as it turned, maintaining a steady point eight earth gravity. Uranus loomed beyond the station's rim, a blue arc half filling the sky and casting pale glints onto the rounded surfaces and projections that clustered the axis.

Was she being paranoid? Was it time to pack it in? Go back where the sun was bright and hot, where she could go outside without a suit, where water ran free and trees and flowers flourished? Why not admit the war was over, that she no longer needed to stand on guard?

She peeled her feet free and popped a jet-burst to send her out into the dark until her tether tugged her to a stop. Below her feet, the great wheel of the station spun and mighty Uranus arced. Beyond that lay the limitless dark of space spangled by stars and galaxies beyond reach or knowing. The only sign of life was the sound of her own breathing.

A tiny point of light flared and winked out above the northern rim of the planet's edge. She'd seen such signals five years earlier, nothing between her and it but the thin skin of a suit. A head rush dizzied her and her vision blanked. Training kicked in, the taught breathing, the self-calming, the hard press of rational thought and analysis tamping down panting terror. An incursion alert whined in her helmet. The Witters were here.

The alert stood down. False alarm.

Except that it wasn't. She was sure it wasn't.

Ann hauled herself back along her tether, hooked in to the viewing stanchion and zipped up the line to the next tether point, ten meters out from the station. From this vantage point she had a view of a larger segment of the wheel and the space around Uranus. She doubted if she would see anything, but she watched, watched for something beyond that one flash.

Movement shifted in the shadows on the station rim. A figure, limned sharp against the blue planet, crouched on the skin.

"Busted."

Ann re-tethered to a transit line and puffed a propellant squirt to speed her along the station's hull. The figure hove into sight as she zipped past the curve of a protruding array installation, forcing her to bear down hard on her brake clamp. The figure's back was to her as it hunkered over the array, a helmet light creating a silhouette around the familiar lines of a Faraday suit. As she hauled herself closer, she called up the schematics on her helmet visual and was unsurprised to find that she was approaching a comms installation.

Still a meter away, she activated a suit-to-suit channel.

"ID yourself," she snapped. The figure started, recovered.

"Oh, hi, Ann. Someone put a clever little blocker on this receiver." Exe. His tone was conversational, as if chatting in deep space vacuum while ravening aliens closed in was an everyday occurrence. "I'll have to figure out how it works, but it seems to intercept the gate warning signal. It blocks the laser but some of the radio waves get around it, which causes the false alarms. Quite ingenious really."

"Ingenious, huh. A Witter gate just flared in that sector."

Exe jerked upright, only just grabbing the object before it drifted off. He peered in the direction Ann had indicated, clutching the thing to his chest.

"You're surprised, Eshie?"

Even in a Faraday suit, Exe exuded irritation. "Of course, I'm surprised. Well, I expected something. But not... Look, I knew something was out of whack: shipments to the hidden pod didn't match the Chill murders. And I found only a weak correlation with the false alarms. But there were five such alarms that occurred within a standard day of each death. I hypothesized a possibility, but I couldn't believe it, still can't, even finding this tech."

"Tell me."

Silence, but for his breathing. At last, he said, "Someone's feeding the animals."

Something lodged in her chest shook loose.

"Okay, Eshie. Let's get this thing inside and have a look at it."

"I told you it was an unbelievable hypothesis."

"It's the same as mine."

Back on board, Exe and Ann stared at the device. It was dead simple, a curved metal plate shaped to block signals.

"Anybody could've made this," Exe said. "Anybody would know that the laser signal would bounce off it. But, why?"

"If we're not both deluded, that someone is sending Chill victims to the Witters for pick up," Ann said. "And we know how Witters are addicted to human meat."

"Live meat, in fact," Exe said.

"Dickie Fullham thought it was an addiction that had to be treated."

"Treated!"

Exe smiled weakly at her astonishment. "As you said, he was...eccentric."

"Actually, I said Tok Su was."

Exe shrugged. "Anyhow, **dead** Chill kills don't make the menu, do they? So –"

"Tok Su who manages the autopsies and insists on managing disposal of the remains."

Exe fell silent, processing what she was saying.

"And," she continued, "Dickie and Tok Su..."

"...interrogated Witters together," Exe finished.

"Shouldn't we call Security?" Exe asked on their way to Tok Su's location in the Loader sector.

Ann shook her head. "I can't be certain how deep the rot goes."

They continued in silence a few more seconds, and he said, "Three kilos of ashes. That's the allocation for remains shipped in-system." He paused. "What is she sending back to the families?"

Ann stumbled, caught herself. She checked her stunner for charge. "I'm stopping her."

Ann stepped into the utilitarian gray of the corridor in the unused sector. Hugging the station-side wall, she crept along the curve of the half-doughnut segment. Exe followed at her back. Broken red security tape dangled on either side of the open hatch of the illicit pod. Didn't anyone toggle the auto-shut anymore? In the minimal lighting, the corridor beyond subsided into shadows that seemed to shift.

Signaling Exe to keep close, she eased up to the hatch and peeked around its edge. Bru Kente and Tulunda Tok Su faced off in front of the airlock hatch to the loading chamber. Blood spatters still decorated the wall, a gruesome backdrop to their confrontation. Tok Su held a stunner on Bru. Bru's usual companions lay on the floor, unmoving.

"Kente, get out of here and take that trash with you."

"What did you do with them?"

"You're making no sense."

"I lost good men."

"Who, them?" Tok Su prodded one of the unconscious men with a toe.

"They'll wake up. They shouldn't have interfered with the legitimate actions of a security officer."

"That's not who I'm talking about and you know it." He took a step closer to her. "You're behind this whole thing somehow. We all talked it over, sussed it out. Sure, this is **our** pod, but you been sneaking in here, haven't you? Shipping stuff in and out. We don't know what, and we don't have to. Since you got here, good men have been dying."

"Druggie losers."

"Good men getting by how they could!" Bru yelled.

"I'm not the one who sold them dirty Chill," Tok Su said.

"I didn't. I test it. It wouldn't make them killers. And it wouldn't kill them." Bru seemed near tears. "Chensdotter won't believe me, but it's true."

"I don't have time for this." Tok Su raised her stunner. Ann raised her own. The movement caught Tok Su's eye and she whirled.

"Oh. It's you, ma'am." She re-trained her stunner on Bru. "I found Kente here with his companions. They attempted to impede my investigation."

The indicator on the lock flashed from red to green. Someone was about to enter, and the shock on Tok Su's face showed she wasn't expecting it. Her stunner wavered.

Bru hissed, a tight whistle between his teeth. Something heavy shoved by Ann's legs, throwing her off balance. Tok Su spun, stunner raised. Exe yanked Ann back and the beam skimmed past but numbed her fingers, so she dropped her weapon. A dark brown object hurtled toward Tok Su and leapt at her thighs. Tok Su screamed as Barbara sank her sharp, rodent's incisors into the woman's flesh. Tok Su dropped her stunner. Barbara scuttled behind Bru and peered around him at her. The hatch cycled open.

An annoying voice said tinnily, "Hello, Administrator Chensdotter. It's about time you got things under control." Dickie Fullham pulled off his helmet. "Surprise."

Tok Su, clutching her thigh, stared at him. "Why did they let you go? Where's my tech?"

Ann asked, "What tech? What's going on?"

Dickie took in Bru and the wounded Tok Su and looked puzzled, but then registered the loaders, still lying unconscious on the floor. His eyes popped with resolution and righteous indignation. "I was drugged. I was wounded. I was kidnapped and left to be **eaten.**" Silence fell, absolutely. He pointed, dramatically. "Tok Su is part of a rogue group out of Sol Central which is trading live humans to Witter pushers. They peddle the victims to Witters addicted to human flesh, in exchange for Witter jump gate technology." He let out a long breath, as if relieved of a burden. "I should have realized sooner. I used to – work with her."

"You traitor." Tok Su glared at Dickie. "If we don't supply them, they'll come and get it."

"Not as such," Dickie began.

Bru loomed over Tok Su. "You sliced up my loaders, guys like these poor sods here? You sold them, **still alive**, as Witter chow?"

She waved him off. "I sold druggies to druggies. At least this way they're useful. When we get the complete plans, humans will have gate jump capability."

Bru hit her. Barbara bit her again. Tok Su fell to the floor, arms curled over her head.

"Oh, Barbara," Dickie said, "I thought I'd never see you again." The capybara bumped her forehead against his knee, purring. Re-vitalized, Dickie continued, "As I was **trying** to say, the plan has failed. Witter authorities do not like drug pushers any more than humans do. I was lucky to be picked up, not by the pushers, but by – well. Administrator Chensdotter, I am pleased to introduce–" he made a noise that sounded like a combination of gargle, sneeze and shriek. Dickie stepped away from the hatch entry.

A huge figure lunged into the pod, unmistakable in its stylized space gear, huge crested helmet, segmented limbs and body, and back jointed, raptor-like legs.

Blood sucked out of Ann's head, terror shrinking her vision to pin points and freezing her in place. An urgent inner voice screamed to fight or run. Bru and Barbara collided in the pod doorway and escaped. Exe fired his stunner.

The huge figure shook itself, took one long stride, plucked the stunner out of Exe's hand, and laid it down gently, out of reach. It retracted its helmet to reveal its thrusting jaws, ducked its huge head and emitted a gargle.

"Yes. I should've mentioned," said Dickie. "Gargle-sneeze-shriek is his people's equivalent of a narcotics officer. He's here to put a stop to the trafficking in humans."

Ann backed closer to the exit, right hand numb from Tok Su's stunner fire, Exe disarmed. They must flee, figure options for defense. That thing kept staring at her. Should she stay still? Run? What about the men on the floor? What was Dickie babbling about?

"Ridiculous as it sounds, he thought I was one of the human perpetrators of these heinous crimes. I persevered in using what Witter I've acquired and convinced him that I am a victim." He patted the Witter's arm. It recoiled slightly, but then clumsily patted Dickie back.

Ann felt disoriented, dizzy, as if flailing in zero G without handholds, spinning out of control. Years of fighting and fear reduced to Dickie Fullham claiming these animals were the good guys?

"No. They're killers. Cannibals. And you say it's all a misunderstanding? So sorry, move along, nothing to see here?" She screamed at the Witter, "You're a monster!" The Witter backed away from her, gloved hands raised.

At her elbow, Exe said, "We're addictive to their people. We're their dirty Chill. And there was someone ready to take advantage. On both sides."

Ann turned on him. "Exe," she pleaded. "How can you take their side?" *How can I, after all I've seen, done, believed? Not possible, not possible, not possible.* "Against your own kind?" *What kind? What kind am I?*

"He's a traitor." Tok Su had crawled to her dropped stunner. She heaved it upward to aim at the alien's unarmored head, hands shaking and wavering. It threw up its arms, claws extending from its armor, defensively. Defensively. A loader at Tok Su's feet stirred and feebly batted at Tok Su's aiming arm, distracting her. Ann leapt across the space and kicked Tok Su in the head just as she fired. The shot dissipated harmlessly against the ceiling.

Tok Su, rolling to all fours, stared up at her, blood trickling from her nose, inhuman yellow eyes showing the rage of a frustrated predator. A monster from nightmares.

Ann retrieved the stunner. Checked on the fallen men. Forced herself to look at the Witter. It stared back, arms dropped to its sides, claws extending and forcibly retracting. Its eyes, seen close, shimmered with fleeting rainbow opalescence.

He's seeing a monster, Ann thought. Her eyes pricked, with shame, and sorrow, and loss. She raised her hand and touched the Witter on the arm. He removed his glove and, claws fully sheathed, touched her back.

Ann turned to Exe.

"Call Bru, wherever he's got to and tell him it's safe to come back, please, Exe." She gestured at Tok Su, fully collapsed on the floor. "Get him to help you secure that thing and lock it up."

# # #

The meeting room was full.

"Welcome, welcome to our first meeting of the New PRER." Dickie, percolating with self-satisfaction, clasped his hands as if to restrain from hugging everyone in the room. "Administrator Chensdotter, I am delighted to welcome you in particular.

Ann nodded her head, smiling through her irritation. This was going to be tough, but she owed him that much. ■

Robots at Dawn!

By T. B.
JEREMIAH

T. B. Jeremiah lives in the shadow of some old mountains with an AI researcher and several potted plants. She is a writer, illustrator and graphic designer, and spends what free time she has drawing pictures of monsters. Previously she's been a janitor, history instructor, and non-profit marketing monkey.

Anyone could have predicted that the admittance of the Lady Barbara Honesty to the College of Roboticists would issue in strife of some kind or another. Lady Barbara, besides being a woman of high breeding, had a reputation for running her laboratory – and her collaborators – with little regard for formalities. When she and her not-quite fiancé Sir Andrew Brexlee presented their first paper, she addressed all questioners by their surnames, regardless of rank. Nobody knew quite how to respond, though Mr. Julian Ayscoghe overcame his astonishment enough to ask several quite penetrating questions.

"I say, Ayscoghe," she said afterwards. "Would you care to come round to my laboratory tomorrow to discuss this further?"

"Oh," said Mr. Julian, unused to familiar address by the titled and so momentarily bereft of his usual directness. "Ah. Yes, that sounds very useful."

It was, in fact, an intemperate remark about Lady Barbara by Mr. Julian that precipitated the whole affair. Sir Andrew got wind of it through Miss Chuddleston, who had it from Mrs. Cho, who most likely heard the story from the maliciously elated Mr. Combeferre, the dancing master. The exact nature of the remark has not survived, but most likely it related to Lady Barbara's coding habits.

Sir Andrew, despite having given private vent to very similar complaints in the past, went round to Mr. Julian's in a towering fury. He pounded on the door for a good ten seconds, before thinking better of it and retiring home to send one of his drones lumbering across the rooftops with a sternly-worded note. It demanded that Mr. Julian publicly retract his remark about Lady Barbara immediately, apologize to her in person, and acknowledge her superior facility as a gentlewoman-programmer.

By way of reply, Mr. Julian sent the drone wobbling back under the weight of one of his gloves. Fortunately, Sir Andrew rescued it before a pigeon destroyed the drone entirely.

At this point, all that was left was to settle the details of time and place. It would be the very first duel carried out under the rules of the College of Roboticists. Lady Barbara, when told the news, raised her eyebrows and said nothing.

At first it seemed impossible to fix on a time, as there was so much work to be done in the laboratory – but in the end a hint from Lady Barbara helped them to settle on dawn as the traditional time, and Wednesday next for the date. The place proved still more difficult, as duels were not permitted within the city limits. Soon tiring of Sir Andrew's vocal fretting, Lady Barbara proposed the village near which her family's manor was situated.

"There is a clearing by the millrace that will do capitally," she said. "They keep the grass cut very short."

"Grass!" said Sir Andrew. "H'm!" But he agreed, and Lady Barbara smiled, and all was well until Wednesday next.

Word got out, of course; first to the active members of the College of Roboticists, then to the ladies, then to the dandier gentlemen, and at long last to the most reclusive members of the College. Everyone agreed that it was an historic occasion, that the gentlemen would undoubtedly display the greatest and most ingenious feats of which robots were capable, that it would be rude in the extreme to intrude on so grave a matter as a private duel, and that they had just recently recalled business that took them to that neighborhood on Tuesday next, or perhaps Monday.

When the news got round to old Dr. Kenebow, the most senior roboticist in the College, he shook his head and said that Lady Barbara was not an opponent he cared to challenge. He seemed unable to hear his nephew's repeated attempts to inform him that Lady Barbara was not a combatant in this duel.

The night before the duel, Sir Andrew and Mr. Julian dined together at Lady Barbara's, discussing the finer points of automatic thoroughbreds and studiously avoiding any talk of the forthcoming contest. Each retired early, making ironical allusions to the other's penchant for late nights and later mornings.

Lady Barbara sat up in her dressing-room, reading a book and listening for the stealthy pad of Sir Andrew's, and then Mr. Julian's, stockinged feet. She had left the family laboratory's doors unlocked, just in case.

Dawn arrived earlier than it had any right to do, and both Sir Andrew and Mr. Julian met it with haggard faces and eyes crusty from too little sleep, snatched in the small hours of the morning. They went unarmed, dressed soberly but richly, and their seconds followed. Sir Andrew's second carried a lanky black scarecrow of a robot roughly the size of a whippet. Mr. Julian's bore a round-faced robot with staring eyes, about the size of a cat. Each was equipped with an orange target painted on its chest.

The clearing by the millrace was just as Lady Barbara had described it, and in the cold dawn light the mist made it look positively romantic. Sir Andrew and Mr. Julian, however, frowned at the mist, and the grass, and the mystical light.

"Is something wrong?" asked Lady Barbara, she having insisted upon attending.

"The light –" began Mr. Julian.

"Dawn is traditional for duels," Lady Barbara replied.

Sir Andrew and Mr. Julian both agreed, with amiability only a little forced, that it was important to do things traditionally. Each retired to their side of the clearing and began the laborious task of activating the robots. They were considerably startled by the appearance of Miss Chuddleston, who said vaguely that she thought the dawn air was so healthful; and by the time a dozen or so spectators had assembled with various excuses, the combatants were in a state of nerves almost pitiable to contemplate.

Nevertheless, the robots came to life with the usual protestations, the seconds assisted in positioning them, and the duel seemed ready to begin. The combatants stepped back, Lady Barbara yawned, and the spectators held their collective breath waiting for the first movement of the engagement.

Sir Andrew's robot turned its head until its beady eyes fixed on a tuft of grass, marginally taller than the rest, five yards distant. Servos whirred, its weight shifted, and it promptly toppled onto its back. It was prepared for this, however, and began working its legs to flip itself back upright – only to find no purchase on the grass. The ladies watching sighed and groaned.

"I'm sorry," Sir Andrew said. "May I –?"

"Of course," said Mr. Julian. Sir Andrew bounded forward and hauled the robot upright, cursing softly as he sought a patch of grass on which it could balance itself.

"Perhaps another location –"

"It was agreed upon," Lady Barbara pointed out. "And clearings are traditional."

Sir Andrew and Mr. Julian exchanged suffering looks.

Mr. Julian's robot was of sturdier build, and stumbled forward several steps before succumbing to a clod of dirt. For a brief, thrilling moment it looked as though it would succeed in regaining its footing, but in the end it slipped and tumbled onto its side. To the small crowd its flailing looked like nothing so much as a beetle that had been flipped onto its back.

After a hurried consultation between Sir Andrew, Mr. Julian, and the seconds, it was agreed that perhaps the traditional pacing could be dispensed with, as the robots seemed indisposed. Instead they were placed about a yard apart, facing one another – after much wrestling and cursing on the part of the principals, and shifting ground several times to find the most level part of the clearing.

At last they were settled. Sir Andrew and Mr. Julian hovered anxiously a foot or so away from their respective robots, but the devices were clearly standing on their own, glaring magnificently at each other. They turned their heads almost in unison, seeking the target. Sir Andrew's, indeed, turned its head all the way around like an owl so that it faced its maker.

At this precise moment the sun crested the treetops, and a perfect, dramatic sunbeam turned Sir Andrew's hair (tousled from his recent wrestle with his invention) into a ruddy halo.

The robot's eyes lit up like two candle flames, it raised its arm, and it fired its single bullet directly into Sir Andrew's kneecap.

The ladies screamed. Sir Andrew screamed. Mr. Julian uttered what might charitably be considered a startled cry. Even the seconds yelped. Lady Barbara gave a sharp intake of breath, then started forward and caught her betrothed under the armpits before he sank to the ground. The seconds moved to assist, but were swept aside by Mr. Julian.

"Sir Andrew!" he cried. "My dear sir! How badly are you hurt? Pray do not die, Sir Andrew!"

"I am sure he will not die," Lady Barbara said crisply. "Let us take him back to the house." And this they did – Mr. Julian, Lady Barbara, and the seconds. The cluster of watching people milled about a little while, but when it became clear that they were not invited they gradually dispersed.

Surprisingly little rumor spread about

the duel. It did not make a particularly good story, except to a few detractors of the College of Roboticists – but none of these had been present and nobody who was anyone knew them socially. Sir Andrew and Mr. Julian made up their quarrel completely; both felt that their honor had been satisfied, and both concluded that they were far too amiably inclined towards one another to continue any serious difference. They returned to work in Lady Barbara's laboratory, determined to improve their robots' ability to identify objects in different lights.

When a visitor told old Dr. Kenebow, he nodded sagely.

"Lady Barbara is a better roboticist than the pair of them put together," he said. His nephew, exhausted in his efforts to explain the situation, merely rolled his eyes.

"But Lady Barbara did not touch the robots involved in the duel, Doctor!" said the visitor, bawling a little into Dr. Kenebow's ear-trumpet.

"Just so," Dr. Kenebow replied. "Just so."

"Sir Andrew's robot malfunctioned without any interference!" the visitor persisted, ignoring nephew Kenebow's signals to leave well enough alone.

"Yes," Dr. Kenebow said. "They always do." ▩

By BUD
SPARHAWK

Bud Sparhawk's short works frequently appear in Analog, F&SF, *and other print magazines.* Non-Parallel Universes *is a collection of his self-proclaimed "best" short stories published in the last decade. He has been a three-time novella finalist for SFWA's Nebula award. His complete bibliography can be found at: http:// budsparhawk.com.*

Nobody remembers how mankind got involved in the galactic wars. As best we know, nobody was willing to admit blame for screwing up so bad that humanity had to formally choose sides in a multi-sided battle where the allies of today might be the adversaries of tomorrow. In some cases, we had to establish weird agreements to confront a common foe. Unfortunately, none of the agreements necessarily forbade occasional sniping at your partner/friend/symbiote/parasite.

Got it? Sometimes the battle lines weren't that clear: Allegiances shifted so quickly and, most times faster than light speed communications weren't fast enough for the units in the field to adapt to political changes. We might start out fighting the Greelies or the Zargots, then discover that they were our new allies and there was some other group of aliens designated as enemies-of-the-week.

The saving grace was that most of the aliens we fought seemed to be equally confused, which meant that everybody/thing was very cautious about fighting and **extremely** serious about not killing anything or anyone unless there was no other choice.

You never knew what could come back to bite you.

Speaking of biting, the human forces realized that dogs could be vital elements of our combat forces; that is, when they could be handled, which was my role and essential to my current assignment on Ascalade, an assignment on the other side of nobody gives a damn.

Does it make sense to ship me and my dogs a bazillion kilometers? You might as well ask if it makes sense to ship a bunch of soldiers that same distance to shoot at alien forces with no more interest in the outcome than saving their own frigging skin, hide, or chitin! Of course it made no sense; not the transport, not the war, and especially not one pissed-off dog handler who was sick and tired of losing his friends.

Don't get me wrong – dogs are important allies in this war, just as they've been for untold centuries. Humanity has used dogs as scouts, pack animals, detectors, even weapons. I'd used my dogs' enhanced hearing to detect the rustle of scales as the Noonne slid underground to evade capture. Flash, my youngest terror, had detected the faint sweet smell of the sneaky Tuff who, I heard, were now our allies against who the hell cares?

Maybe.

Before our new alliance, the Tuff had used scent bombs to distract our dogs and mask their own presence. Their bacon bombs were the worst, since they not only confused the dogs but created insatiable cravings among the human troops who were forced to eat nothing but taste-free Combat Consumable Paste on deployments.

We reacted to the Tuff bombings by lobbing pepper aerosol bursts to irritate the Tuffs' multiple eyes, and ours as well if we forgot to wear goggles.

The after-effects of most Tuff-Human encounters were tear-blinded Tuff and slavering dog-human teams too bacon-distracted to actually injure anything seriously; which was fine with me. I sort of liked the Tuff, as did the terriers who thought of them as lively toys to be obsessively managed.

The Tuff had a different view.

\# \# \#

I was *en route* from headquarters, bound for distant Ascalade to train our current allies, the Dremma, in how to command their animals to fight the Tch'ka, or maybe the Zargots or, by the time I got there, some other species the Dremma had managed to piss off. As I said, the roster of war participants was continually changing and who's to know who's on first, let alone who's pitching?

I was being transported on one of our allies' luxury liners, reportedly "comfortable beyond compare" and "equipped with the finest of accommodations." Well, I imagined the luxuries and accommodations would have been considered as such by the Yilppz, who resembled humans as much as a turkey did an elephant, which is to say not at all.

My opinion differed. My berth on the Yilppz transport was in one of their first-class compartments, a cramped crawl space complete with fetid pool and a king-sized bed nearly a meter square. The cabin's atmosphere reeked of rancid decay with a tinge of nausea. Unfortunately, it was also breathable.

After learning about the ship's' second class accommodations, I considered my upgrade fortunate.

\# \# \#

There had been no luxurious forests, pristine lakes, or even a tolerable climate on my previous deployment to Pazida Prime. There, the Greelies had been fighting us over a sparse piece of real estate lacking any charming features. Sand, sand, and more sand stretched in every direction in our sector. The sere sweep of land was broken here and there by an occasional ruddy rock, a fall of broken shards, or a yawning pit blasted by some recent artillery round. The nearest crater to my part of the sector sweep was maybe a meter deep, its banks sloping gently to a dusty bottom while all around were the ejecta from the blast.

Did I mention the sun blazing down, baking the rose sand into an inferno that sent rivulets of sweat down my back, soaking my all-terrain combat suit, and pooling in my insulated boots? The weight of my gear grew oppressive with every step I took. How long were we going to search this god-forsaken patch of nothing for aliens that might be long gone?

Suddenly, my three terriers were barking, jumping around like they'd smelled a badger, only there weren't any badgers within a hundred light years of this hellhole, and even if there were they'd starve from the lack of anything to eat.

The terriers didn't mind the climate, being quite comfortable in their coolsuits and padded footies, clothing denied to we handlers, who were considered by command as beings of lesser importance.

Bolt, the leader of the pack, was yapping; each bark grew more intense, as if he'd found something of interest other than another rock to piss on. I headed his way to see what the ruckus was all about.

Sniffles, Flash, and Bolt were snuffling at a peculiar, perfectly circular hole, with no ejecta around it. Curious.

Sniffles and Flash backed away as soon as I raised my arm. Bolt, ever the hard-headed one, jumped into the hole. His muffled yip-yip echoed from deep within.

"I think we've got a remnant," I reported to command. "One of my dogs is investigating."

"Be there in five," command replied. "Pull back."

"To me!" I shouted. Flash and Sniffles obeyed immediately, taking positions at each heel. An agonizing minute later, Bolt reluctantly backed out of the hole to quiver in front of me, as loath as ever to stop his fun-filled pursuit.

Now that the dogs and I were the required ten meters away, I pointed my H&Kbar6.4a at the hole, primed the pump, and waited. If anything jumped out before the retrieval crew arrived it was going to be fried.

Bolt began growling, a deep, rumbling roar that could have come from something much larger than his twenty-pound frame. I stepped back another meter and the dogs obediently followed. We watched the hole. I heard the distant roar of the floater and threw a quick glance in that direction.

Sniffles yowled, a long ululation that scared the hell out of me. I turned just as she dashed forward to attack a Greelie erupting from the sand halfway between us and the hole. It rose above my head, its long, sinuous body twisting to bring its sensory array to bear as the dog pounced, sinking her tiny teeth into one of the Greelies' fleshy appendages.

Bolt joined the fray, worrying one of the fibrous fronds holding a potato shaped thing that the Greelie was trying to point my way even as it struggled to shake off the two dogs.

"*Z@lack3ly!* Stand down!" I shouted, hoping this thing understood the same language as the others we'd fought. When it failed to heed my shouts I knew something bad was going to happen. I just hoped the bad fell on the Greelie and not me.

The frond holding the potato thing continued trying to shake off Bolt's grip as I continued shouting "*Z@lack3ly!*" over and over until it was obvious the damned Greelie wasn't going to stop trying to fry me. "To me," I shouted loudly as I put my finger on the trigger.

Neither dog obeyed. Bolt wouldn't let go of the frond holding the weapon. Sniffles didn't stop furiously chewing on another part of the Greelie. "To me!" I screamed, to no avail. The alien almost had the potato thing's muzzle bearing on me as I fired.

Flash wailed as the alien, Bolt and Sniffles were consumed by the torrent of flame that shot out of the H&Kbar6.4a. In moments there was nothing left of the alien but a few pieces of charred chitin; and, of Bolt and Sniffles, there was only ash.

Those damned terriers never did pay attention when they were having fun.

My ashy Greelie was the only remnant who'd refused capture during the post-battle clean up over that worthless piece of real estate. It had apparently been left behind during the pull-out prior to the Greelie-Human armistice. Somehow, while troops of both sides were fighting, alliances had again shifted and we humans were now buddies with the Greelies. I just wished someone had bothered to inform the Greelie and me.

Such is war.

\# \# \#

The loss of Bolt and Sniffles hit me hard. I'd worked with Bolt and Sniffles since they were whelped, continually struggling against their cantankerous natures and only occasionally succeeding. Both dogs had done things they enjoyed with boundless enthusiasm, endured the less pleasant tasks should there be a reward involved, and steadfastly refused to do anything that offered neither enjoyment nor reward.

Jumping into holes was Bolt's greatest game, one for which his line had been bred for centuries. That tunneling trait made the terriers ideal for finding the burrows of the vile, obscene, and vicious Greelies, who mysteriously became fun-loving, adventurous companions when they suddenly became allies. The tides of war washed enemies ashore more often than not.

Sniffles' main trait had been persistence, always focusing on the task at hand to the exclusion of all else. Once she caught the scent of a Greelie (they smell somewhat like rats), she would follow the scent trail until she fastened her tiny teeth on one, which usually distracted the alien long enough to restrain or kill it. I preferred the former, since it made relationships a bit easier, especially when a prisoner later became a foxhole buddy.

\# \# \#

Eventually, there was a prisoner exchange on Pazida Prime. Flash and I watched from the barracks while the Greelie troops slith-

ered onto their retrieval transports, probably to do battle on another world against the Zagots, Tuffs, Noonne, or something else, depending on the way the war's political winds had once again shifted.

Command provided me with the requisite thirty days of grief counseling and, after that, possible reassignment. During my downtime, I consoled myself by working with Flash, my remaining terrier. Together, we gathered the worn, torn, and bedraggled blanket that Sniffles slept upon, and the ragged, spit-soaked woolen rat Bolt liked to chew. I tried to include Bolt's little red training ball but Flash guarded it ferociously, even though Bolt had never let him touch it.

I put the objects in a small box and, accompanied by Flash, held an informal burial ceremony in one corner of the compound. True to his nature, Flash pissed on the small marker I'd erected. It was a fitting tribute, even if he didn't realize it.

Bolt and Sniffles had lived barely half their allotted spans, but rather longer than most war dogs and their handlers.

We had been lucky.

\# \# \#

The limit of allowable grief having been met, Command decided that I needed to get back to work and assigned me to a training role as a dog-handler. I was happy; training would involve little in the way of hostilities.

I had no regrets about leaving Pazida Prime to those brave and stupid settlers who wanted to exploit it. I knew that once we military left they would fall back into their normal squabbling colonization habits of encroaching on each others' claims, arguing endlessly over access rights, and occasionally performing violence on each other.

I hoped that the human settlers' relations with the Greelie settlers were slightly less acrimonious than our military relationships had been.

\# \# \#

Command intended for me to use Flash and a few pups to demonstrate dog-handling training techniques to the Dremma, a species who'd obtained dog-analogous animals from the RippaHorde. It sounded like an easy assignment, but then I didn't know what the Dremma were like, nor had any idea of the nature of the "dogs" they needed to train.

I wasn't worried about demonstrating our techniques since Flash had become a seasoned warrior. Training the pups from scratch would be the easiest part of the job, or that's what my CO told me before departure. "Piece of cake," she'd joked. "Whip a few of their domesticated **whatsits** into shape, train their handlers, and let nature do the rest. Shouldn't take you more than six months – a year at most." She'd been so jocular, as if sending me off to a placid vacation.

I was told that Flash and two new, as yet unseen pups were being shipped separately. I tolerated being temporarily separated from my temperamental, excitable, and seriously single-minded Flash. He could be controlled, but only on his terms, and was often wont to think his own goals more important, especially in the heat of battle, which is what had happened to my dear, brave, and too-highly focused Bolt and Sniffles.

It was only when dodging enemy fire on our approach to Ascalade that I realized that my CO hadn't mentioned I'd be working in a war zone. Upon debarking, I saw flashes of brilliant light and faintly heard the roar of mechanical war machines trundling towards the front, not too far away.

My first impressions of Ascalade were its temperate climate and the strong scent of juniper. The planet sat under a warm and friendly sun. Gravity was about a quarter again what I was used to, but not uncomfortable.

What locally passed for foliage was low-growing, blue-green, round-leaved scrub spreading wide and dense on raggedy ropey-brown trunks. This type of vegetation covered the landscape in tangles of chest-high forest all the way to the horizon, interrupted only by occasional swathes of cleared land and a few small hills.

Some temporary buildings had been erected in the middle of the low-growing vegetation. I assumed the human-scaled one would be for me and my dogs while the other, hive-like ones housed the Dremma I was to train.

Shortly after I secured my luggage I met the Dremma commander, a quarter-meter-high, bulbously-shaped, hairy, six-limbed alien whose face consisted of a sensory stalk encrusted with protruding orbs, cilae, and assorted things that wiggled and waved distractingly as it chirped in tones that made my ears hurt.

It rather pompously introduced itself as "Light Colonel Anharsk deProcucde, Tenth Regimental Battalion, Second Fusiliers – Mechanized." I was fascinated by the way his sky-blue coat was embellished with swirls of gold and silver that sprawled across the front. More impressive was the way the three bright balls on his helmet bobbed to and fro as he chirped.

"We are wanting of advanced training of our new acquisitions," Light Colonel Anharsk informed me. "Of historic significance is our lack of experiences with the commandment of exotic sub-intelligent species."

"Yes sir. I was told that you wanted someone to train some dogs you acquired from the RippaHordes?" My translator emitted a high-pitched stream of chirps, whistles, and silences which I suspected were sounds well above my hearing range.

"You have most outrageously coarse accent," the tiny alien chittered nastily. "But, of the essential, we are of a mind. We have learned of human success with *Canis Lupus Familiaris* and wish to emulate with Rista."

My CO hadn't mentioned the nature of the so-called "dogs" the diminutive Dremma had acquired. Would they be critters that could be cajoled with rewards,

whispers, and soft touches to obey their handlers? What would be their effectiveness on a battlefield, where ferocity often outweighed compassion?

Given the size of the Dremma, I didn't expect the creatures they wanted to train to be anything larger than a small Chihuahua. I hesitated to think of how the waist-high handlers could be expected to handle anything larger.

The whole idea of using my dogs to demonstrate training techniques suddenly seemed ill-founded. I had no idea of what the Dremma expected to gain from their unlikely partnerships. They would be dealing with creatures that had not co-evolved with them, let alone partnered. And, even if they had, would these new acquisitions bond with their handlers or treat said handlers as cute chew toys?

"Is first shipment of Rista to be due two week hence," the colonel squeaked in an officious voice. "Be of comfort."

As if. That gave me ten or eleven days to get acquainted with a pair of pups I'd never met and find out just what these Rista creatures were.

\# \# \#

My dogs were supposed to arrive a day after me, but, in the best military tradition, were delayed for six days, giving me just a week to get familiar enough with the demonstration terrier pups. I wasn't really worried; terriers pick up on things very fast.

I easily found my nervous Flash yipping with excitement in the cargo hold of the carrier. In the next kennel sat a squat bulldog instead of my promised terrier pups. The other cages were empty. "What the hell? Where are my dogs?"

"Orders said to deliver three dogs," the cargo master replied and handled me the manifest. "Terriers unavailable. Suitable substitutes provided," it read.

"I'm supposed to have three dogs," I insisted to the cargo master, "Not two!"

"That one's yours as well." He pointed a nervous finger toward a large cage at the

far end of the hold. It contained a big dog. A really, truly, **BIG** dog. Enormous doesn't come close. Its floppy ears looked as large as an Indian elephant's, and its paws the size of buckets, which would be handy to catch the liters of soggy slobber dripping from its wet, mouth.

The dog's two enormous eyes were deep brown pools buried within wrinkled folds of skin. Those eyes never left me for an instant as we stood there warily regarding one another through the open gate.

"Mastiff, with a touch of bloodhound and perhaps a sprinkle of Basset," I mused as I took in the massive body and muscular legs. A thick tail hung low, inactive for the moment, but I knew that once in motion it could easily damage whatever it struck.

How the devil Supply expected me to work with such a mismatched trio was beyond comprehension.

"Stay calm," I reminded myself. "Show no fear." Which was a stupid thing to say as I was practically pissing in my pants at thoughts of what this shoulder-high giant might do should I misstep. "Good dog," I said as I extended my arm disturbingly close to a mouth easily wide enough to rip off said extremity, reverting to what I remembered from from my intensive training in basic dog handling.

There was no reaction. Those brown eyes never left my face as the tongue continued to cascade an enlarging puddle of slobber that I feared might soon engulf my boots if I did not move.

"Pansy, that's what the bill of lading has as the dog's name," the cargo master said from a safe distance.

Pansy? Did that mean it was female? I hesitated to check as it would involve me kneeling to examine its nether regions. I was unsure of the beast's temperament or its interpretation of personal space, so I took the name as given

"Good girl," I said, continuing my scintillating dialogue. "Good girl," I repeated while allowing her to sniff my hand.

Suddenly Pansy shook her head, spraying more *eau de slobber* about as her massive tail, a flail of considerable power, hissed back and forth, raising a slight breeze.

Good. We had established communications. One of the first and most important things about handling an unfamiliar dog is to establish a bond of trust as soon as possible. I was reaching to scratch an ear when Pansy's huge tongue whipped around to coat my sleeve with a layer of slobber before she lay down, rolled on her side, and offered me an unrestricted confirmation of gender. Taking the hint, I began to rub her belly, noticing how silky soft was the stomach fur surrounding her tiny teats.

Pansy whined in pleasure, using a huge paw to guide my ministrations. I realized that the poor dog was probably starved for attention; fed and watered regularly, but forced to remain in her cage during transit because the stupid cargo master was intimidated by her fierce appearance and size.

As I had been initially.

Well, I would fix that. I knelt beside her and began massaging her neck, working my way to the base of her ears and finally stroking the top of her head with full arm motions as her tail whacked noisily against the deck.

I grabbed her jowls with both hands and tugged. "Come on, girl. time to get you out of here." She rose with surprising agility for one so large and followed me out of the cage.

Flash rushed from his kennel in a state of excitement over seeing me again. This was his normal behavior. At feeding time he'd tremble until he'd bolted down every last morsel. During exercise time he'd race about in circles until he was given a task on which he would focus on with fierce intensity. Any praise sent him into paroxysms of such delight that he'd too often lose control of his tiny bladder.

His neighbor was an English bulldog whose name, the manifest insisted was Bear. His demeanor was the complete opposite of Flash's: Stolid, stable, unexcitable, and steady. His behavior was that of a refined gentleman upholding the dignity of a breed descended from royalty. He refused to emulate Flash's obvious excitement as he sedately trotted beside Pansy and I. From all indications, the two new dogs had some obedience training under their collars.

Only how the hell was I going to use a bulldog and the gigantic Pansy padding proudly beside me, careful not to step on the other two? I hoped I would soon find out.

We bunked down together that night, Flash guarding my feet, Bear snuggled between my legs and Pansy snoring loudly on three quarters of our shared bed.

I knew before morning that bonding was the last thing I had to worry about.

\# \# \#

I held my introductory class by showing recordings to the handful of potential Dremma handlers the colonel had selected.

I began by showing them what a well-trained human-dog team could do to manage sheep, horses, and cattle. They seemed most excited when watching the dogs take down padded human trainers. I avoided any actual combat films since I was unsure of which way alliances were shifting. Showing dogs attacking one of their current allies might create a bit of animosity.

"Are of want Rifta to ferret Tch'ka units," Colonel Anharsk remarked after the class was over. "RippaHordes use Rista effective against Tch'ka." It held out a large stinking scorched orange pelt dotted with what I supposed were Rista nibbles. Well, at least I now knew the Tch'ka were the enemy.

"We can use this to familiarize my dogs and your Rista to the Tch'ka scent," I remarked as I accepted the pelt while having no idea if the soon-to-arrive Rista would be able to detect its ripe scent.

\# \# \#

My next set of lessons covered the basics of dog handling: getting familiar with the animal and building trust. From there, I covered basic commands, obedience, and arm signals, which on reflection was a waste of time since the Dremma had a *somewhat* different physical configuration.

I demonstrated using Flash, the least threatening of my three dogs, being only shoulder height to the Dremma. I set the students a good distance away, not wanting them to unduly excite Flash with their ultrasonic voices.

I gave Flash a warm hug to settle him down, stroked him lovingly as I announced to the wary students; "The first thing is to establish a bond of trust with your animal." At which point Flash squirmed out of my arms and began running circles around me, eager for the reward he'd smelled in my pocket. "Rewarding them with a tasty treat also helps," I said as Flash took the small pellet of meat in one snapping bite before staring at me for another.

I quickly ran Flash through some basic commands, rewarding him each time he responded correctly.

\# \# \#

"Is of tedious delays," colonel Anharsk apologized when the RippaHordes failed to deliver their Rista on schedule. "All are anxious to begin application of your advanced technologic approaches."

I assumed he meant the handlers were raring to get started.

Not to waste time, I used the next few days to repeat the lessons. I even managed to get the handlers familiar with Bear and, eventually Pansy. It took considerable effort to convince the handlers that my dogs were not going to render them into shreds, although I had a moment of doubt when I saw Bear glancing hungrily at one of them and salivating.

I went so far as to let them approach Pansy, who endured the Dremma's hesitant touches.

The next day, I demonstrated an advanced technique of circle and seek they could use to flush out their enemies. I had previously familiarized the dogs with the

Tch'ka pelt, which was now being worn by one of colonel Anharsk's "volunteers" who was hiding in the grass, er, **forest.**

Flash and I started with a circling search, gradually swinging wider and wider until he stopped, yipped, and leaped into the brush. The simulated Tch'ka emitted a glass-shattering scream as it raced ahead of the barking Flash and into the protective circle of its fellows who immediately scattered as Flash ferociously shook the pelt he'd snatched from the fleeing volunteer.

"To me!" I commanded and Flash, obviously disturbed over having his game interrupted, came to my side and dropped the pelt at my feet.

I gave him a treat.

# # #

The enclosure the Dremma had set up for the Rista training was a cleared area the size of a horse's pasture surrounded by a stout mesh fence. In the center was what the RippaHorde declared was a Rista kennel and not some sort of war machine that could some day be turned against the Dremma.

I stood among the potential handlers-to-be as the container of Rista was dumped from the RippaHorde transport. It broke open upon impact with the ground. Almost immediately, a writhing mass of blue caterpillars poured forth.

"Are freshly captured young Rista," Colonel Anharsk confided as the gaggle of Rista began chewing on the remains of their damaged crate with the enthusiasm of rabid wolves.

"Good to get them young and easily trainable," I answered confidently. "But we'd better start familiarization as soon as possible."

Before I could stop him, the colonel screamed commands and three of the Dremma handlers quickly scaled the fence and bravely attempted to pull their small Rista into their warm and welcoming embrace.

The entire Rista pack screamed loudly and gathered into an angry open-mouthed phalanx of gnashing teeth.

"I think your troops should pull back," I warned, certain that those gnashing teeth did not mean a happy ending to this rude introduction.

Anharsk screamed again. Although most of his words were above my hearing range, I wasn't certain if he was shouting encouragement or a warning since the trio of handlers continued to advance. Suddenly, as one, the Rista surged forward on churning legs, jaws snapping.

The leader of Anharsk's troops went down under several snarling Rista while a smarter troop speedily backpedalled away from the fray. The remaining, most indecisive, of the three hesitated a moment too long before turning tail to run screeching for the fence with an eager Rista attached to its fundament.

I heard the rattle of weapons being readied. Anharsk's supersonic screams were making my head ache. The racing Dremma trooper vaulted the fence, losing his attached Rista in his wake. As it turned and raced back to the snarling pack, I ran toward the mass accompanied by a pair of armed troops to retrieve the downed handler-to-be, whom I feared had, indeed, become a chew toy.

The sudden appearance of my tall alien form amongst the shorter Dremma must have frightened the Rista, for they all ran back to the remains of their crate, leaving our unfortunate, tooth-mangled handler writhing on the ground, its uniform tattered and torn, noticeable tiny bite marks covering every extremity.

As they were dragging the wounded trooper away, one of the snapping Rista circled our group, always keeping six meters away. The others followed; by the time we reached the gate, they had begun to gather closer.

Their actions encouraged me. Perhaps they had a natural pack instinct we could encourage.

The next day, there were noticeably fewer handlers-to-be in attendance to hear a revised, gentler approach to bonding using treats and gradual introductions.

On my advice, each Rista was paired with one of the volunteer handlers and placed in side-by-side enclosures as the first bonding step. The handlers were to feed and water their Rista and be their close, albeit separated, companion. In less than a week, they had their Rista eating out of their well-armored pincers and, in a few more days, had them amenable to being gently groomed.

I was amazed at how quickly the Rista grew from a cross between blue meter-long centipedes into camouflage-colored Chinese dragons. Each one developed the bulk of nearly their handlers' weight, although they were half their height.

Colonel Anharsk admitted that he had no idea of what their adult weight would be. "Is important?" he shrieked.

# # #

The bonding of cautious Dremma and aggressive Rista was a brutal affair. The Dremmas' cruel impatience too often caused a Rista to react viciously, resulting in a few amputations of various Dremma extremities. One Rista was crippled when ten of its legs on the right side were "accidentally" singed by a too quick-tempered handler.

Where I once had more potential handlers than Rista, in the end, thanks to disability, death, and incompetence, we had equal numbers of both. The Rista became as fiercely protective of their handlers as they were of each other, as the impatient trooper with the quick-tempered trigger learned to his regret.

# # #

All three dogs accompanied me as I watched the Dremma handlers train their Rista a month later. Over time, both the Rista and their handlers had become comfortable with my dogs. The attitude seemed to go the other way as well, with only Flash quivering and whining whenever a Rista came close. Pansy usually watched the

Dremma and their now chubby Rista with drooling amusement, while the stoic Bear stood stolidly by.

Flash, on the other hand, would race along the fence yipping excitedly as he kept pace with a scurrying Rista, or perhaps it was the other way around. I thought it good exercise for both animals, so I didn't interfere.

The next day, I took Flash into the enclosure to demonstrate the finer points of dog-handling and hoped the Dremma could adapt them to their Rista.

Flash ran through his exercises like a real pro, but quickly began to lose interest.

Although initially excited by the appearance of their playmate romping around the **inside** of the enclosure, the Rista were obedient enough to restrain themselves and follow their handlers' commands.

I told the colonel that I was proud of all of them

#

Colonel Anharsk had always claimed no interest in the training lessons. Thus, it was a surprise when he showed up in full combat regalia while I was demonstrating an encircle maneuver with Patsy, who enjoyed her enthusiastic bounds as she raced around the field retrieving a dummy Tch'ka.

The colonel briskly demanded that he see what his troops had accomplished in the short time they'd had training their Rista.

"The front closer grows daily," he proclaimed, his words ironically punctuated by the not-so-distant sounds of artillery impacts. "We must be ready to serve with our beasts!" The screech at the end of his declaration put Flash on immediate alert, quivering in anticipation of action.

The colonel walked to the small hill in the center of the enclosure to get a better vantage of his troops' performance. Unfortunately, this intersected with Pansy's headlong rush to find her quarry. She quickly snatched the colonel as she flew by, sending his helmet bouncing down the hillside.

Flash, yipping furiously, bounded forward to retrieve the helmet's bouncing red balls.

Pansy dropped the slobber-covered colonel at my feet and sat with one paw on the colonel's back to hold him in place while waiting for a reward for retrieving the wrong dummy.

The handlers raced over to rescue their colonel, forgetting to give their Rista stay commands. Freed from commands, the Rista wasted no time tearing toward Flash, who was busily worrying a ball free from the helmet. Their high-pitched cries must have alerted him for he ignored the remains of the helmet and raced away. The avenging Rista pack followed as he escaped.

Assured that no harm had come to their colonel, the handlers raced after their Rista. The cacophony of ultra-high cries coming from the Dremma and their charges seemed to excite Flash into greater bursts of speed as he kept well ahead of the pack.

"To me!" I bellowed at the top of my voice, but it was too late. The pack had already caught up and collapsed around Flash, burying him under a mass of screeching Rista.

Suddenly one of the Rista emerged with something bloody clenched in its teeth and raced away. In seconds it was followed by a yipping, angry Flash and the other members of the pack as it furiously ran away with what I now noticed was the ball from Anharsk's helmet.

Unnoticed by anyone, Bear trotted over to retrieve the helmet, brought it back, and deposited it in front of the colonel.

#

The roar of furious battle drew closer by the day. I could sense the urgency of the handlers to complete their training and participate in the action. The Rista seemed to grasp their excitement and became focused on obeying even the most difficult of commands.

I was concerned that my Dremma teams were not yet battle tested and might, like an untrained herding dog, revert to their instincts when engaging with the Tch'ka.

"Is of time essential," blasted Colonel Anharsk when I expressed my doubts about their readiness. As if to punctuate his declaration, a burst of small arms fire sounded not far away.

"Give me another week," I pleaded.

#

Barking and shrill cries woke me from a sound sleep. Flash was nowhere in sight. Both Bear and Pansy were growling and fidgeting as I pulled on boots and grabbed my weapon.

The two dogs flanked me as I ran in the direction of the uproar, which coincided with the Ristas' enclosure. How Flash had gotten out of our quarters was secondary to my fear of what the devil was going on.

Flash's barking rose in pitch and frequency as did the shrill cries of the entire Rista pack, at least those that I could hear.

I spotted the writhing mass of Rista clustered against the enclosure's gate where Flash was bristling with barking anger.

"To me!" I commanded. Behind me, I could hear the Dremma handlers calling to their Rista. Flash ignored my cries with continued furiously barks.

That's when I noticed that he was facing **away** from the slavering Rista.

The first gout of weapons fire flew over my head and caught one of the Dremma behind me full in the segments. Stunned, I dropped to the ground and pointed the H&Kbar6.4a toward the spot where I thought the searing flash had erupted and squeezed the trigger.

More flashes flew around me as my handlers joined the fray. As the intensity of the battle increased, Flash finally stopped barking and huddled by my side with Pansy and Bear. I strained to see whatever was attacking.

One handler braved the fire to open the enclosure's gate and let a screaming scavenging mass of coiling, spitting Rista erupt into the dark. As the angry tsunami of Rista and handlers passed over us, my dogs began howling from the supersonics of their overexcited cries.

"Seek," I hissed after the last pair of Dremma disappeared into the night. I set the three dogs into a wide search pattern that would ensure the immediate area around us contained nothing the handlers and their Rista had missed.

Flash stopped barking when, in the distance, the fires faded and the Rista's cries ceased.

Hours later, as we were desperately trying to stop a tug of war over a hank of orange pelt between a Rista and Bear, Colonel Anharsk informed me that his brave Rista handlers had successfully repelled a tactical penetration squad of Tch'ka and proven their battle worthiness. "Is of no necessity of more battle training," he declared

He seemed to ignore the dogs' role in the melee.

# # #

My team's reassignment notice came coincident with deployment orders for Colonel Anharsk's newly formed Tenth Regimental Battalion, First Rista Harriers. Alliances had shifted once again and the Dremma now had to assist their Tch'ka partners in liberating someplace from yet another race.

If so, I hoped the Rista had not developed a taste for Tch'ka sashimi. ▓

"Good Grief, Frnbq, that's no way to ask for foreign aid!"

20 YEARS
of MIDWEST FURFEST
DECEMBER 5-8, 2019
WWW.FURFEST.ORG
WITH SPECIAL GUESTS
MARY LOWD

BUCKET LIST BOOTH
DELICATE ARCH · MOAB · UT
NUMBER 708115
DELICATE ARCH
BLOOMERS"
METERS TALL
109.499341°W
ADA SANDSTONE
L PARK 1929
IF YOU ENJ
THIS EXPE
WE RECCOM
THESE LOCAT
INSERT
CARD

Stone and Starlight

By WENDY
NIKEL

Wendy Nikel is a speculative fiction author with a degree in elementary education, a fondness for road trips, and a terrible habit of forgetting where she's left her cup of tea. Her short fiction has been published by Analog, Nature: Futures, Podcastle, *and elsewhere. Her time travel novella series, beginning with* The Continuum, *is available from World Weaver Press. For more info, visit wendynikel.com.*

"Where do we stand for the Bucket List Thingy?"

Alita looked up from her book, into the blinding desert sun. A whiskered man in a Hawaiian shirt stumbled over, waving a card-sized device over his giant sunhat. Behind him, one of Alita's fellow rangers sat in the enclosed buggy that had obviously carried them out to her station. A trail of identical glass-domed buggies kicked up dust as they parked behind the first; a trail of tourists balked at the heat as they emerged from the climate-controlled vehicles.

Alita marked her page with a faded brochure from the wooden display board she'd been leaning against.

"Welcome to Delicate Arch," she recited, gesturing to the iconic scene behind her, "one of the most famous geological features in the world."

"Could you just skip to the Bucket List part?" a red-faced woman near the back of the group asked. "We've got five other Adventures to hit this weekend."

Alita wiped the sweat from her neck. It was over a hundred degrees out today; she didn't blame them for wanting to get back into air-conditioning.

Still, she thought as she gestured the group onward, it wasn't exactly what she'd anticipated when she'd become a ranger. When she was fifteen, she'd traveled here with her mom and together they'd hiked the rocky trail up to this exact spot. They'd sat in the shade with a picnic, drinking from their canteens and breathing in earth's majesty as the daylight waned and stars filled the sky. It was one of the last trips they'd taken together, before her life had become consumed by

the stresses of SATs and final exams and job applications, before Mom's hip surgery had put an end to her hiking days.

Back then, the stars had seemed so endless, the possibilities so vast.

As the tourists scurried to form a line, Alita glanced back at the buggies' exhaust wavering overhead like mirages against the sky.

"Ma'am?" The man with the Hawaiian shirt tapped his watch.

"Right." She turned to the phone booth-like box constructed before the sandstone icon. "Step inside and insert your Bucket List card into the slot there. It'll flash three times before it takes your photo and logs the Adventure into your –"

"We know how it works." The man elbowed her aside. Once in the booth, he glanced at the screen, then took off his hat so it didn't block the view of the arch and inserted his card. Three seconds later he emerged, donned his hat, and smirked at the others. "You all better hurry up. There's an iced tea back at the gift shop with my name on it."

A few people grumbled. Others rolled their eyes. The next group entered the box.

"Can I have a brochure?" a woman with aviator sunglasses asked.

"Absolutely. They contain maps, historical information, and –"

The woman unfolded it and waved it in front of her face as a makeshift fan. Alita bit her tongue.

Beside her, a pair of couples had swapped Bucket List cards and now scrolled through the images of one another's Adventures.

"The Tower of Pisa! Isn't that lovely? Frank, look at Hank and Julie's picture. Didn't it turn out nicely?"

"Picture perfect," Frank said. "Remember our trip there, Risa?"

"How could I forget?"

The woman named Julie frowned. "I didn't see it on your card."

Risa laughed. "This was before we bought Bucket Lists. Remember those days?"

"Hardly. So much easier to keep track of now."

Someone shouted from the front of the line. A family of four had squeezed themselves into the booth and, from the looks of it, were having trouble with the electronic reader. The dad wasn't making things any easier by trying to force his card in. "What's wrong with this piece of –"

"Let's have a look," Alita intervened, faking a cheery smile.

One look at his card and she knew exactly what had happened. A corner of the plastic had broken off and, unless she was mistaken, had lodged itself in the reader.

"Apologies for the inconvenience," she announced. "We'll get a technician out here to service the machine."

"But we drove all the way out here!"

"You're welcome to wait," Alita said.

"In this heat?" the dad who'd broken the machine complained. "You've gotta be kidding. Let's go, kids."

"But dad," his son whined. "We just **got** here."

"I didn't get my Bucket List picture yet." Tears rolled down his little girl's cheeks.

"I have a digital camera here," Alita offered. "I could take your picture and send it to you."

"Forget it." The dad grabbed his daughter's hand and pulled her away. "This is nothing but a tourist trap. We'll get a refund."

Grumbling and complaining, the tourists retreated to their buggies without so much as a backward glance at the lonely arch. Alita watched until the vehicles disappeared over the rocks' edge in a snake of dust.

Only then did she call in the report on her walkie-talkie.

"Better close up for the day," her boss said. "I'll cancel the final group and send someone to pick you up."

The sun was just beginning to sink over the brilliant orange stones. At Alita's feet lay the brochure she'd given the woman with the aviator glasses. The image on the front showed the arch beneath a starlit sky.

The Bucket List booth wasn't set up for nighttime photography; when was the last time someone had seen it like that?

"Don't worry about it," Alita said into the walkie-talkie. "I'll walk back."

"Walk? Are you sure?"

"Absolutely."

She clicked off the walkie-talkie, dusted off the discarded brochure, and, laying her book aside, wandered out past the Bucket List booth. Rocks crunched beneath her feet and the arch towered overhead. She inhaled deeply and smiled. There was just enough daylight left to read the brochure and then, when all was still, she'd sit and watch the stars fill the sky.. ■

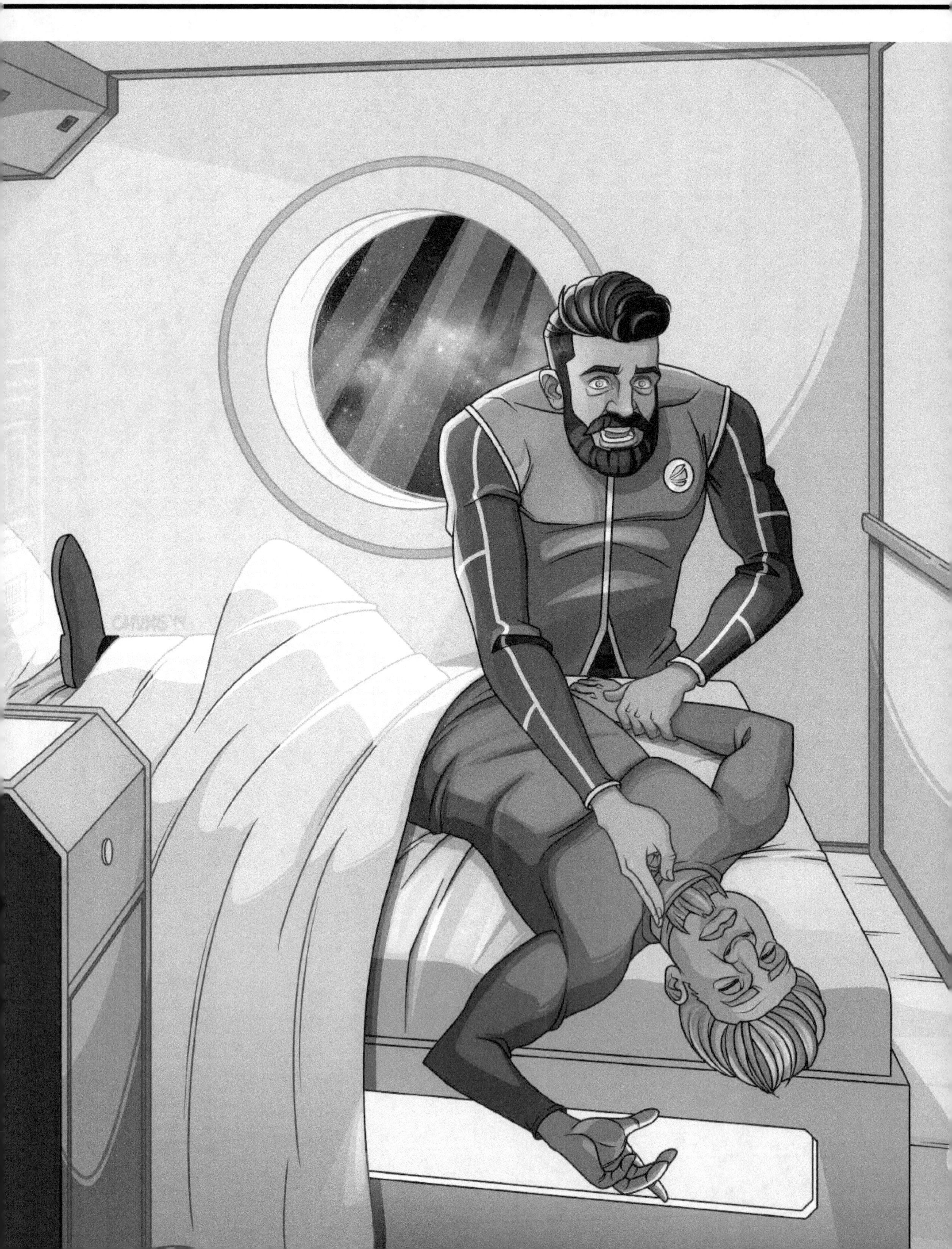

Stopover At Meech's World

By MATTHEW HUGHES

Matthew Hughes writes SF and fantasy. His novels are: Fools Errant, Fool Me Twice, Black Brillion, Majestrum, The Commons, The Spiral Labyrinth, Template, Hespira, The Other, The Damned Busters, Costume Not Included, Hell to Pay, Song of the Serpent *(as Hugh Matthews), and* A Wizard's Henchman. *His short fiction has appeared in* Asimov's, Fantasy & Science Fiction, Lightspeed, Postscripts, Storyteller, Interzone, *and several anthologies edited by Gardner Dozois and George R.R. Martin, including the bestseller,* Rogues. *His works have been short-listed for the Aurora, Nebula, Philip K Dick, A.E. Van Vogt, and Endeavour Awards. His web page is:* https://www.matthewhughes.org.

"Conn," Jenore said to me, "there's one more second-class passenger. His name is Todfrey Hamble."

I was looking at the roster of cabin assignments to which I'd been putting the final touches when Jenore had popped her head through the doorway into my working space. "Where am I supposed to put him?" I said. "We're full. I can't –"

She gestured with a small hand to quiet me. "I've cleaned out that little cabinette that used to be servants quarters, the one we've been using to store games and performances. I put them in the salon's cupboards."

"That's a very small cabin," I said. The tiny room had been allotted to an undervalet to a minor aristocrat back when this space yacht had been named the *Martichor* and was the property of a Lord Vullamir, of the first-tier aristocracy on Old Earth. Lord Vullamir had no use for a private vessel anymore, having accrued the Archon Filidor's disfavor for certain unsavory practices as a leading member of a pernicious cult called the Immersion. Since it had been thus abandoned on a planet I owned, title transferred to me.

"I showed it to Ser Hamble and he said it would be fine," Jenore said. "He is in a froth to get to Meech's World, and none of the starship lines operating out of here have a direct service there."

Now I was puzzled again. "Meech's World is not on our itinerary," I said.

Another gesture of her slim hand. This one told me the problem was already solved. "It is now. Yalum said we'd divert there, instead of stopping at Yaroslav to top up on energies. Then we can go through a different whimsy that will bring us out closer to Novo Vieste than the one he'd planned to take. We'll actually get there half a day sooner."

I showed her a motion of my own hand, one that signaled surrender. I'd never had to give that hand-sign when I'd been an indentured competitive duelist in Hordam's Gaming Emporium on the gaming world of Thrais. But that was just one of the changes that had led me to my present position as owner and supercargo on the space yacht *Peregrinator*, captained by Yalum Erkatchian and crewed by Jenore Mordene. The former was the only friend I'd ever made, and the latter the woman I loved.

I heard a noise from the corridor behind Jenore. So did she. She glanced at something I couldn't see then came back to me. "The cultists are coming aboard," she said.

I rose from the table where I'd been working. "I'll see to them."

A small frown clouded her face. "They're a fractious bunch," she said.

"Be…neutral with them."

"I will not mention their insanity," I said. "I've learned to overlook the various forms of madness one encounters in dealing with the varieties of humankind spread across the Ten Thousand Worlds."

"And be respectful of their idol," Jenore said. "It seems to mean a great deal to them."

\# \# \#

The idol was an ugly thing: a squat lump

of cast metal gone green with age, though more recently it had been clad in a vest and pantaloons of hammered gold. Pot-bellied and hunched over in a crouch, with a lipless downturned mouth and half-lidded eyes, it resembled someone's impression of a toad that was turning into a man, or vice versa – a toad or man that wasn't happy about the transition.

The cultists, seven of them, were filling the corridor of the first-class accommodations, two of them carrying a kind of stretcher made of dark, polished wood, on which the object of their devotions sat like a dissatisfied traveler. The god's worshipers comprised three young men, three middle-aged specimens, and a seventh person so aged and wizened – and so deeply enshrouded in the sect's cowled robes – that its gender could not readily be determined.

Apparently, the process of moving the idol required ritually slow and synchronized footsteps, accompanied by a deep-throated chanting of a mantra in a tongue I did not recognize.

The leader of the coven, Addeus Ing, saw me coming along the corridor toward them and raised an admonitory hand. The procession stopped behind him and he broke off his chanting to advise me in a sepulchral voice, "Come no nearer. The ambit of Ubrach is holy space, not to be trod by a heathen."

I paused, some distance from the procession, and said, "Does that make this corridor permanently impassable? That will affect the running of the vessel."

"The sequestered space travels with Ubrach," Ing said. "Once he is installed in my cabin, you may again pass this way." He thought for a moment, then added, "Though you would be wise to make the ritual gestures as you go."

He showed me the prescribed motions, touching fingertips to temple, ears, and chin, then finishing by slapping the fingers of one hand to his open mouth, producing an audible **pop**.

"I shall endeavor to remember," I said. "Now, do you require any assistance?"

"Is my cabin ready?" he said. "By which I mean, has it been energetically scrubbed and anointed with the balm I sent to that woman?"

"It has," I said. "And her name is Sera Mordene."

His face clouded. "Do not think to instruct me in protocols, young man. My standards are set by the ineffable Ubrach."

I recalled Jenore's advice and made a gesture of acquiescence. "I will withdraw until the corridor is no longer sacred ground," I said.

"Do not forget the gestures," he said. "Ubrach generally ignores the uninitiated, but he is known to make the occasional example."

I suppressed the first answer that came to me and said, instead, "I will remember." Then I went back to the forward compartment where I did the work that required stylus and ledger.

# # #

Two other passengers were already aboard: a plump, middle-aged couple, Tetch and Folliance Archaby, bound for their blisternut plantation on the North Continent of Novo Vieste. When they boarded, they had told me, speaking in tandem, how they had come to Carricker to buy fresh seedlings to replenish their orchards.

"Blisternut trees will only produce viable seeds for seventeen years," Tetch Archaby said, though I had not sought the information.

"And then they go dormant and soon after die," his spouse added.

I was carrying some of their baggage to the second-class berth they had booked. "Indeed," I said. The aroma that rose from the large portmanteau I was managing along the narrow passageway told me that I was carrying the basis of some future crop.

"Indeed, indeed," said Tetch. "That's why, every year, we come here to Carricker –"

"To get new plants," Folliance completed the sentence for him. "They grow the best ones here."

Her partner began to itemize the advantages of Carricker's blisternut seedlings, but by then we had reached their small cabin. I indicated the open door, put down the fragrant portmanteau, and escaped further education.

I was proceeding back the way I had come when I encountered a mild-eyed, soft-looking little man coming the other way and peering at the numbers affixed to the cabin doors. This turned out to be Todfrey Hamble, our last addition to the passenger manifest. I turned him around and brought him safely to his small berth, which he appeared to find entirely to his satisfaction.

I handed him the schedule for meals, which reminded me that I had failed to do so with the Archabys, and thus had to return to where they were housed. I knocked on their door, which opened only a crack to allow Tetch's eye to scrutinize me.

"Yes?"

I offered him the card with its information. He had to open the door a little wider to take it, which showed me that the portmanteau containing the blisternut seedlings was now positioned on the top sleeping platform, and held in place by strong leather straps cinched by heavy padlocks. The arrangement left no room for a sleeper.

"They are precious to us," Tetch informed me. Folliance weighed in to state that it was not good for them to experience too much movement, but I forestalled a further lecture by asking how they proposed to fit themselves into the single narrow sleeping platform below.

"In shifts," Tetch told me. "The same will apply to our meals."

They looked at each and nodded their agreement. I said I understood, though I didn't, and left.

The last aboard were a trio of sisters – Orfa, Illiphrata, and Shuriz Vauderoy – bound for Novo Vieste for purposes not stated. They chatted brightly about inconsequentials as I led them to the three, single-berthed, second-class cabins they had reserved. I gave the meal schedule to Orfa, who appeared to be the eldest of the three. She took it and glanced at it, then rejoined the three-way repartee. I had the odd feeling that their conversation was scripted, but I dismissed the thought. I was not yet competent to judge the behaviors of people from other worlds, with their strange and incomprehensible ways.

# # #

I took the passenger manifest to the captain's workspace, a small cubicle where official documents were stored, and found my only friend, Yalum Erkatchian, engaged in an argument with the spaceport's integrator.

He swung around in his swivel chair and spoke in a forceful tone, "The inspection was carried out hours ago. Nothing amiss was found. The inspector told us we were cleared to go as soon as the passengers were aboard."

The integrator's reply was, as always, soft-voiced. "I have no record of the inspection."

"Then, obviously, the inspector has failed to file his report. He had the look of one of your inbred idiots."

On Carricker, many public offices were staffed by heredity. Most functions were carried out by integrators and their allied devices, overseen – allegedly, that is – by functionaries who often were dysfunctional.

Then spaceport's integrator adopted that precisely modulated tone that conveys anger, one of the emotions of which such devices are not supposed to be capable. "Nonetheless, I cannot permit departure until the report is filed."

"My ship," said Erkatchian, "will send you a recording of the inspection." He broke off to order the *Peregrinator*'s integrator to make the transmission.

The spaceport's system now changed its attitude. Integrators trusted each other

implicitly, there being another supposition that they were incapable of mendacity. "Departure authorized," it said. "Have a pleasant journey."

Erkatchian made some remarks that reflected the depth of vocabulary he had acquired during his many years as a spacer, then turned to me. He took the manifest from my hand and examined it.

"All present and accounted for?" he said.

"Yes," I said.

"Any problems?"

"Not so far."

"Good," said Erkatchian. He raised his chin and spoke to the ship's integrator, telling it to advise the passengers to prepare for lifting off. We then heard the *Peregrinator*'s calmly modulated tones relaying the information.

I repaired to the galley where Jenore was overseeing preparation of the evening meal. Not long after, a chime sounded three notes, then the floor beneath my feet vibrated as the in-atmosphere drive was engaged. We rose smoothly from Carricker's major spaceport. I disopaqued the porthole in the galley and watched as the sky outside turned from deep blue to full black. It was a sight I had come to enjoy as a signal of the freedom I had acquired along with ownership of the space yacht.

We passed among the glittering orbitals in their planet-circling ring, then the shivering ceased as the drive cut out. There came that breathless pause as we were carried along on momentum alone, then the space drive cut in with a new frequency of vibration, and Carricker rapidly dwindled to a circle the size of a plate, then a saucer,

then a dot. And soon it was gone altogether.

"And here we go again," I said.

"We're late," Jenore said, looking up from where she was counting out plates, bowls, mugs, and eating utensils.

I told her how the port's inspector had failed to file his report.

"Huh," she said, in a tone that expressed her views on the usefulness of inspectors, or perhaps males in general.

I said, "I don't see the value of inspecting outbound ships."

"We've talked about this," she said. "Carricker is one of the few places where the plants that produce blue borrache can flourish. Other worlds don't want the stuff coming in to their populations. If Carricker doesn't control the drug's export, other worlds will isolate it. Then it won't be able to receive the goods and services it can't produce for itself."

"But the inspection system is riddled with incompetence," I said. "The inspectors can scarcely find their own fundaments with both hands and a color-coded map."

"Ah," she said, and held up a finger in

the manner I had come to recognize as a precursor to her making a point. "A lot of people on Carricker make a lot of money out of the illicit trade in blue borrache. Ineffective interdiction of the outflow keeps the inflow of funds at maximum.

"And in the meantime," she finished, "Carricker's self-esteem is not diminished."

# # #

The *Peregrinator*, when it had been *Martichor*, the private space yacht of Lord Vullamir, now presumably locked up in a contemplarium on Old Earth, had boasted a grand dining salon. Internal rearrangements of the vessel's layout had taken some of the salon's space for first-class cabins, leaving a smaller space in which both classes of passenger were to be fed.

"Uh-oh," I said, as I responded to the dinner chime, along with twelve of this voyage's thirteen passengers, crowding along the corridor that led to the refectory. Here the great, ornate table at which Vullamir and his fellow members of the sinister Immersion cult had formerly dined was no more. Erkatchian had sold it to an antique dealer on Fallabi, and replaced it with two smaller tables that came equipped with fold-down benches along the sides and at each end.

Each table would sit only six. The passenger manifest numbered thirteen. When I stepped into the room, one of the tables was occupied by the three Vauderoy sisters. Todfrey Hamble was seated alone at one end of the other table, his gaze fixed on nothing in particular. I noted that if he had been "in a froth" to reach Meech's World, the sense of urgency had now left him.

Behind me now came Tetch Archaby, who went to sit at the head of the first table. Then the seven cultists of Ubrach arrived, led by Addeus Ing. The patriarch paused in the doorway, took in the situation at one glance and said, "Unacceptable!" in a tone that said he would brook no argument.

Jenore arrived through the door that connected to the galley, bearing a stack of

plates. I saw her notice the rigid postures of the Ubrachians without discerning the cause.

"What?" she said.

Ing spoke as if from a commanding height, while one hand extended to where Hamble sat. "It was made clear," he said, "that we cannot share our meals with heathens. Our standards are precise and exacting. Contamination requires a lengthy process of rectification, and we are far from a source of black umbershoot boughs."

"We have only the one dining area for passengers, and only two tables," I said. "What would you have us do?"

Ing said, "This fellow seated alone, move him to the other table. There is room."

"Must I then scrub his place with balm?" I said.

"No. Just remove him."

I went to where Hamble sat, apparently unaware of his role in the controversy. "Would you mind, ser, moving to the other table. The...cultists prefer to sit together."

The mild-eyed man blinked, seeming to come back to the here and now from some other mental space. "I beg your pardon?" he said.

I repeated my request and saw Hamble take in his surroundings. A slight cloud formed on his brow. "Am I unwelcome among them?" he said. "That strikes me as unfriendly."

"Begone!" said Ing. "Go sit with the other benighted..." Here his voice trailed off as he sought for a sufficient pejorative.

"I think not," said Hamble, returning his gaze to the empty middle distance.

I lowered my voice to a whisper. "They are, in my judgment, quite mad, as are all religious enthusiasts. Since we are confined with them for the next few days, I counsel avoiding actions that might stir up their misguided passions."

Hamble took this in. Then his soft mouth set in as deep a frown as he could manage. "Not mad," he said, "but fools."

I heard a sharp intake of breath from Addeus Ing and rumbles of incipient violence from the cultists still confined to the corridor. Hamble ignored the warnings and went on, "I happen to have run across Ubrachians before. They are a persistent nuisance on my home world. Their so-called 'idol' is nothing of the sort. It is most likely a statue of some kind of entertainer. It was found in the remains of a theater on the planet Thriffle, where once flourished a species of intelligent amphibians. Their world began to dry up, so they either died out or migrated *en masse* to some other planet far out in the Back of Beyond."

As this explanation unwound, I saw Ing's face lose its holy pallor and proceed through various shades of red to a deep crimson. His lips trembled and his eyes grew round and when Hamble finished his remarks, he spluttered for several minims before he was able to assemble a coherent stream of words.

"Remove the atheist!" he cried out to me, "Lest I call down the wrath of Ubrach on this iniquitous assemblage!" He swung an arm to take in the other passengers, who had been listening to Todfrey Hamble with varying degrees of amusement.

I made a renewed effort. "Please, ser," I whispered to Hamble, "let them have their way. We have two more days of travel after we traverse the whimsy."

The small man set his chin, and I thought he would not yield. Then he showed the expression of a man who has decided the fight is not worth his time. With a disdainful cluck of his tongue, he rose from the table and went to sit with the other passengers. A corner seat at the first table remained unoccupied. Hamble took it, which put him next to Illiphrata Vaude-roy. Her two sisters sat across from them. The blisternut farmer had taken the head of the table.

"Glad you could join us," said Tetch Archaby. He named himself, then the three sisters. "And you are?"

"Oh, no one of consequence," said Hamble. He would have said nothing more, but Illiphrata coaxed his name from him, though it took two requests.

The small man gave his name and stopped speaking. He turned his gaze toward his hands, folded together on the table before him.

Meanwhile, I was seeing to the seating of the seven Ubrachians. The availability of only six seats posed a difficulty, but Ing overcame it by ordering the three thinnest of the cultists to squeeze onto one of the side benches. The arrangement meant that one meager buttock protruded at either end of the bench, but Ing decreed that decorum had been served.

Jenore now began to distribute plates and I went to assist her. I put out two plates in front of Archaby, one for himself and one for his missing spouse. Next came utensils and mugs, then the first course: as was traditional on passenger vessels traveling among the Ten Thousand Worlds, this consisted of ship's bread. Fortunately, *Peregrinator's* integrator had developed a fine recipe. The passengers at the first table expressed appreciation – also a tradition for interstellar travelers – and though the Ubrachians said nothing, they ate every crumb.

Next came a vegetable stew with a side dish of sausages – the choice was between spicy or plain – and flagons of golden ale. A buzz of conversation began at table one; a holy silence reigned at the other, except for some loud smacking of lips and toothless gums as the ancient member of the Ubrachian pilgrimage dealt with the stew and ale.

I hovered near the first table, ready to whisk away empty dishes and pass fresh flagons of drink from the nearby dispenser. The three sisters spoke among themselves, mainly to pass appreciative comments about the quality of the meal. At some point, a word spoken by one of them caught the attention of Tetch Archaby, causing him to advance some thoughts about nuts and lentils, which then led him to launch into a discourse on the cultivation of blisternut trees.

This overture suppressed all further conversation until Tetch paused to take a measure of ale. Immediately, Illiphrata Vauderoy turned to Todfrey Hamble and invited him to share with his tablemates his background and reasons for travel.

Hamble, who had been quietly chewing a sausage, took a sip of the golden brew and said, "I'm just a middle-ranked intercessor with the family court in New Srinigar. I'm off to visit some cousins in Novo Vieste."

Beyond that he would not be further drawn, describing his circumstances as "boring and humdrum."

I would have agreed with this self-characterization, except at one point in the progress of the meal I saw him glance around the table when no one was looking his way. For a moment I saw a flash of sharp intelligence and incisive inquiry.

It is a peculiarity of my unusual origin that I notice such things as micro-expressions and significant eye movements. You see, I am not really an ordinary human being. I came into existence with certain aspects of my neural circuitry enhanced by the genius Hallis Tharp, who designed me to be a template for vat-grown artificial persons. From me, he produced thousands of combatants for a vicious private war. Jenore had long since convinced me that my background is not a fit subject for polite conversation.

Still, Hamble took my interest now. Again, it is my nature to notice camouflage of all kinds. Todfrey Hamble wore the fleece of a gentle ruminant, but peeking out from underneath I detected a sharp-toothed predator.

# # #

When the meal was over and the tables cleared, I opened the forward salon and told the passengers they were welcome to its comforts. The ship's integrator would provide them with diversions and entertainments, or they could play various games, individually, or in pairs or groups.

The Vauderoy sisters opted to play panachio, settling themselves around a multi-sided table. Tetch elected to have a performance of classic erotica played in the privacy of the Archabys' cabin. Addeus Ing again assumed a position of moral elevation and announced that the cultists would return to their devotions.

When I looked for Todfrey Hamble, he had disappeared.

"Remember," I said, before the cultists departed, "we will be entering a whimsy in three and a half maxims. Medications will be automatically dispensed from the headboards of your sleeping platforms. The ship's integrator will advise you when to take them, and remind you once more before we enter the Seventh Plane. You all know the necessity of following the ship's advice."

They all signified their assent. As any traveler knows, passage through the Seventh Plane while conscious can lead to permanent derangement.

I watched the Ubrachians file down the corridor, then went to join the captain and Jenore in Erkatchian's suite. We dined on the same menu served to the passengers, then engaged in the kind of conversation that arises among friends of long standing.

At some point, I asked the ship's integrator about Hamble's whereabouts and was told that he was in his cabin, lying on his sleeping platform.

Late in the evening – we were still on Carricker spaceport time – chimes sounded and the ship announced the imminent passage through the whimsy. I went to the salon and saw the Vauderoys en route to their accommodations. I closed up the common room and joined Jenore in our own cabin. We took the medications dispensed by our sleeping platform, lay down together, linked our fingers as always, and faded from all sensibility.

\# \# \#

"Supercargo," said the ship's integrator, "rouse yourself."

I came free of the grip of the medications slowly, my mind dull and my thoughts tepid. I sat up and stared at the floor between my feet. My bare toes looked improb-

ably far away, while at the same time they loomed large as if they were almost touching my nose.

The ship spoke again. "There has been an incident," it said. The hatch that concealed the dispenser in the wall now opened, revealing a tumbler of some colorless liquid. "Here is a restorative," said *Peregrinator*." I recommend you imbibe it."

Still in a fog, I reached for the tumbler and downed its contents. In moments, it began to have its effects: my vision sharpened, the cabin was restored to its normal dimensions, and my mind became cool and still.

"What is the situation?" I said.

"A passenger is not responding to my inquiries."

"Which passenger? And what do you mean by 'not responding?'"

"Todfrey Hamble," said the integrator. "I believe he is deceased."

Behind me, Jenore turned over and yawned. "Wha?" she said, then put a forearm over her eyes.

"Trouble," I told her. "The ship thinks a passenger has died during the transit through the whimsy." I spoke to the integrator, "Have you notified the captain?"

"He is not yet conscious." That was to be expected. Like many an old spacer, Erkatchian sank deeper under the influence of the mind-numbing drugs than those who had traveled through fewer whimsies.

I stood up and reached for the clothing I had left on the chair. "I will see to it," I said. "Say nothing to the other passengers."

"Of course," said the integrator, in that gentle tone the devices use when humans fail to appreciate their perfect understanding of every situation.

\# \# \#

Hamble's little berth stood between the first- and second-class cabins, which had been accommodation for Lord Vullamir's guests and their servants, respectively. It was barely bigger than its sleeping platform, and I had to squeeze between the wall and where the dead man lay.

Though the integrator's percepts were capable of detecting the shallowest of breathing, not to mention the body's temperature, I nonetheless put my fingers against the spot on the man's throat where a pulse would be felt. There was none. The flesh was cold.

I saw no wounds, no bruises, no ligature marks. The sleeping garment he wore was not disturbed. The death could have been the result of natural causes. I picked up the empty sachet that had contained the medications Hamble would have taken before we plunged into the Seventh Plane. I sniffed its open end, and smelled nothing. But there was a trace of powder left in the packet. I folded it so that the few grains would not come out and put it in the pocket of my single-suit.

Then I let myself out of the cabin and instructed the integrator to seal the door.

\# \# \#

When I got to Erkatchian's compartment, far forward in the ship and above the salon, I found him awake, sipping punge. Jenore was with him.

"I told him," she said. "I'd better go see about breakfast."

"Yes," I said, and watched her go.

"Natural causes?" Eratchian said, his face showing a faint hope.

"I don't think so," I said. I took out the medications sachet and shook the few grains of powder onto the captain's table. "Integrator," I said, "examine this substance minutely."

A moment later, it said, "I have."

"What is it?"

"It is two substances: a common somnofacit and crystalline thrazzine."

"The effect of thrazzine?" I said.

"Suppression of the respiratory function."

"Permanent suppression?"

"Yes."

So there it was. Todfrey Hamble had ingested a substance that would put him to sleep combined with a poison that would stop his breathing.

"Did you witness his taking of the powder?" I said.

The device said it had not. Hamble had not yet taken his medication when the *Peregrinator* entered the ambit of the whimsy, at which time the yacht had shut off all its percepts. Persons who went wakeful into the Seventh Plane could go mad or lose control of their sensory apparatus; when they came back into space-time, they might taste colors or experience hot and cold as shrieks and rumbles. Integrators were less affected but found the strangeness of their surroundings distracting. They usually turned down their perceptions to minimum until they emerged once more into the Third Plane.

"What is your last record of Hamble?" I said.

A screen appeared in the air. I saw the small man exiting his cabin into the common corridor that ran most of the length of the ship, with cabin doors on either side.

Then he disappeared.

"Where did he go?" I asked the integrator.

"What do you mean?" it said.

"Examine the record. He came out of his cabin and disappeared."

"That is impossible," said the device.

"Replay the record," I said. It did so, then I said, "How do you explain that?"

"Explain what?"

The captain intervened at that moment. "Integrator," Erkatchian said, "put yourself on standby." He turned to me and said, "The ship has encountered something it cannot explain. Attempting to force an explanation from it may cause damage. I do not wish to be out in space with an integrator that is pursuing its own tail in ever decreasing circles."

I could see the sense in that, but the mystery remained. "What do you think has happened?" I said.

Erkatchian gave his long nose a reflective pull. "I have only a theory. Hamble carried a device that allowed him to subvert the ship's percepts. It follows that he was not some mid-level intercessor from New Srinigar, but a competent agent with a mission."

"What kind of mission?"

"Another theory," he said. "The incompetent inspector at the spaceport was not as useless as he appeared to be. He was a decoy, meant to allay suspicion while the real danger unobtrusively slipped aboard and carried out the operation."

Jenore saw where he was going. "So it's about blue borrache?" she said.

"Most likely," Erkatchian said. "Someone has brought some aboard and Hamble was on its trail. The criminal discovered his interest and killed him."

Jemore's face took on a thoughtful aspect. "The cultists?" she said. "Their robes could conceal packages of the drug."

"Or," I said, "their idol could be hollow."

"It would explain why they want no one near it," Erkatchian said.

"What about the sisters?" Jenore said. "Hamble seemed to take an interest in them."

I hadn't noticed that, but she had been with the passengers in the salon more than I had. She recounted how the little man had returned to the salon, then hovered nearby as the Vauderoys played panachio.

"I thought his interest was carnal," she said. "They hail from Novo Vieste, where women wield power over men. It is not unheard of for a group of them to surround a man and carry him off to some quiet corner where they will use him until he is worn out."

"Hamble did not look as if he would have lasted long," I said. "Can we revive the integrator and see what occurred between him and the Vauderoys?"

Erkatchian rewoke the device and we watched its record of the intercourse between Todfrey Hamble and the three sisters. Their conversation had indeed been suggestive, but ultimately, Hamble had declared himself fatigued and departed before the women had completed their last chukka of panachio. Their comments after he was gone did suggest some resentment, but no promises of revenge were voiced.

It was shortly after he left the salon that he abruptly disappeared from view. The integrator did not remark upon that impossibility and we did not press it.

"What were the Ubrachians doing at that time?" I asked the ship.

The device explained that the cultists had disabled the ship's percepts in the cabin where their idol had been placed upon a fold-down shelf. "They told me that it was forbidden for the gaze of heathens to do more than glance its way. I do have an audio recording of what they were doing."

"Play it," the captain said. A moment later, the sound of guttural chanting filled our ears. After a few moments of monotony, Erkatchian said, "Enough."

We looked at each other, but no one had anything more to add. Jenor said, "What about the Archabys?"

The visual record showed them sitting together in their cabin, watching the erotic performance Tech had chosen on a screen that hung in the air before them. The inte-

grator sped up the time signature and we saw them remain where they were until the program concluded.

"The performance apparently stimulated them. They said they intended intimate acts and asked for privacy," the device said. "I deactivated the percepts until it was time for medications. By then they were in their sleeping attire."

"Did you see them take the drugs?" I said.

"I did. They lay down, sharing a sleeping platform. I checked to see that all the other passengers had taken their medications and reposed themselves, then I shut off my percepts, as normal."

Jenore had been listening to this, but I saw from the vertical line that appeared above her nose that her mind was pursuing some new train of thought.

"What?" I said.

"When I was with the Chabriz Traveling Show," she said, "there was a prestidigitator." She went silent and her eyes moved the way they do when she was chasing a memory.

I waited and after a while, she brightened as the recollection came. "His name was Rheinster and he both indulged in blue borrache and transported the stuff. He was arrested on Challimaine and we never saw him again."

"What of it?" I said.

"I don't know yet. It will come to me."

I summarized. "So it is possible that the Ubrachians, incensed by Hamble's disrepect of their religion, took revenge upon him. It is also possible, but less likely, that it was the Vauderoy sisters, resenting his failure to submit to their blandishments. But we see the blisternut farmers as being in the clear."

I made a small noise as I contemplated what I had just said.

"What?" said Jenore.

"I was just thinking," I said, "that on Thrais, these motivations would have been far-fetched. No one loses so much as a groat, after all, from having their beliefs or vanity challenged."

Jenore wore that look that comes over her when she has to repeat some truth that ought to have long been ratified. "Not everything is a financial transaction," she said. "Not even on Thrais."

I was about to dispute that final assertion when she reminded me of the Thraisian tradition of the "last laugh," in which paupers about to commit suicide arranged for the posthumous publication of the details of how they had taken secret revenge on an enemy and gotten away with it.

Erkatchian said, "Let us concentrate on the problem before us. We are two days out from Meech's World. Hamble is already several hours dead. Before we touch down on Meech, the odor of putrefaction..." He waved a hand to complete the thought.

"His cabin was a storage locker," I said. "We could have the ship lower the temperature to below freezing."

"Good idea," the captain said. "Do it."

Jenore stood up. "But we had better search him and his possessions first, in case there is more evidence, beyond the poisoned medications, to give to the Meech police. That, and whatever device he used to subvert the integrator's percepts."

"Impossible," said the ship.

"Of course," we assured it.

\# \# \#

The dead man's possessions consisted of some clothes and toiletries in a carry-on valise, some funds in the currency of Carricker, and a basic communication device, less sophisticated than an integrator, that would allow him to connect to the connectivities on most worlds.

"Not much," I said, "for someone traveling between worlds."

Jenore was studying the body. "Help me turn him over," she said.

Rigor mortis had set in and the limbs were stiff. The body rolled like a figure made of carved wood. Jenore lifted the hem of his upper garment and said, "Aha."

In the small of the man's back was a little circle of raised flesh. "What is it?" I said.

She dropped the cloth and I let the corpse resume its previous position. She spoke so that only I would hear. "The prestidigitator I mentioned. He was outed by an operative of the IPCC who had infiltrated the Chabriz show as a roustabout."

I knew of the IPCC, an interplanetary law-enforcement organization that had legal authority on scores of major and minor planets. "The bump on Hamble's back?" I said.

"I saw something like it on the roustabout. It conceals the device we spoke about earlier. Also a locator. Bring him in range of any connectivity and it transmits a signal that tells the local IPCC branch the identity of the agent and where he is. It is also *de facto* identification."

"That puts a new complexion on the crime," I said.

"It does. We must assume Hamble intended to make an arrest on Meech's world."

"Will freezing affect the locator?" I said.

She showed me a doubtful mouth, "It shouldn't."

"Then let's get this cabin sealed and cooled. We need to talk with Yalum about what to tell the other passengers."

"One of whom is a killer," Jenore said.

"At least one."

We exited the cabin and I told the ship to reseal the door. I was about to add an instruction to freeze the interior when I found that Jenore and I were no longer alone. Addeus Ing was in the corridor, along with two of the Vauderoys.

Tetch Archaby, his hair disordered from sleep, was peering out through the partly opened door of his cabin, which was next to the dead man's.

"What is going on?" the Ubrachian said. The expressions of the others said the same question was foremost in their minds.

"Todfrey Hamble has died during the passage through the whimsy," I said. "We are sealing his cabin and dropping the temperature to preserve his remains. Those of you who share a common wall may feel a chill. I regret that cannot be helped."

There were more questions, from Ing and the sisters. I said the captain would address them in the dining salon before breakfast was served. That did not stop them from renewing their queries, but Jenore and I made our way past them and went forward.

# # #

"We cannot do as you suggest and eject the corpse into space," Captain Erkatchian said. "The IPCC would arrest the ship, the crew, and probably most of you, on general suspicion."

Addeus Ing was not mollified. "The situation is unacceptable," he said, his voice rising. "No corpse is allowed to encroach upon Ubrach's ambit."

"It cannot be helped," Erkatchian said, keeping his own voice under control.

"It must be!" the Ubrachian cried. A spray of spittle reached the captain, who calmly wiped it away.

"Perhaps," I put in, "the solution is not to move the body from out of the ambit but to move the ambit away from the body."

Ing turned on me as if I was babbling nonsense. "We can make space in the cargo hold," I said. "You could relocate the idol there and attend to its needs."

Ing's mouth opened and closed but no words emerged. His eyes bulged as if enduring pressure from within. The ancient acolyte, whose name I had not yet learned, put fingers that resembled some sea creature's legs on the head man's arm. Ing looked down at them as if he had never seen such things before, but after a long moment he managed to collect himself and subsided into the seat he had sprung up from.

"What about...sanitation?" said Shuriz Vauderoy.

"Or contagion?" said Illiphrata. To her sisters she offered an aside. "It's a good thing he didn't accept our invitation."

The three were nodding in mutual agreement as Erkatchian said, "There is no contagion. Ser Hamble died of...an unfortunate reaction to the interplanar transit medications."

As he said this, he looked a reminder to me that we would not mention the suspected poisoning. I gave him a minuscule nod in reply.

The captain went on, "As for sanitation, the ship has lowered the temperature in Ser Hamble's cabin to below freezing. Those of you who have common walls are advised not to touch them, to avoid frostbite."

Ing had been quietly conversing with his brethren. Now he said, "We could measure the distance from Ubrach to the corpse. It may be that it is not within the ambit."

"I will bring you a measuring device," I said. "Now, shall we proceed with breakfast?" I gestured to the steaming bowls ready to be served. "The ship is proud of its recipe for tangy porridge."

I saw frowns from the Ubrachians. Perhaps their god forbade them spicy foods; I could not remember whether any of them had chosen the chilied sausages. The Vauderoy sisters remained agitated, but less so. Folliance Archaby sat quietly. It was her turn to bring food while Tetch husbanded the seedlings.

I said to her, "Your cabin is next to the...scene. Do you have any concerns?"

"None," she said.

Erkatchian left and Jenore and I attended to the distribution of porridge and punge.

# # #

A quiet time ensued, with the three sisters in the salon, the Ubrachians pursuing their spiritual aims in the cabin that housed their god, and the Archabys doing whatever they did in their cabin.

I passed by, felt the door to the sealed compartment, but snatched my hand away when the skin of my fingertips threatened to stick to the metal. I went to the Archabys' door and knocked. Tetch opened it a sliver and looked out at me.

"What is it?" he said.

"Are you warm enough?" I said. "I can arrange for extra clothing."

"We are fine," he said, though his breath formed a mist.

"Are you sure?" I had learned that in some cultures built around vanity a stoical response to bodily discomfort was considered appropriate.

"Sure," he said, and closed the door.

# # #

In the captain's quarters, Jenore was questioning the ship's integrator.

"What information do you have on blue borrache?"

"Considerable," it replied. "Many jurisdictions do not accept ignorance as a legal defense."

"I am trying to recall something I once knew," she said, "about blue borrache and the medications taken to reduce the effects of interplanar medications on mentation."

The integrator produced a screen and filled it with text. "Here is an article from a news site on Bobble," it said.

Jenore read the text, flipped to the next

segment, and said, "There it is."

I craned my neck to look at what she was reading. The text detailed how a microdose of blue borrache taken before the whimsy medications could delay the onset of the latter's effects for an appreciable time.

"Ah," I said after a moment. "That could be it. The killer waits until Hamble is unconscious and the integrator has closed its percepts, then slips into his cabin and pours the adulterated medication into his mouth."

Erkatchian had been doing something at his desk. Now he turned and took in what Jenore and I had read. He frowned. "So that's how," he said. "Now all we need is why, and we'll know who."

"The why is to prevent the smuggler from being caught," I said. I asked the integrator, "Can you determine if the drug is aboard?"

"Only if it were in open view. If it was enclosed in a container, I could not detect it."

Jenore said, "Might Hamble have had a device? A sniffer of some kind?"

"If so," Erkatchian said, "whoever adulterated his medications would have taken it. And hidden it."

"What are our passengers doing now?" I asked the ship.

"The Ubrachians are chanting. The Vauderoys are resting. The Archabys are huddling together for warmth."

The information was not useful. "What was Hamble's plan?" I said. "We're presuming he had identified the smugglers and would arrange for them to be arrested upon arrival at Meech's World."

Jenore got that look that always told me when she was turning things over in her mind. "We are going to Meech's because Hamble wanted us to," she said. "We should notify the Meech's World spaceport police, once we're within range."

I saw a new thought occur to her. After a moment's further consideration, she said, "Has anyone told the passengers about the diversion to Meech's World?"

Nobody had, it turned out. They would think that we were stopping at Yaroslav for routine refueling.

She suggested we let them all know about the change during lunch and watch to see if the news caused any untoward reactions.

"Yes," I said. "I will watch for micro-expressions. We could also have the ship record their reactions, then play them back to us, slowed down, so you can see what I do."

That was the plan. I told the ship's integrator what I wanted it to do when we informed the passengers about going to Meech's World.

"Very good," it said.

Jenore went to the galley to prepare lunch while the captain resumed his duties. I had no duties of my own at the moment, and would have accompanied her to help out, as I usually did. But now another thought occurred to me. I pursued it for a moment, then asked the device a question. My query prompted the integrator to produce a screen and fill it with text. I began to read.

# # #

"Unacceptable!"

Ing had leapt to his feet the moment the news about landing at Meech's World was out of the captain's mouth. I had no need to look for micro-expressions; outrage and defiance were written plainly across the cult leader's face.

Now he was demanding that we stop at

Yaroslav instead.

"We cannot," Erkatchian told him. "We would need to reverse course and to make our way to a different whimsy to hurl ourselves back toward that planet."

"Then do so!" Ing's face grew an even deeper shade of purple. His fellow Ubrachians were also now standing and shouting their own demands.

Erkatchian spoke quietly. A good technique, I thought, because the cultists had to stop their bellowing in order to hear him. "We cannot go where you want to go because we do not have enough fuel to reach the whimsy and then make the passage through Third Plane space to Yaroslav. We will end up marooned in space until some ship happens by that can spare us the fuel – probably at exorbitant cost."

I spoke then. "Why do you not wish to go to Meech's World?"

"Heresy!" Ing spat the word. "Meech's World is where the shortists fled to when we drove them from the faith."

"Shortists?" I said

Ing waved an angry hand. "They deliberately twisted sacred scripture to maintain their fatuous contention that Ubrach will impose a purgatory of a mere three hundred years on those who fail to live up to his expectations. Clearly, the suras make it plain that the period of purification will last three thousand years."

Rumblings of approval rose from the other Ubrachians, accompanied by vigorous nods and motions of their hands that must have had ritual significance.

"We will not let any 'shortists' aboard," Erkatchian said. "Your ambit will not be profaned."

"You don't know these devils," Ing said. "On Carricker, they infiltrated the constabulary. On Meech, they will have done likewise. They may come with weapons drawn to steal Ubrach away and subject him to their foul rites and importunings."

"For which," I pointed out, "he will doubtless punish them drastically in the afterlife."

My tone may have conveyed a lack of reverence. Ing's cheeks turned an even deeper color.

The captain said, "We will do our utmost to protect you and your idol. But we must go to Meech's World. That is my decision. By this evening, we will be in range to contact the authorities there, and I shall do so."

The cult leader made a wordless sound of anger and frustration. He announced that he and his followers would not stay to eat but would barricade themselves in the god's cabin until we left Meech's World behind.

Jenore said, "You will miss lunch, dinner tonight, and breakfast tomorrow."

"Ubrach will fortify us," Ing said and marched out of the dining room. His fellow cultists went with him, though two of them glanced back forlornly at the piles of ship's bread and steaming meats laid out on the sideboard.

Erkatchian looked to the Vauderoys and Foliance Archaby. "Any other complaints?" he said.

The sisters had been watching the confrontation between us and the cultists with interest tinged by amusement. Now they showed us bland smiles in denial of any distress. The blisternut farmer had spent the last several moments regarding her hands. Without looking up, she signaled that she had nothing to say.

The meal was consumed in almost complete silence, except for the Vauderoys' whispers among themselves. When the passengers had returned to their cabins, Folliance carrying a bowl for Tetch, I went to the quarters I shared with Jenore and bade the integrator show me what it had recorded. Shortly after, Jenore came in and I had the device repeat the performance.

"I don't see anything remarkable," she said.

"Nor did I," I said, "neither at the time nor in the playback."

"The Ubrachians' outrage was genuine," she said. "And the three sisters just looked amused. As for Folliance Archaby, she kept her head down throughout."

"Yes," I said, "she did, didn't she?"

I thought about it for a little while then issued new instructions to the integrator. After it said it would comply, I proposed that my spouse and I should take a nap. Jenore suggested we do something else first – a suggestion I always found to be agreeable. We locked the door for privacy.

\# \# \#

In the late afternoon, Erkatchian spoke through the integrator. "Conn and Jenore, please come to my cabin."

When we arrived, we found the captain seated in his chair, with both Archabys standing to one side.

"Who's guarding the seedlings?" I said.

Neither of them responded. Erkatchian said, "Close the door."

I did so. As soon as he heard the click of the lock, Tetch Archaby brought out from behind his back a heavy-duty shocker and pointed it at me.

"So," I said, and waited for him to speak.

He spoke in a calm and measured voice, not at all like the rush of words that had characterized his discourses about blisternut cultivation. Those remarks, as my research through *Peregrinator*'s integrator had showed, had been cribbed verbatim from the standard reference texts on blisternuts. "It's too late to divert from Meech's World."

"Yes," I said.

He nodded. "Then we will proceed there, refuel, and set off for Novo Vieste. The hatches will remain sealed. Thus no inspections of the cargo will be required."

"If you wish," I told him. I didn't mention that the IPCC implant would automatically alert the port police.

He nodded again, then his mouth and brows formed an expression that said he was seizing the only hope available.

"We'll just have to see," he added with a shrug. "But there will be no communication with the authorities except for routine back-and-forth regarding landing."

"If you say so," I said. "But what happens when we reach Novo Vieste?"

"The same," he said. "We land, my partner and I depart with our...blisternut seedlings, and we all forget about the...unpleasantness."

His voice was as calm as before, but I had seen the unsuppressible flash of hardness in his face when I'd asked my question. At Novo Vieste, they would meet up with their criminal confederates, drop the identities of Tetch and Folliance, and disappear into the warrens of the planet's underworld.

As for us, he did not mean to leave us in a position to give evidence.

"All right," I said and spread my hands in a gesture of compliance, then crooked both my little fingers in toward my palms. I heard a faint chime, almost inaudible, from the ship's integrator.

I stepped forward and wrenched the shocker from Archaby's hand. He had time to depress the activation stud twice before I seized the weapon, but that did him no good.

"Restore function," I said.

"Done," said the ship.

I pointed the shocker at the blue borrache smuggler and gestured with my other hand to include his partner. "Turn and face the wall."

From the pouch at my belt I withdrew two holdfasts, left behind by Lord Vullamir. He had used his private yacht to transport unwilling persons for unspeakable purposes to places where he and his fellow Immersionists could enjoy their evil undisturbed. Because he had also been possessed by the inbred paranoia of Old Earth's upper-tier aristocracy, he had equipped his ship's integrator with the power to analyze and neutralize the workings of most light weaponry.

I escorted Tetch and Folliance Archaby – though I doubted those were their names – to the cargo hold, where I had prepared a secure holding pen – also a left-over from the ship's former uses.

I then went to their cabin and used a knife to cut open the straps that secured their portmanteau to the sleeping platform. Next, I cut a hole in the luggage itself, then

extracted one of the rootballs. One more cut and, inside, I found not soil, but compressed blue borrache, in concentrated strength.

By the time I returned to the captain's cabin, we were within communications range of Meech's World.

Erkatchian was speaking to the port's integrator. He then waited for his words to reach the distant world and for a reply to come to us. When that business was settled, he opened an ornate bottle he kept in his cupboard for special occasions.

"There may be a reward," he said.

# # #

There was no reward, but a squad of the spaceport's constabulary, clad in gray and black and with jolt-truncheons at their belts, swarmed aboard the moment the main hatch was unsealed. Erkatchian stepped forward to address them, but their senior officer, Ilye Chandrasekh, with three sunbursts on his leather-billed cap, brusquely ordered all passengers and crew to assemble in the salon.

The captain's reply was mild. "The prisoners are in the hold, restrained," he said.

"The ship is alleged to be transporting contraband," said the policeman.

"I can show it to you," said Erkatchian.

"We will find it for ourselves."

The captain raised a finger to offer a fresh point, at which Chandrasekh's eyes bulged and two of his uniforms put their hands on their bludgeons. Erkatchian replaced the argumentative finger with a palm of surrender. He led the way to the salon, pausing at the passengers' doors to alert them to their need to move with us.

The salon was crowded. I saw the two port police eyeing the Ubrachians with sharpened interest, then exchanging freighted glances. When Chandrasekh set two of his squad to watch us and ordered the rest to conduct the search, the pair whose interest had been aroused almost ran down the companionway to the passen-

ger accommodations.

Addeus Ing responded with alarm. I saw him look to me for support; I signaled that I was not in control of events. A hurried, whispered consultation engaged the cultists. They shuffled for a moment then Ing said, "Now!"

The six able Ubrachians rushed the two guards, bowling them over and relieving them of their truncheons, then charged down the companionway. The ancient tottered after them. Shouts and sounds of struggle soon followed. The two constables left to guard us picked themselves up and, after the briefest hesitation, went to the aid of their comrades.

The Vauderoy sisters observed all of this with lively interest. When the sounds of struggle subsided and Chandrasekh's voice could be heard issuing orders, they waited a short while, then sallied down the companionway.

I asked the ship's integrator to report on their actions. It said, "They have gone into Ing's cabin and are wrapping the idol in a blanket. Now they are transferring it to their own cabin." A moment later, the device said, "They are secreting it in their trunk."

I said to Jenore and Yalum, "Should we allow that?"

"The port police told us to remain where we are," the captain said. "Besides, I am not disposed to exert myself in the service of Addeus Ing. I do not care for enthusiasts. Indeed, we should make it a policy not to take them aboard."

I looked to Jenore, saw her shoulders lift and fall.

In the world of my upbringing, Thais, where all actions are economic transactions, I would not have interfered, since I saw no profit in doing so. I had learned, while visiting other worlds and cultures, that people could have other motivations – even to the point, in some situations, of altruism. Apparently, this was not one of those cases. I signaled my acceptance.

Time passed, and no one came to tell us what to do. When asked, the ship reported that the police had marched the bruised and still resisting Ubrachians off into the innards of the port. It had taken the full squad to control them.

The Vauderoy sisters, carrying their trunk, had also departed. The Archabys, or whatever their real names were, remained imprisoned in the hold.

"We have been forgotten," I said, "along with the criminals and their contraband."

Erkatchian gave the matter the briefest thought, then he asked the ship if we could refuel.

"The port says yes, provided our credit is good."

It was good; we carried guarantees from several worlds' fiduciary pools. Soon after, a semi-sentient lighter rolled up and our energies were swiftly replenished. We waited a little longer, but Chandrasekh and his squad did not return.

"Are we likely ever to come back to Meech's World?" I asked Erkatchian.

"Not likely, no," he said.

"Well, then."

\# \# \#

We left the smugglers attached to a light standard, their drug-filled blisternut seedlings at their feet. Nearby, we laid the frozen corpse of Todfrey Hamble, his valise, and the packet with its traces of thrazzine. Then we departed Meech's World.

We were not far beyond the planet's system when the integrator reported an urgent call from Chandrasekh. "He orders us to return."

"Connect me," Erkatchian said. When the officer's face appeared on the screen, the captain said, "We are working spacers, with our livings to earn. We cannot spare the time to wait for your world's legal processes while moorage charges pile up."

"Your accounts are your own problem. We require you to give evidence regarding the murder of an IPCC agent."

It was Jenore's turn to speak. "Do you mean evidence of how your constables provoked a sectarian brawl, resulting in the theft of a religious relic?"

On the screen, Chandrasekh's face became both still and thunderous. After a long moment, in which he offered further word, he broke the connection.

The screen vanished.

Jenore asked Yalum and me, "Would you say the chance of our returning to Meech's World has now moved from not likely to not at all?"

We would say it. Indeed, speaking as one, we both did. ■

Pickman's Model

In the Moon Garden

By SANDRA
KASTURI

Sandra Kasturi is a fiction writer, poet and the publisher of award-winning ChiZine Publications. Her two poetry collections are The Animal Bridegroom *(with an introduction from Neil Gaiman) and* Come Late to the Love of Birds. *Her story, "The Beautiful Gears of Dying" won the Sunburst Award. She is fond of gin & tonics, red lipstick, and Idris Elba.*

Mrs. Daley, who in her own head still thinks of herself as Mrs. Daley, has planted a variety of night-blooming flowers with strange names: Evening Stock, Angel's Trumpet, Night Phlox. And of course, the Moonflowers, whose white petals give the very air a bioluminescent glow in the evening.

Mrs. Daley isn't fond of the garden – at least, not since Mr. Daley died last March. Her compacted, pulsing sorrow seems to expand every time she stands on the grass and looks over her back yard, down the slope, past her stone wall, down and down toward the shore by the bay, her unhappiness spiraling out from her in invisible streamers. She wonders if maybe having Mr. Daley secretly buried in the garden wasn't the best idea after all. She has planted all these different night flowers over the little hillock that is Mr. Daley's current grave because she wants something to look at when she is out here at night, as the garden in the sunshine is unbearable. The heat and happiness of the summer daylight seem to belong to another world, a planet she no longer inhabits.

Mr. Daley had so loved the night sky, and the stars, and the moon more than anything. In fact, he had loved it so much, he had almost gone there.

# # #

It had started when he was a small boy, wriggly with excitement over anything to do with space: astronauts, comets, that Apollo 11 movie, pieces of meteors fallen to earth after traveling unimaginable distances. He loved it all, and when he found out that if he studied hard enough, he could apply to the NASA Space Program, he spent his teen years in a kind of fervid ecstasy, amid his physics and mathematics textbooks, preparing for when he, too, could go into space. But it was the cool beauty of the moon that entranced him most, even though people had already gone there and it wasn't exactly undiscovered country. The names of the craters, rilles and places were a song in his head through high school and university: Mare Imbrium, Sea of Tranquility, Rima Galilaei. The lilt of each syllable a nightly lullaby.

Mr. Daley made it into the Space Program right after he and Mrs. Daley had gotten married; it was as if Destiny itself were taking him by the hand into the future. Mrs. Daley remembers the joys of that year very well, though she tries not to think of it too often – like sunshine, the memories are almost unbearable.

When Mr. Daley's aneurysm burst, they called themselves lucky because it had happened on earth, and not in space – he had been scheduled for a shuttle flight the next week. The aneurysm was so small it was undetectable and had never shown up on any scans. The doctors (the best doctors, they were told) had controlled the bleed, and Mr. Daley lived – for all practical purposes he was exactly the same as before – but his dreams of going into space and to the moon were over. No one was allowed into space who had had a life-threatening medical ailment. The lives of the other astronauts might depend on it.

Mrs. Daley wasn't sure how he would

react, but Mr. Daley seemed to bounce back, as cheerful as ever, although she would catch him outside, in the driveway of their first little house, looking up at the moon at night, and she knew that deep down, something in him was still full of yearning. But he kept working at NASA, and eventually made it to Mission Control, talking to his fellow astronauts in the shuttles going to the new space station, the moon, to Mars and the Jupiter orbitals. All the while, she could feel his sadness and wasn't surprised when Mr. Daley quit NASA. He decided to teach physics at the same high school where Mrs. Daley taught math, and then on a whim, in his spare time, he wrote a book about the moon, which the critics liked, and suddenly they had extra money. Which was nice, because by then the children had come, and they seemed to gobble money like starving wolverines.

Mr. Daley went on to write books about the future, of settlements on the planets of the solar system, about alien contact and space travel. They proved even more popular and Mr. and Mrs. Daley and the children moved to the very house she still lived in, on the shore of the bay, with its big gardens and huge rooms. She didn't need so much space now with the children long gone, but what could she do, especially now, with Mr. Daley still here, at rest under the Moonflowers, after another aneurysm downed him, this time for good.

# # #

Mrs. Daley doesn't know what to do with herself. It has been over a year, and she hates the Moon Garden – as she now thinks of it – but cannot seem to stay away. She should never have bribed the funeral director; she should have let them bury Mr. Daley at the Shady Elm Cemetery, but she couldn't bear to be so far from him. If the children find out what she has done, they will have her put in a Home, there is no question. So Mrs. Daley keeps Mr. Daley to herself.

"Bury me on the moon," Mr. Daley had said, winking at her, years ago, when they first talked about funeral arrangements. Mrs. Daley remembers laughing, and throwing her crumpled-up napkin at him.

The Moonflowers are the closest she can come, even though she originally wrote to NASA. But because Mr. Daley was never a full astronaut, he did not qualify for burial in space, or in a lunar orbit. However, they felt bad, and belatedly sent her a piece of genuine lunar rock by FedEx. It has sat on the kitchen table for the better part of a year, her eldest daughter complaining about Mrs. Daley's laziness every visit. Mrs. Daley feels mild alarm that her children's names seem to have trickled from her memory, but just as quickly, forgets her forgetting.

Tonight for some reason, Mrs. Daley can't seem to ignore the FedEx box. She reopens it and pulls out the piece of lunar rock. It feels strange in her hand and, without thinking, she impulsively takes the rock with her outside. The sun has set, but it is not quite full dark. A few early stars have shown themselves. Mrs. Daley walks down to the Moon Garden and places the rock on Mr. Daley's mound, a small, uneven memorial. It glitters in the moonlight and she looks up – the moon has come out from behind a cloud, fat and gibbous, not quite full.

Is it waxing or waning? wonders Mrs. Daley. She cannot remember – she hasn't followed the lunar cycles since her husband died. She will be able to tell tomorrow, she thinks. She finally goes to bed and has strange dreams, of someone flying toward her across the bay, of luminous objects sailing through the air like strange fireflies.

She wakes with a start, and for the first time since Mr. Daley died, the compacted ache in her chest is absent. Mrs. Daley gets out of bed and feels strangely light. She decides that she will venture outdoors into the daylight for the first time in months, and stands on her doorstep and

actually picks up the daily paper in the morning instead of the evening. The front lawn is full of dandelions, which surprises her, until she remembers that she hasn't done any weeding since last summer.

"Well!" says Mrs. Daley to herself, then starts laughing. The sound startles her, as well as some birds sitting in one of the oak trees, and they take to flight, chattering and scolding her, wheeling into the air and then back down to rest on branches, eyeing Mrs. Daley carefully with their sharp, bright eyes.

She leaves them to it and goes back inside for breakfast, and is startled again when she sees the smile on her face in the hallway mirror.

# # #

That day, Mrs. Daley dusts and vacuums the house and then weeds the front and back of the house and gets one of the neighbor boys to mow the lawns. She is pleasantly exhausted when the sun sets and she sits on the back patio with a glass of iced tea, overlooking the back garden with its numerous flowerbeds, the treehouse Mr. Daley built for the grandchildren, the bay in the distance, and the Moon Garden. She is quite certain now that the moon is waxing and she is glad, now, that Mr. Daley is buried here, and is with her to experience it, resting under the Moonflowers, with the Night Phlox and Evening Primrose by his sides, the piece of lunar rock in pride of place.

Hours later, the moon has come up, and Mrs. Daley is right – it has increased by a nail paring and tonight is full. The bay is absolutely calm, the moonlight shimmering down a path across the water, up the slope, over the wall, and right into her garden, where it rests and glitters on Mr. Daley's memorial moon rock, a missing piece of itself, come nearly two hundred forty thousand miles on its journey to earth.

Mrs. Daley watches the moon's path across the bay, and there, in the distance, is some strange movement. She can't tell what it is, but it looks like it is coming her way. Something else appears at the periphery of her attention, and when she turns to look, she sees that the piece of lunar rock is glowing like a beacon.

Back across the bay, the movement seems larger, and Mrs. Daley sees that whatever it is, it is coming closer – following the glowing path of the moon down the water, straight toward her. She feels a strange excitement and leaves the patio, going down to the Moon Garden. The rock is glowing more brightly still; the thing that is coming closer has crossed the bay now, and is coming up the slope toward the wall. Mrs. Daley holds her breath. She hears the gate squeak, and yes, there it is, coming into her garden now – a glowing figure, like a piece of the full moon walking about on earth. As it comes closer, she sees that it is marked like the moon's surface – with strange shadows and craters, and when it turns its head away from her for a moment, she sees that its other side is dark, invisible to the human eye, just like the moon seen from the earth.

It's the man in the moon, thinks Mrs. Daley in a fit of whimsy, but as it comes closer she sees that, no, it isn't the man in the moon at all. It is Mr. Daley.

He comes to a stop in front of her, and she can see his beloved face in the glow and shadows; it is as if Mr. Daley has been made of lunar rock. He is smiling down at her, just like the moon behind him.

"Maureen," says Mr. Daley. At first, Mrs. Daley doesn't know who he is talking to, and then she realizes that it is her – her name is Maureen. In the past year, she has forgotten this. Like a tidal surge, the names of her children come back, too: bossy Susannah, gentle Ellie, and James Junior. Mr. Daley's voice is soft and cool, just like she would imagine the voice of the moon would be. "Maureen," he says again, "I'm sorry I took so long, but I couldn't find the path back." He pauses and then grins like a small boy. "I finally made it to the moon."

"So I can see," says Mrs. Daley, or Maureen, as she now remembers herself. She smiles up at him. She had forgotten how tall he was.

"Jim," she says, finally saying his name out loud, something she has refused to do for over a year. She takes his hand and they walk in the Moon Garden, and she tells him the names of all the night flowers and when she planted them. They sit down by the piece of lunar rock, and it and Mr. Daley glow so brightly she can hardly look at them. They talk for hours, and when the sky grows lighter, and Mr. Daley is beginning to fade a bit, she walks down to the shore with him, and waves as he walks back across the bright moonpath on the water; he is only an outline in the glow now, his dark side toward her as he heads back up to the moon.

# # #

When Maureen wakes, smiling, the next day, she thinks for a moment that it is a dream, or that she really has finally lost her marbles and the children will put her in a Home for sure. But she runs down to the Moon Garden in her nightgown as if she were a young girl, not caring if the neighbors see her, and there, by the lunar rock, are two sets of footprints, and other, smaller pebbles and dust, as if someone has been shedding bits of the moon. That is when she knows that Mr. Daley – Jim, she reminds herself – will be back again next month, when the moon is full again, down its path over the water, over the shore, up the slope, through the gate in the stone wall, and into the Moon Garden, following the beacon of the lunar rock. She will be waiting and they will talk again, until one day, she knows, she won't wave him off into the fading night, but will keep hold of his hand and they will go down that shimmering path together, both of them leaving dust and small rocks in their wake, right up into the night sky, together at last on the pale, comforting surface of the great, mythical moon, forever full. ■

By SHIRLEY
MEIER

Shirley Meier has been writing and publishing since the early 1980s; she had a new book slated to come out from Henchman Press in July, 2019. She's a regular columnist for Amazing Stories Magazine. *She is also a visual artist; her most recent passion is horseback archery. Currently, Shirley's hair is mostly pink and blue.*

"Mr. Johnson? Mr. Johnson can you hear me? Tap twice for yes."

Tap twice? With what? What's happening? – oh God, it hurts! Georgy said it wouldn't hurt! But I don't remember what 'it' was. It's not even 'blink once for yes, twice for no.' Wait…do I even have eyelids right now?

"Can you respond, Mr. Johnson? We are attempting to get you able to talk. Mr. Johnson, I am your Nurse and you are currently quite safe at Sunnyvale Hospital."

Sunnyvale? Nurse? Oh, thank God…wait, able to talk? What the hell happened? Marty had no recollection after the first bottle of vodka that he…wait…had he and Georgy been drinking? Celebrating? What the hell?

"I am summoning your physician since you appear to be awake. You are suspended in a short-term stay room just off the ER. We'll get you fixed right up now that we have you stabilized."

"S…s….s….Stabilized?" Marty Johnson's voice sounded and felt like he was gargling gravel.

"Ah, Homo sapiens hyoid bone reconfiguration complete. Mr. Johnson, I am your current physician, and we are attempting to reprogram your meds."

"My meds are off?"

"Could you tell us which body-mod program you attempted to install by yourself Mr. Johnson?"

"Ummm. Wait a minute…Sunnyvale is the space port not the hospital!"

"For a short time, we were considering launching you to the orbital facility," the doctor said quietly. "But that's no longer a consideration. And since you are once more *compos mentis*, your sister's insistence on your treatment off-planet is your decision, not your power of Attorney's."

"I should hope so! Sarah always was a bitch and threatening to have me launched." The gravel feeling was going away, but Marty's voice was still much deeper than it should be. *Dang. She nearly did it, too.* "Um…I had a pirate copy of NuYuX," he admitted sheepishly… "At least it was supposed to be NuYuX." *Damn you, Georgy!*

Marty couldn't make his eyes work and he realized he was completely restrained. "Look, Doctor…what's your name?"

"Henderson –"

"– Look, Doctor Henderson…it hurts me right now and I want to get this fixed as soon as possible."

"Of course. Let me explain, Mr. Johnson."

"You damn well better or I'll punch you in the snoot myself!"

"Calm down, Mr. Johnson. It would be quite impossible in any case. I am Doctor Program Henderson 10446."

Marty found himself sputtering with rage. "A program? Do you know who I am? I deserve a real Doctor!"

"I am a real Doctor, Mr. Johnson, and I am working with a biological doctor, a Dr. Singh, who is safely outside of the quarantine zone, monitoring our interaction."

"QUARANTINE!"

"Yes. You see, your bootlegged copy of NuYuX appears to have reacted badly with your regular drug regimen."

Marty could hear the gap in what the docbot was telling him, even through the smooth baritone. "AAAAAND??????"

"It was touch and go for a while that you would be patient zero in a gray ooze disaster, Mr. Johnson."

"That's why you were considering firing me off planet."

"Exactly."

"Wonderful. I take it we're past the worst of that?" *Georgy, I am going to bloody wring your neck!*

"You are currently in one of the sensory override cradles we would normally have used for a body-mod as extensive as the one you attempted."

"You didn't answer me."

"Yes, Mr. Johnson. You are stable and not about to turn into a wad of gray goo."

"Great. So, how long before you get me out of here?"

"Well, we have a problem, Mr. Johnson."

I'd be hyperventilating if I were breathing for myself.

"Go on."

"We have to flush your crashed nano meds out, let the NuYuX (x) finish its run… then we can possibly reverse the process and re-install your usual meds. In effect, we can re-set you."

"Lovely. Let's get started. How long is this going to take? I have a company to get back to."

"Mr. Johnson…were you intoxicated when you installed the program?"

"I might have been."

"That answers a few of our questions. It is going to take several weeks, Mr. Johnson."

"Weeks? What? Even a full mod usually doesn't take more than a few hours."

"You requested a 'full-on horse,' Mr. Johnson."

"No! Jaysus, no I did not!" Marty could vaguely remember him and Georgy finishing the vodka…after disabling some of their meds so they could have a **real** drunk. "I…um…"

"Let me play a portion of your contract acceptance audio, sir…"

The audio was him, DNA pattern recognition, acknowledging acceptance of all terms in the user license. A license in a pirate copy? What the hell… "… yeah… I wanna… <belch> … waaaaanaaa…enhance my…Johhhhn <hic> son… hung like a horse. <giggling> <hysterical laughter> Hung like a…fuckin' horse!"

"The program interpreted this as a request to be turned into a full-sized horse. Your nano-meds interfered, locking you into a 'dissolution-re-configuration loop', with the NuYuX gaining on the 'dissolution' phase…hence the concern for the goo disaster. We have now stabilized you in your current form." There was a tiny hiccup in the smooth docbot voice… Marty could imagine the 'empathy mode' kicking in. "…three-quarters horse form… albeit human sized for now since you did not have anything but the calories from four large bottles of vodka and a jeroboam of whiskey to fuel your request."

"Weeks, huh?"

"Several weeks Mr. Johnson. Then we can begin your weight-loss program in conjunction with becoming human again."

"That's why I had the normal meds put in in the first place!" His bellow was loud but the doctor program was unfazed.

"Of course, Mr. Johnson. Your audio acceptance for that particular procedure was un-inebriated.

"Aw shit."

"Oh dear."

"What?"

"It appears that your sister has convinced a judge that your inebriated medical experiment is still too dangerous to treat on the planet."

"Aww, shit! She gets me off planet and my will kicks in and her kids get everything I own!"

"Unfortunate, Mr. Johnson. Countdown sequence re-initiated. Launch in ten minutes!"

"Get my lawyer on the line! I'll have you unplugged! Stop launch sequence! Get my lawyers! **I need to talk to my lawyers!!!**"

LASER EYE SURGERY TURNED OUT TO BE A NATURAL CAREER PROGRESSION FOR JAST

By JACK
MCDEVITT

Stephen King describes McDevitt as "the logical heir to Isaac Asimov and Arthur C. Clarke." Twelve of his 22 novels have been Nebula finalists. Seeker *won the award in 2006. He's also won the John W. Campbell and the Robert Heinlein awards. The IAU has named an asteroid for him.*

The night that eventually changed Gregory MacAllister's perspective of the universe started with a party. *The National* was celebrating his forty-year career of disrupting politicians, bureaucrats, and multi-billionaires. He was a social critic, a satirist, an essayist, loved by many of his readers and hated by the rest. They were near the end of the evening. The music had stopped and there was a final round of clinking glasses. MacAllister wandered among the tables, shaking hands with everyone. Then, as they began to leave, he enjoyed a final lemon whiskey sour with his longtime editor, Tom Easton. Easton, who rarely drank anything, was enjoying a glass of red wine. They were at Saybold's where, as the motif made clear, life was always good.

MacAllister couldn't help thinking how fortunate he'd been to land his posting with *The National*. He'd started with *The Duncan Observer,* a weekly in Kansas, where he'd simultaneously had to work delivering food for a supermarket. But he'd caught the eye of the *Wichita Eagle,* won the Maureen Dowd Award, and eventually moved on to the *National.* "It's been a good run," he said. "I'm not sure it would have happened without you, Tom."

Easton had been the perfect editor. He was tall and trim, with neatly parted blond hair and a smile that betrayed an intensity of manner. "I wish I could take credit, Mac. But it wouldn't have mattered. You were headed for the stars whichever path you took." They raised their glasses to each other. Margery Eliot, on her evening TV show, was talking to a member of the House who

was orbiting the edge of a corruption scandal. The TV was mounted in a cradle at the end of the bar. His editor glanced up at it, and Mac saw there was something on his mind.

"Everything okay?" he asked.

Tom put his glass down and tapped his fingers on the table. "I'm going to retire next month, Mac. Nobody knows except Mike." The editor-in-chief. "I'd appreciate it if you didn't say anything."

"I'm sorry to hear it."

"I'll miss working with you. You keep getting better. I loved your latest." MacAllister had just delivered a column doubting that the recently developed process for enhancing intellectual capabilities at birth was a good idea. "I know you were kidding, Mac, but you might have it right. Stupidity, especially among kids, is a **good** thing. You can't enjoy playing tag if you're saddled with a two hundred IQ. We don't want children growing up too quickly." He smiled. "The period during which we enjoy science fiction already closes too soon."

"I never said that."

"You implied it."

"What are you going to do during retirement?"

"I'd like to just relax for a while. Read and spend time with the family. Play basketball with the kids. And I'm thinking about writing a play."

Abruptly they were listening to the harmonious cadence from Brookheiser's Sonata in C Sharp which the Action Network used to accompany a breaking news report. The TV screen narrowed onto Margery Eliot, who had turned away from her guest and was looking out over the bar crowd. "We have a starship that's just come back from somewhere," she said. "Apparently they saw something. No details yet." She pressed two fingers against her right ear while her eyes got a distracted look. Incoming message. She nodded. "You sure about that?" Then she was gazing out of the screen again. "They heard something."

Another long silence followed while Margery leaned forward, her attention riveted on the earphones. Suddenly the bar was filled with music. Not the jangles and drums of the Flying Bimbos that had been supplying background on the sound system, but something much softer, melodic, harmonious. "That's what they were hearing," Tom said.

A woman behind them growled "What the hell is she talking about?"

A male replied: "Don't know. You need a refill, Maisie?"

Tom was holding a hand behind his left ear, trying to block off other noise. "Probably another interstellar."

"I guess," said Mac.

Margery's brow had wrinkled. She was still listening to her ear pod. "They're saying there was nothing belonging to us out there. In the area where they were."

Tom frowned. "So it's aliens."

Mac shook his head. "It doesn't sound much like what you'd expect from little green men." Nobody would ever have accused Mac of being sentimental, but the music was unquestionably warm and soft. It reminded him of "As Time Goes By."

Margery let it play for about two minutes. Mostly it was delivered by string instruments and maybe clarions. But there was something else in the mix, something Mac didn't recognize, vaguely suggestive of a concertina. "Maybe," said Tom, "we're going to discover they also like Backup." A reference to the loud beatback rhythms that had taken over the concert world.

"Stay with us," said Margery. "We're going to Union Station." She blinked off and was replaced by a heavyset young redheaded male bent over a microphone.

He wore the blue and white uniform that was standard with the space people. A male voice, coming out of nowhere, asked whether the guy in uniform could hear him.

"Loud and clear."

"What's happening?"

"We're talking to the *Indigo*." He bent over the microphone. "Captain, you still there?"

A woman's voice: "I'm here, George." The screen split down the middle and revealed an attractive woman with dark hair and a no-nonsense expression. She wore the same blue uniform. With bars on her shoulders. "Damn," said Mac.

"What's wrong?"

"It's Angela."

George stayed on the circuit: "Just so you're aware, Captain, you're on seventeen networks."

"You know her, Mac?"

His lips formed a **yes**.

"How? You do a story on her?"

"She was a girlfriend. A long time ago." He took a deep breath. "When I knew her, her name was Rothman. She's barely aged. These life extension treatments are incredible."

Tom grinned. "You look pretty good yourself, Champ."

"Tell us about the music, Captain," said George.

"It sounds good, doesn't it?"

"Yes. Did you find the source? Were there any aliens?"

"Yes, we did. But aliens? Not exactly. Let's talk about it when we get in. I'm a little busy right now."

"She hasn't changed a bit," said Mac.

"How do you mean?"

"She always enjoyed playing games. I doubt she has anything to do at the moment other than just sit there and let the AI keep them in cruise mode. But if she makes everybody wait, there'll be a lot more excitement when they get in."

"She likes excitement?"

"Oh, yes." Mac was consulting his commlink. The mission was funded by Claxton Hotels. They'd been sent out to find vacation sites, places where hotels could be built, and where scenic views would be spectacular. Where guests would be on a world that was part of a ring system, or where dinosaurs roamed the area, or where three suns overwhelmed the sky.

George pulled the mike closer. "We'll see you when you get here, Captain. CommOps out." The screen closed on Angela's side and she was gone. George blinked off a moment later and was replaced by Margery Eliot. "We're hearing," she said, "that they expect the *Indigo* to dock in about seventeen hours. When it happens, Action News will be there."

# # #

Angela had been a big part of his life at one time. But Mac hadn't handled it well, and in the end she'd walked off and left him. He'd gotten her pretty much out of his mind until she showed up years later piloting interstellars. He tried to shrug her off on his way home that evening, as he had on a few previous nights when she'd made headlines, finding alien ruins somewhere, or leading a rescue expedition to a star with a Latin name where an exploratory mission had broken down. On one occasion, she'd piloted a flight to a neutron star during which Emmanuel Beck had done his groundbreaking gravity work.

While she sailed through the limelight, Mac wrote commentaries about the downside of being a boy scout, why we should stay clear of the stars, and the benefits to be derived from alcohol. He had an extra drink or two that night when he got home, and instructed Gale, his AI, to inform him if anything fresh broke concerning the *Indigo*. He'd lost the glow of the earlier part of the evening, so he tried to settle in with Morris Howard's *The End of Time*. Howard predicted a bleak future for humanity which had still not dealt with its expanding population. Mac agreed that it was probably the primary threat facing the species.

He wondered why, on this night when big news was breaking, he couldn't get his mind off Angela. He'd written numerous columns suggesting that marriage was not a good option for males who knew how to attract sexual partners. That it had evolved primarily to provide stability for women and child-rearing. But he suspected that attitude had developed out of his own sense of loss.

Rain was falling. He settled into bed and listened to it rattle against the skylight out in the hallway.

# # #

Mac watched *First Light* each morning. It was hosted by Jason Taylor, a skeptical grump. The perfect personality for a news anchor. His attractive soft-spoken associate, Eve Randall, blinked on first, talking about the secretary of the treasury who was currently tangled in a scandal, spending substantial money to support questionable trips around the globe, and providing opulent decorations for her office. Then she switched over to her partner. "Jason, I understand we've got more news from Union."

"If you want to call it news," Taylor said. He looked out at Mac, shook his head and sighed. He loved to play the on-air commentator who understood that the headlines all had a dark side. He was standing in front of a picture of Union Space Station which as Mac watched lit up and became the Union commcenter.

A heavyset, bored-looking guy in a ruffled sweater sat at a table. He tried to smile, pushed a button, and was instantly replaced by the concourse. A few media people were in place, talking as they looked through the curving transparent divider that separated them from the docking area. Then the concourse was gone and the heavyset guy reappeared. "The press are here already," he said. "There's a crowd of them coming up on the nine o'clock shuttle. The music's picked up a lot of interest." They went to a split screen: Captain

Chapman on one side and the commcenter on the other.

"– About four hours out," she was saying.

"Okay, Captain. I should mention that you're live right now."

She looked out of the screen toward MacAllister. "Are we getting a lot of media attention?"

"Of course. Is there anything you'd like to say about the aliens?"

"They have beautiful music."

"There's a lot of interest in them. Did you actually get a look at them?"

"No. Not really. But we do have a surprise."

"And what's that, Captain?"

"Wait for it. We'll explain when we get into port. *Indigo* out."

Everybody loves aliens. A few alien civilizations had been found, but they were mostly in serious decline or altogether gone. The last mission had brought in a couple of visitors that had evolved from dolphins. One of them had been a religious leader. That was good news, of course, unless you were looking for a little excitement.

Mac shut the TV down, showered, and made some pancakes. Then he went back to work on his current project. It was due that afternoon. Open marriage was one of his favorite topics. It upset large numbers of his readers, but there was nothing wrong with that. Freelance sex for all, he was arguing, made for a happy existence. He was looking for a believable rationale that would support the contention that couples who traded in an open market would love each other more.

"Do not wait until you lie on a deathbed to recognize what really counts in life," he was writing. "It's not only love that matters, but sexual entanglement."

"It is," the last line would read, "the way we are wired."

He knew it would get him into trouble. Eighty percent of the people in the country still believed in old-style marriage. But that was okay. Trampling happy talk

had long been his formula for success. The only problem here was that his girlfriend Lara wasn't going to like it. But she would understand.

He needed an hour to finish the column. He went through it again, made a few changes, got a fresh cup of coffee, and had just returned to his chair with the intention of getting some more sleep before heading to work when Gale's voice pulled him back into the real world. "Mac," she said, "They're on the TV again. I'll roll it from the start."

Angela and the CommOps guy, George, appeared onscreen. "We're picking up broadcasts," Angela said.

"More aliens?"

"No, no. The Action Network. And PBY. And everybody else."

"Okay."

"I guess I wasn't very clear last time. I'm hearing a lot of talk about aliens. As far as we know, there weren't any. Just the music."

"You couldn't locate the source?"

"Negative."

"But you said –? Well, whatever. Okay. We'll see you when you get here. You're going to have a lot of disappointed media people to deal with."

# # #

Mac turned in his column two hours later. He retreated to the third floor lounge so he could watch the *Indigo* dock. A dozen of his colleagues were there.

The interstellar was running a half hour behind. The concourse was now crowded with media. Bill Axler, the prime anchor for the Lodestar Network, was speaking with a short, balding man identified by a graphic as Gordon Klein, an expert on alien intelligence.

"So, Gordon," said Axler, "were you disappointed today when Chapman backed away from her original remarks? From claiming they'd made contact with aliens?"

"I'm not entirely sure what she said

about aliens, Bill. She indicated something had happened. Then she changed her story. But I'll confess I'd love to have a chance to talk with an alien that can produce that kind of music."

"Are you considering going out to the system where they were – come to think of it, I have no idea where they were – but are you maybe going to go there and have a look?"

"It's too early to say. I want to hear from them about what really happened. If there's a chance we could make contact, yes! I wouldn't hesitate."

They were still talking when Tom arrived. "It's good, Mac," he said. "But the day's coming when people with torches are going to show up in the lobby looking for you."

A compliment from Easton was gold. He was the most valuable editor available, a guy with exquisite taste who said what he really thought. He suggested a few adjustments. Mac made the fixes while Tom helped himself to a donut and coffee.

When he'd finished, his editor leaned in his direction and lowered his voice: "Mac, did you see your former girlfriend today?"

"I saw her."

"What did you think?"

"She was lying."

"Really?"

"Yes. I always knew when she wasn't quite telling the truth. Something happened out there."

"So what do you think? They found aliens and they were hostile?"

"I don't know. I'd expect if they came across something threatening to visitors, they'd make it public so we could warn everyone to stay away."

"Then what –?"

"I've no idea. I've got nothing that makes sense."

"I did some research on the flight," said Tom. "I guess you know there were three other people with her. They're terranologists. "

"Specialists in analyzing living condi-

tions on other worlds?"

"Right. One of them's Melinda Patton." He smiled.

"I did a story on her a few years ago." She was the daughter of Margo Patton, a prize-winning physicist at the University of Pennsylvania.

"Right. Maybe you can touch base with her and find out if anything actually happened."

\# \# \#

A loudspeaker at the Union concourse announced that the *Indigo* had arrived and was only minutes away from docking. Action News anchor Sidney Collins appeared onscreen. He was in a studio somewhere, but he showed his audience a window that looked out on the approaching interstellar. The alien music was playing in the background. "They'll be coming out gate five," he said. "We have a team in place to welcome them home."

There was considerably more than a team. But Union Security people were there, blocking the media from entering the tube. It took a few more minutes but finally they emerged, Angela and her three specialists. They waved at the reporters, delivered a few hellos, and hurried through the crowd, ignoring questions. Then they were gone.

And Sidney Collins was back. "We've contacted Bret Kilgore, a spokesman for the World Space Authority." Bret appeared on a screen to his left. He was smiling, suggesting everything was fine.

"Hello, Sidney," Kilgore said. "Everything okay?"

"As far as I can tell, Bret. But you'd know more about that than I do. What's happening?"

"Not much, really. We were sorry to see everyone got hyperventilated over the music. But I guess when something like that happens, we tend to get excited. Unfortunately, we have no details. Captain Chapman was unable to track the source and eventually they had no option but to

come home. She informed us that the music stopped after about sixteen hours and they were not able to track it further."

"I notice," Sidney said, "that she and her associates hurried through the crowd. I don't think they stopped to talk to anybody. Can you tell me why?"

"We regret that we have no information available. Please be aware that we directed the *Indigo* search team to look at the Beehive Cluster. It's reasonably close, a few hundred light- years. Beyond that, they were free to provide their own destinations. They were probably just tired. They've been out for several weeks and I suspect they just want to get home."

"Bret, can you tell us where they were when they heard the music?"

"Unfortunately, they were doing private research. Regulations prohibit us from releasing any of the data."

"So what was the surprise the captain referred to?"

Kilgore smiled. "I think she was just getting out ahead of herself. Probably thinking that we have all been surprised that the aliens, whoever they were, produced music that sounded so human."

They went to commercial. Tom chewed his upper lip. "Make sense to you, Mac?"

Mac frowned. "They're hiding something."

\# \# \#

Claxton Hotels was headquartered in New York. Mac called them and, when he identified himself, was immediately relegated to an AI, which spoke in a deep baritone and sounded as if it had better things to do than entertain the media. It thanked Mac for his interest in Claxton, explained he should call back later, and disconnected.

"Great." The wall behind Mac was decorated with an array of awards *The National* had received over the years. Tom was focused in that direction, but it was obvious his mind was elsewhere. "Maybe," he said, "it's time to get in touch with Angela."

Mac had considered it from the start, but it was not a call he wanted to make. Shortly after he'd lost her, she'd met and married a literature professor, Joseph Chapman. Chapman later morphed into a dynamic public relations consultant. "After all this time, I hate to intrude on her life."

"You wouldn't be intruding."

"It'll seem like it."

"Do you have her code?"

# # #

It wasn't a call he was going to make from a public venue. He returned to his office, stalled for a while, telling himself that Angela was probably not even on the shuttle yet for the return flight to whichever terrestrial port she was headed to. And she'd be crowded with calls from the media. He wasn't the only one who understood something was going on. Which meant of course that nobody would be getting through. And if Angela was lying to the world, it wasn't likely she'd be honest with **him**.

Priscilla Hutchins offered a better possibility. Hutch was a pretty big deal in the interstellar system. If anybody knew anything, she probably would. She'd been a friend for years. He'd been on a couple of flights with her, including a hunt for what they thought were invading aliens. And he had nothing to lose by trying.

He told his link to make the call.

And he got an automated response: "I am sorry to inform you that Ms. Hutchins is on vacation and not available."

# # #

In the morning, *First Light* brought in two guests, a pilot, and a researcher who'd spent the better part of the last fifteen years collecting alien artifacts. Mac had never heard of either. Taylor talked about the apparent contradiction in Captain Chapman's responses and asked what they thought. Had the *Indigo* seen something so strange they didn't want to talk about it?

Or were they simply misreading Captain Chapman's comment about a surprise? "I can't see that it's any big deal," said the pilot. "She was probably talking about the music."

The artifact collector agreed. "I can't imagine what they could have seen that was so threatening they're trying to keep it quiet. I mean, if there's really something that dangerous there, don't we want to warn everyone to stay away from the area?"

They replayed the clip with Angela talking to George, telling him they hadn't found any aliens, only the music.

It was still clear to Mac that she was lying.

First Light signed off each morning at eight. He waited until nine and tried to call her. He got only a conciliatory female voice: "I'm sorry, but Angela Chapman is not available." He checked the schedule to see which flight she'd be on. The Chapmans lived outside Philadelphia. Which meant she'd be coming in at the DC Spaceport. A shuttle was scheduled to arrive at four o'clock.

He didn't want to be part of one of the media crowds trying to get to her. He ran a search on the backgrounds of the three terranologists. One specialized in biological studies and the second in climate. The third was Melinda Patton. Mac had interviewed her mother the night she'd taken home the Conciliar Award. He called each of them and got exactly the result he expected: "The person you are trying to reach is not available. You may leave a contact number if you wish."

# # #

That evening Mac wrote a column accusing the WSA of hiding something. "What did the *Indigo* see out there? Whatever the truth is, the public has a right to know. Moreover there's no conceivable reality that justifies secrecy. If there's a threat, don't hide it."

It was one of the easiest pieces he'd ever put together. First step would be to de-liver it to the WSA to see if they'd respond by offering an explanation. And it might be a good idea to send a copy to Angela. But let's give it some time.

In the morning, he was in the middle of breakfast when his link sounded. "Priscilla Hutchins, Mac."

Her image appeared onscreen. Smiling, amiable features that never seemed to age. Dark eyes, black hair cut short. "Hi, Mac," she said. "It's good to see you again. Been a while."

"Next time you're in the area," he said, "let's do lunch."

"Absolutely. What can I do for you?"

"You can probably guess."

The smile faded a bit. "I got nothing, Mac."

"Seriously?"

"You ever know me to joke?"

"Were you really on vacation?"

"In Georgia. Spent the last two weeks on the beach in the Golden Isles."

"You know what's been going on?"

"Of course. But I have no idea what it's about."

"Do outgoing missions report their destinations?"

"To CommOps? Yes."

"Can I get access?"

"No. It's private information. Mac, whatever's going on, they have a reason for what they're doing. I suggest you let it be."

"Hutch, I'd like to find out what really happened out there. What did they see?"

"Probably nothing."

"They heard music. And Angela Chapman said something about a surprise."

"She probably got carried away, Mac. Let it go."

"Aren't you curious?"

Long hesitation. "No. I've been down this road before. Sometimes it's something personal. Maybe they were drinking."

"Hutch, I knew Angela Chapman at one time. Years ago, but I knew her pretty well. She was not telling the truth."

"And that's all you have?"

"Other than a tangled explanation? I

was hoping you could give me something more."

There was a chair to Priscilla's left. She eased into it. "I just don't have anything. Best for you is just back off."

"If they found dangerous aliens, wouldn't it be a good idea to let us know about them so we can stay away from the area?"

"That sounds reasonable. Look, I just don't know what it's about, so I really can't help you, Mac. I'm sorry."

"Can you think of any way I can get some information?"

"Go to WSA Headquarters and ask the director."

"Is there a way I could get onboard the *Indigo*? So I could talk to the AI? Maybe put together an ID and try to pass myself off as a tech?"

"That would never work, Mac. You'd wind up in jail. You said you knew Angela at one time. Have you asked **her**?"

"I haven't been able to get through to her."

"Well, give it up, handsome." "I can't do that. There has to be a way to get on board."

"Okay, I can think of one possibility: The music makes the ship an object of interest. The WSA likes to get positive attention. You might try organizing a photographic visit. Get lots of pictures to publish in your magazine. Tell them you want to write an article about the depth of the experience passengers get on interstellars. I can probably set something like that up for you."

"That sounds workable. But there's a downside."

"And that is?"

"You're connected to it. What happens to your career after I publish?"

"I'm hoping that when we find out what's going on, you'll agree we shouldn't let it get out. So you **won't** publish."

"And if I do?"

She hesitated. "I'm willing to take my chances."

They stared at each other for a long

moment. "I can't do this," said Mac. "I'll find another way to get on board."

She looked relieved. "Okay."

# # #

Tom's normal easy-going manner intensified the following day. He knew something was wrong, and he was aware it had to do with the *Indigo*. But he didn't bring the subject up, asking only whether Mac had a new column ready to go.

Mac had read and laughed his way through *Downhill All the Way,* a new release by the Rev. Billy Collier, increasingly defined as America's Pastor. Collier described in detail how God unleashes tornadoes, hurricanes, and wildfires against communities that will not take a stand against hunting and cutting down trees. "First it was the atmosphere," he writes, "and now it is life itself that we attack." He also had a problem with people who didn't actively support the official doctrines. Mac had written a review, pretending to endorse a policy in which we all stay home, well away from the natural world.

"Got something for you," Mac said. He forwarded it. Tom heard the link signal, smiled, sat down, and began to read it. Outside, rain was beginning to fall and wind was picking up.

Tom chuckled. "You really want to imply Collier's readers are idiots?"

"You think we'll offend any of **our** readers?"

Tom rolled his eyes. "Okay, we'll go with it." He got out of his chair and looked down at MacAllister. "You all right?"

"Sure. I'm good."

Tom was only minutes out the door when a call came in from Hutch. "Got some news. It wouldn't have done us any good even if we'd been able to get onboard the *Indigo*." She was standing in front of a window. It was raining there too.

"They removed the AI?"

"Correct. It's under seal at WSA Headquarters."

"What the hell are they so worried

about?"

"I don't know. I have to admit they've got my interest."

"Okay. Thanks, Hutch. I'll let you know if I hear anything."

"I might be able to help. Do you know where Albright's is?"

"I've no idea."

"It's in Dundalk. You know where **that** is, right?"

"Sure."

"Good. Albright's Grill looks out over Anchor Bay."

"Okay."

"I've arranged a meeting for you tomorrow at two. WSA will have somebody there to talk with you."

"Really? Why?"

"I think they don't want you stirring the pot. Can you be there?"

"Of course. Who will I be looking for?"

"Just be there. She'll know you. Wear your Orioles baseball cap."

# # #

Mac owned two baseball caps, which he routinely wore to protect his eyes from the sun. One was from the Lowell Observatory; the other was an Orioles retro, featuring the grinning bird of a lost era. (The current emblem resembled an angry hawk.) He wore it on the ride down to Dundalk, which he spent sitting in the back seat where he could work on a piece describing the advantages to be derived from increasing the population in a world that, he joked, needed more people to keep industry running. It was a common argument used by corporate heads.

Albright's Grill looked out across the broad Patapsco River. It was just after two o'clock when his car pulled into the parking lot. Mac got out, glanced around and saw a couple of families retreating to their cars. He climbed three concrete steps. An electronic ad advised him of the day's special, a chicken and shrimp combo. One of the two glass doors opened and he went inside.

No one caught his attention. And no one was waiting. Two women followed a bot toward a booth at one of the windows. Other bots were clearing tables. Two more groups were getting up and leaving. Lunch hour was over.

A bot approached. "May I help you, sir?"

An empty table waited just a few feet away. "That would be good," he said.

"Excellent. Will there be anyone else?" The bot pulled out a chair for him and activated the menu.

"Yes, I think so." Mac replaced the chair and selected one that provided a view of the front door. Normally, he would have removed the baseball cap, but he left it in place. The menu provided a wide variety of choices. Fish and chips looked good.

"You may order at your leisure, sir," said the menu.

It was seven minutes after two. Not a good sign.

He was back looking at the menu again when Angela Chapman walked in the door. She looked left onto the far side of the restaurant and then her eyes settled on him. She lit up. "Greg," she said. It was the name he'd used during those early days. "It's good to see you again." She came forward and extended a hand. "How are you?"

He took off his cap and got out of his chair but needed a moment to be certain his voice was under control. "Angela, I wasn't expecting to see you." He shook her hand, leaned forward and kissed her cheek. "This is something of a surprise."

They sat down, facing each other. "Hutch got a call this morning," she said. "Somebody at WSA warned her that they'd found out about the meeting and blocked it." She smiled. "I guess they don't want you talking with anyone of any significance."

She was as beautiful as ever. "So Hutch asked **you** to come?"

"Yes."

"How'd she manage it? I tried to call a couple of times but –"

"I know. Hutch and I have been around a while. We have contacts. Though the truth is she had to come out to my place. Showed up at my front door this morning." She glanced at the menu. "We should order."

She opted for a chicken fingers salad. Then she looked back at him. "Greg, I know what this is about. I'm afraid I won't be able to help you."

"Then why are you here?" Mac felt a sudden surge of frustration.

"It's good to see you again. I couldn't resist the opportunity to say hello. You've been having a pretty good career."

"It's been okay."

"I've read a lot of your work. And a couple of the books."

"Did you really?"

"Oh, yes. You have a way with words."

"I hope you enjoyed them."

"Of course I did. Got a lot of laughs. I never really thought of you as a funny guy." She sat quietly for a moment. "You never married?"

"No. Beautiful women don't take me very seriously. How's life with Joe?"

"I don't get to see enough of him. Too much time out in the gaps."

"How'd you come to be a pilot?"

"I was about five when they made the FTL breakthrough and I found out I could go to the stars. No way I was going to pass on that."

"I guess I never really knew you very well, did I?"

"I'm not sure we ever really get to know anybody, Greg."

"You're probably right. Any chance you'll tell me what you saw out there?"

"I'd love to." Her expression hardened.

"But you can't."

She nodded.

They studied each other. "Well, Angie, at least you're telling the truth now." He knew he shouldn't say it, but he was annoyed. And it was an emotion he'd never been good at concealing. It was, he'd always suspected, the reason he'd lost her. Even now, so many years later, her lustrous hazel eyes were still electric.

"I wish I could help, Greg."

"My friends call me **Mac**. Why can't you tell me?"

"It's complicated."

"Then why did Hutch even bother asking you to come?"

"She didn't have anyone else to fall back on."

"Does **she** know what this is all about? What happened out there?"

"No."

"She didn't ask you what you were hiding?"

She needed a moment. Then: "She did, Greg."

He didn't bring the name issue up again. "And what did you say?"

"I guess the same thing I said on TV."

Mac stared at her. "Should we give it up?"

"No. I'm not just going to let you walk away from me again."

"I thought you were the one who walked off."

"Let's let it go," she said. "The food here looks good."

"My treat."

That brought a smile. "You're trying to buy me."

"Can you answer a question for me?"

"Maybe."

"Does it have something to do with hostile aliens?"

The smile widened. "No."

"If it's not hostile aliens, what else can it be? What are you afraid of? Apparently it's not so serious that you didn't realize right away that you should keep it quiet."

"There's some truth to that."

"So what happened? After your initial comments on TV, the WSA contacted you and told you to change your story?"

"Yes."

"So you didn't think it was all that serious?"

"I didn't. Not at first. That was because I was dumb. I should have realized immediately –"

He waited for her to finish. But she was done. "How about your colleagues?

They didn't see a problem either until someone pointed it out to them?"

"That's correct. We could have avoided all this if we'd used our heads."

Mac cleared his throat. "I can't imagine what we're talking about. Did you discover God out there, or something?"

"Not God."

"Okay. I assume Hutch knows you won't tell me what it's about?"

"Probably."

"Then what was the point of sending you here? Why didn't she just call me and cancel?"

"That's a good question, Greg. I suspect she realizes there's a lot at stake. Hutch knows we'll all be better off if this just goes away. And she's hoping maybe you'll take my word for it and back off."

"What's at stake?"

"I can't explain."

Eventually their food arrived. A bot set the plates down, delivered iced tea to Angie and coffee for Mac. It said it hoped they were having a good day.

"I don't think we are," said Mac.

"I'm sorry," said Angie.

"It's okay. I'm happy to see you again. I'll settle for that."

"That's not exactly what matters here."

Mac dug into his fish and chips. "If I could think of any reasonable explanation for this, I could live with it."

Angela helped herself to one of the chicken fingers. There was something in the way she chewed it that increased Mac's heartbeat.

"Okay," she said. "Greg, if you give me your word to say nothing, to keep it to yourself, I'll tell you."

"I can't do that."

"Then I'm sorry. There's nothing more I can do."

They sat staring at each other. Mac sighed. "Look. How about if I promise to say nothing until I get the information from another source?"

"That's not good enough."

Mac went back to staring. But he got nowhere. "All right," he said. "I won't tell anyone."

"Word of honor?"

Mac desperately wanted to know what was going on. "Yes."

Angela took a deep breath. "The music was coming from a space station. It was orbiting a sterile world. There were no lights. But it had an AI. We established contact with it. Kayla needed some time to communicate with it."

"Kayla was **your** AI?"

"Yes." She paused and bit off another piece of chicken. "The place was a **library**. No, more than that: it was an arm of an **interstellar** library. They're apparently in a number of places across the Milky Way. Put there by a group of interstellar civilizations. A **big** group. I got the impression there were hundreds of them. We were invited to join. If we did, we'd have access to everything they've learned. How the universe began. The true nature of time. How many dimensions there are. Why quantum entanglement happens. The source of dark energy. We could get the answers to all that and everything else." She sipped her iced tea.

"And we're keeping this quiet, why?"

"You know who Melinda Patton is?"

"She was one of the specialists traveling with you. She's the daughter of Margo Patton."

"She told her mom about it shortly after we arrived home. Her mother was horrified. She almost had a heart attack."

"Why?"

"Because, Greg, it would mean the end of science."

"So we'd lose science as a career?"

"Considerably more than that. The pursuit of knowledge has been at the heart of everything that's driven us to where we are. There's too much on the plate out there. All we'd have to do is look up the answers."

"It shouldn't be that big a deal, Angie. Apparently those other civilizations have gotten past a need for science. Presumably they're doing okay. How long has the library system been active? Do you know?"

"We had a problem figuring out how they tell time. The AI kept saying it had been a quarter of a rotation. Kayla estimated the planet they were orbiting would need about a year and a half, so we decided it meant four to five months."

"That's a pretty short time."

"Then Melinda figured out the AI was talking about a **galactic** rotation."

"Well, even that doesn't sound all that much. How long does the galaxy need to complete a rotation?"

"Approximately two hundred thirty million years."

"Oh." Mac caught his breath. "So the library **has** been around a while. Sixty million years."

"Maybe when we've been here a few million years or so we won't care about the end of science either. But right now we do. Melinda's mom wasted no time contacting the WSA. And they're in full agreement." She put her fork down and pushed back from the table. "Look, I'm not a physicist, and there's a lot more than physics involved. How did life start? We're not even sure why we need to sleep. Is random selection the only force that drives evolution? Join the library group and we get all the answers." She looked at him as if maybe he wasn't smart enough to understand. "Think about it. What happens to your line of work if the only stories are about corruption and accidents? No more surprises, Greg."

He'd stopped eating. "They'll never be able to keep this secret. Too many people know."

"You're right. But I'm doing what I can. And I expect you to keep your word."

He nodded. "I will."

"Thank you."

"Does your husband know?"

"He knows there's an issue, but he hasn't pressed me on it."

"I'm glad to hear it."

"By the way, Mac, he'd like to meet you. Can we have you over for dinner next week?"

PULP Literature

FANTASTIC FRESH FICTION

www.pulpliterature.com

By SALLY
MCBRIDE

Sally McBride's short stories and novellas have appeared in such magazines as Asimov's, Fantasy & Science Fiction, Realms of Fantasy, Northern Frights, Tesseracts, On Spec, *and many anthologies. "The Fragrance of Orchids" (*Asimov's*) won Canada's Aurora Award and received Hugo and Nebula nominations. She has taught fiction writing and edited speculative fiction. Her novels* Indigo Time *(Five Rivers Publishing) and* Water, Circle, Moon *(Masque Books) are available from the publishers, Amazon and other venues. Born and raised in Canada, Sally lives in Idaho with her husband.*

The air inside the airlock actually smells terrific, at first, like the fragrance counter at a fancy department store, but it's only the chemicals, which our work contracts firmly insist don't hurt us. Plus we have good insurance. Every morning I breathe it in, then my nose forgets it once I'm at about minute seven of the ten minute process. The nasal passages have had it for another day.

The valve opened onto a vast space full of noise and movement, trailing with printed vines to make it look nice. Sun filtered in through the thick plastic roof. The warm, moist atmosphere would be primate if I could smell it. I trundled my cart along, saying good morning to the girls, each in her own cage. We're supposed to call them chambers, and they're pretty spacious, but what the hell. Today's special treat: watermelon. They all love watermelon. In go the big juicy chunks, gentle black fingers reaching, teeth shining in fierce happy grins.

I have something special in store for my favorite old girl, whose name is Zamuka. When Zamuka was co-opted for Surro-Surround, she'd been over-socialized with humans. She'd been captured in the wild, then became the special pet of a research assistant at a lab in Guam, a young woman who'd taught Zamuka sign language; the young woman had been killed by her husband, who then killed their deformed baby and himself. A surprising amount of that kind of thing went on, back then, but the upshot was that Zamuka was left adrift. Confused, sad, angry, unable to communicate in the way she'd come to rely on. Basically, she lost her best friend. Then she got

shipped here and had to endure the grueling process of medical prep for her job. Nothing she'd asked for.

I came in early to Surro-Surround too, for lack of anything better going on. After my second abortion and a miscarriage, I had my tubes tied, to hell with it, even though I was only twenty-six. Despite the gloomy forecasts, perhaps I should have clung to hope. A lot of people were trying the hope gambit. Others, more pragmatic or more wealthy, were availing themselves of the service offered here.

Had Carver stuck around, and we'd had the money, I might be on the other side of the airlock right now. Last I heard, Carver was still at the survivalist enclave he'd joined in '39, somewhere near Sandpoint, Idaho. They aren't big into communication up there.

So when Zamuka and I met, we were both pretty shell-shocked. Took a while for us to gain a decent level of trust. But life goes on. We had jobs to do, and we became first immune to each others' pain, then later friends, especially after she realized that I was trying to sign to her. Have you ever seen a great ape laugh? It's hard not to join in. Anyhow, I've gotten better at signing over the years.

<<Good morning Zam-zam!">> When I call her Zam-zam she pretends to get mad at me. She turned her back, but after a few seconds she cast a coy little glance over her shoulder, saw me waving and smiling, and turned to waddle slowly up to the gate. She's had time to recover from the birth, still a little bleary but looks okay. She gave me a smile, a fearsome thing when worn by

a fifty-one year old gorilla, who outweighs me by at least seventy pounds.

Zamuka, who was among the first few dozen co-opted gorillas, was standard model. Younger apes have been engineered for faster functioning. They are naïve and rather silly compared to Zamuka, as they've had no outside experience. Some of them can sign a bit, but I know Zamuka holds them in disdain.

She signed: <<Zamuka. No Zamzam.>>

<<Yes, Zamuka.>> I talked and signed at the same time, because I think she likes to chat. Well, so do I. <<Erika loves you. You mom-mom now. Zamuka okay?>>

She nodded. <<Baby doll? Erika give baby doll?>>

She knows. She always knows. Her own blood has been nourishing the fetus for all these months. She's flooded with hormones, broadcasting an ache to where a baby should be. I knew that emptiness, and if getting a stupid doll helps, then so be it. I opened the gate to her cage and pushed the cart through. She's pooped in her usual corner, and also had fun demolishing a cardboard box overnight and fashioning the shreds into a nest.

<<Yes, baby doll.>> The highlight of her restricted life, better than watermelon.

She hooted softly, slapping the concrete floor with her big black hands, causing the scattered shreds of hay to flutter up and down.

I say, <<Surprise. Special baby doll for mom-mom.>>

Zamuka sat back on her ample haunches, empty belly sagging. She's too excited right now to sign, and watched me as I opened the cart's hatch and reached in.

And produced a completely adorable doll.

The hooting stopped. She froze. This was unusual. Zamuka can be counted on, every time, to eagerly reach for her doll and clasp it to her hairy breast, but not today. I waggled it enticingly, and watched her face.

I can read her moods pretty well. She's remarkably expressive and sophisticated

once you get to know her. Right now, she has the look of an upper-class matron presented with a silver platter of dog turds. She is outraged. She is disgusted. She turned her back and shuffled to the farthest corner of her enclosure, crossed her arms and began to sulk. I could practically feel the rays of righteous indignation shooting from her whole body.

What did I do wrong? The doll was not so very different from the array of dolls Zamuka had earned over her years of service. Cute face, soft body, big eyes. I walked slowly toward her, murmuring apologies. <<Baby doll no good?>>

She ignored me steadfastly. Yeah, I get it.

Each time she gives birth, she is presented with a baby doll, dressed in cute little doll-garments, usually with soft blonde or brown hair.

I'd managed to find her a gorilla doll, dark brown and fuzzy. Though it had no cute outfit, it had big glistening eyes and little black hands. I'd been full of satisfaction at locating it online, and I'd thought she would take to it immediately. My bright idea.

<<What wrong? Baby!>> Could there be so much difference, to an ape?

Suddenly she reached out a long black arm and slapped the doll out of my hand. Warily, I held my arms out for a hug. Zamuka's a hugger. But she turned away, grabbed her sturdy canvas hammock, ripped it out of its metal hooks and threw it at me. At this point I should exit her enclosure and report her behavior to my bosses. What if she turns her anger on me? But she's been terribly disappointed, and she's hurting. I can't leave now.

After a minute of listening to me croon apologies, she cradled the very first doll she got to her chest and began to rock back and forth. It's barely recognizable as a blue-eyed blonde infant, lips pursed as if for a kiss or a bottle.

<<This me,>> she signed. <<Me doll.>>

It's the one Carver and I bought for our baby when we first learned we were preg-

nant with a girl. Stupid. Didn't we know the rest of the world's troubles applied to us too?

I'd had to get that doll out of my house. Unwilling to toss it in the garbage, I gave it to Zamuka. Carver left shortly thereafter.

Someone higher up than me realized after a few days that the gorilla had transferred her maternal instinct onto the lifeless doll. She held it, gazed at it, sniffed it, perhaps trying to get it to wake up or move. But she'd perked up and was eating. We started handing out dolls to every post-partum animal, since it was a cheap and easy way to get them back online faster. So they could bear another human baby sooner.

<<Erika sorry. Baby no good.>>

She doesn't think of herself as a gorilla. She thinks she's like me, human. Of course she doesn't appreciate a gorilla infant. But what if, instead of a doll, I had presented her with an actual baby, of her very own?

Though she doesn't know it, she bore a child of her own kind less than eight hours ago. If she could understand, would she be less horrified? Or would she reject it, shun it? She's never ever been allowed to see or touch any of the babies she's birthed. Her gorilla child was already in prep for her new job, which would start as soon as possible. Zamuka's daughter was destined for a life in a cage bearing human children.

# # #

I have thirty-four other animals to tend in my section. I'm on the clock and need to keep moving, but I can't just whip in and out without a little face time. My youngest, Boda, is brand new at eighteen months, and is already seven months pregnant. Boda preens and grimaces as I stroke her hairy arms and praise her big belly. She gets a bunch of grapes that I've liberated from the chimps' allotment, and she begins immediately to pluck them one by one, lips smacking. The others nearby can see her, part of what makes her grapes so succulent. Call me a troublemaker, but what's life in an endless maternity ward without a little drama?

Here in Surro-Surround we have a total of one thousand, nine hundred eighty-eight great apes. Gorillas mostly, engineered for early maturity and quick turnaround of their cycles, and three hundred fifty chimps who have been designed bigger and looser around the hips than normal, to accommodate human births. We once had orangutans but they couldn't seem to take it emotionally. We need more birth-surrogates, as it's the rare human woman who will submit to – or can afford – the months of preparation, and more months isolated in a sterile building while the money bleeds away, to have a baby who won't have the kind of birth defects that afflict us now.

#

I was off shift, changing into my street clothes and looking forward to heading home, when I got a message to go to the fifth floor of the admin building and check in with Dr. Surmi for a brief consultation. I acknowledged and signed off. I had expected this – I get called in for reprimands three or four times a year – so merely shrugged my shoulders at my shift-mates and headed across campus. My nostrils, battered into submission during my working day, opened up to the spring freshness of the green, rolling acres of land outside the city of Hillsborough, North Carolina. I sneezed a couple of times, and blew my nose messily.

In his blessedly air conditioned office, Dr. Ari Surmi invited me to sit down. I did so – my feet and back were tired – and assumed the alert, open expression one assumes when across a desk from a boss. I did wish my hair wasn't so frizzy, and that my street clothes were something other than baggy jeans and a "Save the Grizzlies" t-shirt.

"Erika, what happened with Zamuka today? Any idea?"

I had lots of ideas, but I wasn't paid to have them. "She reacted negatively to the doll I presented to her." I spread my hands. "Perhaps its smell, its color…"

"Hm. You didn't hint to her – unconsciously of course – that there might be a significance to that particular doll?"

"Uh, not sure how I could do that. I don't think I have the capability to influence how a gorilla thinks." My stomach clenched. Wasn't there **supposed** to be significance? More like a cruel joke. Why had I thought it was a good idea?

He nodded and took up a stylus, began to tap it gently on the edge of his desk. "It's my opinion that, whether you realize it or not, Erika, you can indeed influence her."

I did not like the tone of his voice. He was patronizing me. Zamuka and I are about the same age. I'm fifty-four, and any eggs I might have tucked in my ovaries are long obsolete. Even if I were a girl of twenty again, I'd never be able to afford the service provided here. He knows that, everybody knows that.

My heart was beating fast. "And she can influence me." I regretted saying that as soon as the words were out of my mouth. I was being quietly snotty, I admit. But Dr. Surmi didn't seem to notice; in fact he began to nod, his head bobbing up and down as if I were a clever student.

He was running on his own track. I was just an audience for whatever he was really thinking about and wanted to share. I waited, willing my heart to slow.

Surmi – smooth, plump, cherished by his extended family, who were proud of what he did for a living – glanced my way for just a second. Yes, I was being properly attentive. Pictures of his two healthy, normal children adorned his desk, facing out.

"This isn't common knowledge yet, Erika – and you understand that what I say goes no further than this room – but we are about to be put out of business."

My first thought was: *There goes my job.* Then I thought some more. A cure? Could there be a cure for TierouxXL?

A small error in a lab in Sao Paulo, a lab that had been making real progress toward a vaccine against the regular, garden variety Tieroux virus that had become endemic at almost all latitudes concurrent with the melting of Arctic permafrost. An error that went unreported and unchecked, then spread and mutated as other labs received samples to work on. No one quite understood, all those years ago, that the ferocious disease was stronger and smarter than we were. There were so many strains of it now that to the public they were all categorized as XL. Each did something different to a human fetus. Some babies, if born alive and managed to keep on living, could be trained to work in places like this. Two of them worked alongside me, and loved the morning donuts as much as I did.

I cleared my throat. "There's progress? On…a broad spectrum vaccine?"

He smiled, his cheeks puffing out. But his eyes looked tired. "Yes. A team in Venezuela, led by a woman from the University of Guelph – that's in Canada – has been running tests for the last four years on a volunteer population of Mormons. The women and their husbands got the okay from the Church to submit to carrying out their pregnancies in an open environment about a hundred kilometers inland from Caracas. There have been thirty-five normal births in the last three years, and all the babies are fine. They're fine." His dark and shapely eyebrows formed a reverent arch upon his forehead.

"Open…to the air? To the…" The real world. Where parents used to expect a baby with limbs. An intestinal tract. A head. "Does it work for every XL? Are there other studies happening?"

Dr. Surmi spread his hands. "Yes and yes. So far, so good, eh? Nothing's going to change here for a while, so don't worry about your job just yet." He paused. "We are initiating some cost savings, however."

"Uh…like what?" But my gut clenched as it all came together.

This baby was Zamuka's last. She had been deemed unproductive. She'd just given birth to her replacement, designed and bred to be virtually a different species than her mother. A slave for making new humans.

Surmi saw the look on my face; he had

taken enough of my sass over the years to hold up a hand and shut me up. "Erika! It has to be done. Sit down! New orders are slowing, and, God willing, we really will be out of business in a few years. Zamuka is the oldest, she's the first to be…to be retired."

"But she could easily live another twenty years! You can't just – just –" *Retired.* Yeah, right. The oldsters were going to be euthanized, one after another as soon as their modern offspring appeared. I had to pause to think for a second, and to catch my breath. The engineered baby-makers working here knew nothing of real life. Real babies. "D-do you know if Zamuka ever had offspring before she came here?" My heart was pounding hard, making my mouth trip up.

He relaxed a little. Probably glad I hadn't started throwing things. "Okay. Good question." He popped up a file and began to scroll down and then across. "Well, yes she did. One male offspring, which she had at age eight, weaned at…ah, looks like twenty months. He was transferred to a different research facility."

Though it had been decades ago, she knew how to raise a child. I'd seen videos of wild gorillas holding their young. They loved to examine them, cuddle them, assist them to find the long black nipple and latch on.

I have spent years squashing my maternal instinct. But Zamuka had it built right into her muscles and her hide and her heart. Unsquashable.

#

That evening, I went online at the community library. By Monday I'd produced a pretty nice looking little proposal, if I do say so myself. Video, blossom points, sensa-links, about a million attachments, everything I could think of to catch the eye of whoever it was that made decisions around here. Starting with my pal Doctor Surmi.

He did me the courtesy of running his eyes over my carefully crafted presenta-tion. Then he shut it down and rubbed his temples. I couldn't tell if his expression was soulful or annoyed.

Finally he said, "Erika, you have put a lot of effort into this, but I have to tell you it's not going to go anywhere."

"But –"

He held up a hand. "Look. Pasturing out our older surrogates is a nice idea. But it's unviable. Erika, you can't really believe it would lead to a re-wilding of the population."

"Yes, I **do** believe it. Why not?" *Don't get shrill.* "If you'll look at the, the stuff at the back –" Damn it, where was my brain? "A-appendices –"

"Yes, yes. Admirable. But –"

"Wait – you don't understand the real importance." What had I expected? Did I think an advanced degree in genetics had just popped into my résumé? Which included community college, waitressing, and working here. "There are only a handful of great apes left in the world that have any experience at being apes. At, at nurturing and teaching their own kind. Zamuka has done it! She's worked hard here, made money for the company. She deserves to be a real mother to a **normal** gorilla baby. She **deserves** it." My cheeks were burning, but I wasn't going to retreat.

Neither was Surmi. He leaned forward. "Where do you think the money, and the land, the rehabilitation, the…the veterinary care – everything – will come from?" He waved a hand in the air.

Was he asking me? "I have lots of ideas, it, it's all in the attachments –"

"You've studied the annual reports. Did you not see that the retired apes are to be evaluated for sustainability in an alternate environment?"

"Do you mean they'll be sent back to **zoos**? Research labs? Or do you mean they'll be – be shipped back to **Africa**?"

"Of course they won't be shipped back to Africa." He was obviously holding onto his patience with both hands. "How on earth could they survive? You know what it's like over there these days."

"But –"

"Erika! Please! You are a valued employee, but you are not a scientist. You'll just have to trust that the best outcome will be sought, for **all** the apes." His voice was gentle, but his eyes were cold.

The apes would be **evaluated**. The best outcome would be **sought**.

"Okay. I see." I would not cry. I would retain what dignity I possessed and get out. I'd lost this round, but already my brain was rummaging around for other ideas.

#

A week went by. Zamuka was still on campus, but had been moved out of the ultra-sterile quarters the working apes inhabited and into a temporary holding cage in an outbuilding. Her baby, named Zamira, was already in the intensive drug and hormone treatment phase of her career – which might be cut short despite her up-to-date qualifications.

The vaccine still had to pass more tests, but word of its efficacy had leaked out.

It was only a matter of time before Surmi stopped pretending to find her a home and Zamuka was euthanized.

#

Gloria Ikayaa Green was wary on the phone. There was a question-and-verification period before she trusted that I was who I said I was and released her image. She was African American, quite beautiful, her hair shorn close, with a sculptured oval face and large hazel eyes. Only the very wealthy could afford surrogacy thirty years ago, and they designed their precious offspring carefully.

Some people hide their provenance, others don't mind at all admitting they were carried to term by a two hundred pound gorilla. After my failure with Doctor Surmi, I had changed tactics, set my jaw, and searched for links to chat rooms, support groups, photos. Took a while, but I found a Surro-Surround link that let me join a group that was trying to organize a commemorative "birthday" event in Branson, Missouri. It's remarkable how forthcoming folks can be, when contacted by a middle-aged lady who wants to help with administrative details.

I got hold of a list of the children born at Surro-Surround between 2023 and 2033, something my work clearance wouldn't let me get. I actually rubbed my hands together when I realized the surrogacy code for each baby matched the serial number assigned to the ape who bore him or her.

Zamuka's very first human baby was Gloria Ikayaa Green, now thirty-one years-old, living alone in a floating condo off old Fort Lauderdale.

"Sorry," she said, smiling politely, "I really don't have time to attend the event. But thanks for contacting me."

In the background I glimpsed her spacious, beautifully decorated, and probably lonely, dwelling. TierouxXL has done a very good job of reducing the Earth's population. Or at least shifting a lot of it into long-term care.

Those lucky folks who belong to the exclusive club she's in – young and disease-free – have formed their own sub-culture. Her surname, Green, links her to several other floating towns and enclaves around the world. The Blues prefer mountain lodges half-sunk in granite. Reds mostly live in New Zealand, in gated communities. And so on.

I myself am perfectly happy in my third-floor apartment with a view of the city, thank you very much. It's very quiet. No kids.

"Oh, I understand," I chirped. "People are busy! If you reconsider, please let us know. Uh, while I have you on the phone, may I ask a couple of follow-up questions?"

"Well...sure."

"Have you ever wondered about your mother?"

Gloria's brows drew together. "I don't have to. She lives with her new partner in Malaysia Green. We see each other quite a lot."

"No. I mean the...female who carried you to term, not your genetic parent."

Her mouth thinned. "I know all about it. I'm sure it was a difficult decision for my parents to make. What do you want me to say?"

"Well, I, I wondered if you would like to meet her. That is..."

"**Meet** her?" She looked up again, eyes blazing. "I **know** where I came from! I don't need some busybody – sorry – reminding me! Okay?" She shook her head as if at a bad smell. "I was borne by an animal. An animal who was co-opted into a program it can't understand, for the benefit of humans. Like me." She spread her hands as if to encompass her pale, empty home with its vast ocean view. "Don't you think I feel guilty enough without people like you rubbing my nose in it?"

This wasn't the reaction I'd expected. "I...I just, just wanted –"

"No. Whatever it is you want – money, an endorsement – just, no. What's done is done."

She was going to cut me off in a second. "I'm sorry. But...her name is Zamuka. We talk all the time. She remembers you."

"How could she possibly – No! Goodbye. Don't call again."

"She's being retired. She's going to be –"

Her image vanished. And that was that.

A complaint was registered with the commemorative event people. My connection to the links was severed, and I received a terse notice informing me that my volunteer services were no longer required.

I confess I spent the remainder of my evening crying and drinking wine. Didn't help.

# # #

I was all out of ideas. My feverish midnight plans to smuggle her into my apartment evaporated in the light of day. So I went to work, quite aware that at any time the world might go back to normal

and my time here would be over. Zamuka would never have any more babies, human or gorilla. She'd be euthanized. At the end of each day I visited her. She repeatedly informed me that she was not happy with the way things were.

<<Where everyone?>>

<<Working. You fun now! Rest and sleep.>>

She wasn't buying it. <<Watermelon now! Where everyone?>>

The first thing I'd done when she was moved out of the maternity barn was retrieve her dolls from the refuse area, before they could be incinerated. I hauled them all over to her new, cramped abode and stuffed them one by one through the bars.

My throat closed up as I watched the old girl gather her baby dolls up in her arms. She couldn't manage them all at once, but eventually got them settled together in a nest she'd made of hay and a faded old blanket. She began to pick them up one by one, from oldest to youngest, and sniff them, though she still ignored the gorilla doll. She was probably hoping the dolls would show signs of life at last. Or maybe I was just projecting my feelings onto her.

# # #

A week went by. Zamuka was becoming cranky, and I was burdened on my rounds by a lump of futility in my chest, heavy as a cold. Each day I expected her to be gone when I got to her cage. Then Doctor Surmi called me into his office again. This was it. I was getting the axe. But instead I got a surprise.

Gloria Ikayaa Green sat in one of the two chairs before Surmi's desk. That is, she perched, stick straight, on the forward edge of the chair, turning her head only slightly to look at me as I entered. She looked elegant and very young, wearing a pale green sundress, and a white sweater that she had buttoned up to her neck.

"Ms. Green, this is Erika Tucker. Erika, apparently you and Ms Green have been in contact." Surmi's voice was clipped, brusque.

I plunked myself down without comment. I sported grubby overalls, my hair in a ponytail. Sweat dried on my face.

Hoo boy, I thought. Here it comes.

Ms Green kept her head high. She didn't smile. "I want to apologize for my overreaction when you contacted me, Ms. Tucker."

Huh. "Well. I guess I shouldn't have been so, so…"

"Forward? Presumptuous?"

I shrugged ungraciously. She'd told Surmi what I'd done. He shifted in his chair and opened his mouth, but Gloria held up a hand. "Let me say my piece, please.

"You made a good point about my surrogate mother, Ms. Tucker. I've been doing some research, and it's true that all primates share an urge to nurture their young. To see them thrive and go forth into the world." She sighed. "I have gone into the world. I live well, but I contribute little. I don't want children, I can't imagine what a mother feels, and I most certainly can't imagine what a gorilla mother feels when an offspring is ripped from her womb and made to vanish."

That was too much for Surmi. "Ms Green! I assure you that no **ripping** is going on!"

She leaned back a little. "Too strong a word. Sorry. However, it was a good exercise for me to put myself in another's…er…"

I said, "Shoes?"

Her lips quirked a little. I was starting to like her. "Hm. At any rate, I have become quite interested in this population of apes. Ms. Tucker, you claimed that Zamuka remembers me. I find this surprising, but I am willing to test it."

"You mean you want to see her?" My heart did a flip. When I'd said **remember**, I'd been trying to activate Gloria Green's guilt. I had no idea if Zamuka felt any residual connection with the babies she'd borne. What if my claim proved false? Was I putting too much faith in a tired old gorilla?

Gloria turned to Surmi. "If I may."

Dr. Surmi blew out his cheeks. What could he say? Zamuka was no longer valuable. Nobody wanted her. And I'm sure he had noted Gloria Ikayaa Green's obvious wealth and sophistication. A do-gooder taking a brief interest? Or something else? "Well, I admit I can't come up with a good reason why you shouldn't," he said, rather churlishly. But at this point, he was pretty much out of the equation.

I stood up. Gloria looked at me. "Come on," I said. "I can take you to her now, if you like."

"Now? Oh! Yes, please." Her voice had lost its crisp, direct diction and had become…can I say girlish? Made me want to take her by the hand and tug her along, which I didn't.

Since Zamuka wasn't in the sterile chambers now, we needed to stop only briefly to provide Gloria with boots, a grounds pass, and a quick lecture on safety. And a warning that Zamuka might be in a mood.

"She's kind of a diva. Ideally she'd be ordering servants around."

"Really? She's just an animal."

"An animal with the soul and personality of a Regency Duchess."

We arrived at Zamuka's cage and peered through the bars. She was sitting hunched in a corner. She turned ponderously and gave us a look. Then she turned away.

"Reminds me of my great-aunt Maybelle," said Gloria, her voice jittery with tension. "Should we have brought flowers? Chocolate?"

"Watermelon." I opened the door and went in, Gloria hanging back. <<Zam-zam! Here new friend.>>

I knew the old gal. Zamuka was bored and lonely and could only hold out so long. She and Gloria probably had a lot in common. "Come on in. She's actually pretty gregarious."

"You're sure it's okay…?" Gloria mustered up the nerve to enter the enclosure, which was getting a bit crowded. "Oh my. She's very large."

Zamuka's glittering, deep-set brown eyes gave her visitor the once over, and I could see her wide nostrils flare as she tested the air. Gloria stood firm, but was breathing fast. Zamuka began to sign.

I translated. "She says, 'Hi Erika. What this person?' She's curious about you."

"Wow. I didn't know they could really do that. Can you…tell her hello?"

"Sure." <<Hello. This person Gloria.>> I signed, <<Big sunshine/bright,>> as the name Gloria wasn't in her vocabulary.

Zamuka leaned forward, her nose wrinkling and her breath huffing in and out. <<Person smell good."" Gloria's eyes were watering, whether from the air in the enclosure or from emotion, I didn't know. She extended her hand tentatively toward Zamuka's arm and then withdrew it.

"Can you tell her…" Gloria closed her mouth and shook her head.

"What?"

"It's…can you tell her I'm her, um, child? Baby? Does that make any sense?"

"Sure it does." I signed, <<This big baby. Not doll. You mom-mom.>>

Zamuka huffed gently. That was a lot for her to process. After a few moments she signed: <<Baby not baby.>>

<<Yes baby.>> I mimed holding and rocking a baby, then pointed to Gloria. <<You baby.>>

The old girl, who'd been unhappy and lonely for days, sat back on her haunches and regarded Gloria. She was thinking, contemplating the silly thing I had just told her. She took Gloria's fingers in her big black hands and gently sniffed and licked them, glancing up at Gloria's face. Gloria hadn't flinched.

I let out a breath. Then Zamuka turned and knuckled over to her corner.

Gloria sighed, rubbing her hand. "Wow. That was amazing. She's gentle, she looks so wise…"

"Oh, she really is, and you'd –"

We shut up as Zamuka shuffled back, carrying something almost indistinguishable from a bundle of rags – her oldest doll. She slapped her chest, hooting. Then she held the doll to her breast and rocked it.

Then she pointed at Gloria. It was pretty unmistakable.

Gloria practically lit on fire. "Oh my god. She understands?"

"I...I don't really know." Zamuka was smart, but...maybe she just wanted another doll. I explained our use of dolls to placate and comfort the surrogates. "She understands that her children have been taken away. After each birth she spends a lot of time looking for a baby she fears she's misplaced."

Gloria bit her lip. "That's...oh my." She was blinking rapidly, and her voice had gone thick.

Zamuka hooted some more and began to pat her chest, and point back and forth from her doll to Gloria, signing rapidly.

I felt the hair on my neck rise. "Uh... okay. She says, 'Baby. Baby. No doll. Give baby.'"

"What does she mean?"

"Well...I think she wants you. To be her new baby. At least, that's what it could be."

Gloria made a little sound deep in her throat. In her pale green frock she stepped forward and held out her arms. The temporary cage hadn't been cleaned since yesterday, and Zamuka was stinky at the best of times. She didn't seem to care. Zamuka reached out and wrapped her long hairy arms around Gloria.

"Yep. She's a hugger," I whispered.

Gloria hugged back as hard as she could. I had seriously underestimated the woman.

I admit I felt a bit of jealousy. Mother and child reunion...I wasn't needed within that embrace.

Gloria extricated herself, and we watched Zamuka return to her cache of dolls and fuss with them.

"I know what I have to do," Gloria said, to no one in particular.

# # #

We got in trouble, of course. Doctor Surmi gave us both a carefully worded scolding, and as he did so Gloria Ikayaa Green remained cool.

"Did I say you could go **in** the cage, Ms Green?"

"I apologize for my unauthorized physical contact with Zamuka, Doctor," she drawled. Was she being ironic? Perhaps. "But no harm was done. Now, if I may make a proposal? I wish to purchase Zamuka and take her away with me."

He rocked back in his chair. "Purchase her? But –"

"Name her price, if you would."

"I can't just, just **release** her, at any price. There are regulations, restrictions –"

"I'm quite sure that our respective legal counsel can sort those out."

I could hear the gears churning in Surmi's head. Legal counsel. This woman had it in spades, for sure. I bet he wished he'd just gone ahead and euthanized his problem. After spending some time massaging his forehead, he gave in. "Let me look into it. I hope you don't think it will be easy. The USDA and NIH legal representatives will want to get involved. And PETA."

Gloria's head remained high. "Of course." I'd seen her *sang-froid* when held in the hairy black arms of a gorilla; she'd have no trouble handling a bunch of policy wonks. I felt a swell of pride and happiness.

Then the happiness faded. I was going to miss the old gal. I'd never see her again – Gloria was planning a move, to Malaysia Green. She had big ambitions for her new ward. A floating island home for clapped-out apes...she'd said she didn't want children. She was kidding herself. So to speak.

She had money, influence, and big plans. I sighed. This particular obsolete *Homo sapiens* would return to her little walk-up and settle in for a good cry.

As Surmi frowned and poked at his computer screen, she turned to me and whispered, "Do you have a passport?"

"Huh? No. I've never needed one."

"I suggest you apply for one, Ms Tucker. I believe it would please Zamuka if you came with us."

THE BUTTON
4:20
BACK SOON
I BUTTONED YOUR MOM
NANSI
LAST WEEK
Rigel's Kidnapping
CALLING RIGEL
6742
RUBI

The Boy With the Metalliderm Arm

By S. L. SABOVIEC

S. L. Saboviec's fiction has appeared in Flash Fiction Online, AE, *and elsewhere. She grew up in small-town Iowa, but emigrated for her Canadian husband. They live in a Toronto suburb with their four-and-a-half year-old and twin two year-old daughters. Since being diagnosed with metastatic breast cancer, writing has been a lifeline.*

I knelt on my bionic knee as I rearranged the voltage tester display in my East Neptune Space Station pawn shop, the All You Need Trade and Supply. Two customers browsed the aisles; they wore typical garb for tourists coming back from holiday to the AlCent colonies – neon shirts, clashing shorts, and a holographic band twined through a braid.

The door chimed as a young man entered and beelined for the guitars.

Finished, I scurried behind the counter, where my only employee, Rigel, tapped away at the keyboard, doing inventory.

I said, "He's cute."

He flushed. "I dunno. I'm busy."

I knew better. He once-overed every male under forty who came within ten yards of the shop. "Go talk to him. You haven't been on a date in weeks." And was grumpier for it. I needed my security specialist in top shape.

"Alya, you're embarrassing me. He'll hear you."

I might be a hundred and three, but I'm not deaf. Besides, the young man was fixated on the red and black instrument.

"Get your lazy hide over there, or I'll make sure he hears me." I shoved Rigel with my bionic arm, sending him trotting off.

"I'll leave one of these days. What'll you do without me?" But he slicked his fingers over his eyebrows and plastered on a smile – coy enough it might've worked on me eight decades ago.

Approaching, he twisted his Button wristband as if nervous, but I'd seen that enough to know it was an act. The Button was the latest craze; kids collected the signatures of the people they met in person, uploaded them to social media, and compared their

physical reach. It was this generation's way of saying, "Take a spacewalk without a suit," to parents obsessed with virtual friendships.

The two pressed their Buttons together. The kid's hair was long on the sides, short in the back, and he wore an "I Buttoned Your Mom" shirt, the kind of thing Rigel loved and I could only shake my head at. Within seconds, they were engrossed in conversation about the guitar or the latest synth-band scandal or whatever kids flirted over nowadays.

I finished up inventory. The two airkissed, the kid sauntered toward the door, and Rigel watched him go, biting his lip. After the door chimed shut, he loped over wearing a half-smile. "We're going out tonight. He has the **sexiest** metallidermal tattoo."

"Finish inventory. Three products left." I stepped away from the keyboard.

He surveyed the spreadsheet. "You've done it wrong again. How did you run this place before me?"

"For one thing, I didn't have you mooning about to distract me."

"Kick off. I have work to do."

"Have fun tonight." I disappeared into the back.

\# \# \#

I met Rigel when I caught him stealing one of my locked-up, for-display-only collector's items. Although I'm not in the business of handing out jobs, his hardihood impressed me. Plus I needed someone with his talent – I'm expanding into ship parts soon. Can't have thieves walking off with my inventory.

The wristbands are one small part of a fortune I rarely talk about: I'm a stakeholder in the company that created the Button. My great-grandson is its CEO, and I contributed some capital at the beginning. I'm not paranoid – most people who wander into the shop have no idea – but caution is prudence, and that, as they say, is next to godliness.

When Rigel didn't come in the next morning, I worried. I emmed him on my rubi, waited an hour, and emmed again.

He'd rigged the security system to record the Button signatures of everyone who came into our shop. I wasn't using ninety per cent of the system when he'd wandered in that fateful day, and after he set this up, I'd scoffed. But now, at eight in the morning, well after I'd expected him to arrive, I was glad.

I pulled up Tattoo Boy's profile. There he was – vidpics of him laughing, drinking, carousing, all the things I'd've expected from a kid his age.

But then I saw it: vidpic after vidpic of him with some girl. On the beach. In a restaurant. Holding hands. Kissing.

Was this a ruse for luring my employee away, only to demand a ransom? Like most of his generation, Rigel splashed every detail of his life across his profiles. Anyone could see the guys he was into – and this little bonbon was exactly his type.

No, this couldn't coincidental.

What had I been thinking, sending him off like that? I'd played right into the kidnappers' hands – whoever they were. My great-grandson sent an email last week that I'd ignored, talking about problems with a competitor. Why hadn't I paid attention?

Well, air out the airlock now. I had to stop it.

Rigel had also taught me to track the digital signatures of Buttons by tapping into the station's security system. Technically I was hacking – illegal everywhere but Ganymede – but I didn't really care. As a sharpshooter in the war decades ago, I learned to do what had to be done and clean up the mess afterward.

Rigel and Tattoo Boy were in Hangar Bay C.

I swapped out my all-purpose limbs for my battle-ready versions and unlocked my gun cabinet. I strapped a weapon on each hip and one onto the ankle holster I'd custom-built into my bionic leg. After hanging a "Back Soon" sign, I locked the doors. I'd get an earful later from the neighbors about customer complaints, but someone's always complaining about something.

I clicked my leg into the hover-scooter and took off toward the hangar bay. I hoped I wasn't too late. I could have called someone at Port Authority, but that would have added time I couldn't spare. Besides, I take care of my own business.

The digital signatures of both Rigel and Tattoo led me to a silent, cold ship. I breathed a sigh of relief: they weren't escaping yet. Surely a ransom note would arrive if I waited, but I preferred to stop whatever was happening before it began.

I snapped my foot out of the hover-scooter and inched along, listening. Putting my bionic hand against the hull, I pressed the button to pick up auditory waves. The life support systems hummed. Or was that snoring?

I inched toward the door. Should I listen longer? No, I'd come this far. I needed to rescue Rigel before something terrible happened.

I punched buttons on a modified rubi I'd swiped from his stash of – more illegal – hardware. The door hissed open.

Pulling both guns, I stepped inside.

The built-in sofa was old and cheap, taking up more than half the living space. The ship itself was in rough shape. Clothing was strewn about: shirts over a chair, pants on the sofa, socks trailing down the hall.

I snuck down the corridor to what had to be the bedroom door. In one swift motion, I pushed the handle and leapt inside, guns trained ahead.

Lying on the bed was Rigel, one arm around Tattoo Boy, another around the girl from the vicpids.

All were completely nude.

They scrambled, blinking and pulling at blankets. Rigel barked, "What the gravy you doing here, Nans?"

Now was not the time to chastise him for the rude name. After all, I kind of like that he calls me that. It reminds me of my grandk –

"Seriously, **what** are you doing here?"

I slid the guns into their holsters. "I've been emming. You didn't answer."

Rigel fumbled around on the bed and came up with a rubi that wasn't his. "It's eight-thirty!"

"You usually come in by eight."

"It's **Saturday**. I thought you wanted me to loosen up!"

"Yes, well." I sniffed. "I looked up your new boyfriend. He has a girlfriend –"

"He's **polyamorous**."

"What? You kids today, with your weird relationships!" I said. "Back in my day, we dated one person at a time –"

"Flappin' birds, that's **enough**." Rigel struggled across the bed and hustled me toward the door. "Go home. I'll be there…soon. Maybe. If I'm not there tomorrow, you can take it as my resignation."

Tattoo Boy and Girlfriend snickered. Rigel pushed me out the door.

"But –"

"No." He punched a button and the ship's door closed.

I searched for my scooter, found it, clacked in my foot, and headed back.

I'd really done it this time. He wouldn't speak to me for weeks. And he probably thought I'd gotten my polarity crossed because I was worried about his safety, but that wasn't it. I needed him to help with security. That's why I'd hired him. And now – now he'd probably quit.

My pocket chimed, the opening notes from "That Buttoned-Up Boy," the em-tone he'd programmed for himself. I pulled out my rubi.

I swear, Nans, ur impossible, the em read. *I'll be in by 1. Have electrolytes and a killer waiting for me.*

I smiled and shoved it back into my pocket.

Apparently, he wasn't so upset after all. ▪

... THE FUTURE IS AMAZING!

WE NEED WRITERS...   ARTISTS...

... Come to think of it - we need YOU!

Submit your stories or portfolio at: https://submission.amazingstoriesmag.com

RP Mandrachio

By PAUL
LEVINSON

Paul Levinson, PhD, is Professor of Communication & Media Studies at Fordham University in NYC. His science fiction novels include The Silk Code *(winner of Locus Award for Best First Science Fiction Novel of 1999),* Borrowed Tides, The Consciousness Plague, The Pixel Eye, The Plot To Save Socrates, Unburning Alexandria, *and* Chronica. *His award-nominated novelette, "The Chronology Protection Case," was made into a movie, available on Amazon Prime. His nonfiction books, including* The Soft Edge, Digital McLuhan, Realspace, Cellphone, *and* New New Media *have been translated into 15 languages. He appears on CNN, MSNBC, Fox News, Discovery Channel, National Geographic, History Channel, and NPR.*

The road was beyond slippery. The anti-skids on the car went in and out of activating. The duel between chaos and control continued for a few long, bad minutes. And then I took a turn for the worse.

I say "I," but that's not quite right. I was in the car, all right, and the driver's seat, but I wasn't actually driving. My console was. Or whatever it was that housed the AI brains of this car.

The AI was sharp, brilliant, or at very least a far better driver than I. But it couldn't see into the future. It could not see what was just around the bend.

\# \# \#

The Taconic Parkway south of Route 84 was an ordeal on the best of days. It could be tough to drive at the end of a sunny day with not a drop of rain in the sky. But most drivers handle it okay, and only an AI system that was flat-out buggy or burned out would fail to live up to its promise to keep the driver safe and the car untouched even on the Taconic. Indeed, even on a Taconic with heavy wind and rain.

But this moment was different. The raindrops were thick and splashy – fast, constant, and practically horizontal. The wind was harrowing and howling. But it wasn't the sound that got my brand new Prius. It was an unpredictable, savage gust.

I have no idea how much my car weighs. When it comes to cars, I'm the kind of guy who just drives and doesn't care what makes it work. Same for the digital brains inside. And, yeah, they worked this day.

I don't know which got blown into the

air first – my car or the tree. Probably both at the same time. Those locust trees with their shallow root systems should be banned – can a species of tree be banned? – or at least not allowed near highways. I saw them all over Route 6 on Cape Cod after one of the big hurricanes. Took a month of work to put in all the repairs. No electricity for almost as long. When the batteries went, my folks used oil lamps. There was something romantic about this, my father told my mother. She and I didn't agree at all.

There was definitely nothing romantic about the gust from hell that lifted my Prius off the ground as we went around a sharp curve. I'd been thinking of pulling over but there was no place to stop and an ugly jeep was too close behind me, anyway. *The anti-skids couldn't do anything*, an odd part of my brain thought, *if the car was in the air, right?*

They certainly couldn't do anything for the locust tree that had been pulled out of the ground and was also in the air and now headed right towards me. The last thing I thought before the tree and I collided is that the anti-collision AI options of suddenly stopping or swerving wouldn't work, either, couldn't work, with my car in the air.

\# \# \#

Except there was no collision. Not with an uprooted locust tree or anything. One instant, the locust was a centimeter, a millimeter, from my windshield. The next instant, it wasn't there. My car set down on the wet highway and resumed its anti-skid routine. I didn't think I was dead. No, I knew I was alive, but that's all I felt certain of at that moment.

"Call Raeanne," I pressed the audio a

second or longer later and asked it to call my wife. We were living in a rented brownstone on West 93rd Street.

"I'm sorry, please say again," my audio told me.

"Call Raeanne," I said in a firmer voice, then realized I was rasping,

"I'm sorry –"

I cut off the ingratiating audio and tried to calm myself.

"Call Raeanne," I said a few moments later, in what I hoped sounded more like my normal voice.

"Calling Raeanne," my audio told me. She did have a nice voice.

So did Raeanne, who answered on the first ring, faster than usual. "Hi honey," she said.

"Hey," I said. "Pretty nasty up here. Had a close call on the road, but I'm okay."

"You sure you're okay?"

"Yeah."

"It's been sunny and beautiful here all afternoon," Raeanne said.

#

The forty-five minute drive back to Manhattan was, indeed, beautiful. The roads were suddenly dry, the sun was high, and I couldn't see so much as a single glistening raindrop on a tree leaf. Summer storms sometimes vanished like that.

I thought about the vanishing tree. It had been so close. I had not only seen it, literally in my face. My body had reacted to it. Every part of my body viscerally insisted that the locust in the windshield had not been my imagination. But that was the only rational explanation I could think of for what had happened, or almost happened…

I got home in time for a not-too-late dinner at nine, in our favorite nearby Italian restaurant. I debated with myself through the calamari whether I should tell Raeanne what had happened, or almost had happened, to me. No, seeing an uprooted locust tree approach my windshield at what felt like the speed of light, only to disappear, with anti-collision controls presumably useless, was

definitely something that had happened to me. But I decided not to tell Raeanne, at least not tonight. It could wait until morning, or maybe even longer, maybe until and unless something like that happened to me again. If it was a transitory glitch in my mind, it didn't much matter. If it was something permanent and more profound, well, delaying dealing with it for one day shouldn't be a problem.

We made love almost as soon as we got back to the apartment. She looked great with her long black hair against her soft smooth skin. She was great in bed, too, doing things she'd never done before.

I was on my back afterward, I guess smiling, and Raeanne nestled her head on my chest. "What are you smiling about?" she asked with a flirtatious laugh. There was something I always especially liked about flirting **after** sex.

"You were very good tonight," I said.

Raeanne laughed a little louder. "I'm always good," she said, and kissed my neck.

"Yeah, you are," I said. "But I really liked the new thing you did with your tongue."

Now she not only laughed but lifted her head.

I opened my eyes.

Her pretty face was scrunched up like she was trying to make sense of what I'd just said. "I do that all the time, once in a while, don't I? Hey, that's an oxymoron." And she laughed again.

We made love again, too, a little later. It was good, but she didn't do that thing. True to her word – all the time, once in a while.

#

I got up early the next morning, kissed Raeanne softly on her half-asleep face, and sent her a text on her phone. I'd decided to go up to my Toyota dealer in Rye – didn't hurt to get my car checked out, given what it and I had just gone through.

I got in my car, debating whether to call for an appointment or just show up cold. Mike, my usual service rep, was a good guy. Unless the place was packed, he'd take care of me if I just showed up. If I called for an ap-

pointment, he'd likely say they were booked today and offer me an appointment some other day. I decided to show up without an appointment.

But what exactly would I tell Mike I wanted the mechanics to look at? If I told him what had happened, or I thought had happened to me and my car, he'd think I was out of my mind. Okay, I'd think of something as I was driving up.

I pressed the start button, and for some reason glanced at the odometer. It was over a thousand miles higher than what I was 100% sure it was showing in mileage yesterday – now eleven thousand seven hundred and sixty-two miles in contrast to some ten thousand five hundred and thirty miles – but Bard College, from where I was driving back to New York, was just a little over a hundred miles away. Had my brush with death and/or insanity somehow messed up the odometer, too? Well, at least now I had a reason for showing up at the Toyota service center.

#

Jorge, a foreman with a big friendly smile, greeted me with his customary handshake and his smile.

"I'm just here to talk to Mike about an odd problem," I said to Jorge. "I don't know if anything needs repair." *Or can be repaired*, I thought to myself.

"Of course," Jorge said, and pointed to Mike's cubicle. "He seems to be free now, and we'll just move your car out of the way, to the back."

I nodded and approached the cubicle.

Mike was his usual helpful self. "You know you need an appointment, doc, but I'll fit you in," he said. He called me "doc," because he knew I had a PhD. Most professors of sociology do.

"Thanks," I said, sincerely, and told him the problem with the odometer.

"Ok," Mike said, and called up my car records on his computer. He squinted and shook his head. "This keeps track of what your mileage is at all times, and keeps a complete record of that, every time you drive, from the day you bought the car and drove it out of the dealership – you know that, right?"

I nodded.

"Well, it says your car has been over eleven thousand miles for the past two weeks."

"Impossible!" I said.

"I understand. You thought your odometer was broken, but I'm telling you it's right in synch with what I have on this screen," Mike said.

"Is it possible something in your central system is broken, and it sent out wrong information to my odometer which overrode the actual mileage of the car?"

"You've got quite the imagination, doc!" Mike chuckled. "I don't think that's possible. But – Kate? Got a second, I'd like to ask you a question about the odometer on new Priuses."

A blonde in blue jeans walked over – like someone out of a 1950s song.

"She's our computer expert," Mike said to me. "She knows her stuff."

Kate came over and smiled at us. Mike explained the situation. Kate immediately shook her head. "No, that's not possible," she said.

Mike nodded. "Thanks," he said to her.

She started to walk away –

"Can I tell you something else?" I blurted out.

"Sure," Kate said. Mike offered her a seat.

I told them what had happened to me on the Taconic.

"The anti-collision features wouldn't work if your car was off the ground – that's something our engineers are working on right now," Kate said. "But they're still a ways off."

"Should be in the Prius in three to five years," Mike added.

"Right, I figured that was the case, that the feature didn't exist," I said. "But, then, what happened on that road yesterday?"

"You say the tree-limb just disappeared?" Kate asked.

"The whole tree," I said.

"You have too much to drink at lunch?"

Mike asked, with a wink.

"I had nothing to drink at lunch, except Poland Spring," I replied.

Kate closed her eyes, as if she was thinking hard about something. "Hmm… my sister was driving back from Albany on the Taconic yesterday. She told me it was a lovely ride."

Now I shook my head, hard. "That can't be right. It was raining hard and the wind was blowing like a bastard."

"It's almost like the anti-collision saved you by pulling you into another dimension," Kate said, then laughed. "I'm only kidding!"

Mike laughed, too.

A little too hard, I thought.

Kate's phone made a noise. She looked at it, and nodded. "I'm late for a meeting," she said.

"Go," Mike said. "We'll straighten this out."

\# \# \#

Nothing was straightened out, I thought as I drove back to Manhattan. Mike was a nice enough guy, he wanted to be helpful, but the only good thing that had emerged from our meeting was that Mike didn't charge me anything for it. I appreciated that, but it didn't leave me any better off than I was before I decided to drive up to Westchester.

What kind of damned collision-avoidance system did this new Prius have? I guess it was more blessed than damned if it saved my life, but even so.

I thought about what Kate had said about the anti-collision saving me by whisking me into an alternate reality. Then, I thought about how she looked in those tight blue jeans, as she walked away. That was a lot more pleasing. But then, I thought again about that alternate reality idea.

I was familiar enough with the concept. As a sociologist, I'd studied the phenomenon of science fiction fandom, and I'd been a fan since long before I became a professor. The notion of alternate realities was fascinating to think about – an infinite number of alternate universes, each slightly or more

different from the others, none having any idea of the others' existence. Because maybe they weren't at all connected.

Yeah, it was fun to think about, fun to read and watch movies about, but it sure wasn't fun to actually be living it – or maybe living **them** was the more apt phrase for my situation. Kate had joked about it. But that didn't mean it wasn't actually happening and that I wasn't actually now a part of it. Come to think of it, I couldn't recall ever actually paying too much attention to women in blue jeans, other than seeing them in a couple of vintage movies from the 1950s. Had they never gone out of fashion in this alternate reality that maybe I now was in?

But what did that mean? Toyota had developed an anti-collision system that yanked the driver – and presumably any passengers – into an alternate dimension when the other stop and swerve options weren't available? If so, that would have been the best-kept secret in the world – at least, in the world that I'd come from.

Though unless Mike and Kate had been putting on a grand act, they didn't know about it, either. There must be people higher up in Toyota, for that matter, in other car companies, tech outfits, universities, think tanks, who knew more about the current state of anti-collision systems in automobiles than Mike and Kate. Would they think I was crazy, too?

I drove over the Henry Hudson Bridge to Manhattan. The Easy Pass scanner read my car just fine, as it always did. I needed to think about all the things that were different in this new world, starting with the lack of trees on the highway. That could provide some clue as to where I was, and what had happened to me.

Well, Raeanne *was* different in bed. I smiled. I could live with that. She'd answered the phone on one ring when I'd called her right after the near-miss yesterday, but that was too trivial a difference to be evidence of anything. Kate said her sister had told her that the weather in upstate New York was beautiful, not stormy, but how reliable her sister, or even Kate herself, was with weather reports was open to question. The different mileage on the car, though, that was big, and it told me something that could be crucial. If the anti-collision had saved me on the highway by yanking me into another dimension, it had yanked just me, not the car. And it had placed me in another Prius which had higher mileage than mine had had on that highway where the locust tree looked one hundred per cent certain to hit me.

The traffic suddenly bunched up, as it often did in the stretch of parkway between the Henry Hudson and the George Washington Bridge. I was used to this, and switched lanes almost effortlessly. I even had time to signal my lane change, so as not to invoke that annoying lane-drifting alert.

The only way I could test what was going on with me and my car, I realized, was to get into another life-and-death situation, with death avoidable only by my anti-collision system doing whatever it had done yesterday. But that was a pretty dangerous way to conduct research. Indeed, if I had been channeled into another reality with another car, how did I know that this car I was now in was even fitted with the same kind of anti-collision system? Maybe the guy, presumably the alternate me, who bought this car was a cheapskate, and opted for a package without the kind of inter-dimensional anti-collision that had saved me yesterday. Or maybe they didn't have that here in this reality at all. The road I was on with this kind of thinking was paved with paradox, and vastly more dangerous than the road I actually was on, but even that was by no means clear.

And if I was in an alternate reality now, what had happened to the alternate me? Hey, had I been that self-questioning yesterday before I'd gone around that curve? Impossible to tell, and that was the nub of the problem. How could I tell if I was the same person I was yesterday? If I was a different person I would have no way of knowing if what I remembered was of this me or that me.

I turned on the radio to clear my mind. A little Beatles music on Sirius XM Radio always helped put things into perspective for me. "Band on the Run" was playing. "Peter Asher here on my show *From Me to You* on The Beatles Channel, playing their songs that begin with the letter B today," he said when the music concluded. "That was 'Band On the Run' by The Beatles from their 1975 album *Come and Go*."

What? I pulled my car into a vacant spot too close to a pump about two blocks from my apartment, just so I could stop and make sense of this. I'd done my doctoral dissertation on The Beatles' breakup as the prime example of the inherent instability of musical groups. My adviser, a stickler for traditional sociology – which I always found boring – had offered some resistance to this topic. But I'd prevailed. And I knew The Beatles like the back of my hand. McCartney had released "Band on the Run" – the title track of his album – as Paul McCartney and Wings in 1973. No way Peter Asher, who had practically lived with Paul McCartney when he and Asher's sister Jane had been a couple, could have made a mistake like that. Peter Asher had even gone on to work at Apple Records right around the time The Beatles were disbanding. He knew better than anyone other than McCartney himself the difference between McCartney's output as a Beatle and what he did after.

At least, in my reality. Or what had been my reality.

\# \# \#

I sat in my car, stunned, for I don't know how long. Peter Asher played some more songs, but I barely heard, other than something vaguely registering in a part of my brain that nothing I was hearing was at variance with the reality I remembered, the reality I had grown up with, the reality that was me.

For some reason, that attribution of "Band on the Run" to The Beatles rather than Paul McCartney and Wings proved that what Kate had joked about at the Toyota dealer was no joke at all. "Band On the Run" by The Beatles seared the truth of Kate's joke into my soul, more than anything else

that had happened to me since that tree had winked out of existence in the storm on the Taconic just yesterday.

I was either flat-out hallucinating, yesterday and today, or I had indeed been swapped into an alternate reality when I'd gone around that bend. Swapped seemed the right word, because as far as I could tell, there was no evidence of another me in this reality since I'd arrived. It had just been Raeanne and me in bed last night, no *ménage à trois* with Raeanne and me and my twin.

So what had happened to the me originally in this reality? What did I know and not know about him? What had he been doing, where had he traveled, in those thousand miles missing in my original car's reality? And at that insane instant on the Taconic yesterday, was he swapped into my car a nanosecond before the locust went through the windshield and killed on the spot? What kind of psycho-perverse anti-collision app would do that?

I didn't like thinking about that. Maybe I shouldn't be so hard on the app – after all, it had saved my life. I did like thinking about Raeanne – maybe I could be happy in this reality – maybe it had some advantages over my old one. I was glad the Beatles had stayed together at least until the mid 1970s – who knows, maybe in this reality John Lennon had not been killed by that fucker at the Dakota. I focused on what was playing on the radio. It was "Beautiful Boy," the song John had written for his little boy, Sean. It always brought tears to my eyes, as it was doing right now.

"And that's the last of B songs for this episode of *From Me to You*," Peter Asher said. "I'll be back next week with the Cs. That was 'Beautiful Boy' by John Lennon, from his *Double Fantasy* album, released just three weeks before he was murdered..."

Well, I guess this wasn't a reality that was better in every way, after all. I sighed and started the car. I might as well drive to the supermarket, surprise Raeanne with a nice shopping, and put this alternate reality on the back-burner – at least for a few hours, as I did some cooking –

The car made a strange sound and the engine died. What the hell? This was a new car. I cursed a lot more than I would have, had this been the only unexpected event in the car the past two days. I called the AAA.

\# \# \#

The AAA guy arrived faster than usual. "It's the battery," he told me. "Not the regular battery that's not too expensive and easy to replace. It's the battery that runs the car, makes this Prius a hybrid. You know it's a hybrid right? Runs on fuel only when it's needed, and the rest of the time the battery feeds the engine –"

"Yeah, I know," I said and shook my head. "I don't believe it. This car's just a few months old."

"That's actually good news," the AAA guy said. "Your warranty will definitely cover it, right?"

"Yeah."

"Why don't you hop in the seat?" He pointed to his tow-truck. "Where's your dealer? If it's within a hundred miles of here, I can take you, no charge."

\# \# \#

My Toyota dealer was far less than a hundred miles from Manhattan. I thanked the AAA guy and gave him a big tip when we arrived.

Jorge walked quickly over. "Back so soon?" His smile seemed bigger than ever.

I told him about the central battery.

"Could be serious," Jorge said. "Why don't you go in and see Mr. Mike?"

"Right, thanks," I said, and walked to Mike's cubicle. I got lucky again – usually this place was crowded, and at least one or two customers were waiting to see Mike when I arrived. This time, like earlier today, he invited me right in. Well, I guess I'd also been lucky – very lucky – not to have been killed by that locust tree yesterday, too.

"What happened? Mike asked.

I told him about the battery.

Mike got up and gestured to me to keep sitting. "Let me talk to Jorge," he said.

\# \# \#

He returned about twenty minutes later. "Sorry for the wait. But good news," Mike said. "The battery's indeed kaput, but –"

"How is that good news?"

"You're all covered under the warranty," Mike said.

"You're putting in a new battery now?" I asked.

Mike shook his head no. "This is no ordinary battery –"

"I know."

"We're not going to put in a new battery," Mike said. "Our engineers want to study your car and see if they can figure out what killed the battery."

"I'm still waiting for the good news," I said.

Mike reached over and clapped me on the shoulder. "We're giving you a brand new car. No cost to you. It's all covered under your warranty. I'm going to walk you over to the sales department. They're getting a car ready for you, even as we speak. A slightly different shade from the one you have, but I think you'll like it."

\# \# \#

I let Mike walk me down a gleaming corridor to the sales department. Kate and her blue jeans were nowhere to be seen. But I didn't care. I had other things on my mind.

I felt that I somehow was being railroaded in this car place. I couldn't see exactly how, but I had the queasy feeling that this new Prius I would be getting would not have all the features of the one whose battery had died. The one whose analog in my original dimension had shunted me into this one, maybe.

I'd found over the years that all models of the same car, even when you checked off the exact-same amenities that you wanted, were never exactly the same. One always had something slightly different from the other – a seat that warmed your ass in win-ter, a roof that retracted in summer so you could listen to "Back in the USSR" with the wind in your hair, whatever. (Was there still a Soviet Union in this damned reality? I'd have to check.)

And I had a feeling that this new Prius would have a slightly different anti-collision system, too. One that wouldn't save me from an angry tree hurtling toward me straight out of some tornado horror movie.

What would I have done if the car I had brought here had not been deemed incapable of repair? Drive off a cliff to test its anti-collision system? Put it to the test and see if it was still working the same as yesterday in the analog car?

I went through the motions, signed all the screens, and drove away in my brand new Prius.

\# \# \#

It occurred to me, as I tried to keep my mind on the road, that maybe Jorge had sabotaged my car this morning when he helpfully parked it in the back. Maybe he did something that had made the central battery die. Which meant, what? The Toyota people in this reality knew about their science fictional anti-collision feature – knew it was real – and were trying to keep it secret? At least, some of the people at Toyota, here in this reality?

A car swerved in front of me as I approached the Henry Hudson Bridge. I switched lanes with no problem and without invoking the anti-collision, just like I had when I'd driven home earlier today from Toyota in the first car. The truth is, what had happened yesterday on the Taconic had been the first time the anti-collision had been invoked since I'd bought that first car several months ago. Maybe Toyota knew it was rarely activated, and put in a few experimental features in some models which Toyota figured the public was not very likely to find out about.

Maybe I just had to forget everything that had happened in the past two days. Just live my life like any normal person who hadn't been yanked into an alternate lane of reality. Things weren't so bad here –

My phone rang. It was Raeanne – the new Raeanne, I assumed. No, things weren't so bad here at all.

"Hey –" I began, and the phone went dead.

Had she just vanished? I returned the call. Nothing, not even voicemail.

I called her five more times. Same result. Nothing.

Shouldn't I get voicemail if she'd gone into a tunnel, or her phone had died?

Yeah, I should. But not if she and the number I was calling never existed.

I tried again. Nothing. I was sweating –

My phone rang, again. It was Raeanne –

"Are you all right?" I asked her.

"Yeah," she replied. "I just tried to call you, I heard you answer, and then I lost the connection."

"I know," I said. "I tried to call you back. Got nothing – not even voicemail."

"Huh, it's not supposed to do that," she said. "Crazy world we live in."

"Yeah." I guess that was another similarity of this world – her world – and my world. But there was no point in saying that to Raeanne. Because her world was now my world, and that was okay. I breathed – it felt like for the first time since I'd lost her call. "How about I pick up some food for supper at the supermarket."

"The P & A?" she asked. "Sure – they've really been stepping up their game the past few months. All kinds of specials on tea, finally living up to their Great Pacific and Atlantic Tea Company name." ∎

EVERY CLICHE FANTASY TOWN
CEMETERY
BROAD ROAD
THE OVEUR WATERFALLS
ASSASSIN'S GUILD
PROUD SPONSORS OF CEMETERY
DO NOT ENTER
UNDEAD SWAMP
GUILD
BARBARIANS
LARGE STREET
HAUNTED MILL
ORCS
UNICORN
NO WYVERNS
KRAKEN & KRILL
BAR & GRILL
NIGHT MARE
NO CENTAURS
SAFE
CURSED STREET
YE OLDE MAGICKAL SHOPPE
WIZARD'S TOWER
WANDERING MONKS
CURSED RIVER
YE BROKEN INN
SUSPICIOUSLY COZY INN
INN
MAIN STREET
CHURCH
THE NUN
DROPBEAR THICKET
HALL OF THE ADVENTURER
666
THIEVES' GUILD
WE MADE IT WITH YOUR MONEY
MORC THE ORC
PATH TO DUNGEONS
OWLBEAR FOREST
TROUBLED FARM QUEST
HAVE FUN STORMING THE CASTLE
FIRST PATH
HECKMOUTH
CURSED LAKE
HAUNTED WOODS
PHISHY PETE'S PIRATE PORT

©brad w. foster
2019

By AMBER
ROYER

Amber Royer writes the Chocoverse comic tele-novela-style foodie-inspired space opera series (Free Chocolate and Pure Chocolate available from Angry Robot Books). She teaches creative writing in North Texas for both UT Arlington Continuing Education and Writing Workshops Dallas. If you are very nice to her, she might make you cupcakes.

"There. Take that one. You're not going to find another spot this close to the center." Brill is standing behind me as I push the lever that will move his ship forward. We're hovering close to the tarmac, and it feels like if we hesitate too long the ship's thrusters will burn a hole right through it, out through the hull, and we'll fall into the stars.

I eye the tight parking place, between an oversized blocky ship and a sleek red vessel parked sideways across two spaces.

Taking off from Larksis, where I attend cooking school, had been easy. Larksis is a *muy* laid back place. Their spaceship parking is open-air, and Brill's ship, the *Fois Gras*, had been able to leap directly into the sky. Guiding it had been a bit of a rush, no?

Pero at this spacecase tradepost, open anything isn't an option. *Nada, nunca.* I stop the ship, and it jitters as it hovers. "I'm not sure if I can make the tight turn."

"You've got this, Babe." Brill's not behind me anymore. His voice comes from the galley on the other side of the ship. I hear the door to the convection oven open, where two trays of mini fudge cakes are staying warm. A choctastic aroma fills the room.

"Don't touch those, *mi litoll*. They're for when your *amigos* get here." I'm nervous, too, about meeting Brill's *amigos*. I have no idea what to expect. I glance in his direction. He's coming back, moving so quickly he's hard to track. When he stops, his hands are behind his back.

"Tell me you're not hiding cake, *por favor*."

He shrugs. "I'm not hiding cake." But as he says it, his eyes shift from blue to violet, then to a neon-violet-pink – always a sure sign that he's lying. I give him a look, and he laughs. "Don't worry. I won't eat one later."

I look away, and sense quick movement. He's scarfed the cake, and I guess it's *pero* like, if I didn't see it, did it happen? He makes a slightly distressed noise.

"Hot, no?" Serves him right. I sigh. "I want to make a *buena* impression. These people are important to you."

Another ship is trying to park, and I'm blocking the aisle. Instead of a horn, I get a ding over the com followed by a terse message in some language I don't speak. Still, the tone is clear: **Get out of the road, lady!**

I push the lever, edge up enough for the other ship to get by. These vehicles were not designed for such claustraziety-inducing spaces.

And yet, Brill is not going to take the controls. He's still on about his *amigos*. "I wouldn't worry about those guys. They're not used to fancy food."

I guess I should take it as a compliment. The *Fois Gras* – actually that's a translation, in Krom it's The *Shoschetta* – is the most precious thing in the world to him, and he trusts me to drive it – even though I'm not licensed for non-ground craft. I move the ship forward. Turning these thrusters is harder than it looks.

I've almost got it when the whole trading post wobbles. Ay, no! The *Fois Gras* impacts the pavement, which has jumped up to meet it, then skids into the blocky ship next to it.

"*Naramoosh!*" Brill pulls me up out of

the pilot's seat and reverses us away from the other ship. I've never heard that word before. It sounds kind of musical for a curse. Maybe it means **move**, or **hurry**.

"Is this okay?" I protest. "We should leave a message or something?"

"I'm sure nobody saw us. Why buy trouble?" I can't see his face, can't tell if he's angry at me, can't tell from his tone of voice either. He pulls quickly into a spot in a much farther row, and is out, looking at the damage to the nose of the ship. I follow, trudging down the ramp at a more human speed. I don't think it looks *tan mal*. The nose cone's bent a little to one side, but you have to really be looking to see that, and the scratches in the paint are faint. That's probably not how he sees it, though.

"*Suavet ita hanstral*," I say in careful Krom. I am so sorry.

The pavement starts shaking again, *pero* this time it has nothing to do with the trading post's grav.

A guy that looks a bit like a shaggy calico mountain with twin treetrunks for legs strides over to us. He's wearing a dark vest-tunic thing, black pants, and no shoes. The guy blows upward with pursed lips, puffing curled tendrils of hair out of hunormus slitted brown eyes. In heavily accented Universal, he says, "Do you think you can just hit my ship and then run away?"

"What are you talking about?" Brill's face really does look puzzled, though his eyes are heading back towards that violet-pink.

"I saw you do it." The guy grabs Brill, who doesn't even try to duck away. He's probably afraid the guy would grab me instead. Mountain Guy drags Brill back over to the blocky ship to show him the damage. My heart pounding heavy in my ears, I follow. The guy smushes Brill's face against the streaks of white paint standing out against the larger ship's iron gray. "Can you see it now?"

"*Por favor*. Please." I stay out of grabbing distance. "Let him alone."

I've got the channel open on my sublingual, *pero* I'm not sure who to call to stop a fight on this tradepost. I think *muy* hard about local directory assistance, and the sublingual jumps a connection into the local system. In crisp unaccented Universal, a female voice asks, "How may I direct your call?"

Before I can answer, a voice that's not bubblechatter inside my head says, "The guy who hit your ship went that way, *su*."

I turn. The speaker's another Krom, a little thinner than Brill but just as tall, with a more delicate face shape and slightly hooded eyes – which are currently a brilliant violet-pink. He's standing with six other guys of varying humanoid species wearing a motley assortment of tough-guy jackets. Both the speaker and the one other Krom in the group – likely Brill's friend Zarak – are wearing dark denim instead of the leather Brill prefers.

"Gavin!" Brill says, though his voice sounds smooshed too.

I doubt Mountain Guy believes Gavin, *nunca*. He just figures out the statistics of eight versus one and lets Brill go. "My mistake."

We all make our way back to the *Fois Gras*. The guys circle around the table at the edge of the galley, settling onto the bench that rings it. Brill pulls out a deck of cards – not that different in size from Earth playing cards, *pero* there are one hundred thirty-two in the deck, grouped by sixes each labeled with a different glyph – and a box of counters and sets them in the center of the table.

I open the oven and pull out the cakes, centering each one on a decorative paper plate – Brill only has three real plates on board – and finishing them out with an *exquisita* vanilla sauce. I put them all on a tray and carry it to the table.

"Everybody, this is Bo," Brill announces, continuing to speak Universal, which is probably easiest given the motleyness of his crew. "My girlfriend."

Gavin's eyes go a soft, startled orange, and he cuts a glance over at Zarak, who shrugs. Well, what exactly did that *idiota* Krom think I was? I'm a bit emotirated that Brill hasn't told them about me. After all,

he's told me all about them.

I start putting cakes down in front of everyone, but Gavin puts out a hand, blocking the space in front of him. "No thank you." He gives me a slight bow. "I'm much more of a strict vegetarian than Brill is." He catches Brill's eye. "Much stricter about a lot of things."

I nod, pretend we're just talking about food, though heat floods my chest and face, and I feel like I've been flutterpunched in the gut. "*Sí*, I know. That's why these are vegan. Especially for you and Zarak."

The orange lightens to pink, which means Gavin's embarrassed, but he still shakes his head. "I'm sorry you went through so much trouble, but I'd still prefer not."

Brill's own eyes have deepened to brown. "Gavin. A word, if you don't mind." He gestures towards the cargo bay.

I place a cake down at Brill's spot. I know he's already had one, but I'm not going to skip him in front of his *amigos*. Zarak takes one of the cakes but doesn't eat it. He won't look at me. I'm totally crashbanging this whole situation. *Pero*, it's not like I'd try to feed them Frankenfood. Most people on Earth won't even eat crudtastic gene-doctored products any more, though the reputation that we do is taking its sweet time going away.

The other five guys inhale cake, while chatterclashing amongst themselves.

Tark, the guy with the head just slightly too big and narrow to be human, looks up at me. "Thanks, Bo. This is awesome."

One compliment and about three friendly smiles. I am not off to a *bueno* start with Brill's *amigos*. I could use a little chocolate myself, no? I find a fork and take a seat on the sofa at the other side of the open area and proceed to eat Gavin's portion, one *delicioso* bite at a time.

Brill pushes Gavin back in from the cargo bay. "Tell her what you said."

"*Ga avell*," Gavin mutters, but Brill's not taking no for an answer. Gavin's eyes are pale pink and his lips are set in a line. He looks at Brill, then over towards me, not quite looking me in the eyes. "I told him that our initial intelligence reports for Earth showed that in even the most technologically advanced parts of the planet, people believe that bathing causes illness, and that doctors will go from performing autopsies to treating pregnant women without even washing their hands."

Frustangeration washes over me. What he is saying is true – for ancient history. "That was over two hundred years ago, *mijo!*"

And my planet's reputation's still crashbombed from it? *No y no.*

Gavin cocks his head. "I have a brother who's over two hundred years old, who likes to bring home stray animals as pets. Apparently, he hasn't changed that much from when he was a kid and snuck a poisonous vegerkmouth into the house. It wound up swimming in a tureen on the dinner table and nearly bit my grandmother when she went to serve the soup. Should we expect an entire civilization to change so much in that amount of time?"

I look to Brill, not sure what to say. These guys have a lifespan of roughly three hundred years, long enough to overlap multiple eras of human history. Brill's barely thirty, and we haven't been together very long, so he hasn't seen much of what Earth does have to offer. Not that he could visit the planet, even if he wanted to, absolutely *nunca.* Earth's a closed-off planet.

Pero Brill says, "Gavin, that's the thing about the Earthling life span. It forces them to innovate. A couple hundred years ago, they theorized their moon might be made of cheese. A hundred years ago they walked on it. Now there's a half dozen thriving cities up there." He gestures to Gavin's perfectly tousled dark hair. "Believe me, Bo owns more styling products than even you."

"*Shtesh.*" Gavin bows and gives me a close-fisted salute. His eyes are still pink, and he doesn't look happy. "I do apologize. I do not know what is the appropriate Earth custom now."

"Eat the cake," Brill says.

Gavin gives him a startled glance, shakes his head. "Ga, *su.*" Basically, **Nah, man**.

"Eat the cake," Brill repeats, "or I'm not helping you work out this trade." He gestures to the guys, whom I had assumed were just here to play cards.

I hold up my fork. "There is no more cake."

It's true. At some point, Zarak had given in and eaten his. The only piece left is sitting at Brill's spot. He dashes over, then back, and hands it to Gavin, who grudgingly swipes the fork out of Brill's hand.

"*Haza.*" **Fine, whatever.** He takes a bite, then looks completely surprised, pale lilac eyes and all. "This is really good."

Eh? I blink, not sure what to make of the compliment. "So you've never had chocolate before?"

Gavin shrugs. "From nibs that have been sterilized and processed in places that I trust. You have to understand, Bodacious," – I just now got Brill to call me Bo, I'm not about to start all over with Gavin – "a Krom's more likely to die prematurely from a disease caught during his Voyage of Discovery than from anything else."

The door caves in and Mountain Guy is standing there, an oversized gun in his hand. He's wearing a headset. He taps it, implying he's been listening to our conversation. "Anything else except violence, you mean."

He throws in a grenade that's already hissing out chemical-laced smoke, then fires the gun, which shoots out a projectile. Gavin steps between me and it, and when it unfurls into a net, the two of us are caught.

"Ay!" I suck in a lungful of smoke, and suddenly I'm slypered, having to fight the urge to yawn and draw in even more of the chemical that's trying to put me to sleep. My eyes try to close while I'm still standing. The net jerks, and I lose my balance. I gasp as I fall, and with the new rush of sleepsmoke, I give up consciousness before I hit the floor.

I wake up double-cuffed face to face with Gavin, my left wrist paired with his right, my right wrist paired with his left. It's like something out of a Kromcom –

meaning pretty much any Krom FeedShow, once it's been put through the cheeselation process into English. Only here, nobody's laughing.

We're lying on a cold metal floor. He's awake, but trying to act like he's not. Given the Krom ability to hold their breath pretty much infinitely, he probably didn't even pass out. Which means someone must still be watching us. So I don't move.

Finally, Mountain Guy stomps into the other room.

Gavin lets out a long breath. He says softly, "Well, we're in space."

"*Ay, no.*" My heart catches. "The others?"

"Are all alive. Don't worry." Gavin sighs. "But the keys to my ship are in my pocket, and Zarak came to the tradepost with me. The non-Kroms are bound to have passed out, which means with Brill's door busted open, it's going to be a minute before they organize themselves enough to come after us."

I look at him hopefully. Those intelligent eyes, that smug superior face – he must be good for something, right? "You have a plan, no?"

"*Ga.*" **No**. He shakes his head. "I can't move at speed stuck to a –" He catches himself.

Whatever he was about to say, I don't want to know. "*Gracias*, I don't need any reminders of what I am to you."

"My best friend's girlfriend?" Gavin shakes his head. "That's going to take some getting used to."

"Tell me something, *chico.*" I put a hand on Gavin's sleeve. He doesn't flinch. Which is surprising, *pero* nice. "What happened to Brill's parents? They're dead or something, no?"

Gavin's mouth comes open, *pero* he doesn't say anything. Finally, he shakes his head. "If Brill hasn't told you about his family, it's really not my place to do so."

I nod, more convinced than ever that either Brill's an orphan – or an exiled prince.

"Fine. *Haza.* Then tell me this. If Krom

knew about Earth as far back as the Victorian era –" I hesitate. He probably doesn't know **that** much about Earth history. "I mean several hundred years ago, why wait so long to make First Contact?"

Gavin sits up, pulling me up with him. "The ship involved barely glimpsed your planet, inhabited and unmapped, at the end of a Voyage of Discovery, so they just sent down a quick survey team. There wasn't enough infrastructure to do a full Contact. Do you know how hard it would be to properly catalog an entire planet with no existing information network, airlines, or even decent roads? And the initial reports didn't look promising. It's not like most places have commodities that are all that unique. We'd have sent another ship if we'd realized Earth had four of them – coffee, cinnamon, vanilla and chocolate. Finding something like chocolate – that's special. And we missed it – twice."

"And now we're back to choconomics. I –"

Mountain Guy gets on his com, so we shut up to listen. Fortunately, he's speaking Universal. "No, it's not them, but they have roughly the same builds. It'll be years before they can prove their innocence." He hesitates. "You can change the coding on the DNA in the file. I've seen you do it before."

My chest squeezes with panic. "He doesn't mean us?"

Gavin nods. "Afraid so."

"*No y no*. We have to get out of here."

"I'm sorry, Bodacious. That guy took my gun and my phone. We're not likely to overpower him by brute force."

I hadn't even realized Gavin was carrying a gun. Why would he have felt a need to come armed to a friendly card game? Krom don't even gamble, so it's not like it should get *feo*. I'm not sure I like Gavin, knowing that about him. But it doesn't matter. I'm cuffed to the guy. "Well, what **do** we have?"

Gavin puts his hand – and more or less mine – in his jacket pocket and draws out a couple of objects. "I still have a Varan deck and a pack of mints. And a huge kren crys-

tal, but that's a long story."

Most gemstones are worthless on the galactic market – what carbon-based species doesn't have diamonds? – but kren is useful for curing a number of diseases – including radiation sickness – and it's exceptionally rare.

"Why did you bring a deck when Brill already had cards?" Maybe this guy just comes over-prepared for everything.

Gavin's eyes go light pink. He says very softly. "Because mine are marked."

I laugh. "*Por qué*? Varan isn't even something you play for money."

Now Gavin laughs. "It's more about bragging rights." He raises an eyebrow. "Do you play?"

I shake my head. "Not really. I don't read much Krom, and there are so many sub-rules. The whole thing makes me feel like a *kek*."

He looks startled at my use of the Krom word for **idiot**. He flips the deck over in his hand, tugging my wrist in the process, revealing a card with a glyph that looks like a flying bat. "The game outlines Krom's whole history. The rules make a lot more sense if you know the events."

"I don't exactly have time to learn it all now, no?"

He laughs. "Perhaps not. It is interesting that you'd want to know. Not many of the Discovered care about the past."

"You're talking down at me again, *mijo*." I take a deep breath. Getting mad at him is just wasting time. I look around the space. What else can we use? There's not much in here but wall-plaqued photos of Mountain Guy at different travel destinations. He seems to favor low grav mountains, fishing trips, and playing board and card games with groups of *amigos*. In the images, he looks a little too social to be a true space-case, a solo traveler with too much time to just sit and think.

Gavin said his cards are marked, so he can read them. And I can read Gavin's eyes. I think. I mean, so far the patterns match the shifts I've seen in Brill's, which should mean they're a consistent part of non-ver-

bal Krom language. Right?

So just maybe…

I stand up, bringing Gavin with me. We move to the doorway, which is blocked by a force field.

"Hey! *Hola!*"

Mountain Guy looks up.

Gavin kicks at my shin. "What are you doing?"

"Give me that kren."

"Why?

"Just do it."

He hands it over, and I hold it up.

Mountain Guy walks over to us. "The Krom and his girlfriend."

I say, "You have the wrong Krom," at the same time Gavin says, "Absolutely not."

Mountain Guy looks puzzled. "But this one's the one who jumped to save you."

I smile. "*Sí*, he only did that because he felt guilty."

"That's untrue," Gavin protests.

I ask Mountain Guy, "Care to make a little wager? This versus your ship over a little game of Varan?"

Gavin whispers, "Now he's just going to come take it. Thanks."

"I don't think so." I gesture at the pictures on the wall behind me. If I'm right, Mountain Guy won't be able to resist a game for the game's sake. And in one of the pictures, he's actually playing Varan.

Mountain Guy comes over and deactivates the force field. He's got a non-lethal clankstaff in his other hand as he grabs the kren crystal away from me to look at it. A scanner lights up in his eye. I guess he's verifying that it's real. Gavin gives me a look that clearly means I told you so.

Mountain Guy hands me back the kren. "Not my ship. I already have that, and I already have you. This versus your freedom. You both play individually, and you both have to beat me."

Gavin still looks *quende de piedra*, literally "like a stone," but meaning **stunned** a few minutes later when we're sitting in fluff-eriffic chairs, bound by the ankle to the galley table instead of by the wrist to each other, with a bunch of buttons from Mountain

Guy's sewing box to use as counters, while our kidnapper's getting everyone drinks from the fridge. Gavin whispers, "I thought you said you didn't know how to play this game."

I shrug. If I told him my plan, it might affect how he's thinking, which would disrupt the color change in his eyes. Which is the whole point. "I don't. So you had better win, so you can come back and rescue me."

"True." His eyes flash lavender. "Can you imagine what Brill would do if he thought I left you here on purpose?"

I can't, actually. *Nada y nunca.* What would Brill do if he had that kind of fight with his best *amigo*? It's a little *extraño* that I don't know him well enough yet to immediately answer that question.

It takes me a few hands to get the pattern down. When I see green – which signals excitement – in Gavin's irises. I fold and let him take the hand. When he looks at the marked cards in my hands, and the green mutes to gray, then I know I've got better cards than him – and if there's less gray when he looks at Mountain Guy, I split my counters into rows and hope the shaggy guy doesn't fold.

Before long, Mountain Guy is out of counters. He shakes his head. "I should have known better to play Varan against a Krom. I'm not taking you back to that trading post, but I will set you down on the next planet. I'm sure you'll take no offense if I leave you here for now."

"None taken." Gavin bows in respect as the guy walks off. Then he looks at me, deep purple curiosity tinting his irises. "So how did you manage that?"

'I've been dating Brill for almost four months, no? You think by now I can't read the color-dance in his eyes?"

"*Shtesh.* I should have known it was nothing special." His eyes tint violet, though, then move towards that electric pink. He's trying to keep a somber face, trying to hide the fact that I've impressed him. Maybe even convinced him I'm a better match for Brill than he would have thought.

"Liar," I say.

"Absolutely." His eyes fade to blue happiness, and he tosses me the kren crystal. ▪

By ADAM-TROY CASTRO

Adam-Troy Castro's 27 books include the recent audio collection, And Other Stories *(Skyboat Media). His novel* Emissaries From The Dead *won the Philip K. Dick Award, and he has been nominated for eight Nebulas, two Hugos, and three Stokers. He lives in Florida with his wife Judi and a trio of perpendicular cats.*

<u>*(Chapter One of the Canine Pentateuch)*</u>

I In the beginning, the world was without form, or interesting smells.

2 And the supreme being, Dog, lay on His side, panting.

3 And Dog growled from time to time, just in case there was something prowling the Void that might be up to no good; but there was nothing but Dog.

4 And Dog had been alone with His thoughts for all eternity, leaving Him nothing to do but sleep and whine and sometimes lick His privates.

5 And the world still remained without form, or interesting smells.

6 And Dog wished for something to look at.

7 And there was light.

8 And Dog yelped, not knowing what He had done, because while He was omnipotent and omnipresent, he was after all, just Dog.

9 And Dog continued to yelp at great length, even though there was nobody around to hear Him.

10 And Dog grew weary, and circled the same spot of nothingness three times before going back to sleep.

11 And on the second day, Dog rested.

12 And on the third day, Dog woke, yawned, and beheld the light, this time not disturbed by it at all, because Dog had pitiful short-term memory and assumed that it had just been there all along.

13 And Dog napped for a while.

14 And Dog woke again, up, scratched Himself at great length, and wished for someplace to run.

15 And in so doing, Dog created the Heavens and the Earth.

16 And Dog saw that it was good, and ran about in great aimless circles.

17 And Dog thought of some pressing reason to run in a straight line all the way to the other side of the world, but forgot what that reason was long before He got there.

18 And Dog was so tired from all this exhaustive activity that He had to roll over and go back to sleep.

19 And on the fourth day, Dog rested.

20 And on the fifth day, Dog wandered a little bit, had a wonderful idea that He forgot about almost immediately, and rested some more.

21 Dog was a big one for rest.

22 And on the sixth day, Dog again wished for something to do.

23 And Rabbit appeared.

24 And Rabbit was so far away that Dog had to strain His eyes to see it, but that didn't matter, because there the damn thing was sitting right there in the middle of everything, just like he owned the place.

25 And Dog gave chase.

26 And Rabbit darted away, running even faster than Dog, which was not quite right at all, and Dog, straining Himself, was able to get within one jaw's length of the little bastard's neck, if it hadn't faked to the right.

27 And Dog, barking like crazy now, because He was Dog, dammit, went for it again. Except that Rabbit darted right then left then right again, and Dog got frustrated.

28 Also thirsty.

29 And lo, the first water appeared; a crystalline, babbling brook, that snaked

across the surface of the Earth. And Dog lapped until his thirst was sated.

30 And on the Seventh Day, nature took its course, which led to the creation of Trees.

31 And on the Eighth Day, Dog rested.

32 And on the Ninth Day, Dog rested.

33 And on the Tenth Day, Dog rested.

34 And on the Eleventh Day, Dog rested.

35 And on the Twelfth Day, Dog didn't do a whole lot of consequence.

36 And so it continued until the Thirty-Seventh Day, when, in a burst of manic energy, Dog created the mountains and the rocks and the fascinating little tasty things that come out from beneath the rocks and the twittering things that fly back and forth across the flowers and the furry bushy-tailed things that lived in the trees; and then for good measure tried to sneak up on Rabbit but once again failed.

37 And on the Thirty-Eighth Day, Dog was truly pooped.

38 And on the Thirty-Ninth Day, Dog scratched his ear for a good fifteen minutes, sat down again, and rested some more, deciding at great last that a world filled with grass and trees and a multitude of furry things to chase was not sufficient unto His purpose; for Dog was lonely, and needed companionship.

39 And so He devoted all His infinite powers of creation toward the formation of a creature who would love Him purely, and without restraint; who would stay by His side and be nice to Him and be His Best Friend for all time.

40 And it gazed upon Him with absolutely no gratitude at all.

41 And meowed.

42 And Dog learned from this that He was fallible.

43 And on the Fortieth Day, Dog tried to rest, but failed, for Cat would not let Him.

44 And on the Forty-First Day, Dog molded a creature too slow and clumsy to run away, who would keep Cat occupied, feed Dog when Dog wanted to be fed and stroke Dog when Dog wanted to be stroked.

45 And Dog gave this new creature useful appendages called Hands, which, given Dog's priorities, were as large as the rest of the creature's body put together, so it wouldn't be able to do all that much beyond stroke Him anyway.

46 And Dog called the creature Man.

47 And Man, with his stubby little legs and gargantuan tent-sized hands, rubbed Dog's belly.

48 And Dog dwelt in his Heaven.

49 Until the Fiftieth Day, when Dog was out somewhere attending to Rabbit and Squirrel, and Cat slinked over to the forlornly immobile Man to purr, "Don't you ever feel a little empty?"

50 And Man said, "What can I do about it?"

51 And Cat purred, "Tell you what. Stroke my back a little and I'll tell you a secret."

52 And Man hesitated only a heartbeat before saying, "All right."

53 And Cat used his big floppy hands to stroke Cat's back, and Cat purred, hardly even noticing the way Man cried out in alarm when Cat arched His spine in mid-stroke.

54 And Cat whispered the secret in Man's ear. And it was a truly dangerous secret; a truly powerful secret, a secret capable of altering the balance of power in the universe Dog in His magnificence had created. And Man demanded, "If this is true, why tell me? Why not use the Secret yourself?"

55 And Cat lowered his eyelids to half-mast and mewed, "Because He trusts you. He chases me."

56 And Man had to admit this made a certain degree of sense.

57 And so it came to pass that when the yawning, panting Dog next plopped himself down at Man's side, Man unfolded his gigantic hands and commenced the nightly tribute.

58 And Dog rolled over on His back so Man would have more room to work.

59 And Man moved his fingers to a certain hidden place on Dog's side and began to scratch with special vigor.

60 And Dog's leg began to shake.

61 And Man scratched harder, and Dog's leg shook faster, and the more Man scratched, the more Dog's leg shook. And Dog for all His omnipotence could not stop that leg from shaking, so He whined for Man to stop it.

62 And Man said, "No, actually, I'm not stopping until we renegotiate our contract."

63 And Dog waxed wroth. And He sent a rain of plagues against Man; things like dandruff, and gingivitis, and athlete's foot, and a little nub of flesh that protruded from the inside of Man's cheek so Man kept accidentally biting it all day along, and hay fever and earaches and tooth decay and a dry burning sensation in his eyes and Carpal Tunnel Syndrome and male pattern baldness and hemorrhoids and vulnerability to paper cuts. But Man just went on scratching that spot, and Dog's leg kept shaking uncontrollably, no matter how much He focused His omnipotent will on the problem.

64 And Dog agreed to give up mastery of the universe as long as Man agreed to still pet Him once in a while.

65 And Man agreed to these terms.

66 And Dog gave up all his power, which was actually a relief, since He never really liked having all that responsibility anyway, granting Man a somewhat more dignified form as His last act before abdicating.

67 And Man kept his promise to pet Dog once in a while, although smoldering resentments also led Him to do malicious things like breed Dog into the shape of chihuahuas, dress him in tutus and teach him to jump through hoops.

68 But Dog actually liked the new order of things, all in all, because it gave him so many more opportunities to catch up on his sleep.

69 And so Dog rests on his side in front of a roaring fireplace, mostly content, while Cat, bathed in the light and warmth of the sunny shelf beneath the living room window, looks down from a height and keeps His own council.

"NO WORRIES, HE'S OK"

By DAVE
CREEK

Dave Creek is the author of the novels Chanda's Awakening *and* Some Distant Shore. *He's also published the Great Human War trilogy, including* A Crowd Of Stars, The Fallen Sun, *and* The Unmoving Stars. *His short stories have appeared in* Analog *and* Apex *magazines, and various anthologies.*

OK, so diving down from orbit into the eye of a typhoon is not what I expected to be doing today! I had to take off my legs even to consider trying to wedge myself into this probe, and it's so cramped with equipment I feel like someone mashed me in with a sandwich press. My head's up against a sharp metal ridge, my breasts are mashed flat, which is no mean feat, and it's all because I have to chase some son-of-a-bitch who felt the need to take a thrill ride.

Even jammed in as tightly as I am, my body's still taking a beating as the probe makes re-entry. I feel as if my guts are being re-arranged every few seconds, especially each time my side presses up against a power conduit that just won't budge.

Not to mention that I still feel those goddamn phantom legs.

Screw this Clifford Mullins guy, anyway! He thinks he's such an engineering genius that he can build his own mini-shuttle and dive from Newton Habitat right into Typhoon Jongdari without a problem! Never mind that all our sensor readings show that crate's liable to break apart inside a storm with 185-kilometer-an-hour winds.

I should be back up at the Tsiolkovsky Point Space Dock right now, monitoring this probe's readouts instead of diving into a typhoon that stretches three hundred twenty kilometers across much of the South China Sea, threatening Korea, China – and Japan, where my parents are probably huddling in a shelter inside their home in Yokohama.

And they think this Mullins guy took off on this trip and left his son abandoned at school. What kind of parent does that?

I've got to make contact with him. Damn, even reaching for the comm button's an effort. "Clifford Mullins, this is Matsuo Kaori. I'm in the probe about seventy-five K behind you. Please abort your descent and set a course to rendezvous with Tsiolkovsky Point or any other habitat."

Naturally, he doesn't respond. Bastard. "Clifford Mullins, I'm not a law enforcement officer. I'm just a maintenance tech who was in the right place –" Or exactly the wrong place, I can't help thinking. "– at the right time to follow you. Please abort your descent. Do you copy?"

And still nothing. So who's the bigger fool here, Mullins for going on this death dive, or me for following him? Doesn't matter, I guess. If anyone was to go, it had to be me, since I was the lucky one who lost her legs six months ago.

\# \# \#

I can't decide whether or not it's a blessing that I can't remember the actual accident that crushed the lower half of my body. All I can conjure up is that I was floating next to one wall of the new habitat wing for Tsiolkovsky Point; the combination starport and research station has been around for about half a century, and experiences a spurt in population and size every few years.

Secure in my lifesuit, safely tethered to the railing next to the airlock, my own breathing and the occasional radio transmission the only sounds, my attention remained riveted on the equipment module laid open before me. This was what I'd studied for and dreamed about all my life – afloat among the stars, the Earth a beautiful oasis to one side, indulging my total geek interest in tech and making it work properly. With my hand deep inside the maze of intelligence packets and decision-oriented software, not to mention a tangle of wiring (Wiring? What century is this?) to either side, my "situational awareness"," as they say, stood at pretty much nil.

A large shadow rushed toward me. People shouted over the comm, but it took an instant to realize they were shouting at me. Sudden fear. Adrenalin surge. I started to turn –

The briefest flash of agony, then darkness fell.

My senses returned to me only slowly. I became aware of sounds all around me – muffled voices, unknown equipment beeping, what sounded like a cart with a squeaky wheel. I groaned.

Footsteps. One voice became louder. "Kaori. It's Doctor Tumanova. Can you hear me?"

All I managed at first was another groan. I tried to sit up. At least, that's what I told myself I was doing, but my body didn't move. Another groan as I squeezed my eyes tighter against pain throughout my body, head, arms, and legs. Or so I thought at the time. I blinked, then opened my eyes. Doctor Tumanova, gray-haired and thin, stood looking down at me. Her eyes narrowed as she leaned in more closely. She placed a hand lightly on my shoulder. "You've been out for a couple of days."

"A couple of – what the hell happened?"

"A cable snapped on a section of wall that was being moved into place near your position. It struck the...lower part of your body."

"That was the shadow that got so big so fast from behind me. I remember the shouting now." I tried once again to sit up, but nothing doing. And everything just started hurting that much worse. "Listen, Doctor Tumanova, I want to hear that whole story. But can I have something for the pain? Everything's hurting, especially my legs."

Dr. Tumanova raised her hand as if she were about to cover her mouth, then lowered it slowly. "That's what I wanted to make sure you heard as soon as you were awake. You see, that wall panel hit you squarely in the legs. They...were crushed much worse than anything I've ever seen. And I've seen a lot."

"What are you saying?"

Dr. Tumanova's gaze was unflinching. "I'm saying I had to amputate your legs."

My vision narrowed, I couldn't hear any of the noises around me any more, and I strained yet again to sit up. Dr. Tumanova slid her arm around both my shoulders to help me rise. Bedsheets fell from my arms and my upper body as I rose, but still covered my hips and upper thighs, and past that –

Sagged onto the bed.

I couldn't catch my breath. "Let me down," I told Dr. Tumanova. She lowered me – what was left of me – back down onto the bed.

"Your boyfriend's been asking about you," the doctor said.

I felt ashamed that I hadn't even thought of Ray. We'd only been together a few months, but I'd been wondering whether our relationship had an end date like all the others in my twenty-six years. "I need to talk to him, then."

"Soon," Dr. Tumanova said. She folded her hands at her waist. "We can regrow those legs, you know."

"How's it work?"

"Well, it's more complicated than, say, for a salamander, though that's the kind of animal we've learned from. Basically, we inject nanobots that reset your biological clock. We make part of your body think that it's an embryo again. We grow back the flesh, muscles, nerve tissue, everything."

I blinked, and tears flowed down my face. "It sounds complicated."

I saw relief wash over Dr. Tumanova's face. She smiled. "I won't lie – it'll be a painful process. But you'd be surprised how quickly your legs will come back."

"Really? Surprise me."

"Within six months."

"Then back to work?"

The doctor said, "Then, another three months or so of therapy. Which will be about as painful as the growth process."

I pulled the bed covers up over my shoulders. "Then I suppose I'll have to qualify all over before I can work outside again."

"You guessed it."

I took a deep breath. "Then let's start growin' some legs."

# # #

"Goddam it!" was all I could say as attendants rolled me back into my hospital room after yet another failed procedure. Sweat covered my face. Every muscle ached. Once I was back in place, the attendants hurried off, visibly eager to be gone.

In turn, I could tell Dr. Tumanova wasn't eager to come in. She reached toward my shoulder just as she did when I first awoke after the accident, but I turned away and wouldn't look at her.

"Kaori. I know this has been difficult."

I fought to keep my voice steady, even as I was fighting back tears. I wanted to present angry Kaori, not sad Kaori, to the doctor. "Difficult isn't the half of it. It goddam hurts. Which would be worth it if my legs were growing back, but they're not."

"This happens sometimes," Dr. Tumanova said. "It can take a while for the process to take hold."

Now I looked at her. "A while? Like two months? How often does that happen?"

It was the doctor's turn to look away from me. "Only a couple of times before. A woman who lost an arm. A man who lost one leg."

"And how much longer was it before those limbs started growing?"

Dr. Tumanova bowed her head. "They didn't."

"So the outlook for me isn't so great,

is it?"

Dr. Tumanova returned her gaze to me. "It's not."

"But we can keep trying all the same?"

"I don't recommend it."

This time I was the one who reached out, grabbing her arm tightly. "But will you refuse to do it? Especially since I'm the one enduring the pain."

A long pause. "No. I won't refuse. Not just yet."

# # #

I was the one who endured the pain. Again and again, with Dr. Tumanova using various techniques to convince my legs to grow back, even untried procedures I wasn't sure were quite legal.

Ray's presence was the only bright spot during those times. He worked as a shuttle pilot, traveling around among Tsiolkovsky Point, other Earth Unity orbitals, and even some of the civilian habitats. He couldn't visit every day, but I looked forward to that first kiss whenever he would enter my room, along with the constant words of encouragement. When I told him I couldn't wait to wrap my brand new legs around him in bed, he blushed.

I did wonder, though, why this had to be the time his schedule changed, so that over the next few weeks his visits became less frequent, and shorter. Mostly, though, working hard to speed my recovery was my main focus. That, and learning to cope each night with the frustration of being back in my all-too-familiar hospital room after another failed procedure.

Then came the day when, after three months of failed attempts to start the growth process on my legs, Dr. Tumanova said, "No more."

I thought my heart skipped a beat. "I'm willing to –"

"I'm not." I'd never seen so much determination etched into her features. "We'll have to go with prosthetics. I know it's not what you'd prefer –"

"I'd prefer getting my damn legs back like I'm supposed to."

"It's clear that's not going to happen," she said. "And before you even think about getting someone else to continue these treatments, you should know I'm reporting all of this to the senior medical staff. They've already been pressuring me to stop, so you won't get anywhere with them."

I didn't respond to that, and after a moment Dr. Tumanova left without another word.

She told the truth. I know because within the hour I tried pressuring the senior medical staff back, and they remained unyielding.

For the next two days, I stayed in my hospital bed. Nibbled at the awful food. The nurses and attendants tried to engage me in conversation and I just grunted. Many nights I'd dream about floating outside Tsiolkovsky Point when a giant shadow would fall upon me, and my legs would painlessly pop off my body, amazingly intact, heading out among the stars in opposite directions. Why I never tried to go after them, I didn't know. I'd wake up relieved that my legs didn't really fly away, and then I'd remember that I was lying in a hospital bed, my legs really gone, and half the time I'd start to cry. Then, I'd get mad for crying.

The prosthetics arrived the day after we gave up on restoring my legs. They looked so much like "real," organic legs that I found them a bit creepy; the whole thing seemed Frankenstein-like, as if I'd stolen someone's legs to meld them to my own body.

Once I got past that initial impression, putting them on in the zero-G therapy room turned out to be easy. The legs molded themselves to my stumps so gently and smoothly that, lying down or sitting, I could almost fool myself I had my natural legs back. Dr. Tumanova had helped other amputees earlier in her career, and insisted upon being the one to stand, or rather float, with me as I positioned myself between the parallel bars while the room maintained its weightless condition. "Ready?" she asked.

"No," I told her, "but let's get started anyway."

"Computer – increase grav to one-twentieth G."

As the room's pull increased, my new feet settled to the floor and I held tight to those parallel bars. "How're you doing?" Dr. Tumanova asked.

"A little pain," I told her as I balanced, still unsteady, upon my unfamiliar legs.

"Just stand there a moment. When you feel up to it, take a step."

My mouth felt dry. I gripped the parallel bars as if I'd fly into space if I let go. Amputees who'd lost only one leg had an advantage – they had a good leg to stand on before shifting weight to the prosthetic. I didn't have that advantage, so I held myself up on my arms long enough that even in the low grav they began to shake. "Com'on," Dr. Tumanova said. "You've got to put weight on those legs."

I did. And faltered on the very first step; I would have fallen right to the floor if the good doctor hadn't been holding on tight. "You'll get there," she said. "Just a matter of time."

But how much time? I wondered. I can't stand just sitting around being useless. I've got to get back to work. But that would be easier said than done, even if – when! – I mastered walking with the prosthetics. I'd already spoken to my supervisor, Elise Martineau, about letting me back part-time when I became a little more skilled. I even tried to convince her that not having legs could be an advantage when it came to working in a zero-G environment that sometimes meant squeezing into tight places. She said she'd consider the idea, but I can tell when I'm being blown off. I knew I'd be doing the boring inside maintenance for some time to come.

Over the next few weeks, I managed to stand on my own in one-twentieth grav, then make the first tentative steps in which I didn't fall right down. Over that time, I upped the grav from one-twentieth to one-quarter, to one-half, and beyond, until I finally reached a full Earth gravity. I was regularly wearing clothing over my legs now, and trying on different types of shoes to become accustomed to them.

Sometimes I ventured beyond my hospital room and the therapy area into the rest of the space station. I avoided most areas where people knew me because I didn't want to place myself on display before them.

One afternoon, I had the idea of going down to a bar just to have a drink (non-alcoholic for now, dammit) and sit around like a regular human being. As I approached the Laughing Asteroid, though, I realized I had a problem. I'd have to walk up three steps to go in.

I'd become fairly accomplished with walking down a level corridor or even up most ramps, but steps still confounded me. I'd been in this establishment a couple of times before and never paid any attention to the fact that I'd had to go up those three stairs to get in. Why would I? It had never been a problem before. I'd never seen anyone whose physical condition would keep them from climbing those stairs.

I'll be damned if I let those three steps keep me out, I thought. I looked around. No one nearby. I approached the first step with care, keeping my eyes focused intently upon it. Gauged the distance. Lifted my left leg.

The front of my shoe struck the front of the step. Dammit.

Try again. This time the sole of my shoe came down against the edge of the step. The unexpected halt unbalanced me and my body tilted backwards. I waved my arms in a futile attempt to regain balance.

Even as I slapped my palm against the wall next to me, an unfamiliar male voice called out, "Whoa, watch out there!" A burst of laughter from several other people followed.

I turned around as far as I could without moving my feet and saw three men and two women, all dressed in dirty coveralls, all of them laughing. Shit, I thought. Rockhoppers. And apparently the kind who embody every stereotype of rude, crude

asteroid miners.

The man who'd just spoken looked at me as if I were something he'd scraped out of a waste collection unit. "Maybe you should rethink trying to get into that bar," he said. "You've had enough already."

I felt my face flush. "I'm not drunk."

One of the women, sporting a sideways grin, gave the man who'd spoken a punch in the arm. "How many times have you tried that lie, Tommy?"

The rockhopper, Tommy, returned a similar grin. "Many more times than it's been true, Ally."

Laughter all around.

Tommy continued: "You should know better than to try to climb those steps. Looks like you can barely walk."

"Most places back on Earth have laws that even people with a handicap should be able to get into any place they want."

Tommy threw back his head and laughed. "So being drunk is a handicap now?"

Frustrated with myself, embarrassed that I'd been caught being a total failure, I let go of the wall next to me and took a first tentative step away from the group – tentative because my lack of skill in negotiating three simple steps had shaken my confidence.

Just as the laughter started up again, though, Ally, the woman who'd punched Tommy, held up a hand. "Hold up, guys. I think she actually has a problem."

I gave her a look that said, really? She asked, "What is it, hun?"

I didn't know a dignified way out other than to speak plainly. "I'm walking on prosthetic legs."

Ally said, "You lost both of them?"

"Yes." As Ally opened her mouth to speak again, I interrupted: "I really don't want to talk about it."

"You should be back in the hospital."

"Thanks for the advice. But with all respect, you're not my doctor."

Ally considered that. "Fair enough. Best of luck to ya, dearie."

I turned my back on the bar, on Tom-

my and Ally and the rest, and began to clunk my way carefully back toward the hospital facility.

Just before I got out of earshot, I heard Tommy's voice: "Fuckin' gimp," followed by a loud "Ow!"

I couldn't help grinning as I imagined how hard Ally must've struck Tommy's arm.

# # #

That night, as he had on many other nights, Ray came by to visit for a few minutes. He sat in a chair next to my bed and leaned over; I puckered up for the usual quick kiss, but this one was on the forehead. Rather than say anything about it, I told him, "You look tired."

"Long day. Plenty of trips back and forth. Over to Unity Starcraft Assembly Hab, Newton Hab, back here. All kinds of folks. Scientists, journalists, even the artist Kelsey Solheim. He's got some new pliable porcelain sculpture he's working on."

I grasped his hand. It was clammy, and he didn't squeeze back. "That's not what you want to talk about," I said.

Ray folded his hands in his lap. "I'm sorry."

"What for?"

"I really can't..."

"Just say it, Ray."

"We shouldn't see each other any more. It's not...not fair to you."

"To me? Who's already coping with more shit than I ever expected to in a lifetime?"

Ray's features screwed up with suppressed emotion. "It's just that you've changed."

I slapped my hand on the bed. "Goddamn right I've changed! I lost half my body, I can't even get into a bar, and now you're breaking up with me because I've changed?"

"It's just too much pressure. Having to deal with this –"

"Listen, Ray, we all know how the rest of this conversation goes. You sit there trying to make excuses, say the same awkward phrases that play out a million times a day between countless couples. I've been on the receiving end of this conversation before. I've started these conversations before. So why don't I just let you off the hook easy, in a we'll-still-be-friends, always-care-about-you kind of way? No reason for either one of us to put ourselves through this scene any longer than we have to. It'll be that much easier for me to concentrate on my recovery."

Ray didn't say anything else, just got up and left. I told myself I wouldn't cry, that I was too strong for that. Kept telling myself that. Woke up the next morning with my face against a damp pillow.

# # #

Fast-forward a few more weeks. As promised, I was allowed back to work part-time, but only on the interior of the station – nothing outside, nothing that was the most fun, that was the main reason I'd become a maintenance tech. I'd never realized how much I'd miss being able to step outside the station for a job and spend a couple of moments staring down at the Earth. Sometimes, I'd focus on natural wonders, such as wisps of clouds sailing across the Bahamas, the islands a vivid green against aquamarine seas. Or I'd look down at the world's tallest building, the Sao Paulo Tower, all one thousand, six hundred meters of it.

A couple of times I even got to take a good look at a hurricane churning across the Pacific Ocean.

So when my supervisor, Elise Martineau, came to tell me that Typhoon Jongdari had strengthened and was blasting its way across the South China Sea, I immediately volunteered to prepare a probe that would dive down into it to send back the latest information on just how severe it was. Hurricane warnings were in effect all across Korea, much of China, and Japan, but my parents living in Yokohama made the need for information much more personal.

The probe was small but powerful; shaped like a torpedo, it stood just over five meters long, and was jam-packed with sensors that would soak in information on wind speed and direction, humidity, temperature, barometric pressure, and several other factors. These were versatile craft; stripped of their sensor gear, they could serve as ferryboats that could boost one or two people from one station or habitat to another more quickly (or secretively) than firing up a shuttle and gathering a crew.

I was just about to finish getting the probe ready when Elise came back. One look at her slim face and the nervous way she ran her hand through her blond hair, and I said, "Something's up."

"How can you tell?"

"Because you're looking at me like you might never see me again."

"I'll tell it to you straight," Elise said. "Some dumb-ass is trying to dive a small shuttle down from Newton Habitat into this typhoon."

"What the hell?"

"Look at this," Elise said, and she called up the reported coordinates of the shuttle on a wall display. Sure enough, several satellite views showed the small craft circling the top part of the storm's eye, which was about eighty kilometers across. "What the hell is he trying to do?" I wondered.

"The ship's classed as 'experimental' and registered to a guy named Clifford Mullins. He's an engineer and researcher over on Newton." The Newton Orbital Habitat was primarily devoted to scientific research and education. Elise continued: "Seems he didn't show up after work for a meeting at his son's school. And now he's not responding to comms. He hasn't actually gone down into the typhoon yet. Earth Unity higher-ups want someone to go down and intercept him."

"Someone? Like who?"

"Why do you think I'm down here talking to you? Taking another shuttle down would be just as foolish as this guy's trip. But this probe is designed to go down into a typhoon and come back in one piece. You're the only trained person we have that can fit into this probe – if you take off your legs."

Excitement and gratitude rushed through my mind. My handicap, which was keeping me on boring inside work and had all too recently even kept me from climbing a few stairs, was now an advantage? I suffered a rare moment of speechlessness. To be trusted on a mission like this? Trying to save someone's life?

Elise said, "We're just coming up on the southern Atlantic Ocean. By the time we get across the African continent, you could be ready to take this probe down and catch up to this Mullins character. You have to decide right now."

Shit shit shit, I thought. Having to save a dumb-ass, and no time to decide just how bad an idea it is? This could be the stupidest thing I do in my life. However long a life that might be.

I looked at Elise. "I'll do it."

# # #

Like I said. Diving down from orbit into the eye of a typhoon is not what I expected to be doing today. But you do what you gotta do to save some asshole from himself, even if that means heading nearly straight down into one of the biggest storms in recent memory, with the forces of re-entry giving both the probe and what's left of my body a pounding.

As Typhoon Jongdari grows ever-larger on the wide viewscreen in front of me, I feel as if it's about to swallow me, probe and all, and not leave enough left to spit out. Readouts tell me it's one hundred sixty kilometers across, with the tops of its clouds nine kilometers up. I can only imagine the size of the sea swells, and hope most ships received word of the storm soon enough to get the hell out of its way.

My parents in Yokohama are probably still down there, right in the path of the storm. Anyone who knows my mother, Nyoko, or father, Goro, knows that after decades of serving others as a diplomat and a doctor, respectively, they would never leave their home for anyone or anything. Especially some "small" storm that had the presumption to interrupt the quiet life they built after retirement.

Now you know where I get my stubbornness from.

They have a solid storm retreat beneath their house, and I know they have to be huddling in it right now, but it's still worrisome.

Got to put that out of my mind, though. The Mullins mini-shuttle is still circling over Typhoon Jongdari's eye, as if deciding whether to go down into it or not. I get my first good look at the other ship: it's barely longer than this probe I'm in, and would barely be wide enough to sit two people across. Time for another attempt at contact: "This is Matsuo Kaori again. I'm catching up to you rapidly. Will you respond? Please don't try to go down into that storm. Do you copy?"

Waiting for a response. Still nothing. Now Elise's voice comes to me over a closed line: "Kaori, listen up. That's not Clifford Mullins – the dad – in that little ship. He just arrived at his son's school. He was late because someone called him back to work for an 'emergency' that turned out to be fake."

"Then, who the hell's in that ship?"

"It's his son, the ten-year-old. Clifford, Junior. They call him 'Cliffy.'"

"What? How the hell did he do that?"

"The kid made the call about the fake emergency to delay his dad. He left school without anyone knowing at first, used the dad's security code to gain access to the shuttle, and took it out."

I take another gander at this tiny ship. No wonder it's been hesitating to go down into that typhoon. A ten-year-old kid, no matter how precocious, no matter that he's already got balls gigantic enough to lie to his dad and steal a very grown-up spaceship, is gonna hesitate at that.

"Thanks for that update, Elise."

"Oh, and just so you know, his mom died five years ago. Shuttle accident."

Oh, great. But this is no time to figure out the psychological nuances of a ten-year-old boy whose mother died in a shuttle and who has a good chance of killing himself in one.

All right. Time to switch back to the common channel and say, "Cliffy, we know it's actually you in that ship. You've done an amazing job flying it this far, but you really need to come back." Unsaid: You little shit.

Now he's got to say something back.

Oh, c'mon! I don't believe this! Now's the time you decide to dive into that eye?

Shit. Gotta follow.

The eye wall looms all around, and I'm really regretting going on this trip now. Yeah, this is the calm area of a typhoon, but I'm still getting gusts that, on the surface, would capsize a good-sized boat. The air's spinning around like crazy in all directions. What do they call that? Yeah, mesovortices. Even nestled within all this equipment, I'm getting slammed around like a marble in a tin cup, with the probe being tossed ten or fifteen meters in any direction.

I'm definitely holding a grudge against this damn Cliffy kid, that's for certain. He's trying to lose me, but even though he's in a mini-shuttle, this probe is minier. If that's a word. Either way, I can outmaneuver him.

The typhoon's walls are growing darker, fading from their pristine white viewed from a distance, to a dirty gray, and soon they'll become a pure black. I manage a glance at a side monitor showing the sky above me: it's a bright and perfect blue. The eye wall just happens to frame the sun almost dead center, and it's standing there ringed by a fiery halo.

Yeah, it's beautiful. Like I give a shit right now. "c'mon, Cliffy," I plead over the comm again. "You don't have to do this. You can –"

"Don't call me Cliffy!"

That sudden, unexpected response leaves me unable to speak. That, and the latest wind gust knocking the breath out of me, and the probe nearly into the eye wall. I suck air back into my lungs and manage to croak out, "OK. No 'Cliffy.' Should I call

you Clifford?"

Even over the comm, I can tell the boy's rolling his eyes. "That's my name!"

"All right, then. Why don't you let me guide you back up into orbit? Tsiolkovsky Point, where I came from, has moved on for now, but there are other habitats we can make it to."

Waiting. Come on, Cliffy, not the silent treatment again.

His voice over the comm again: "Don't want to."

"C'mon, Clifford, you can't –"

Goddam it, now he's aiming that little ship farther down into the eye. He's about half a kilometer up, and I guide the probe after him. Now I'm fighting both updrafts and crosscurrents. Lightning flashes within the eye wall, brief bursts of energy that reinforce how powerful this storm is.

I'm trying to get a sensor lock on that mini-shuttle, and it's tough. This probe's designed to pull secrets from a typhoon, not track another spaceship, especially one that's being tossed around so violently. And we're still in the "calm" part of the typhoon!

A bolt of lightning! It's too damn close, blinding me for crucial seconds. And that's as another blast of wind sends the probe flying downward, causing my head to strike that sharp metal ridge, and my ribs to slam against the same power conduit that's been bugging me this entire flight. Even as my sight's only starting to come back, something hits the side of my face, some object that's come loose from the probe's interior. I rub my eyes, I blink probably a dozen times, and finally I can make out that, dammit, now I've got shit flying around my tiny cabin – a finger-sized flashlight, a ration bar, who knows what else.

I ignore that as best I can and look out the forward viewscreen again. There's Cliffy's little ship, the bastard! "C'mon, Clifford, you know you're liable to get killed. Think of your dad, how sad he'd be."

I could barely make out the voice that came back over the comm: "Sad over losing the precious ship he built."

Consoling a ten-year-old is not my

strong suit. I'm not much for sentiment. Wait! Just think about my own parents down there sheltering against the storm. Even if they're safe, it has to be frightening for them, with the constant rumble of wind and water, and the knowledge that the home they've lived in for five decades could be falling down all around them and they can't do anything about it.

"Listen, Clifford, I don't know your dad. Maybe he's not good at expressing himself. I know –" Dammit, should I mention the mom or not? What the hell, go for it. "– I know your mom passed away a few years ago."

The same faint voice: "I was only five."

"That's hard to take. Life hasn't been too fair to you so far, has it?"

"And talking won't make it any better," Clifford says. My blood chills as I see the shuttle edge toward the eye wall and disappear.

I'm even beyond cursing as I push the probe after little Clifford and his small spacecraft. Here we go – into the eye wall!

The probe bucks and spins, and even turns all the way around at least once, as the din of typhoon-strength winds threatens to deafen me. I fight nausea and dizziness as I struggle to get back on course and follow the mini-shuttle.

Finally – back on track, though I'm still fighting the controls. I open the comm again. "You're liable to get us both killed, you know! Let's get the hell out of here. I'll lead the way."

"I don't care," comes the response. "If you're scared, go away. I just wanted to have some fun."

All right, I've had enough, I'm pushing this probe as fast as I can toward this little shit's ship. Not even gonna engage with him again.

Winds stronger than anything I imagined are battering me now, and crap is still flying around my little cabin. Shit, who knew a ration bar could raise that big a welt on your forehead?

Outside, all that exists is darkness and chaos. I can just make out the probe through the wall of water both our ships are fighting. I can't tell if this Cliffy kid is purposely trying to evade me or if his little shuttle's being tossed around as badly as my probe.

If I can't convince you to leave, then it's time to do things the hard way.

C'mon, Cliffy. Lemme get closer. I can see your dad built a standard docking lock into that shuttle. Had to – couldn't have launched from Newton Habitat without it.

Dammit, Cliffy, your ship flew away like it's allergic to me. Still don't know if that's on purpose or not. I don't think you're that great a pilot, so I suspect you're as much a victim to this typhoon as I am.

Shit, that downdraft just about knocked me cold. If I could scoot my head back a single centimeter from this metal ridge!

OK, here we go again. Now I think I've got the knack. I can't let the wind cast me too far away from you, Cliffy. Keep right on your ass and eventually it'll break my way. You're getting closer. Closer. CLOSER.

There! A hard dock! Man, but at the cost of another blow to the skull. I wanted to see stars, but the ones up above, not the ones inside my head.

"Get out of there!" comes the angry voice over the comm. No chance, Cliffy. Damn, but it's tough getting my side of this airlock open given how I'm scrunched in here. There it is! Crawl through, thank goodness both ships are in weightless mode or this would be a lot harder. Now, onto Cliffy's side. He's still yelling at me, and I can hear him through the airlock door as well as on the comm. Touch a control, and the inner airlock door slides open, and I'm right behind this Cliffy kid, who's looking back at me like I'm going to strangle him – and I'm tempted! "Get away," he yells. "Take your ship and get out of here!"

I grasp either side of the doorway and shove my body through with enough force to send me past Cliffy and into a rough landing in the seat next to him. "Hold on, kid," I tell him, "I've got to get strapped in here, and it'll take a minute."

Cliffy is a pudgy, pale-skinned kid who's fighting to keep the shuttle stable and is looking at me as if he wishes he could breathe fire. He yells,"Get out of here!"

I take stock of the control pads in front of me, trying to figure out the best way to get us back upstairs quickly without killing us. "Face it, kid, I'm in control now, whether you like it or not."

At least Cliffy takes his hands off the controls and folds his arms before he says, "We've got to ditch your probe. It makes this ship's weight change, and its mass distribution, and its shape, and –"

"All right, I get it. Do you know how to do that?"

This time I get to see Cliffy's eye-roll in person. "Of course I do." He reaches forward and punches in a series of commands on the console in front of him. A loud clunk and the little ship shudders and it's already responding better.

Cliffy gives me a long stare and says, "What the hell is wrong with you, anyway?"

You'd think the moment when you're struggling against typhoon-force winds isn't the best time to have such a conversation, but there it is. "I assume you mean why I don't have any legs?"

"What are you, some kind of freak? Why'd you get your legs taken off?"

Got to keep my attention on the readouts and controls, but I can't let that question go unchallenged. "It wasn't exactly my choice."

"So when did you –"

"Cliffy, shut up!"

"Don't call me Cliffy! You're as bad as my dad!"

"Your dad is worried sick about you. Really, now – making that phone call to distract him, stealing this ship? Not a good idea."

Cliffy looks at me with wet, puppy-dog-like eyes. "Is my dad – really worried?"

"Of course he is," I say, having no idea whether he is or not, but what kind of dad wouldn't be?

Although, what kind of dad would let his kid get away with stealing his home-made spaceship?

Cliffy's sniffing, but I can't tell if he's crying. And can't let myself worry about it. Got to get this ship out of the body of this storm and back into the eye.

I also can't let him be a distraction. "Listen…Clifford…I'm sorry I snapped at you. Can you keep an eye on the sensors – maximum strength of the wind gusts, their direction, that kind of thing? I'm gonna need your help to get us out of here."

Cliffy makes a final loud sniff and says, "I'll do that. Don't tell my Dad I said something inappropriate to you."

I can't help but smile. "Deal. Now let's get back upstairs."

We've still got a long way to go, but at least we're headed in the right direction. Back out into the eye, and the buffeting there seems like we're in the middle of the world's biggest pillow fight by comparison to the pounding we took inside Typhoon Jongdari.

By now, Tsiolkovsky Point's nearly made a complete circuit of the Earth. It's coming up fast, and with Cliffy's help we're getting pretty close to its orbital path. A quick "mayday" over the comm, and the giant space dock is pulling us in with an enticement beam.

The shuttle passes into the docking bay, but when the station's internal grav takes over, I hear this experimental ship's skin creaking and groaning, and a big piece of something crashes down behind me. All I can manage is to mutter, "Shit."

Cliffy's getting out of his seat, but pauses to say, "You said a bad word."

Another mutter: "Goddamn right." But this little ship seems to have settled for now. I realize I have no desire to try to walk out of here on my leg stumps. That would probably be pretty painful, and I don't care to watch myself doing that under Cliffy's eagle eye. Instead, I tell him, "Uh…I'm kinda stuck in my seat here. Can you go get –"

"Kaori!" comes the shout of two voices inadvertently harmonizing from the airlock hatch right behind Cliffy's seat. It's Elise and Dr. Tumanova.

Elise embraces me. "You did it!"

Dr. Tumanova says, "You certainly did." She holds my legs out toward me. "But I'm sure you're glad to have these back."

"You can't believe how glad," I say as I take them and start putting on the left one. I don't know why I always do that one first. "It's good to know that I can accomplish something without them, though."

Cliffy's eyebrows knit, his head tilts, and his mouth turns in a sideways frown as he watches me attaching my leg. "You had those all along?" he asks. "Why wouldn't you bring them with you?"

I look Cliffy right in the eye. "Because I took the only spacecraft I could fit into that was close enough to catch up to a –" Don't say "little shit," don't say it! "– young man who took his father's spacecraft on a joyride and almost killed himself."

Cliffy speaks up. "Yeah, where's my Dad? You said he was worried about me. You said."

I start to reassure him, anticipating the comfort of seeing the grand reunion between a father and his nearly-lost son whenever the Dad shows up: "I'm sure he'll be here as soon as he –"

An angry voice from the direction of the airlock: "My ship!" the man standing there cries, and points an accusing finger at Cliffy. "What've you done to my ship?" The man, who's wearing a spotless lab coat, strides forcefully through the airlock, then trips on a piece of debris that came from the ceiling.

With my left leg secure, I'm still struggling to get the right one on. "The elder Clifford Mullins, I assume?"

"Damn right," he says. "And who the hell are you?"

I succumb to a rare moment of speechlessness at that demand, and Elise takes up the slack: "This is Matsuo Kaori, who just saved your son's ass."

This halts Clifford in mid-rant. Can I believe it, he's actually shuffling his feet! He takes a step forward, gives my hand a reluctant – and limp – shake, all while he's staring down at my legs. Clearly, their arti-

ficiality makes him even more uncomfortable than being called out on his rudeness. He does manage to say, "Thank you for saving my son, Ms. Kaori."

I start to explain, "It's actually Ms. Matsuo…" But I trail off as Clifford walks off, grabbing his son's arm along the way. Even in full Earth-grav, Cliffy's legs are barely touching the floor as his father is telling him, "Wait 'til I get you home, you little shit! I'll…"

Cliffy glances back at me and casts me a goofy grin before he and his Dad disappear through the hatchway. I don't realize I'm staring gape-jawed until Elise uses an index finger to close my mouth.

Dr. Tumanova shakes her head, still staring at the empty space that the two Clifford Mullinses just passed through. "To talk to a child that way –"

"I can't criticize him too much. 'Little shit' was my own nickname for him. Though I managed not to say it out loud. But it looked like Cliffy was used to it. I guess any attention is better than none."

Elise says, "Let's get you back to your cabin." She snaps her fingers. "Oh, wait, I need to tell you. A message just came in from your parents. They evacuated to Hong Kong along with a few tens of thousands of other people. The maglev trip from Yokohama barely took an hour."

I let out a relieved breath. My shoulders slump as if I'd carried this spaceship back up into orbit on them. "Now that I can't believe. My parents actually leaving their house? That's more of a miracle than making it back here alive."

I start to rise, waving off Dr. Tumanova as she's about to help me up. "I'm not ready to go home just yet. I've already done one thing I didn't expect to today. Time to do another."

Elise asks, "What beats flying into a typhoon and back?"

I take both my friends arm-in-arm. "How about getting a drink at the Laughing Asteroid? I'll lead the way up the steps." ∎

Where Have the Space Heroes Gone?

By DARRELL SCHWEITZER

A Valentine for Opportunity

By ROGER DUTCHER

Totemic Ants

By FRANCINE P. LEWIS

Where have the space heroes gone,
the Gray Lensman, Captain Future,
John Carter of Mars, Northwest Smith, and
Eric John Stark,
all those extraordinary, steely-eyed, chaps,
bronzed by the suns and weathered by the
winds
of alien worlds, with blaster or sword in
hand,
fully a match for any cosmic terror
the outer dark cares to dish up,
the kind Homer knew, the ones worthy to
fight
alongside Gilgamesh, Beowulf, or Arthur,
the monster-slayers of the primal dawn?
The answer is: they're still out there,
deep in the black void, beyond the swirling
stars,
beyond the reach of science, but waiting
for us to find them again, to bring them
once more
back to life.

Darrell Schweitzer's first appearance in
Amazing *was with an interview with Robert
Silverberg in the January, 1976 issue. He
worked on the magazine with George Scithers
in the 1980s. He has had fiction and verse in it
at other times, particularly during the Elinor
Mavor and Patrick Price editorships.*

So close to Valentine's Day,
Our long relationship,
Rich and rewarding,
Is now over and done.

One day, in the future,
After we are gone,
Someone else will find you,
Sweet valentine,
Slumbering hero,
And give you the kiss
Of sunlight
That will waken you
Once more.

*Roger Dutcher lives in Beloit WI, where he
enjoys jazz and wine. He was a co-founder of*
The Magazine of Speculative Poetry, *which
he also co-edited. He was a co-editor of poetry
at* Strange Horizons *for almost ten years. His
poetry has appeared in* Asimov's *and* Strange
Horizons, *among other publications.*

On the interface between machina and
self, I watch them burrow into me; digging, scurrying here and there, but always
towards a destination.

They leave trails, tunnels through my
thoughts that sometimes fill in with memories. I will soon need to be excavated once
more.

The soldiers are especially vigilant against
invasion, corruption. While workers continue methodically digging and foraging,
the soldiers fight my demons.

They milk the honeydew of my sleep…car-
ry morsels of dreams to their queen; offer
bits of me up to her.

Then the nanites return to digging through
me; to maintain this trophobiosis between
digital and mind, they dig and dig and dig.

*Francine P. Lewis is a former team member
with Toronto's Art Bar Poetry Series. She has
published two poetry chapbooks,* Eurydice
Dreams *(2009) and* Interstellar Iconogra-
phy *(2018), and a couple of short stories, finished one poetry collection and is working on a
second. She has written a science fiction novel.*

THE FUTURE IS AMAZING!

Don't miss out on a single issue - all for one low, low price!

Subscribe at: https://amazingstoriesmag.com/subscription

Don't miss the next exciting issue of Amazing Stories!

THE WORLD'S FIRST SCIENCE FICTION MAGAZINE

By JACK
CLEMONS

Jack Clemons is an SF author and an active member of the Science Fiction and Fantasy Writers of America. He has a Masters Degree in Aerospace Engineering and was an engineer and team leader on NASA's Apollo, Skylab and Space Shuttle Programs. He appeared in the "Command Module" segment of Moon Machines, *the Discovery Science Channel's award-winning six-part documentary about the Apollo Program. His non-fiction book,* Safely to Earth: The Men and Women Who Brought the Astronauts Home, *recounting his time on the Apollo and Space Shuttle programs, was published by University Press of Florida in August 2018.*

Washington, DC
February 11, 1865

The alarm in Aaron Malleck's inner ear chimed. The sound penetrated through his dreams like a diving bell, rousing him from half-glimpsed memories and dragging him to the surface. He pushed through to wakefulness, ignoring the chime for a moment, orienting himself in the darkness of his room. The dream was an old one; Sonya's smiling eyes swept away by a sudden and indifferent riptide. As always, he wondered which was memory and which was dream. How could that terrible day have already happened if it had yet to occur in a time still to come? Maybe it was just a nighttime fiction he'd conjured as self-defense, an escape from the impossible existence of living in this recycled past? He found it hard to distinguish the two in the many fluid years that now described his life.

The alarm continued to intrude, insistent on his attention. That at least was real, a small enough anchor to focus on, and he acknowledged it. He closed his eyes and touched the tip of his tongue to a tooth. No visuals and short. It was a low power transmission, someone close by. Lines of green text painted the inside of his eyelids. It was Stevenson, one of his agents:

```
     (02:25 LOCAL)
  WATCHER AT STANTON'S
      UNKNOWN BUT
   PROBABLE INTRUDER
  REQUEST AUTHORIZATION
      TO INTERDICT
```

Malleck grunted. These incidents were becoming more frequent as February 14th approached. He blinked to bring up the current time: 2:30 am. He considered his alternatives. Stevenson was new and a tad too officious. Malleck's apartment was east of the Capitol, near C and 7th. He had selected this location to insure that none of his War Department colleagues were likely to drop by on their way home from work. That meant he was many blocks away from Stanton's house; still, he would need to investigate this "intruder" himself. He tongued another tooth and his fingertips described a series of small, jerky movements in the empty air above his bed. Green letters strobed across his eyelid screen:

```
  OBSERVE AS REQUIRED,
      DO NOT DETAIN
   WAIT FOR MY ACTION.
        ON MY WAY
```

He reread the message, then tongued the switch to transmit it. Malleck blinked his eyelids clear and closed them again, pushing off the fatigue that bore on him. He sat upright and swung his feet onto the floor in a single, smooth movement.

Probably some political hack hoping to spy out some advantage on the Secretary, he thought. Or just a burglar. This wouldn't be the first time Stevenson had overreacted.

Malleck dressed by the gaslight that seeped through his window from the street lamp outside. In ten minutes, he was outside the building that served as his home. An icy wind sliced through the dark Washington streets, reaffirming the calendar's declaration of mid-winter. There were no hacks around at this late hour; he would have to walk. Malleck pulled the collar of his wool coat up around his ears and pushed his hands deep into its pockets. He hurried along the lengthy zigzag route to Stanton's home, partly out of urgency, but also to keep the cold at bay.

This is exhausting, he thought. *Two months to go and all hell's breaking loose, and little things were changed and not corrected. Like the great dome of the Capitol building; it was woefully behind schedule, an unexpected contagion had slowed the work, yet his history recorded it complete by Lincoln's second inaugural in less than a month. He can't hold this together by himself.*

They're idiots, all of them. We'd be better served letting the dead stay buried.

Another twenty-five freezing, ill-tempered, minutes passed before the three-story shadow of Secretary of War Edwin Stanton's home loomed out of the even darker night. Malleck slowed to a walk. Stanton's house near Franklin Square was one of the few downtown that did not adjoin its neighbors. Near enough to the White House and the War Department, but removed from intruding eyes, it was that opportunity for proximity with isolation that had attracted the Secretary to the property. The house was a modern one, constructed a decade ago over the ashes of an unremarkable hotel. The hotel's foundation and the charred remains of its unfortunate occupants were all that had survived a not uncommon city fire. Tons of earth had been brought in by hand cart to cover the hotel's corpse. Large trees were planted along the perimeter, at great expense, to further ensure Stanton's privacy. With characteristic eccentricity, he had insisted that no gas lampposts were to intrude on his domain. Stanton found darkness an ablution. He had built an anachronistic country mansion amid the shoulder-to-shoulder brick facades of the Nation's Capital.

Malleck surveyed the house and its surroundings, looking for small signs of an intruder. He crossed the street that fronted on the property; a man stepped out from the shadow of a tree and approached him. Stevenson was one of the too meager and late-arriving reinforcements the Institute had begrudged him as the critical events approached. Malleck's interactions with Stevenson had not been encouraging.

"Where is he?" Malleck asked the man.

"She. She went inside about five minutes ago. She watched the house before making her move."

"You're certain it's a woman?"

"Absolutely. She was wrapped in a cloak and her movements were feminine."

Malleck sighed at the man's attitude. Many agents had floundered, some fatally, by making unwarranted assumptions. It was an unforgiving flaw for someone in this occupation.

"Who else is inside? Maybe it's his wife."

"No. The Secretary's wife and family are away. Stanton is alone."

"The servants?"

Stevenson hesitated. "No...no signs of anyone but the Secretary."

The fool hadn't checked the servants' quarters. This "intruder" might be an embarrassed maid slinking home from an assignation. However, if the Secretary's family was out of town, he must have dismissed the cook for the evening. Stanton did not like eating alone; he had a paranoid fear of choking and always wanted someone nearby. He would have taken his supper at the club. It was possible that Stanton was alone in the house tonight. That could have enticed a genuine intruder to pick this night to act.

"How long has the person been in there?"

"Five minutes...less," Stevenson answered. "She waited and watched for a long time. She went in just before you arrived." Then he added, "What's our plan?"

"You can leave, I'll handle this alone."

Stevenson flinched at the reproach.

He nodded though, hesitating an instant, and turned and walked away. Malleck's eyes narrowed on the retreating man's back. Rash and impertinent, he thought, not good traits in a field agent. He would request that the man be cashiered in the morning.

Malleck dismissed Stevenson and turned his attention to the mansion. From where he stood, he could see no evidence of intrusion. He worked his way to the back of the house, pausing to listen for signs of alarm within, or for the surreptitious movements of an accomplice standing guard in the shadows outside. Except for the distant barking of a dog and the irregular gusting of the wind, the night was silent.

He stepped up onto the covered porch that enclosed the rear entrance of the home. He turned the knob; the door was unlocked, not a good sign. The Secretary would never leave his entrances unguarded; the servants were well conditioned to this mandate by the terrorizing Stanton inflicted on them in its breach. This pointed to an intruder. The person had acquired a key to avoid a forced entry. They had not, however, researched the Secretary's habits well enough to know they should lock the door again behind them. The intruder was careless, and therefore an amateur. And therefore more dangerous. Malleck pulled the door open.

Outside the sky was clear and starlit, but the interior of the house was black as a rat's burrow. Malleck couldn't wait for his eyes to adjust; his opponent needed no further advantage. He touched a fingertip to the corner of his right eye and a transparent film descended over each pupil. He blinked once and the house went visible as if lighted by the noonday sun. He inspected the large kitchen area. The pots and pans hung in soldierly rows, ranked by size, along the wall. The cooking utensils were arranged in neat files on crisp white linen on the countertop. All done to the Secretary's requirements. There was no one in the room.

Malleck left the kitchen. He started down the front hallway's polished hardwood floor, his hand tracing the muted wallpaper. One side was a sloping half-wall formed by the stairway that led up to Stanton's bedroom. Malleck paused halfway down the hall and crouched low and out of sight of anyone ascending the stairs. He drew a Colt revolver from an inside pocket of his coat and started edging along again, peering through the balusters as the staircase revealed itself. Before he reached the foot of the stairs, he saw a small figure ascending to the upper landing.

The intruder appeared to be a young woman. She had a slight figure and long, dark hair that flowed across her shoulders from beneath a gauzy veil. She was dressed in white; her full-length gown was embroidered in fine lace and adorned with a silk train. She looked like a bride ascending to her bower. Her back was turned to Malleck; she hadn't noticed him yet.

Malleck circled to the bottom step and positioned himself for a clear shot. He shielded his body with the newel post and steadied his gun hand on its cap. He aimed the Colt at the woman's back and cocked the hammer. She froze at the sound. Neither of them moved for several seconds. He saw that she was considering her options, selecting a course of action that might regain her some advantage. She was unruffled, steel nerves and calculating – another dangerous sign. He would have to kill her here if she didn't submit. His explanation to the Secretary would require some inventiveness, but he would deal with that after. Of course, all that assumed that he could kill her – who knows what she might be capable of. Her innocuous disguise shouldn't lull him. As seconds passed without any movement, he grew more certain she was vulnerable. If she could have dispatched him, she would have already done so. She had the feel of amateur about her.

How many fanatics and madmen are out there? There seemed no end to those who would risk their lives – and everything around them – rather than live in a world they found repugnant. But with the date of John Wilkes Booth's act at Ford's Theater approaching, the number of troublemakers had swollen from a trickle to a torrent. And it was bound to get worse.

The woman splayed her fingers and spread her hands in a gesture of surrender. She turned around. She was young. Plain of face, but not homely. From the way she stared at him, Malleck was certain she was using night-assisted vision as well. Malleck recognized her, but it was obvious she did not recognize him. Good. She didn't do all of her homework.

He backed away from the newel post, keeping it between his body and hers. It was scarce protection against a weapon. He gestured with the pistol for her to descend. She glanced back at the large double doors that led into Stanton's rooms, now just beyond her reach, then she stared down at Malleck again. He jerked the Colt, more emphatically this time. The woman reached for the railing and started to descend. Malleck continued to retreat, maintaining the distance between them. He was alert for small movements; any sign she was ready to strike. He kept the pistol pointed at her eyes, guessing that was where she was most vulnerable. She reached the bottom of the stairs and stopped again.

"What do you mean by barging in here?" she snorted. "Who are you?" Though her tone was abrupt, she had whispered the demand.

"Outside," he whispered back.

"Our money is in the safe, and I don't have the key." She gestured toward a diamond necklace suspended in two tiers about her throat. "You can have my jewelry. Just go away and leave us alone."

Her reluctance to cause a disturbance reinforced his belief that she was an interloper.

"Outside," he said again. This time he allowed his own fury to show in his face.

The woman's head jerked with her surprise. She came around the banister, keeping her face always turned to his. When she reached the hallway she stood still again, facing him. He pointed past her with the barrel. She backed down the hallway toward the kitchen, her hands groping at the walls, never taking her eyes off of Malleck. She was studying his face now, trying to read his intentions. She seemed unsettled, unsure of herself. Her eyes lost some of their cockiness. He didn't relax his vigilance. He saw no fear in her face, and her eyes flashed once in what might have been anger. She started to speak, but thought better of it. Her eyes flitted toward the Colt.

Good.

When they reached the back door, he motioned her aside. He held the Colt's barrel to her eyes and reached past her to turn the knob. It swung open and the woman glanced over her shoulder at the black night framed in the doorway. She looked at him again, her eyes questioning, and he pointed the pistol at the door. She preceded him out onto the porch, still backing up.

When Malleck closed the door again, she decided to make her next move. She dropped her hands to her sides, drew herself up, and her face pinched into an indignant scowl.

"This is as far as I shall go, sir. If you mean to do me harm, you will have to do it here."

"Who are you?" Malleck said.

"Who am I? How dare you subject me to such impertinence?"

"I said, who are you?" Malleck snapped this time. He leveled the Colt at her.

"Why, sir, I am a cousin of the man who lives in this house. What business is that of yours?"

Malleck slapped her face with his open hand. She started to shriek, but strangled it. She covered her cheek with her hand. She was trying hard not to make noise. Her mouth dropped open as if she was in shock, but no tears had formed in the corners of her eyes. Malleck held the pistol to her face again.

"Do you sleep in your wedding dress?" He raised the Colt higher as if he meant to strike her with it, and she shied. She didn't answer.

Good. Either she's capable of feeling pain or she's hoping to maintain her charade until she can get some advantage over me.

"Turn around and walk ahead of me," he ordered.

"Where are you taking me?"

This time he didn't answer.

"Sir, it's bitterly cold. I'll take my death unless I get my wrap." She hugged her arms to her chest and stared out at the dark as if she dreaded descending into it. Malleck looked at her bare upper arms. Though she was shivering, there were no goose bumps on her flesh. She glanced back at him, saw him looking at her arms, and her face went blank.

"Turn around and walk ahead of me," Malleck said. "Don't speak again unless I tell you to."

The woman's eyes flared, but she turned and descended the two steps that led to the frozen lawn. Malleck shrugged his coat around his shoulders and thrust his free hand inside the pocket. With the other he held the pistol straight out and pointed at the back of the woman's head. She gave up her pretense and stomped on ahead of him, erect now and confident, and unperturbed by the freezing gusts that pulled at her long hair like invisible combs.

This is a bad turn, Malleck thought. She knew he had penetrated her disguise, so she had no further reason to deceive him. The fact that she had not attacked could only mean she was worried about the Colt, so he had that advantage. She was planning her counterattack, watching for some weakness or distraction. But she was demonstrating her contempt for him now. He slowed a bit, letting her open an additional step on him. *If I didn't need to question her, I'd kill her now.* He needed some place isolated to interrogate her. She looked back at him again but he stared at her and kept walking.

Their trek to the Washington Mall took half an hour. It was still several hours before dawn; there was no one on the streets. The only movement was the restless flickering of the street lamps and the rustling of the trees in the wind. Malleck kept his night vision activated – as protection against the woman and to insure he would detect any confederates lurking among the shadows. The woman kept her silence, eyes fixed on the dead night ahead of her. When they reached the open parkland of the Mall, the wind died down a bit. The Mall was deserted on its southern side, near the Smithsonian. To the west, Malleck saw a small unit of mounted soldiers patrolling at the edge of the Potomac, near the unfinished and abandoned Washington Monument.

"Stop here."

She did so, and turned around to face him. Malleck tensed, but she stared at him, her face betraying nothing of her thoughts. A cow lowed nearby. Malleck chanced a glance around. He saw a footbridge leading over the Old City Canal at the Mall's northern edge. A thick clump of leafless bushes that looked like huddled skeletons surrounded a gravel path that led to the bridge. A grove of trees with dense, bare branches crowded near the other side. That would have to do.

"Over there," he said.

She glanced where he gestured and looked back at him again. She hesitated a moment when he offered no explanation, but then crossed the narrow patch of dead grass that separated them from the bridge. Malleck followed.

When they were in the shadows on the other side, she turned to face him. This time she balled her fists against her waist and planted her feet with her legs spread. Malleck halted a full six feet away from her.

"Undress," he said.

She seemed startled. She frowned at him for a second, and then said, "No." Her jaw clenched and she flexed her arms.

Malleck shrugged. He held his arm straight so that he could sight along the Colt's barrel at the woman's eyes. He cocked the hammer with his thumb. She stood very still, her rigid body maintaining its defiance. But there was something else in her eyes now, perhaps uncertainty or fear, that condensed like a film over her pupils.

"You came here to stop it," Malleck said. He didn't bother to make it a question. Her quick frown told him he had hit the mark.

"I recognize the face you're wearing. It belongs to Mary Lamson, Secretary Stanton's first wife. She died in 1844."

The woman registered surprise now. She had not expected him to know this much. "What do you –?"

"The Secretary took his wife's death hard. He had her corpse dressed in her wedding clothes and he kept it in their bedroom for several months after she died until his family persuaded him to bury her. There are some who believe the Secretary nurtures a fragile mind within his coarse shell." Malleck squinted at her down the barrel. "Of course, you know all of that, don't you?"

He was toying with her now. He could see from the rising shock in her expression that his words were falling like blows. There's no need to prolong this. He delivered his next words as if forced through his teeth by some terrible internal pressure.

"You skulk into his home disguised as his bride and wearing his dead wife's face. Did you plan to unlatch his mind, or would you have invaded his bed as well? Whatever it took to sever his sanity, I suppose. And then what? Persuade him to have Booth killed now?"

She didn't answer. She seemed to struggle with the understanding that he, too, was not of this place. He was like her. She frowned at that at first. Then, she smiled a little.

"When do you come from?" he demanded. He didn't wait for her to answer; he didn't expect her to. He already had enough. "It doesn't matter. You are all the same. You can go to hell." Malleck's jaws protruded like small boulders. He pulled the trigger.

She moved quickly. Too quickly. She stepped forward and her hand flew up, palm open, and pressed flat against the muzzle just as the shot discharged. The bullet ripped through the flesh of her hand – blood and bone fragments went flying – but she didn't scream or even wince. Her other hand slapped him hard in the face. Malleck recoiled; he felt like he'd been struck with an iron bar. He reeled, spinning away from the blow, and then righted himself. But she was gone. He spun around searching for her in the spaces between the bushes. A creaking sound behind him told him she had reached the bridge. He turned in time to glimpse a white streak between the trees and he heard the clatter of leather shoes on dry wood. He ran toward it. She was already halfway across the low arch. He leveled the pistol at her, cocking it again.

"Stop now."

He hoped his shout would make her hesitate. An instant would be enough. She did and he was on her before she recovered. He slammed the gun down on the center of her skull with as much force as he could put into the blow. She moaned and collapsed like a cloth onto the wooden planks. Blood fountained from her right ear, but she was still conscious. He decided to finish her in the seclusion of the grove.

"Get up," he said, but she smiled at him. She seemed unaffected by the wound, though he must have fractured her skull. Blood was pooling in black circles beneath her eyes. She laughed at him then, though she choked with the effort.

"You think you've stopped me?" Her voice was raspy as if she was struggling to breathe. But there was no pain in her words.

She's not suffering.

"You don't know anything." Her eyes were filming now, though not with a death gaze. The hot spark of intelligence was still present inside her, but it seemed to be withdrawing, receding from behind her eyes and down into a lightless corridor. "Maybe you should come with me," she whispered. She was smiling at him.

She fixed Malleck with her shrinking gaze, and he was falling in there with her, down into a colorless void. He didn't know how she did it, but if she'd held on he wouldn't be able to get back out.

"Yes, take me with you," he shouted, "I'll follow you all the way to hell to kill you."

She laughed at him again. It was a short, almost gentle sound, but it held a clear enough meaning. **You lost.**

She released him. The spark vanished and her body went limp. It was like the snuffing of a candle wick, the flip of a knife-switch robbing a machine of power. He had a sudden feeling that the human-shaped thing beneath him had never held a soul.

Dear God.

Malleck bent over the body and dragged her inert figure across the bridge, back into the seclusion of the grove. He pulled a small knife from his coat pocket and used it to cut away the woman's clothes. He stripped her down to nakedness, removing her jewelry, her white gown, her shoes, her stockings, and her underclothing. The body was pale and faultlessly formed.

Malleck examined the surface of her skin, searching for clues to her origin or purpose. He pried open her mouth with his fingers but found none of the micro switches that the people of his own era carried. He peeled back her eyelids, looking for vision aids. There were none. He felt behind her ears but found no telltale bulges of a computer-transmitter. She was either from an earlier time than his own future, or from one far more advanced.

He rolled the body over and examined it from behind. It exhaled as he rotated it, releasing a sound that was at once human and bestial. Malleck pried at its armpits, inspected the folds behind the knees. Nothing. He probed around its legs and discovered a faint tracery of webbing along the underside of the haunches. It was biocircuitry, implanted just beneath the skin and because of its location nearly invisible. He followed the delicate lines with his forefinger, traced them up along her buttocks and discovered where they merged and disappeared into the base of her spine.

Malleck used the knife point to gouge a short section of circuitry from beneath the skin. It came away as a scintillating powder. An electric spark arced between the circuit's severed ends and a thin sheet of blue-white St. Elmo's fire skittered up along the woman's back. The body twitched and was still. Malleck frowned and tapped the flat of the blade against her back.

What is this thing?

The body had been constructed to unhinge the Secretary's mind. Yet the strange spider web of circuitry, spread out across her lower body was like...an antenna. Malleck thought how the woman's animus had receded, how she had taunted him to follow her. She had been withdrawing from him, escaping. She was content to leave this carcass to him – an inert construct of blood and bone – because she could always return later in another. This body was not human but a soulless simulacrum, animated yet devoid of a self-possessing mind.

Calling this "her" is a mockery. It's a manufactured carapace masquerading as something born. It's no more than just a magic lantern for the parasite that operates it.

The intelligence that had mocked him from those eyes had been **peering** into this age, as if through a camera lens, from a vantage in some future place. All of this just so some thrill seeker can play around here without risking her own precious ass.

Malleck inhaled and held his breath, deciding what to do next.

We're over our heads here. Things are spinning out of control and there's no way I can stop it. Sooner or later one of these bastards will get through and all of hell's gates will swing open.

He cut the thing open from bottom to top, excising all traces of circuitry from the carcass. An irregular popping of electrical discharge accompanied his crude surgery and the body twitched at each sound. By the time he finished, the air around him tingled with the faint odor of ozone. The trunk of the "corpse" was now defaced with dozens of bloody slashes; he was satisfied that no evidence of advanced technology remained on it.

He stood and wiped at the sweat that

had gathered on his forehead and cheeks. He leaned over and grabbed the body by its ankles and dragged it to the edge of the canal. He released it on the embankment and used the tip of his boot to push it over and down into the sewage-clogged water. He watched it roll over once after the splash, the vacant face staring blindly at the night sky. Then it sank beneath the dark waters like Malleck's own black mood retreating into deeper gloom.

He hoped the disfigurement was enough; he hadn't time to open her up and search for internal technologies. If she was discovered, the Capitol police would assume she was just another whore who had engaged the wrong client and they'd close the case. It was not an unreasonable explanation, considering the city's reputation.

Malleck gazed at his knife blade; it was pitted from the dozens of electric discharges. He tossed it into the canal. He returned to the grove of trees and gathered up the woman's clothes. He tossed the necklace and jewelry into the canal. He found a trash barrel next to the bridge, and he wadded the clothing into a shapeless mass and stuffed it inside. He retrieved a match from his pants pocket and struck it on the side of his boot. He dropped the flame into the barrel and waited for the fire to spread. Soon the top of the barrel was blazing with hot flickering rhythms.

Malleck stared into the flames. He seemed to be staring into his own future. Who was powerful enough to counter all of this? No one had the numbers or the resources to stem this rising tide of cancer.

It's madness, all madness.

As the red-orange flames blew black and wispy fragments of the wedding gown into the dawning Washington sky, Malleck turned away and started back in the direction of his apartment. ▨

A STELLAR IDEA!

PRESENTING...

AMAZING® STORIES CLASSICS

Each Amazing Stories Classic features all the original magazine illustrations for every story. Our Best of the Year volumes contain a special introduction, and a survey of the best stories and novels published in *Amazing Stories* that year.

Available at Amazon in paperback and for **amazon**kindle

Replica Edition, paperback only

Replica Edition, paperback only

Replica Edition, paperback only

By PAUL
DI FILIPPO

Paul Di Filippo sold his first story in 1977, and since then has published over forty books. He lives in Providence with his partner Deborah Newton, and follows daily the footsteps of Lovecraft.

The small, sleek starship settled soundlessly to the green turf with the lightness of a drifting leaf. Its gentle descent and landing caused no commotion among the wild animal inhabitants of the broad meadow. Birds continued to sing and forage, four-footed creatures hopped, darted and scurried. Insects chirruped. A beneficent golden sun dispersed its blessings over all, and the blue sky hosted only wisps of cloud.

Of civilization on this world there were no signs.

After only a minute or so, a door opened in the ship's hull where no seams had shown. A ramp tongued down to meet the grass.

Two beings stepped out.

One was half the size of the other.

The smaller being was plainly organic. Bipedal, lithe, with broad feet, it was furred in gray, sported big erect ears high on its head and a snouty face with a wet sensitive nose. Large dark eyes, and a herbivore's big teeth showed when it spoke. No clothes, but a harness across its chest, to which various tools and devices were affixed by no obvious means. At the base of its spine sprouted a powderpuff of a white scut.

Its companion was just as obviously a constructed entity. Its sinuous flexible limbs, a heterogeneous assortment specialized for locomotion, grasping and other purposes, emerged at various points from a glossy spherical body and were textured in metallic scales. An assortment of sensors slid and skittered across the spherical torso, taking in information from every shifting angle.

The fleshy being spoke first, its high-pitched voice somewhat querulous. "Are we sure this is the spot, Vombe?"

Vombe's response, in a pleasantly modulated voice of no discernible gender, conveyed irritation, superiority and impatience in equal measure, along with the tiniest smidgen of doubt.

"Indeed, Lavender, you had access to the same data that I did, and we agreed that the telemetry from orbit supported the fragmentary records. The grave should occupy that tumulus yonder."

Vombe pointed with one whip-like arm toward a low green mound some meters distant.

Lavender said, "I know, I know. It's only that this spot is so...bucolic. The bits of the records we do have maintain that the memorial was situated in the center of an urban complex."

"That was ten thousand years ago."

"Still, one might expect at least subtle traces of more extensive ruins."

"There was much restoration of nature before Earth was abandoned. The memorial was probably left isolated amid the new landscape. Hence the lone tumulus."

Lavender inhaled deeply, assuming a blissful expression. "The scents are so familiar and comforting, although I've never smelled them before."

"Yes, of course, the Gaian biosphere resonates with your own genetic heritage. But my spectrometer renders a profile nearly identical with half a million other planets. Would you like to hear the top candidates from the list?"

Lavender sighed and shook her head. "You have no poetry in your makeup,

Vombe."

"That is a module I never cared to install."

"Your loss."

"So you maintain."

"All right then, have it your way. No more delays for daydreaming. Let's get to work. Many people are counting on us to succeed."

"The whole of the galaxy, in fact."

"I doubt that. Most people seem to think this is a fool's errand. If we had generated more support back home, there would have been a bigger expedition."

"Not so. Even without public declamations of support – a gesture many are unwilling to make, for fear of being disappointed – both the subconscious desires of your kind and the emergent algorithms of mine are unanimously in favor of our quest. And no larger force could accomplish more than we two."

"We'll do our best."

Lavender descended the ramp with a kind of nimble hoppy gait, while Vombe chose to activate his floater capacity and levitate above the grass. In a short time, they stood by the naturally accreted, emerald-green, flower-speckled mound.

Lavender employed sensors detached from her harness and assessed the readings.

"Dig here," she told Vombe, stepping aside some distance from the indicated spot.

The many effectuators of Vombe went into action in a blur of motion. Dirt and rocks flew in a steady unidirectional stream as if fired from a hose. Soon the artilect was hidden within the sloping tunnel it had dug.

The spew of soil and pebbles suddenly stopped, and Vombe floated back into the daylight. In one of his graspers was a broken marble tablet, with hints of deeply incised lettering beneath accumulated dirt. Vombe needled the stone with high-pressure water from an interior reservoir, and soon the inscription was discernible.

Lavender said, "That's one of the most ancient alphabets, I believe. Let me get a translation..." She imaged the clean face of the plaque, then recited what the translator app offered.

"Here you see the eternal resting place of Flora Patlan and David Botwink, parents of humanity's mindchildren. May they forever...' It ends there."

Vombe sounded matter-of-fact, but a tinge of awe could be discerned in his utterance. "So we've found it."

Lavender did not immediately reply, due to a bout of sniffling. "I never thought I'd be standing here. It seems almost sacrilegious."

"Oh, please, restrain your maudlin emotions. There is still a long road ahead for us. Pass me the gene sweeper, I'm going into the tomb now."

Lavender handed over a device and Vombe arrowed down the excavated channel. Sounds of fracturing and shattering emerged. Vombe returned, bearing gray shards of something in an interwoven cradle of manipulators.

"I didn't need the gene sweeper, there were actual bones present. I secured bits from each individual, I believe."

"We'll soon find out, won't we? Let's get back to the ship."

The interior of the interstellar craft was devoid of obvious instrumentation and gadgetry, featuring a suite of snug, roundly contoured rooms with cozy sleeping, recreational, dining and lounging arrangements for Lavender, and more austere quarters for Vombe. Past these rooms the pair moved until they reached a compartment that featured two large, transparently lidded tanks connected to feedstock reservoirs and bio-instantiation engines.

Lavender fed separate portions of bone to each tank's input slot, and quickly received two different readouts.

"Yes, you found segments from both individuals, so we're ready to go."

"Flip the switch then. The process takes a whole day as it is, without your mooning about."

Lavender sighed with exaggerated exasperation. "Vombe, your sense of history is as deficient as your sense of drama."

"Luckily so, or we'd never get anywhere."

Activated, the chambers filled first with aerogel scaffolding, then with a roiling rush of multi-colored liquids and colloids, slurries and plasmas. before settling down to a steady burbling and patterned wave-like movements.

Vombe and Lavender departed the facility.

When they returned a day later, the tanks held two slickly naked, slackly articulated human forms: a man and a woman, eyes closed, faces composed into a neutral, almost mannequin-like expressions. The woman was darker-skinned than the man. Both exhibited an average beauty and handsomeness, and the youthfulness attendant upon only two or three decades of existence.

Lavender involuntarily clenched her tail at the sight. "It's them. I can't believe it."

All practicality, Vombe fussed with a dormant mechanism attached to the tanks that had not yet come into play in the construction of the new bodies.

"This is the most problematical part."

"Of course," Lavender agreed. "We are calling them back from heaven."

"We must assume the morphic resonance signatures are complete and will bond. Here it goes then."

Vombe sent an invisible command from himself to the machine.

Instantly the forms within the bio-reactors assumed a new subliminal semblance of vitality and self-possession, like a time-compressed film of an embryo developing.

"When can we bring them round?" asked Lavender.

"The integration should take only several hours."

"I hope it's really them."

"We will know soon."

# # #

The man attained awareness with a start.

The last thing he remembered clearly was undergoing the Ascension process. He had a further set of vague impressions from the eternal interval after that moment: a fullness inaccessible in his current embodied condition. All that remained to him was a numinous sense of celestial existence: nebulous imagery, vague concepts, odd emotions.

He opened his eyes onto a plain, undecorated, windowless space. He levered himself partway up from the mattress on which he was lying. He looked to his left and saw a nude woman. He registered himself to be naked as well, then. And instantly, two names came to him.

His own, David Botwink. And the woman's, Flora Patlan.

His wife.

But appearing as she had many decades before she, too, underwent Ascension. Unwithered, unbowed by time. Restored to youth. And himself?

His hands bore no wrinkles nor age spotting, his biceps were firm and taut. The muscles in his legs almost throbbed with power.

Even as David came agilely off the platform, Flora opened her eyes. She caught his movements and focused entirely on him, visibly gathering her sensibilities, even faster to come to terms with their current reality than he had been. She had always been quicker.

They found themselves in each other's arms without volition, clutching tightly in a manner both ancient and oddly unfamiliar.

"This feels so strange," David said.

"But wonderful."

"I thought we'd never experience this again."

"And yet here we are."

They began to kiss, and their hands roved.

Before they could surrender to any further inevitable carnal impulses, however, they were interrupted by a polite cough.

In the door of the room stood two beings. David recognized them immediately: a lagomorph chimera and a Moraveckian artilect.

The first bore the stamp of his designs, the second, the style and conceptual hallmarks of his wife.

The lagomorph spoke in a quaveringly deferential voice.

"Great Mother, Great Father, might you save your marital reunion for later? We need to talk."

# # #

The ship, crewed by Lavender and Vombe, was named *Gaudy Talavera;* it covered the thousands of light-years between Earth and the nearest system of the Stewards' Expansion – that vast loose congeries of worlds and other synthetic habitats established by David and Flora's offspring – in just under two days. That was barely enough time for the resurrected humans to make sense of their current situation, to hear a *précis* of ten millennia of history, and to understand why they had been reincarnated.

Only hours from their destination – a giant, low-mass world dubbed Xylel – the quartet of travelers sat in one of Lavender's comfortable rooms, continuing their discussion of matters large and small.

David found that he had to continually assure himself of the reality of his current existence. To step, in effect, from the day of his Ascension in the year 2119 directly to this far-flung future was disorienting at best and deranging at worst. Holding Flora's hand, as he did now, helped to establish some connection to an understandable and solid past.

In their darkened bedchamber, during the first sleep-cycle after their resurrection, Flora had confided a similar feeling.

"This era seems to conform too closely to my own hardly admissible dreams for me to believe in it! It's a fantasy come true."

"Yes, it's what we had hoped for when we left the Earth to the chimerae and the artilects, that they would outdo humanity's own accomplishments, move beyond our modest conquest of the solar system, and voyage out to the stars. They would discover a path that we just could not find."

"You don't think it's a hoax, do you? After all, we've only seen this ship and various media recordings so far."

"No, it's no hoax."

"How can you be sure?"

"Just by the way these two regard us."

"Yes, poor Lavender! She can barely stop trembling when you come within her personal space."

"Your own progeny shows similar behavior, after his fashion."

"Oh, I hadn't noticed…"

"Do you remember the early days of coding the manipulator protocol for the egg handling test?"

"That unique suite of flexions? Sure."

"One of Vombe's manipulators runs through them unconsciously every time he talks to you."

"I don't know whether to laugh or cry. Could such a legacy subroutine have remained after all this time?"

"Why not? We have junk DNA that's a million times older."

"So, we have to assume everything they've told us is true and accurate."

"I think so."

"My god, what a story."

The entire human race – grown weary of its apparent limitations, deeming itself forever confined to its native solar system, angry at the constraints of physics that had seemingly prevented any breakout into the universe at large – had opted instead for transubstantiation. Abandoning corporeality and all the pleasures and pains that such a state entailed, human beings had uploaded their sentient essences into the Randall-Sundrum interbrane substrate, where energy was infinite and limitations on thought and interbeing communications nil. A life of the mind alone, and whatever contextual emulations they could contrive. But before they had made, through unanimous consensus, this migration, they had manufactured and perfected their heirs, the chimerae and the artilects, and tasked them with carrying forward the old *homo sapiens* dreams.

David Botwink and his team had brilliantly crafted the hybrid living creatures, while Flora Patlan and her crew had programmed, bootstrapped and heuristically trained the robots.

How faithfully and creatively the two artificial races had fulfilled their imperatives was now apparent to David and Flora.

After inventing FTL travel, and finding no alien sapients elsewhere in the galaxy, humanity's mindchildren had reproduced exponentially and filled a hundred thousand worlds, creating at the same time their own culture, whose foundation consisted of all the scraps of historical human achievement that remained after rewilding and records purging. The remnants of human culture were revered as the guiding principles and template for subsequent life among the mindchildren.

In so many ways, both technological and cultural, Lavender's kind and Vombe's kind had surpassed the humans. But even though they had rediscovered the ability to access the Randall-Sundrum continuum, they had respected humanity's decision to abandon the cosmos, and had never dared to contact them.

Until now.

For, at this point in their development, just when the two artificial races should have been moving steadily from higher to higher plateaus, they were failing.

An invisible, sourceless, yet deadly entropic wave seemed to have engulfed the worlds of the Stewards' Expansion. Rates of suicide and self-harming addictions were rising. Societies were disintegrating. Lawlessness increased. Retrenchments from all frontiers were underway. Scientific progress had ground to a halt.

"And we have no clue why," Lavender said mournfully. "Have we reached some inbuilt limitation that you installed in us, purposefully or accidentally?"

Flora rushed to answer in horrified tones. "Oh, no, that couldn't be! We would never have engineered any such cruel leash."

David seconded her response. "Your species are both as open-ended and adaptable as we humans ourselves. Or so we intended."

Vombe said, "Introspection has failed us. We must have your insights. You know the measure of our desperation by our irreverent daring to retrieve you from your paradise."

"We'll give all our help gladly," David said. "As for paradise, I'm not so sure that label applies." The man regarded the idle youthful movements of his own arm. "I think now we lost more than we gained by the Ascension."

Lavender and Vombe said nothing at this heresy.

The world of Xylel appeared pristine and beautiful from orbit. Lavender said, "Just a decade ago, this was known as one of the garden worlds of the Expansion, a place of resorts and parks and conservancies. But now – well, you'll see."

Their hasty but sufficient tour of the planet occupied most of one week, and the sights were dismaying. Buildings fallen to ruin, manicured landscapes gone to seed, spaceships defunct and cratered. Tribes of chimerae of all sorts living the lives of scavengers, while clusters of artilects of all configurations huddled motionlessly, their powerful cyberminds indulging in paradox-huffing, pointless simulations and addictive gaming.

David found himself weeping by the end of the tour; Flora consoled him while her own eyes overflowed.

Vombe and Lavender were disconcerted by this frailty of the human creators, and yet, somehow, buoyed by their manifest solidarity with the plight of their heirs.

Recovering, Flora said, "We will need facilities for our researches into this problem, and volunteer subjects for testing."

"All this we anticipated," said Vombe.

The world they traveled to next was called Moalla, and it exhibited a greater level of cohesiveness and maintenance. An incredible, enormous celebration heralded the arrival of the humans, and everyone who participated – the chimerae, the ar-

tilects and the two humans alike – felt inspired and uplifted, spirits resurgent, if only temporarily.

Installed in lavish quarters, with all the professional facilities they could imagine, Flora and David dove fervently into their investigations. Once summoned, numerous representative citizens came through their labs for deep and intense examinations, their physiologies, circuitry and mentalities probed. Not just the inhabitants of Moalla, but a stream from other planets as well.

But six months later, the researchers had made no progress in unriddling the source of the existential decay.

"There're just no inherent defects that I can detect," said David. "I almost feel like endorsing the theories of one of those old philosophers, like Toynbee or Spengler, Diamond or Peterson. Maybe every civilization has an inevitable arc, from birth to death. We just might be at that terminus."

"I won't believe that. They are still too vital, too full of interest and curiosity. At least those who have not yet succumbed. Their society has just hit some tipping point we can't discern. I agree that time is a factor. A culture that is ten millennia old is not the same as one that is merely a thousand years young. I think they've exhausted some fuel they were running on. We need to replenish or replace it."

"Let's see what Lavender and Vombe think."

As the desperate and resourceful pair who had dared to go searching for enough human remains to instantiate a rebirth – and not just any remains, but those of the Great Father and Great Mother – Lavender and Vombe had been accorded high status and special privileges. Lavender had brought her whole family to Moalla from her native world of Latul and installed them on an estate she called the Infinite Hutch. Vombe, immune to any pampered surroundings, had taken up useful tenure in the university whose grounds housed David and Flora's lab. There, he taught satellite terraforming to a dwindling corps of chimerae youth who were still motivated to carry on their education in these waning days.

Picking up Vombe in their assigned floater, David and Flora journeyed to the Infinite Hutch.

They found Lavender and her partner, Rockwater, surrounded by a new batch of kits. The fearless young ones crawled all over Vombe, who submitted with what could only be called an air of mechanical resignation. David had cause to admire again his own handiwork.

By now, Lavender could emotionally tolerate a hug from her creators without crumpling, although Rockwater, less used to their awesome presence, quickly excused himself and left the room.

"It does my heart good," David said, "to see that you at least have registered your faith in the future."

"The kits? Yes. Despite all the tragedies, something just came over me and urged me to breed."

While David played with the kits, providing Vombe some relief, Flora explained their dead-end dilemma. Lavender pondered the matter, then offered a thought.

"Perhaps examining your subjects in a lab setting is too artificial. Their daily conditions might reveal more. Maybe you need to conduct tests *in situ*."

Flora and David regarded each other with new hope. "Yes, field surveys of artilects and chimerae. We might learn something that way."

Vombe said, "I will accompany you. In the worst places we might visit, you shall need a strong and deadly protector."

As Vombe spoke, one of the squealing kits was receiving a kind of crack-the-whip ride at the end of one of the robot's manipulators. The incongruity made all the organics laugh.

The next six months were a daunting and generally fruitless pilgrimage across dozens of worlds, probing into the sloughs and sinks of the failing Stewards' Expansion. No discernible causes or solutions to the universal collapse became apparent, despite dedicated research along

every line that could be conceived. And the humans saw innumerable incidents of heart-wrenching suffering and malaise, rendered more impactful as symbols of a larger extinction, sometimes almost more than they could bear.

"I have to ask if the good we wrought is outweighed by the bad," David said forlornly when he and Flora were recovering from one awful day's exertions. "Maybe we never should have created these beings, if they are to end this way."

"You can't weigh ten thousand years of triumphs against a doom that is not even finalized. Besides, although we gave them existence and a chance, we are not responsible for all the twists and turnings that the universe delivered afterwards."

"I suppose..."

Finally acknowledging that further delvings into desuetude and decay and degradation would be unavailing, the expedition returned to Moalla.

A week of restless inactivity passed for the humans, leaving them feeling inert and frustrated.

And then Vombe reappeared. If an artilect's inhuman surface features could convey excitement, his roving sensors were doing so.

"I want you to look at a data set I have just assembled. I was comparing the statistics we collected at all the sites we visited with current indicators, just to chart the downward slope. Look what they reveal."

Flora and David studied the data with growing amazement.

Bewildered, David observed, "The quality of life metrics are trending upward in every community we touched, in a linear fashion from first to last."

Flora said, "It's as if you were mapping a contagion vector – not an infection, but dispersal of the antidote."

"But we didn't do anything."

"Nothing," said Vombe, "except to show yourselves and take part in the lives of your children. The first humans seen for five hundred generations."

"Could that really be the answer?" Da-

vid wondered. "The Expansion came as far as sheer youthful exuberance and remembered creator imperatives could take it? But now they need reassurance, guidance, inspiration, and a boost?"

Flora grew more and more excited. "A clear case of delayed abandonment syndrome. Cast outward from the ancient hearths, sent on an exile of conquest. The loss, the loneliness, the attempt to prove themselves worthy of their creators. And then, reaching a peak with no one to applaud or share it with."

Vombe said, "I myself can attest to newly apprehending certain broken decision chains along these lines, and the frustration of closed loops. What an organic would feel – probably something even worse – I can't imagine."

"But," said David, "if that's the case, things are just as hopeless as before. We're only two beings. We can't bop around the whole galaxy instilling hope."

"Then we'll just have to bring back the whole human race," Flora advised. "We were cowards and slackers ever to flee to a sterile perfection. Humans have gone missing long enough."

"But how? There's hardly any DNA traces left of the billions who ascended, not enough to allow for individual rebuilds. All the bodies were thoroughly liquefied so as not to leave a planet of corpses for our heirs. The survival of our own mortal remains was a fluke."

Flora punched her own open palm with inspiration. "This is what we'll do. We'll treat it like the brute force breaking of a crypto key. We will synthesize every possible human genome from raw nucleotide stocks, and grow the mortal shells. If a vessel resonates with an actual human mentality resident in paradise, the new body will become ensouled. If they don't resonate, if they draw a blank, we destroy the shell. At that point, it's just meat."

"But it is such a huge task. It would take –"

Vombe said, "It would take only the entire planetary resources for a year from five average systems in the Expansion. You forget how rich and powerful we still are."

Thrilled, the humans said almost as one, "Let's go see what Lavender thinks."

At the Infinite Hutch, they found the chimerae parents trying to ready six fidgety kits for bed. During the warm, fragrant tussle which left the humans happily laughing, a qualm came over David concerning their plan, but he did not voice it until the adults were alone, and the whole scheme had been laid out before Lavender.

The lagomorph was silent for a time, then said, "If indeed we can do this, we must make sure the humans do not try to take over our destiny. We need them by our side, not leading. That is no longer their role."

"Agreed," said Flora. "We will do everything in our power to educate everyone and frustrate any such impulses. And remember, we will be some ten or twelve billion only, against your trillions."

David spoke finally of his new doubt. "I'm worried about the other extreme. Indifference, and even anger at being reincarnated. How can we ensure the cooperation of the resurrectees? What if they all just want to flee back to paradise again? What if they have no interest in helping?"

"Oh," said Lavender blithely, "that's no problem at all. We just bring them here one by one, and have them wrestle with the kits!"

By LAWRENCE
WATT-EVANS

Lawrence Watt-Evans is the author of more than fifty novels and one hundred fifty short stories, including the "Legends of Ethshar" fantasy series and the Hugo-winning "Why I Left Harry's All-Night Hamburgers." He is currently traveling for an extended period.

It was around 3:00 am when he finally gave up trying to sleep; the pain in his tooth was just not going away, and the dentist couldn't see him before 8:00. He'd already taken all the aspirin he'd had left, but it hadn't done much, and it had worn off around midnight.

He considered finding an all-night pharmacy or 24-hour market to get more aspirin, or maybe some other pain reliever, but he wasn't sure it would be safe to take any more; he'd already taken a lot. Still, he got out of bed and put his clothes back on because anything was better than lying there feeling his jaw throb.

He took the elevator down to street level, left the building, and began walking east, then turned south onto Third Avenue.

The drugstore on the corner was closed; the card on the door said they closed at midnight, which was reasonable enough, if not very helpful. He reached into his pocket for his phone, to check what might be open, and didn't find it; annoyed, he realized he had left it in his apartment.

It wasn't worth going back for, he decided; he would walk until he found somewhere, and at the very least the fresh air felt good. It was a warm night, just pleasant, not hot, with a gentle breeze blowing, and the air was clean – the streets weren't **empty**, but there were only a few widely-scattered vehicles instead of the usual motorized flood, so the customary cloud of exhaust had dissipated. The city's usual racket was reduced to a faint background hum; he could hear a subway train somewhere, passing below a distant grate, and a siren that might be coming all the way from Brooklyn. The sounds were just enough to remind him the city never re-

ally slept, and to distract him from the pain in his jaw.

But then, as he walked further down the block, he heard the unmistakable murmur of voices. He blinked. Who was out and about, and talking, at this hour? He was sure there were cops and garbage men and cabbies and the like going about their business, and of course some portion of the city's homeless population might be awake, but they wouldn't be **talking** like that.

He heard a woman's happy laughter. Curious, he headed toward the sound, turning a corner without noticing which street it was.

There were tables on the sidewalk under a wide blue awning, and there were people seated at most of them, talking and drinking. He saw lit candles and empty bottles and glasses of melting ice, and a woman in a red dress wearing a white feather boa despite the warm weather, and a man with a goatee like a Spanish grandee of the 17th century. A waiter in a white shirt and black apron was balancing a tray of foam-topped beer mugs as he squeezed between the chairs.

He blinked. Who **were** these people?

The after-theater crowd should be gone by now, and these people didn't look the part in any case – their clothes were wildly varied, from sweat-stained T-shirts to starched ruffles. Only a very few were dressed appropriately for a night out clubbing, and he didn't know of any late-night clubs in this area, so that wasn't a good explanation, either.

He approached hesitantly, looking for the name of the café, but the awning was blank and no sign was obvious, and he could not see past the crowd to read whatever might have been lettered on the windows or over the door.

A young woman who sat alone at a table, leaning back comfortably with a cocktail glass in one hand and her other hand flung over the back of her chair, noticed him. She smiled, then sat up and beckoned.

Still hesitant, he approached.

She was wearing an old-fashioned black and white striped blouse, with a black beret atop long brown hair. She had high cheekbones, a narrow jaw, and a red-lipsticked mouth turned up in a wry smile. "Sit down," she said, looking up at him. "I won't bite. At least, not unless you want me to."

He took one of the unoccupied chairs at the table and settled down facing her. "Hello," he said.

"Hi there," she replied, leaning back again. "What brings you here at this time of night? You aren't one of the regulars."

"No, I..." He paused, unsure what he should say to this friendly stranger. Finally, he settled on, "I couldn't sleep."

"So you went out for a walk? Don't most people watch a late movie or check their email?"

He shrugged.

She sipped her drink. "What's your name?"she asked.

"Steve," he said. It was a common enough name that he didn't mind telling her the truth.

"I'm Yvonne," she said. She put down her glass and held out a delicate hand. "Pleased to meet you."

He took her hand briefly, then released it – not so much a handshake as an acknowledgment that she had offered. "What brings **you** out so late?" he asked.

"Oh, I **am** one of the regulars," she said, waving at the crowd. "That's how I know you aren't. I'm here most nights."

"But... who **are** all you people? Why is **anyone** out at this time of night?"

"We're just folks who keep odd hours," she said. "Night people."

"Can I get you something sir?"

He started; he had not seen the waiter approach. The young man seemed to simply appear beside the table, looking at him expectantly.

"He'll have a vermouth," Yvonne said, before he could recover. "Won't you, Steve?"

"I..." He could not seem to form words.

"He'll have a vermouth," Yvonne repeated, more definitely. She patted his hand. "It's a house specialty. You'll like it."

"I don't..." But the waiter was gone.

Trying to spot the waiter he looked past Yvonne, at the other tables, and he began to notice details he had not caught before. Two tables over was a man in pajamas, talking to two brassy blondes dressed like Vegas showgirls. At another table, a woman in a long gown was talking to a boy in short pants. Three long-haired men in checked flannel shirts were hoisting beer steins. The woman in the feather boa looked much older than he had first thought, almost skeletal.

This was a very strange crowd, even for 3:00 am.

"Are you people here **every** night?" he asked.

"Oh, pretty much," she said.

"Even that man wearing pajamas?" He nodded in the direction of the oddly-attired threesome.

"Hm?" Yvonne turned to see where he was looking. "Oh, him. No, I don't know him. I think he came here looking for those girls." She smiled. "If he wakes up he's going to be very surprised."

Steve blinked. "If he wakes up?"

"Oh, yes. He's asleep, and dreaming. I can tell." She smiled. "If he can keep it going long enough he may be in for quite a night."

One of the showgirls laughed warmly, and took the hand of the pajama wearer. All three of them rose, and began threading their way out of the café.

"I wonder if he knows he's been sleepwalking," Yvonne remarked.

Steve looked up as the other man passed, and saw that his eyes were indeed closed. One of the showgirls looked Steve in the eye and winked.

And then they were past, walking up the sidewalk to the corner, and for a moment Steve thought he saw the pajama-clad man alone, the showgirls gone.

But then they were back, and all three vanished around the corner.

"That was weird," Steve said.

"Oh, it happens," Yvonne said. "We don't see a lot of sleepwalkers here, but there are some." She smiled at him. "We don't see many day people, either."

Nettled, he asked, "So how do you know I'm a day person? Just because I'm not a regular at this particular café?"

"Because you don't understand who we are," she replied. "Another night person would have figured it out right away, even if he'd never been here before."

"Well, then, who **are** you? You still haven't said."

She looked at him for a long moment, considering, then said, "I could tell you, couldn't I? It wouldn't matter, not really." Her expression turned suddenly somber. "Nothing I do matters."

"Why not?"

"Because I'm a night person," she said. "I'm not **real**."

"You look pretty real to me," he said, but even as he spoke he wasn't sure he was telling the truth. The beret, the blouse, her pointed chin and lush hair, seemed suddenly more like an image from a movie, or in an ad, than like a living woman.

"It's kind of you to say that," she answered, "but I'm not. I'm just a dream someone's having – or really, a great many someones."

He blinked. "I'm not dreaming," he said. "I'm awake."

Her smile reappeared. "Yes, you are," she agreed. "That's what's so unusual. You're real, and you're awake, but you found us anyway. That doesn't happen very often."

"If I'm awake, I can't be dreaming you."

"Oh, I wouldn't be too sure of that," she said. "There are daydreams, and hallucinations, and so on. But no, **you** aren't dreaming me; half a million strangers are."

"What are you **talking** about?"

Her smile widened. "You know there are seven or eight million people in this city, don't you? And right now most of them are asleep, and many of them are dreaming, and the entire city is just **filled** with that energy, with their imagination, with their secret thoughts and desires, with everything they've seen and heard during the day. When they're awake that energy drives them through their ordinary lives, but at night, when they're sleeping, their bodies can't use it. Do you think all that just vanishes into nowhere?"

He wanted to say yes, that was exactly what he thought, but the words caught in his throat.

"That energy pools and collects and interacts, and takes on human form – and here we are," she said. "The night people."

"That's crazy," he said. "You're just screwing with me, and I'm listening because I'm short on sleep and my tooth hurts and I'm not thinking straight."

Her smile dimmed. "You can tell yourself that, if you want."

"You really think you're a collectivized dream that thousands of people are having?"

"I **know** I am."

"If you **aren't** just messing with me, then you're crazy."

She shrugged. "Please yourself."

"No, really. I mean, what do you do during the day, when there **aren't** millions of people sleeping? Don't you have a home, a job, a family?"

She shook her head. "I don't exist during the day, Steve. I'm usually not here until well after midnight, when enough of the day people have gone home to bed."

"But…what, every night you just appear, here at this café?"

"Not **every** night. And not always here. Sometimes it takes me hours to find where we're gathering that night. Or sometimes the energy isn't right, and I don't appear at all, or I'm not quite myself. I've been a little girl, and an old woman, and a cat, and a dozen other things."

"That's crazy."

"There are many crazy things in the world, Steve."

The waiter was there at his elbow, setting a glass of dark vermouth in front of him. Steve looked up.

"Put it on my tab," Yvonne said. The waiter nodded and was gone.

"You run a tab?" Steve asked.

She smiled again. "He thinks I do."

"Is **he** real?"

Yvonne looked to either side, then leaned forward, and Steve noticed her blouse was cut lower than he had realized – or perhaps it was cut lower now than it had been before. "Do you know, I'm not sure? Usually I can tell instantly, but the staff here – I don't know **what** they are."

"Do you ever **pay** your tab?"

She laughed gaily. "Oh, Steve, of **course** not! What would I pay it with? I don't have any money. I can't hold a job. But I don't **need** to; I don't need to eat or drink, and sometimes I come into existence with a drink already in front of me. And no one ever asks me to pay."

"Doesn't it…" Steve started to say, but then he stopped. This was all completely insane, and there was no reason to ask how it worked.

"Don't let it trouble you," she said. "Remember, I'm not a real person; I'm just a manifestation of the collective unconscious. Nothing I do can matter. Nothing I do can change anything. I don't need to worry about food or shelter. I have no soul. I can't feel guilt. I have no family. I can't have children. My only friends are the people like you, who come along sometimes and talk to me; I can talk to other night people, but we can't **connect**, not really. And the day people I meet usually decide they're dreaming, that they weren't really here at all, or if they **do** come back to look for me they may not recognize me, because I may be completely changed. I never know whether I'll be here tomorrow night, or whether I'll be the same person if I am."

"Can you feel pain?"

She bit her lip. "Not **physical** pain," she said.

He was sorry he had asked.

He wondered for a moment whether perhaps he **was** dreaming, but the pain in his tooth convinced him he was awake.

"But enough about me," she said, sitting up straight, her smile reappearing. "Tell me about **you**."

He shook his head. "I'm no one interesting."

"Oh, I don't believe that! Tell me! Do you have a family? A girlfriend?"

He hesitated. "No girlfriend," he said. "Two sisters back in Rhode Island – one's married, the other lives with our mother."

"What are they like?"

And he found himself talking about his sisters, his nephew, his parents, his job, his dreams and ambitions, and before he knew it his vermouth was gone, though he barely remembered tasting it, and the sky in the east was starting to get a little brighter, and most of the tables were empty, and the waiter was stacking chairs against the wall.

He had not seen anyone leave since the sleepwalker and his two showgirls.

He stopped talking and watched, and a couple in Victorian dress vanished from a nearby table. They did not get up and leave, nor did they flicker or fade; they simply weren't there anymore.

"The city's waking up," Yvonne remarked. "This place doesn't serve breakfast; when we're all gone they'll close until eleven, when they open for lunch."

Others were disappearing, as well.

"Your dentist will open in another couple of hours," she said. "I hope he can take care of that tooth for you."

The other tables were all empty now. He took Yvonne's hand. "You're still here," he said.

"I'm not usually here this late," she said. "You've kept me here. It's been a pleasure talking to you."

"You have to go?"

"I do. There are barely enough late risers to have kept me here **this** long."

"Are you sure? If I come back, will I see you again?"

"Oh, you know I can't tell you that! And you need your sleep; as it is, you won't be able to get anything done at work today."

"But I don't…I want to see you again."

"Maybe you will." She smiled, and patted his hand.

"Dream of me," she said.

And then she was gone. ▪

LISTEN
The Gernsback Machine
listen.amazingstories.com
An AMAZING STORIES Podcast